KILLS
OF THE
FATHER

The Misadventures Of
Max Mason

Charles Sisk

ARCHWAY
PUBLISHING

Archway Publishing books may be ordered through booksellers or by contacting:

Archway Publishing
1663 Liberty Drive
Bloomington, IN 47403
www.archwaypublishing.com
844-669-3957

Because of the dynamic nature of the Internet, any web addresses or links contained in this book may have changed since publication and may no longer be valid. The views expressed in this work are solely those of the author and do not necessarily reflect the views of the publisher, and the publisher hereby disclaims any responsibility for them.

Any people depicted in stock imagery provided by Getty Images are models, and such images are being used for illustrative purposes only. Certain stock imagery © Getty Images.

ISBN: 978-1-6657-2055-7 (sc)
ISBN: 978-1-6657-2056-4 (e)

Library of Congress Control Number: 2022905081

Print information available on the last page.

Archway Publishing rev. date: 04/07/2022

ACKNOWLEDGMENTS

This book was special to write because it's all about FAMILY, and how far the love for family would go to protect each other from anything & everything that happens in our everyday lives.

My incredible wife Kristina takes her duties of being a mother & grandmother VERY seriously. Her incredible sense of doing the right thing no matter how many times people or family tried to keep her down just amazes me everyday. The love & pride she has for our children, and our grandchildren should get her a nomination for "Mother of the Year" which is why I love writing about Karen Tyler and her intense love for family. Thank you for continuing to show me the way to forgiveness, faith, trust, and honor. I love you so much.

Jason, we are SO proud of the man, father, and partner we have seen you grown into over the past few years. I know your sister was the highlight of the first book ("Five Seconds of Dead Air") so it's your turn to shine in this one son. It has been my honor to be your father, and this book is dedicated to you and your family.

Stephanie, walking you down the isle was the biggest, most important event in my life with you, other than your birth. I know I haven't always lived up to the standards a father should have with his daughter, just know I will ALWAYS be proud of you and love you beyond words, and I dedicate this book also to you sweetheart; you will ALWAYS be the Princess in my books.

Albie, I've only known you a little while, but I have seen the way you treat my daughter with love and respect. You look at her the way I look at Kristina, with so much love & pride the way it should be; which makes me so proud to call you my son-in-law and my family.

I wrote police officer David Murphy in honor of you young man; thank you for taking care of my beautiful daughter. This book is also dedicated to you.

Parker, Christopher, Waverly, Alice, Evan, and Nevaeh, and Kaitlyn…you're all still to young to read this book, but when you ARE old enough I want you to understand that the theme of the story was…there is <u>NOTHING</u> Grandpa wouldn't do for any of you…no questions asked.

Grandma & I love you all so much and love watching you grow up right before our eyes.

Rashad…it has been an honor, and a privilege to write you into one of my stories. You have been an incredible friend & brother and I want to honor you with being Master Sergeant Crusher Davis, whose love and respect for others makes him the superhero I know that you are.

Jaime…what you did for me back in the day, I will never forget. It showed me the respect & integrity you have for your friends and family, which is why I wrote Detective Jose Martin in your honor; a small part in "Perfect Score" I thought you deserved a bigger role in this book. Thank you for your friendship young man.

Jean-Marie…I'm so sorry you got left out of the credits for your incredible editing of "Perfect Score" so I wanted to make up for it with one here. You have become and incredible friend to me & Max and we appreciate your support & love for his/our adventures. Thank you.

Raymond Earl; what can I say that I haven't in the previous two books. You have been incredibly supportive of Max's adventures and I hope you continue enjoying them. Thank you so much dude.

And finally, to my younger brother Bruce who left us in 2022 at the young age of fifty-nine. The family loves & misses you brother, rest in peace.

To all the technology & devices we use everyday, remember we all need human interaction. Talk to that person instead of sending a text; enjoy the surroundings you are taking that picture of yourself with, instead of just glancing at it as a background; talk to somebody you don't know instead of having your ear buds blasting in your ears, you might find they have an interesting story to tell. And finally, stop using technology to bully, intimidate, blackmail, and hurt others feelings…remember it could be your feelings that get hurt tomorrow. Technology is here to help us, teach us, not control us.

CHAPTER ONE

It was a breezy, cool Saturday morning in October as Max Mason walked out of his kitchen glass doorway onto his backyard deck drinking his first morning cup of coffee as he watched the sun slowly rise in front of him.

Max slowly sipped his coffee thinking what he, his family, and his friends had been through over the past fifteen months; dealing with the Global Broadcasting Network charity attack, Tanaka Amikura's deadly vendetta, defusing a nuclear "dirty" bomb in Boston on live television, a new Global Security Council alliance, dealing with the Russian mob, and the Stovoski brothers taking over his girlfriend Karen Tyler's hospital during her knee surgery. He stared out into his backyard and changed his thought, thinking he could use a few more small trees back there along the fence line of his yard smiling.

Max heard something behind him and slowly turned to see Tyler in her robe limp through the doorway behind him holding her own cup of hot coffee smiling. Karen Tyler officially moved in with Max after her knee surgery and the infamous "hospital takeover" back in April. Max insisted that he take care of her during her physical therapy and helped push her for the past seven months to get her knee back in shape for duty on the team. It didn't hurt that the two of them were crazy in love with each other either Max thought.

"How are you feeling this morning?" Max asked Tyler who was still walking with a cane. Max took her coffee mug from her and helped her to the patio chair then placed her cup on the table in front of her.

"It's getting less painful, but I hate this "old lady" cane the physical therapist gave me to use" Tyler said with a grin.

She placed the black tubular cane the hospital had given her beside the chair as she finally sat down with Max's assistance, then reached for her coffee mug in front of her.

"I really don't feel like going tonight Max" Tyler said knowing Max was going to try and talk her into it knowing she was feeling self conscious about her limp and having to use a cane.

"I know sweetheart, me either" Max replied. "But it's the Admiral's 70th birthday and both he and Kristina want us to be there to celebrate it with him" Max said watching her take a sip from her cup.

"It's a costume party, how am I supposed to incorporate a limp and a cane into a Halloween costume?" Tyler asked looking sadly at Max.

Max smiled at her and walked back into the house then returned quickly with two large boxes and placed them on the hard wooden deck in front of her. "Interesting you should ask that" Max said to her. "Open them" he requested seeing the suspicious smile on her face.

Tyler lifted the top off the first box to find a round black bowler type hat which she promptly placed on her head realizing it was a perfect fit for her. She smiled at Max and asked "What are you up to Max Mason?"

Max didn't say anything he just smiled at her as she reached down and opened the second box to find a really nice men's black silk suit and pants outlined with gold trim; and a pair of men's black lace up shoes. Tyler picked up the shoes seeing they were about her size then looked at him with a seriously confused look on her face wondering what she was holding and looking at.

"Who is the ONE person that can walk around the room with a limp and a cane at a Halloween party?" Max asked Tyler with a big grin. "You love those OLD movies he's in" Max said to her hoping she would guess.

"Are you serious?" Tyler asked with a big laugh. "You want me to go as Charlie Chaplin?" she asked looking at the suit still in her hands.

"YES" Max said with a huge smile thinking it was a great costume and that she wouldn't feel self conscious about holding her cane or her small limp. "I had the suit custom tailored for you sweetheart" Max said smiling.

"Mikey helped me figure it out, and even sent you a special cane for tonight so you wouldn't have to use your "old lady" cane as you like to call it" he said smiling hoping she would feel better and go tonight with him.

Max handed her the cane that was leaning against the deck railing that Mikey had made for her; which was beautifully crafted with a long circular length, a rubber bottom, and a shiny black lacquer finish. The handle was made out of a gold finish in the shape of an eagle's head.

Tyler thought it was absolutely beautiful and picked her phone up immediately and called Mikey's cell phone forgetting it was 7am back in Oklahoma.

"Hello" Mikey Stevens answered in bed still half asleep.

"Mikey, I love my new cane, thank you" Tyler said into the phone excited.

"Hey sweetheart, how are you feeling; are you getting around okay?" Mikey asked raising up out of bed and looking over at Faye still sound asleep.

"Yeah; still a bit painful but its getting better" Tyler replied into the phone. "Are you and Faye coming for the Admiral's party tonight?" Tyler asked.

Mikey shifted the phone to his other ear seeing Faye roll over still asleep and whispered "No, Faye and I have a set consultant from the cable network coming out this evening to give us a bigger set for the show" he said. "I sent Max an expensive bottle of scotch for the Admiral along with your cane" Mikey said laughing quietly not to wake Faye.

"So whose idea was it for me to go as Charlie Chaplin?" Tyler asked looking over at Max sitting in his chair smiling and sipping his coffee.

"We had a productive conversation last week him & I when he

asked me to make you a new cane" Mikey said. "He told me you loved those old movies and that Charlie Chaplin would be a great Halloween costume for someone who had to walk with a cane" continuing to talk to Tyler on the phone in a low voice. "Your cane is made VERY special, Max doesn't know the detail I went into with this cane and you might not want to tell him" Mikey said to her chuckling.

Tyler looked over at Max still drinking his cup of coffee as she listened to Mikey telling her the details of how her new cane was made that she was holding and admiring. She smiled at Max then told Mikey "That's so cool; give Faye a big kiss from us and we will talk to you soon, okay" Tyler said hanging up the phone.

"A blonde Charlie Chaplin huh?" Tyler asked Max with a smile. "And what will you be wearing Mr. Mason?" she asked with a giggle.

Max watched as Tyler looked into the boxes again sitting on the wood deck pulling the suit coat out and examining it up close.

"First, Stacy will be here by noon; at Kristina's urging the Admiral gave her a weekend furlough to attend the party; she asked if she could spend the night here I didn't think you would mind" Max said knowing it was Tyler's house now and he should have asked her.

"That's awesome; Stacy and I get to play dress up tonight" Tyler said to Max making him feel better about assuming and not asking her about Stacy staying the night.

"You still haven't answered my question Max; who are you going as tonight?" Tyler asked smiling placing her costume back into the box.

"We're making it a family theme night" Max replied with a big grin. "We're all staying in the 1930 era; Stacy is going as Dorothy in the Wizard of Oz, and I'm going as the notorious gangster Al Capone" he said smiling at Tyler who he could tell was getting excited about this party now.

"That's pretty cool, I love you for doing this; I know this really isn't your kind of thing" she said reaching up to kiss him as he stood over her.

"What do you mean girl; I'm a party animal" he replied laughing as he stood beside her chair.

"And besides, you needed to get out of the house; I know your physical therapy is driving you crazy, I thought you could use a little adult time" he replied smiling, grabbing her hand and squeezing it. Max smiled at Tyler kissed her hand then looked into her eyes and said "I love you too".

The front doorbell rang, Max got up and walked through the kitchen to the foyer; looked at the security video screen at the side of the front door saw it was a delivery man and opened it.

The delivery man was there to bring both Max and Stacy their costumes from the costume shop after being altered for them both. Max thought it was a smart idea to get Tyler's costume ahead of time so she couldn't say no to going. Max signed for the garment bags and three boxes, and brought them into the living room just as Tyler walked slowly into the room using her new cane Mikey made for her.

Tyler sat in the chair next to the couch in the living room watching as Max opened one of the boxes, pulling out a small basket with a stuffed dog hanging out of the front of it.

Max smiled at her and said "This must be for Stacy's costume" he said with a chuckle.

"What?; Al Capone can't carry a basket with an adorable little doggie in it" Tyler asked smirking. "Not manly?" she asked with a smile.

"Ha Ha" Max replied with a smirk on his face putting the basket back into the box and putting it aside. He quickly opened the second box and pulled out a miniature plastic replica of a 1930's Thompson sub-machine gun, and a large black brimmed white pin-stripped fedora hat. "Now this is more my style" he said with a laugh holding the toy gun.

Max placed the hat on his head and bent the brim down over his face very slowly looked at Tyler with a grin and asked "Who's YOUR gangster?"

Tyler couldn't help but laugh uncontrollably at Max, thinking how silly and dashing he looked in the big hat. Max pulled the trigger of the toy machine gun and it made a funny clicking sound. "I don't think that's how it sounded at the St. Valentine's Day Massacre in 1929" he said with a grin.

Max put the hat back in the box, laid everything on the couch near the front door and walked back into the kitchen where he proceeded to go into the refrigerator and pull out eggs, bacon, a couple of thin ham slices, shredded cheese, onions, and a green pepper. Tyler followed him slowly into the kitchen with her cane and sat down on one of the bar stools around the oak wood island that was in the middle of the kitchen. Max smiled as she sat down and asked "Southwest omelet for breakfast sweetheart?"

"Yes please kind Sir" she replied. She loved watching Max cook and he was actually really good at it. "What time do you think Stacy will be here?" she asked him with a smile on her face.

"Probably not for another couple of hours" Max said cutting up the green pepper and onion looking at her and raising one of his eyebrows playfully.

"Maybe we should work up an appetite before you start cooking" Tyler said with a sheepish grin on her face.

She started walking towards the stairs up to the bedrooms dropping her bathrobe on the hardwood floor revealing herself completely naked when she turned and asked "Coming?" extending her hand out to take his.

"Yes ma'am" Max replied with a grin on his face turning the burner off and placing a lid on top of the pan he started using. He looked at Tyler and thought to himself how lucky he was to have someone so beautiful and sexy as she is; taking her hand and following her up the stairs to their bedroom.

They "made love" for a VERY long time finally remembering that Stacy would be there any moment, jumping out of bed having to take turns in the shower.

Max kissed Tyler long and hard when she got out of the shower, her wet blonde hair dripping on the bathroom floor as Max got in for his shower. "Hope you saved me some hot water?" he said to her playfully, getting a grin from her as he got in the shower.

"Maybe" she responded, along with a giggle as she left the bathroom.

They both went back to the kitchen after getting dressed continuing to cook where he left off before he went upstairs to "play" with Tyler. Max had just made Tyler's omelet when the front doorbell rang again.

Max looked at the security screen and opened the door to see his daughter standing there with a big happy smile on her face.

"Hi daddy" Stacy Mason said giving her dad a big hug and a kiss on the cheek in the doorway.

"Hello princess, why didn't you use your key?" Max asked as Stacy walked past him through the front door. "How was the drive up?" he asked knowing it was a three hour drive from Va. Beach to DC where she was stationed.

"I didn't want to interrupt something that you and Tyler might be doing by just walking in" she said with a sheepish grin.

"And, it was great; I'm not going to be able to drive for about eight months when we ship out next weekend, so driving right now is awesome" Stacy said with a smirk. "Where's Tyler?" she asked her dad walking into the living room as he closed the door behind her.

"She's in the kitchen eating a late breakfast" Max replied following Stacy into the kitchen.

"Great, I'm starving" Stacy said as she came into the kitchen seeing Karen Tyler sitting there eating an omelet, with toast, and sipping a cup of coffee.

"Hey you" Tyler said to Stacy smiling as she came into the room.

"Don't you look pretty today" Tyler continued.

"Thanks, how are you feeling?" Stacy asked giving her a long hug knowing that physical therapy can be harsh especially for a knee injury.

"Doing okay sweetie, can't run a mile yet but I'm getting there" Tyler replied laughing.

Stacy sat down on the stool next to Tyler while her dad made her an omelet the way she liked it growing up. Stacy didn't like ham all that much so he would substitute it with crispy bacon bits with extra cheese. Max remembered Jacob's favorite was "everything" in his, and that they BOTH inhaled them when he made them every Sunday morning.

Max finally sat down across from the girls to eat his omelet and reminded them both "We need to get dressed, and be at the venue in less than three hours, so NO procrastinating you two" Max said with a stern look at both of them.

The two women looked at one another and then at Max and busted out laughing knowing he had NO control over either of them when it comes to getting dressed and being somewhere on time, they were GIRLS it's what they do!!!

"Where's Uncle Jordy and Uncle Mikey, aren't they coming?" Stacy asked finishing her last bite of toast then wiping her mouth with her napkin and pushing her plate away.

Max picked up the empty dishes rinsed them off and placed them in the dishwasher. He looked back at the two ladies smiling and thinking to himself how lucky he was to have them both in his life.

"Mikey has business obligations he can't get out of in Oklahoma, and Jordy is out of the country on loan to the Global Security Council with Laila Habib" Max replied to her looking over at Tyler with a smile thinking to himself he just had really good sex with her. Tyler returned the same sheepish smile back.

Max went into the living room and came back with Stacy's costume boxes and placed them both on the kitchen floor by Stacy's feet. "I believe these are yours" he said to her smiling.

Stacy quickly opened the first box to find her basket and little stuffed dog and said "He's so cute" looking at Tyler who smiled approving of what she said.

She put the basket down on the table and opened the second box to find a pair of bright ruby red shoes with straps on them. Stacy pulled her sneakers off and tried the shoes on to find them a perfect fit. She smiled at Max and Tyler then ran to Max and flung her arms around her dad's neck, kissed him on the cheek and said "They're perfect; thank you daddy".

Max looked at his daughter and smiled saying to her "The shoes are yours to keep princess; I had them made in your size" knowing she would use them with other outfits as well as her costume.

Stacy squeezed her arms harder around Max's neck and kissed his cheek again saying "Thank you daddy; I love them". Stacy pulled the classic light denim dress with shoulder straps out of the box and held it against her smiling at Tyler and said "I'm off to see the Wizard".

"Yes you are" Tyler replied looking over at Max who was smiling like a proud father should.

Max looked at the clock on the microwave oven to see it was almost three PM saying "OKAY enough of this, the party starts in two hours ladies; It takes an hour to get there, that means WE have an hour to get ready and be on the road" Max said knowing that neither one of them was paying any attention to what he just said.

Max took his garment bag to the Master bedroom and got dressed while Tyler and Stacy took their costumes to Stacy's bedroom down the hallway where Stacy would be sleeping tonight so they could help each other get dressed. Tyler wouldn't admit it but having another woman in the house was a good thing for her, someone she could talk to about how she was feeling about her injury.

Max looked at himself in the full length mirror wearing the black suit with white pinstripes and thought how cool he looked. He tied the black tie around his neck and tucked it inside the vest, then put the jacket on with the two-toned white and black shoes. Max looked like a 1930's gangster.

Max waited in the living room holding his black fedora hat and plastic machine-gun pacing back and forth anxiously waiting for Tyler and Stacy to come down the staircase wearing their costumes.

Max didn't have to wait too long as they both started down the stairs together, Tyler in front of Stacy.

Max was beaming with pride at both of them the way they looked.

Max gave Tyler a big smile when he first saw her dressed in her costume…wearing a baggy black suit with gold trim and tie, with black shoes, the matching bowler hat, and carrying the new cane Mikey made for her. Max spared no expense for her, buying a fake black mustache she could glue on instead of using a black marker under her lip. She WAS Charlie Chaplin.

Stacy had her hair tied up in long pigtails, wearing a white blouse with the light denim jumper, white knee socks, and of course her new ruby red shoes.

She had the basket on her arm with the little brown stuffed dog poking his head out of the front lid. Max was wondering if he had to fight off "flying monkeys" for her because she WAS Dorothy tonight.

"WOW, you both look amazing" Max said to them as they reached the bottom of the stairs now standing in front of him.

"Can we get pictures together?" Stacy asked her dad. "I can't wait to show my shipmates what we looked like for the Admiral's party" she said excited.

Stacy was to deploy next weekend for an eight month stay at sea on the USS Alabama, an armed destroyer to be stationed in the Persian Gulf. Kristina, the Admiral's granddaughter persuaded the Admiral to let Stacy come to this party before she had to ship out also knowing it would be the last time she got to see her father and Tyler before she left.

"The Admiral will have a photographer at the party taking pictures of guests as they arrive" Max replied to Stacy's picture question. "We can get one professionally done before you have to go next week" he said to her with a smile.

"Don't you look handsome" Tyler said to Max looking him up and down smiling. "That suit is you" she said laughing, knowing that Max hated wearing anything with plaid or pinstripes on it.

"Aren't you cute" Max replied to her with a condescending smirk on his face.

The three of them got into Max's large black SUV and headed to the party. It took them about twenty minutes longer to get there because of the overcrowded Halloween weekend traffic which in the DC/Northern Virginia area was normal.

Max hated to be late for anything, especially a party for the Admiral.

Both Max and Tyler noticed the increase in Secret Service and FBI security activity around the Raymond Earl building as they slowly pulled up.

They could see limousines and SUV's taking their turns to let costumed guests out, watching as the valets helped them out before parking their vehicles or directing the drivers where to park.

Max glanced over at Tyler and smiled, then glanced at Stacy sitting in the back seat from the rearview mirror as the three of them watched guests make their way up the steps to the front entrance.

The Raymond Earl building housed the offices of the U.S. Senate right next door to the U.S. Capitol building. Named in memorial of Senator Raymond Earl, a former Speaker of the House back in the 1960's it is a highly secured building protected by several different agencies including Secret Service, the FBI, and the NSA. It also had one of the largest ballrooms for political fundraisers, inaugurations, and parties in the Nation's Capital.

Max drove his SUV up to the security check point and handed the Secret Service agent his invitation for the three of them, along with their ID's out the car window.

The agent looked at his clipboard and acknowledged that the three of them were on the guest list, checked their ID's and handed them back to Max.

"Please enjoy the party Director" the agent said to Max smiling at both Tyler and Stacy looking at him with their own excited smiles.

The three of them got out of the SUV, collected their costume props, situated their costumes, then Max handed the valet his keys who in turn handed Max a valet ticket got in and drove his SUV away.

"I hope he parks it close" Max said to Tyler with a grin seeing her roll her eyes at him knowing he hated to wait for his car when he wanted to leave.

Max, Tyler, and Stacy stood at the bottom of the stone stairs as they watched Max's car drive away.

Max smiled at both Tyler and Stacy tipping his fedora hat to them both then took Tyler's hand and slowly helped her up the stairs, with Stacy walking up beside them.

When they got to the top of the stairs Tyler gave Max a kiss on the cheek and told him "Thank you for being my hero" then started walking on her own with her new cane next to Stacy as Max walked behind them both.

The three of them walked into the grand ballroom that was located on the 1st floor almost immediately next to the front entrance and was amazed at the decorations, the costumes, and even how good the band was playing.

The entire ballroom was decorated in black, purple, and orange streamers, spider webs, black lights, and several fog machines around the dance floor to give it that eerie, scary cemetery effect.

Max looked around the room figuring there were sixty or seventy guests already present, dressed as cowboys, aliens, vampires, superheroes, and zombies, LOTS of zombies Max thought as his gaze went back to Tyler and Stacy smiling at them.

The three of them stood admiring everything when a zombie dressed photographer approached them and asked if he could take a picture of them together. They stood in front of him and smiled as he took a couple of pictures of them together then one each individually handed Max a ticket and said "Thank you, enjoy the party".

Max looked at Stacy and said "We'll get copies made for you before you ship out sweetie I promise".

Stacy hugged her dad again and said "Thank you" then started looking around the room still holding Tyler's hand smiling.

Max, Tyler, and Stacy stood watching the small crowd dancing in front of the stage decorated as a cemetery complete with gravestones, cobwebs, and fog as the band all dressed as ghouls played a popular song.

Max looked around the room at all the different costumes but one costume caught his eye in particular, a female with bright steel blue eyes dressed in a white ninja outfit carrying a white handled ninja sword on her back. Max noticed that her face was completely covered by her white mask except for her piercing blue eyes staring into his; thinking to himself that there was something familiar about them.

Max took his eyes off of her for a split second to look over at Tyler and Stacy and when he looked back the white "ninja girl" was gone. Max thought this odd and quickly looked around the room, finally seeing the back of her head chatting with someone dressed as a cowboy. Max immediately blew it off as someone's date checking him out in his costume after all he did look handsome in it he was told.

"Well Director, nice to see you dressed up for an old man's party" Admiral James Cartwright said laughing behind him his granddaughter Kristina standing by his side.

"You'll NEVER be old Sir" Max said turning to see the Admiral dressed in a complete Roman soldier outfit. Wearing a gold tunic, plastic sword, and a flowered wreath head band.

"You're going to make me guess aren't you Sir?" Max asked with a grin.

"Really Max; I'm Julius Caesar" the Admiral replied with a scowl on his face that quickly turned into a smile.

Max looked over at Kristina and said "WOW" seeing her dressed as Cleopatra, Queen of the Nile.

Kristina had just turned eighteen and was not the shy little girl that survived the GBN attack over a year ago. She wore a low cut, full length, gold evening gown with her hair put up with a gold snake tiara, and gold snake bracelets that wrapped around her arms.

Max took her hand and said "You look wonderful young lady, nice to see you again".

"Thanks Mr. Mason, I'm not so sure grandfather thinks so" she said looking at the Admiral with a smile.

"I don't like the fact that you're growing up so fast young lady" the Admiral said to his granddaughter with a smile looking at Max with an overprotective scowl.

"She graduates from High School next summer, then she's off to college; she'll forget about her old grandfather by then" the Admiral said laughing with pride.

"I love him Mr. Mason, but he's a pain sometimes" Kristina said with a giggle hugging her grandfather getting a look from him.

Max looked at the Admiral and rolled his eyes as if to say to him "What are you going to do Sir?" as he shook the Admiral's hand and said "Happy birthday Sir" with a grin.

"Is Stacy and Tyler here Mr. Mason?" Kristina asked with excitement in her voice. Just as she asked both Tyler and Stacy came up next to Max smiling.

Stacy wasn't sure of the Naval protocols involving a party so to play it safe she stood at attention and saluted the Admiral and said "Happy birthday Sir" with a smile to Max.

"At ease Lieutenant, this is a party" the Admiral said to Stacy with a smile. He liked Stacy's costume and asked "Should we be looking for a yellow brick road somewhere around here young lady?" laughing to make her more at ease.

"Thank you Sir for allowing me to be here tonight" Stacy replied knowing that the Admiral pulled some strings to get her Captain to allow her to come tonight for Kristina, and to see her dad before she shipped out for almost a year.

Kristina screamed seeing both Tyler and Stacy and the three of them totally ignored the Admiral and Max looking at each others costumes and complimenting each other. The three of them kept in touch since GBN and would go shopping and have lunch when they could all get together.

This was the first time in four months that Stacy was able to get back to the DC area to see everyone and knew she had to make the most of it.

Kristina grabbed Stacy's hand and pulled her towards the dance floor to dance with her while Tyler stood by Max's side smiling at him and the Admiral.

"Agent Tyler I like your costume" Admiral Cartwright said to her. "I love Charlie Chaplin movies; how is your rehab going?' he asked with a smile.

"It's coming along Sir, I can jog almost three miles now without pain or swelling" Tyler replied thinking she would be back at full strength by Christmas.

"That's wonderful, keep me informed if there's anything you need let me know" the Admiral stated to her.

"Time to go talk politics while Kristina is having fun" he said to both Max and Tyler looking over at her and Stacy dancing.

As he turned to walk away he looked back at Max and smiled saying "Thanks again for dressing up Max" then started to walk over to a crowd of people he recognized when he suddenly stopped and turned back to Max still standing next to Tyler saying with a smile on his face "I hope you will reconsider accepting the President's promotion, you deserve it; and Admiral Mason has a nice ring to it don't you think" then continued on walking.

"Really, am I that transparent?" Max asked Tyler with a disconcerting look.

Tyler smiled at him and giggled "You do prefer to dress up in camouflage and tactical gear" she replied smiling. "And what's this about a promotion; Admiral?" she asked squeezing his arm.

"It's nothing; I turned it down, you know how I hate those kind of things" Max said to her grinning.

"Did the President make you an Admiral?" Tyler asked trying to get him to talk about it with her.

Max rolled his eyes and sighed not wanting to tell her then said "President Bradshaw wants to make me a Rear Admiral for the Boston situation".

Max could see the pride on her face when he told her but hated all the attention the idea was bringing him.

"Rear Admiral Mason, it has a certain charm to it" Tyler said smiling at him seeing how uncomfortable the title made him.

"Let's keep this between just you and me for now please" Max asked. "I don't need anyone calling me Admiral right now" he said with a grin.

"Okay Admiral" Tyler said laughing then kissing him on the lips. "By the way I'm VERY proud of you" she said holding his hand tighter.

Max gave her a big smile "Thanks; come on, let's go see what kind of food this party has" he said grinning at what she said grabbing her hand and walking slowly with her to the buffet line.

The food buffet was extremely impressive to Max and Tyler it had everything from rotisserie chicken to carved roast beef, salads, and a whole table for desserts alone.

Waiters and waitresses were dressed in white and black tuxedos with zombie makeup serving drinks and champagne to guests not sitting at the tables that were positioned all around the ballroom. Max and Tyler sat at a table and ate then handed their empty plates to a waiter that came by and asked to take them.

Max noticed Tyler watching both Stacy and Kristina dancing together and got up out of his seat, tilted his hat, and put his hand out asking "Would you like to cut a rug with me darlin'?"

"Not right now Max" Tyler said with a smile feeling a little self conscious about still using her cane in public but appreciating Max's effort to not let it bother her with others around.

Max wasn't taking no for an answer, he could see how much she wanted too so he said to her "If you don't dance with me; I'm going to have to embarrass my daughter and her friend by dancing alone right next to them" he said grinning. Max started doing his "gopher dance" as he called it; rocking back and forth with his clinched fists in front of him making her laugh at how silly he looked.

Tyler smiled at him and said "We wouldn't want that to be the last thing she remembers before she goes out to sea now would we dad?" she said laughing as she slowly got up grabbing her cane.

Max and Tyler walked over near Kristina and Stacy dancing in front of the stage. Tyler leaned into Stacy and whispered "You owe me big time" giving her a big grin. Stacy looked at her strange not understanding what she meant but ignored it and went on dancing. Max and Tyler slowly danced together next to Stacy and Kristina with smiles on all their faces.

Tyler noticed a waiter dressed like all the other staff except completely without zombie makeup carrying an empty drink tray walk on the other side of the dance floor behind Max about fifteen feet away, but strangely continued to keep his eyes fixated on just Max. She quickly looked around the room and thought this odd after seeing all the wait staff including the buffet serving staff in zombie makeup to go along with the Halloween theme.

Tyler continued to dance with Max along side Stacy and Kristina a couple of feet away keeping an eye on this man who slowly made his way directly behind Max who had his back to him.

Tyler noticed he was about six foot tall, muscular, shaved head, and was either a "gym rat" or had some kind of military look too him especially the way he looked around the room, noticing where the exits were.

Tyler screamed "MAX" as she watched the man she was observing place his tray down on a nearby table and pull out a handgun complete with silencer and raise it slowly towards Max.

Tyler moved to the right of Max pushing Stacy into Kristina causing them both to fall to the floor, then with two hands she aimed her new cane at the man's tuxedo and pulled the eagle head handle straight back towards her…that sent a loud roar out of the barrel of the cane hitting the man with a single .410 shotgun slug that went into his chest and knocked him back four feet into the wall killing him instantly and knocking down several costumed guests to the floor as he fell.

Stacy realized what was going on and her first instinct was to cover up and protect Kristina Cartwright now lying on the floor beside her. As she watched the man go down from Tyler's shot she glanced around the room quickly as another man came up on the other side of the ballroom dance floor with a gun in his hand.

"DAD BEHIND YOU" Stacy screamed as she watched a white clad figure come out of the crowd, a silver throwing star in her hand raised above her head glistening in the party lights.

She looked around continuing to keep Kristina under her to see scared and hysterical guests running for the exit then she looked back at the ninja.

Stacy looked at the white clad ninja girl and the two starred into each other's eyes for a split second then the ninja girl threw the silver throwing star at the man behind Max embedding it deeply into his skull killing him as Max starred into her eyes after the throw whizzed past his head with ferocious velocity.

Max looked back behind him to see the dead waiter with the steel blade in his head with a gun in his hand then turned back quickly to find the white clad ninja girl gone.

Kristina managed to see the white clad ninja kill the man on the other side as she continued to lie on the dance floor and grabbed Stacy next to her to see if she was okay.

"Are you okay Stacy?" Kristina yelled noticing Stacy was pale as a ghost her eyes darting around the room as if she was looking for someone.

"I'm fine sweetie, thanks" Stacy said to her still looking around the room noticing everyone was still in shock at what just happened.

"Did you see that ninja girl kill that man?" Kristina asked relieved it was over and her friend was okay beside her.

"That wasn't a ninja girl" Stacy said to Kristina, still looking around the room. "That was MY sister" looking at Max with questions, who heard what she said with a serious look on his face.

Just as Stacy finished that statement Secret Service agents swarmed the ballroom with guns drawn yelling at Tyler to put her cane on the floor.

Tyler slowly placed the cane on the floor and stepped back putting her hands in the air. The agent close to her picked the cane up off the floor and yelled for her to get on her knees which she awkwardly complied, slowly, not wanting to get shot over any sudden moves. She watched as several agents ran to the two dead gunmen lying in pools of their own blood and secured the guns that were still in their dead hands.

Tyler looked over at Max who had gotten on his knees as well beside her and smiled "He told me not to say anything about it" she said nervously. "Thought you might not approve that he made it for me" Tyler said referring to Mikey's gift; her new shotgun cane.

Max looked at Tyler and smiled "You & Mikey are MY heroes tonight" he said to her holding her hand tightly as agents insisted they present ID's to them.

Admiral Cartwright came out of the crowd of guests having been in another room with some Congressmen and asked "What the HELL is going on here agent?" seeing both Max and Tyler on their knees with their hands on top of their heads like petty criminals. "GET THESE TWO UP OFF THEIR KNEES NOW AGENT" the Admiral said with authority and anger in his voice.

"Yes Sir" the agent replied motioning to both Max and Tyler

that they were free to get up off their knees, then he handed Admiral Cartwright Karen Tyler's cane.

"I take it this is ONE of Captain Stevens little surprises he likes to make" the Admiral asked Max as he admired the craftsmanship he put into a simple single-shot shotgun making it look like a sophisticated walking cane.

He fidgeted with the cane twisting the eagle head back & forth then pulling it up to reveal the spent shotgun shell. Taking it out of the cane he smiled at Max & Tyler saying "I'll be damn"

He placed the shell back into the chamber then pushed the eagle head down to reload it. "When you speak to Captain Stevens later on; tell him I want one" Cartwright said with a big grin to both Max and Tyler then handing the cane back to Tyler.

The agent whispered softly to the Admiral who looked at Max and smiled. "Seriously" he said with a smile to the agent's statement. "I understand another damn ninja was involved tonight Max" the Admiral asked laughing slightly.

"Yes Sir; sorry about ruining your party Sir" Max said apologetic to his commanding officer. "It seems this time a ninja saved my life instead of trying to end it" Max said a bit confused about the situation.

Stacy rolled off of Kristina and helped her up off the floor, who ran directly to her grandfather hugging him uncontrollably who held her tight comforting her. The Admiral looked at Stacy and softly said "Thank you" knowing she kept his granddaughter safe during the attack.

Admiral Cartwright turned to the FBI agent in charge, now standing beside him and informed him that this was officially Max Mason's investigation now.

"Find out who these guys were Max; and what the HELL was that ninja doing here?" the Admiral ordered.

"Yes Sir" Max replied looking at Stacy with concern who returned his look with one of anger and disbelief.

Stacy nodded and smiled as the Admiral glanced back at her smiling then he turned with Kristina and walked toward the front entrance with his Secret Service detail.

Stacy dusted her dress off and walked over to Tyler and her dad standing over the first body that Tyler had killed.

She watched as Max bent down to search the dead assassin's pockets seeing the big hole in his chest and his white tuxedo covered in his own blood.

The only thing Max found in the dead man's pockets was a small picture with a word on the back of it. Max looked at the single word "DRAGON" on the one side then flipped it over to see his own face on the picture. Max looked up at both Stacy and Tyler and showed them the picture.

"Dad, why does he have a picture of you?" Stacy asked getting upset now.

Max didn't say anything to his daughter, instead he got up and walked over to the other dead body across the floor. Max noticed the precision the silver throwing star hit the man right between his eyes into the right eye socket between the bridge of his nose and his eyeball, impaling directly into his brain killing him instantly. Max thought to himself that there was only ONE ninjitsu Master who taught this particular technique and he was DEAD.

Max again leaned down on one knee and searched the second assassin to find the same small picture of himself, flipping it over to find the word "DRAGON" again inscribed on the back of it figuring out they were working together to kill Max at the party and both given pictures of him to recognize their target.

"Director Mason, I have two undressed dead bodies in zombie makeup downstairs in the parking garage, and two alive but unconscious NSA agents on the second floor, one outside and one inside the security surveillance office Sir" a young African American FBI agent informed him. "The building is now completely secure Sir" he said to Max.

Max looked around the room observing as FBI agents interviewed, and took notes letting the guests leave after they made their statements.

He watched intently as both Stacy and Tyler were being debriefed, noticing they both continued to glance over at him with concern about him almost being killed tonight.

Max walked over to Tyler and Stacy sitting at a table with another agent and stood beside Tyler putting his hand on her shoulder to comfort her. "Ballistics is going to have to take your cane in for processing sweetheart" he said with a smile.

"I made it a top priority so you can get it back tomorrow" he continued as Tyler handed him the shotgun cane Mikey made for her.

Stacy stood up and looked at Max with anger in her eyes and asked "When do we get to talk about this dad?" putting her hands on her hips and starring into his eyes then glancing down at Tyler.

"Not now sweetheart, wait till we get in the car" Max replied knowing this was a conversation they all needed to have. Max approached the lead investigator and asked "Are we needed here anymore Agent?"

"No Sir, we have everything we need from your team Director, you can leave now Sir" the agent said walking the three of them towards the front entrance.

Max Mason looked back to see the FBI's criminal forensic team rushing around the ballroom to process all the evidence they could find then addressed the agent escorting them to the front entrance "Thank you, make sure I get copies of everything on this case in my office by tomorrow morning" Max asked as he followed Tyler and Stacy out the front door of the building. Max looked back for a moment thinking it was a nice party.

CHAPTER TWO

Max, Tyler, and Stacy walked out and stood at the top of the marble steps in the crisp October night air looking down at all the flashing blue lights of the emergency response vehicles that had blocked off all the streets leading to the Raymond Earl building. Max looked at Tyler and said with a sheepish grin "And you say I never take you anywhere fun".

Tyler smacked him in the arm as she was being helped down the stairs by Stacy and replied "You're such an asshole Mason".

"Yeah, but I'm a cute asshole" he said laughing trying to lighten the mood but seeing that neither of them would go along with him.

Stacy helped Tyler all the way down the steps to Max's awaiting SUV, helped her into the front seat closed her door then got in the back. She closed her door and put her seat belt on waiting for Max to get into the driver's side. Once Max got in and put his seat belt on she lit into him "WHERE THE HELL HAS SHE BEEN FOR THE PAST TEN YEARS DAD?"

"You need to calm down Lieutenant" Max said with authority looking at her in the back seat in his rear view mirror.

"REALLY DAD, you're going to pull this RANK shit on me?" Stacy asked, her face turning bright red from anger. "This has NOTHING to do with the Navy, CAPTAIN; but it has EVERYTHING to do with FAMILY and nothing else" she said to her father defiantly.

Tyler reached over and put her hand on Max's shoulder then looked back at Stacy agitated in the back seat saying "We all need to talk about this rationally and figure this out together".

Before Stacy could say anything negative to Tyler Max spoke up "I'm sorry sweetheart, but I SERIOUSLY have NO idea where she's been or why she was here tonight" Max said to his upset daughter still looking at her in the mirror.

Tyler was confused by the conversation and asked "Who was she?" wanting to know who the white clad ninja girl was who saved Max's life earlier.

"She's MY sister Yuki; Yuki Amikura" Stacy replied to Tyler giving her father the evil eye he's known for many years when she got pissed at him.

"We haven't heard from her in over ten years, it was like she dropped off the face of the planet" Stacy continued saying to Tyler.

"And NOW all of a sudden she shows up in the middle of a Halloween party and saves YOUR life from a couple of professional assassins; WHAT THE FUCK IS UP WITH THAT DAD?" Stacy yelled again angrily at Max.

"Wait a minute; Amikura, as in Tanaka Amikura?" Tyler asked out loud to them both.

Max looked over at Tyler and said "Yes, she is Tanaka's little sister; when her father was killed she stayed with us for about eight years until her uncle from Japan came and took her away from us" he replied. "My wife and I tried to adopt her through the military but her uncle was family and refused to allow us" Max explained. "The uncle took her back to Japan and that was the first time we've seen her in over ten years" he explained seeing the sadness in Stacy's eyes.

"We tried looking for her through the military to no avail; she just disappeared, then Stacy's mother was killed in the car accident and I got shipped back to the states with the kids" Max said seeing tears come down Stacy's face in his mirror.

"I know you're confused and hurting princess, I don't have any answers right now; but I'm damn sure going to find them" he said to his daughter trying to calm her down after the sudden discovery that her best friend was still alive, and well, after all these years.

Max pulled into his drive way walked around to Tyler's side and helped her get out of the SUV. Stacy grabbed her basket prop and followed behind the two of them. "Why hasn't she tried to contact us before now?" Stacy asked as Max unlocked the front door and pushed it open.

Stacy seemed to have Max's six-sense when it came to danger and felt something strange as Max opened the front door. She pushed Max slightly and raised her basket in front of him to watch a sharp silver throwing knife stick into it where Max's head would have been as they stepped inside the door. Max flipped on the light switch beside the door to see the white clad ninja standing in his dining room about fifteen feet from the three of them as they stood in the open doorway.

Tyler quickly pulled the small .380 automatic pistol Max kept in the small key & mail table near the front door and aimed it at the person standing there in all white.

Stacy yelled "NO, Tyler don't shoot her" as she took her hand and slowly lowered Tyler's gun.

The ninja slowly lowered her white mask to reveal her face to the three of them. "YUKI" Stacy yelled as she saw her face staring into her big blue eyes. Stacy smiled at her childhood friend and asked "Where have you been all these years?"

Yuki (pronounced "You-Key") Amikura was all grown up now, into a beautiful young Asian woman. She stood about 5'-6" tall, and weighed about 140 pounds with a model build, but her bright blue eyes were what made her stand out. She ignored what Stacy asked starring into Max's eyes and stating "Max Mason you have killed MY father and brother you MUST pay for your betrayal of my family's honor" Yuki said looking back at Stacy.

"Wait a minute" Stacy said to her defending her dad. "He didn't kill your father; Tanaka did" Stacy said to her moving slowly in front of Max. "You've got your facts messed up girl" Stacy said staring her down.

Yuki looked away from Stacy and looked again at Max and replied "I will not kill you in front of my sister, but I am coming for you Max Mason" the young Asian woman said to him.

"WHAT THE FUCK IS THAT SUPPOSE TO MEAN?" Stacy asked her defiantly, knowing she just threatened to kill her dad.

Tyler took a step towards the young Asian girl the gun in her hand still pointing at her and said "You better bring a lunch girl, because it will be an all day thing getting past me, to get to him" she said with a determined stare and a grin.

Yuki looked at Tyler and grinned thinking what she said was amusing then looked back at Stacy "It was nice to see you again MY sister; you have grown up well" she replied to Stacy with a smile.

"Where have you been?" Stacy asked confused, then watched as the young girl ran to the open window in the dining room and dove out into the night air.

Stacy ran to the open window and screamed "YUKI, REMEMBER OUR GAME" she said hoping she heard what she said into the night.

Stacy sat down on a chair in the dining room and started crying thinking she was never going to see Yuki again. Max walked up to her and put his arm around her as Tyler put the gun back in the drawer.

Stacy hugged her dad and asked "Why is she doing this?" as tears continued to roll down her face.

"I'm not sure sweetheart, she's definitely confused about the past" Max said trying to make her feel better thinking that someone has put these thoughts into Yuki's mind to make her try to kill him.

"I'm going to bed daddy" Stacy said standing up and kissing Max on the cheek. "Good night Karen" she said giving her a hug and a smile before heading up the stairs to her bedroom.

"Good night princess" Max said lovingly watching Stacy climb the stairs towards her bedroom thinking she has to be somewhat confused with what's happening with Yuki.

The moon was full and bright shining down on the playground near Max's house as a white clad figure slowly moved in the shadows surrounding the children's swings and slides.

"I didn't think you would show" a voice said from the darkness.

Yuki Amikura stepped out of the shadows and into the moonlight hearing the voice walking towards her from the shadows. "I'm surprised YOU remembered" Yuki said with a smile standing next to the children's slide.

Stacy Mason walked into the moonlight dressed in her all black tactical gear minus her guns with her long blonde hair in a ponytail.

She left her guns at home because she remembered as children Yuki hated guns, refusing to even touch one; she preferred razor-sharp blades instead.

"Where have you been all this time?" Stacy asked as the two young women faced each other. "We thought you were dead" she said.

"My dad and I looked for you, where were you; DAMN IT, ANSWER ME" Stacy yelled tears welling up into her eyes.

"My Uncle Nabu took me back to Japan to live with him and my cousin Noki; he took us into the mountains and trained us to honor the ninja code like my father and brother" she replied to her, looking at Stacy thinking she had grown up to be so beautiful.

"My Uncle told us the stories of how your father killed my father and brother, and then burned the images of their deaths into our brains" she continued as Stacy stood there and listened to her.

"I made a promise to my Uncle on his deathbed that I would avenge our family honor by killing Max Mason; and that is what I'm here to do my sister" Yuki said with a stern look on her face.

Stacy stepped towards her "unofficially adopted" sister and looked her hard in the eyes pointing her finger at her saying "First off, MY father did not kill YOUR father; YOUR fucked up brother did" she said very angrily.

Yuki stood there staring back at her with a scowl on her face refusing to believe what she was saying to her about her brother.

"Second, my father only killed your nut job brother because he was going to blow up a building full of children because of his stupid jealousy issues he had with YOUR father; I KNOW, I was there, he tried to kill me too" Stacy said standing nose to nose with Yuki.

Yuki didn't like the tone of Stacy's rant stepped back into a fighting pose and said "I guess we're not going to talk about this friendly anymore, are we sister".

"I guess not" Stacy said quickly throwing a right hand punch to Yuki's jaw connecting solidly causing Yuki to stagger back wiping away a small amount of blood on her now split lip.

Stacy stepped back to see what she would do, and didn't have to wait long when a round house spinning kick caught her by surprise hitting her in the side knocking her into the metal and plastic sliding board. Stacy grabbed her ribs as she leaned on the slide and felt a bit of soreness; caught her breath and stood back up in front of the white clad ninja girl.

"What do you know about family honor?" Yuki asked angrily at Stacy standing in front of her in an aggressive stance.

"Plenty; I know honor is about trust, family, protecting those that can't protect themselves, and JUSTICE" Stacy said spin kicking Yuki fast and hard in the stomach knocking her to the ground.

"YOU KNOW NOTHING OF HONOR" Yuki screamed at Stacy as she slowly got up from the ground her white ninja uniform now covered in playground dirt.

"YOU ONLY KNOW ABOUT SHOPPING MALLS, CELL PHONES, THE INTERNET, AND ON DEMAND MOVIES" she continued. "YOU KNOW NOTHING OF SACRIFICE, LONELINESS, OR DEATH" Yuki explained pulling her sword from its scabbard behind her back and swinging it to her side.

"REALLY; now you want to fight to the death?" Stacy asked as she reached behind her back and pulled out two steel three pronged sharpened Sai's and brought them out to the sides of her.

"Looks like you are YOUR father's daughter" Yuki said slicing at Stacy who countered with one of her Sai's catching her sword and pushing Yuki backwards.

"You have NO idea" Stacy stubbornly replied waiting for Yuki's next move.

"I loved your father, and he loved me; do you think he would approve of us trying to kill each other" Stacy asked as Yuki swung her blade in anger hearing what she said about her long dead father cutting Stacy on the right arm seeing the blood on her sword.

"WOW" Stacy said stepping back. "That's gonna leave a mark you know" she said laughing reaching up and putting her hand over her cut to stop the bleeding.

Stacy walked away from Yuki and over to the swings throwing her Sai's on the ground in front of her, sitting down on one of the swings looking at Yuki in attack position with her sword above her head.

"I'm NOT going to kill YOU, and you're NOT going to kill ME; so sit down here with me and lets figure this out together like family, like we used to when we were kids" Stacy asked as she rocked slowly back and forth in the swing watching as Yuki lowered her sword.

Yuki walked over to the swing and smiled at Stacy then shoved her sword into the soft ground and sat down on the swing beside her gently rocking the swing back and forth.

"I've NEVER stopped thinking about you, you are my big sister; MY FAMILY" Stacy said to Yuki swinging side by side with her.

Stacy pulled out a 5x7 picture from her tactical vest pocket that showed the two of them smiling when they were young right before Yuki left for Japan, and showed it to her.

"I remember that day, WE were so happy" Yuki said pulling her own 5x7 picture out of her ninja gee to show Stacy she NEVER forgot either.

The two young women laughed together and swung their swings faster and higher, then Stacy slowed down and pulled out a bag of strawberry flavored licorice strings and handed Yuki one as Stacy took a big bite of the one she had.

"I remember Max Mason use to give these to us when we got mad at one another" Yuki said with a big grin. "I haven't had one of these in years" she continued. "He always reminded us that no matter how mad or angry we were at one another we always had each others backs because we were sisters" Yuki said with a tear coming down her face.

"Where do you think I got these; he has a stash in a cabinet in the kitchen" Stacy replied laughing. "When I get upset he pulls them out" she said laughing with tears in her eyes. "It never gets old eating one of these" Stacy said laughing.

"By the way, who is the woman with the gun?" Yuki asked referring to Tyler back in Max's living room.

"Kinda ballsy her stepping up to you huh" Stacy said with a smile.

"Yeah, I wasn't expecting that; I like her" Yuki said laughing.

"She's dad's girlfriend, Secret Service Agent Karen Tyler; I have a feeling soon she's going to be OUR stepmom" Stacy said chewing on her licorice string with a big smile on her face.

"She's VERY protective of you and Max Mason" Yuki replied noticing that she was willing to kill her for both of them.

"Yeah, do me a favor and don't try to kill her, she saved my life last year from your brother's men" Stacy said to her slowly swinging back and forth then looking at her sister with a funny smile.

"She saved my sister's life that makes her MY family now" Yuki said bowing her head to Stacy.

"Lady Tyler will be under my protection from this day on" she said raising her head to show Stacy her beautiful smile.

"LADY Tyler" Stacy replied with a chuckle. "She'll love hearing that one" Stacy said laughing with Yuki.

Stacy went on to tell her what had happened to her and her dad the past few years; about losing his Secret Service charge, the GBN attack with her brother Tanaka, becoming a Navy SEAL, her dad's Boston adventure, the hospital takeover with Tyler, and her being shipped out this coming weekend by the Navy as the two of them chewed on their candy.

"Why did your Uncle Nabu want my dad dead if he knew the truth about YOUR father and brother?" Stacy asked hoping this wouldn't put them at odds with one another again.

KILLS OF THE FATHER

"Plain and simple; JEALOUSY" Yuki replied to her question.

"Max Mason was the ONLY student my father ever trained that wasn't Japanese and my Uncle resented him, and hated my father for training him" she continued.

Yuki went on to explain where she had been all these years; training with her uncle's ninja clan, going to business school in Tokyo, and inheriting her uncle's large multi-billion dollar electronic and telecommunication businesses around the world with her cousin Noki.

"So you're a rich party girl" Stacy said laughing knowing that was the furthest thing from the truth with Yuki.

Yuki laughed and replied "No, I'm just a figure head that signs the checks with my cousin" she said smiling back at Stacy still swaying back and forth on the swing.

"You wanna pay my rent for the next ten years" Stacy asked jokingly with a big grin.

Yuki gave her a big smile and giggle in return.

Stacy slowed her swing down and stood up then bent over and picked up her two Sai's lying on the ground in front of her and slipped them both behind her back into her belt.

"I see your father has taught you the way of the ninja" Yuki said still swinging and smiling knowing her little sister can take care of herself.

"Nah, he just taught me how to kick somebody's ass" Stacy said laughing. "And by the way, YOU cut me" she reminded her older sister looking at the cut on her right jacket arm. "You owe me a new jacket girlfriend" Stacy said to her sister laughing.

Yuki smiled and said "You got my nice white uniform dirty, as well as giving me a bloody lip" laughing back at her.

"That kinda makes US even" Yuki replied smiling.

"Oh yeah, you might want to start wearing black or maybe the royal blue they have available; that would look really cute on you by the way" she said with a grin. "They tend to get less dirty if you get knocked to the ground" Stacy said to her smiling sarcastically.

"What about MY dad?" Stacy asked as Yuki turned to walk away grabbing her sword out of the ground and slipping it back into the scabbard behind her back. "Are you still going to TRY and kill him?" she asked watching her sister head towards the shadows of the trees.

"You understand he's not that easy to kill; RIGHT" Stacy said, her voice getting louder as she watched her big sister start too walk away.

"How do I get in touch with you again?" Stacy asked hoping this wasn't the last time she will see her.

Yuki Amikura turned and smiled at Stacy handing her a business card she pulled out of her now dirty white gee saying "Only you get to use this, understand little sister" Yuki said as Stacy looked at the card with only a phone number on it.

"Tell OUR father Max Mason he's welcome, and that I'll be around if he needs me since his OTHER daughter will be out playing with fish in the ocean" she said waving to her then turning and disappearing into the late night darkness.

Stacy watched as her newly found big sister disappeared into the woods then turned and started heading back to Max's house down the street. Stacy climbed the trellis Max had attached to the house many years ago and climbed in the window of her bedroom to find both Max and Tyler sitting on her bed waiting for her.

Stacy smiled because she knew her dad and Tyler knew where she had been. This reminded her of the time when she was fourteen and her dad caught her sneaking back in around 1am after going to see a boy she liked and HE didn't.

"Are YOU and her OKAY?" Max asked as Stacy pulled her Sai's from her belt and placed them on her nightstand table then sat down on the bed with the two of them.

"You mean did WE try to kill each other?" Stacy asked grinning.

"You do look a little battle worn sweetheart" Max replied seeing the cut on her right arm as she removed her jacket and tactical vest.

"You should see the other girl" Stacy said smiling at the two of them and making a joke.

Max noticed the bag of red licorice sticking out of her jacket pocket and asked "Did it work?" knowing what she used them for then pulling the bag out, grabbing one and putting it in his mouth smiling.

"Maybe; she's a bit confused right now but I think I got some points across to her" Stacy replied.

"She's going to need some time to figure this all out in her head, but I don't think she's going to try and kill you anymore" Stacy said biting down on a piece of candy tearing it in half and giving the other half to Tyler who smiled putting the candy in her mouth.

"Is she coming back; she has a place here if she wants it" Max asked Stacy. "Where is she staying, how is she getting by?" Max asked like a concerned father.

"She told me to tell you she'll be around" Stacy said smiling knowing Yuki gave her a private phone number if she needed her big sister. "Whatever the Hell that's supposed to mean" she said to her dad heading into her bathroom laughing.

"Trust me dad, she'll be fine in the outside world" Stacy said with a grin knowing Yuki was well off and could stay anywhere she wanted.

Stacy turned back and looked at Tyler smiling "By the way; she likes you Lady Tyler, you made a friend for life" she said closing the bathroom door behind her.

Tyler looked at Max with a confused look on her face saying "Lady Tyler?"

"I've ALWAYS thought you were a lady" Max replied to Tyler with a smile.

"Aren't you the charmer" Tyler said with a big grin leaning over and giving him a kiss.

Max smiled knowing his friend's daughter was back in their lives, but still worried about her; not knowing where she was or how she was taking care of herself.

Tyler grabbed his hand as he looked at her and smiled. "She'll be fine, they BOTH will" Tyler said to him knowing that look on his face.

"I'm not worried about them, they can both take care of themselves; what I'm worried about is that we still don't have a clue who's trying to kill me or why; or when the next attack will come" he said to her with concern.

Yuki Amikura slowly and silently opened the window into the bedroom of the hotel she was staying in and climbed through standing beside the bed. As she closed the window behind her she heard a voice in the dark.

"If you insist on climbing in and out of the bedroom window PERHAPS we should consider renting our hotel rooms below the 10th floor" the voice said as the bedroom light came on to reveal a young Asian woman wearing a black pants suit standing there looking at her.

"You know how those high-rise cross winds can affect ones climbing up the side of a building" the Asian woman continued sarcastically with a straight face.

"You're my assistant Ochi, NOT my mother" Yuki said to the young assistant standing in front of her with disapproving eyes.

"Did you see her?" Ochi asked excitedly.

Ochi Okasa (pronounced "OH-KEY") was a petite, beautiful, young Asian woman with short black hair. She has been Yuki Amikura's personal assistant, college roommate, and sparring partner for the past ten years since she was assigned to her by Yuki's late Uncle Nabu when she was ten years old as her personal companion.

"How do you think I got this?" Yuki asked pointing to the bruise and split lip on the side of her face as she slowly took off the dirty white ninja uniform and handed it to Ochi.

"Looks like your little sister has her own skills" Ochi replied looking at the playground dirt all over the white uniform. Ochi put the dirty uniform on the bedroom chair and picked up Yuki's white ninja sword sliding it all the way out of its white scabbard to see traces of blood on the blade looking at it with concern on her face.

"Whose blood is on your sword?" Ochi asked Yuki suspiciously who had her back to her assistant continuing to undress.

Yuki Amikura stood there in front of her friend and assistant embarrassed with her head lowered and said "It's Stacy's blood" looking up at Ochi who was shaking her head with disappointment.

"YOU CUT YOUR SISTER?" Ochi said forcefully to an already guilt ridden Yuki. "Did you hurt her?" Ochi asked hoping a small cut was the worst of it.

"NO NO, she's okay; she even forgave me for it" Yuki replied smiling at Ochi and continuing to explain that she didn't mean to harm her little sister.

"She surprised me, and embarrassed me by putting me on the ground" Yuki said laughing. "I let my anger get the best of me and she taught me how to control it" she continued.

"BUT, I did go to far by cutting her SLIGHTLY" Yuki said trying to show her remorse and get forgiveness from her friend in front of her.

"I know it's no excuse and petty, but SHE did throw the first punch" Yuki said laughing. "I need to order her a new jacket by the way" she said smiling.

"You're right, it's no excuse, she's your family; WE don't KILL family" Ochi said giving her best friend a forgiving smile.

"And you're right, she does have serious skills; she's practically ninja" Yuki said. "But then again, she was trained by HER father who was trained by MY father; so it shouldn't surprise me that much" Yuki continued as she watched Ochi put the sword back in its scabbard and place it back on the bed, then pick up the dirty uniform looking at it still a bit confused how it got so much dirt on it.

"Maybe we should go with a royal blue uniform for now on, I

understand I would look "cute" in it" Yuki said giggling thinking what Stacy had said.

"Do you think she knows?" Ochi asked placing the soiled uniform on the arm of the chair.

"You mean does she know I have been keeping an eye on her for a while?" Yuki asked washing her dirty face with a wet washcloth Ochi had handed to her after coming from the bathroom.

"She seemed really surprised, AND angry to see me; so I don't think she knows" Yuki replied to her assistant's question.

"Your Uncle's business enemies might try to use her against you; you know that don't you?" Ochi asked concerned for Yuki's new family connection.

"That might have some merit after what happened tonight" Yuki said.

"Two professional assassins tried to kill Max Mason at the costume party tonight" she said looking out the hotel window with her back to Ochi rolling her eyes knowing what she was about to hear from her friend and confidant.

"Someone other than YOU tried to kill him; interesting?" Ochi asked with a condescending smile as Yuki turned to look at her.

"YES, someone other than ME" Yuki replied giving Ochi a funny look and sticking her tongue out playfully. "Max's girlfriend killed one, I killed the other" she replied to her assistant.

"So YOU saved his life instead of killing him?" Ochi asked seeing the confusion on her friend's face.

"I actually tried to kill him at his house but Stacy surprised me being there" Yuki said sitting on the bed feeling embarrassed.

"I may have been a bit misguided in my enthusiasm to kill Max Mason for my father and brother" Yuki expressed out loud.

"Yeah I know; you want to say I told you so" Yuki said smiling at her young friend.

"You didn't kill him, so I don't have too" Ochi replied smiling back. "Other than your cousin Noki, the Mason's are the ONLY thing close to family you have" Ochi said smiling.

"You're my family" Yuki said to her with a big smile.

"And you will ALWAYS be my family; but Max Mason, Stacy, and Jacob are your REAL family and they MUST be protected" Ochi said smiling.

Yuki Amikura walked over to Ochi and hugged her. She brushed away a tear and smiled at her long time friend who smiled back appreciating the hug.

"How did you kill the assassin?" Ochi asked Yuki curiously who had her back to her assistant pulling clothes from one of her suitcases.

"I hit him in the eye with a steel throwing star" Yuki replied as she turned holding some clothes to see Ochi putting her sword and uniform away in her specially made tactical bag.

"So if the target was Max Mason; why would someone want to kill him in such a public way" Ochi said thinking out loud.

"I don't know; but I downloaded the security surveillance footage to a flash drive before I escaped from the building; thought maybe you could go through it for me" Yuki replied with a smile handing the small electronic device to her.

"Let's run it through the facial recognition software and see if we can get a hit, maybe through Interpol or the Global Security Council" Yuki asked as she got undressed to take a shower.

While Yuki took a shower Ochi Okasa sat at the desk and opened the laptop sitting there on top of it. She plugged the flash drive into the USB port and booted up the computer. She typed the keyboard feverishly then watched for her results. Ochi Okasa was a computer genius and hacker who work's for Yuki as her private computer specialist in the company.

She fast forwarded the video to the attempt on Max Mason's life zeroing in on the two men that tried to kill him.

She ran their faces through Yuki's suggested Interpol and Global Security Council criminal profiles and came up with no matches.

She leaned back in the chair and watched the video footage a couple of times for anything the two men did leading up to their attempt on Max Mason's life, finally noticing that they both wore the same type of ring on their right hands.

Yuki Amikura finished her shower and walked back into the hotel bedroom wearing bright red silk pajama's that she had taken out of her suitcase, drying her wet hair with a towel. She stood behind Ochi looking over her shoulder at the laptop screen and asked "Anything on them?"

"Not yet; but I did find something interesting about the two of them" Ochi said as she enlarged the captured photographs from the video surveillance footage to show Yuki the rings on both assassin's hands.

"They wear the same ring, so they knew each other" Yuki said out loud seeing the rings on their hands.

The two silver rings had a large eagle holding a U.S. flag in its beak; this lead both Yuki and Ochi to believe they were U.S. military or ex-military.

Ochi continued to type on the keyboard of the laptop while Yuki dried her hair in back of her continuing to look over her shoulder at the brightly lit screen.

"Looks like they ARE ex-military" Ochi said looking at the U.S. Military Personnel website on her screen after hacking into their secured server and running their faces through her facial recognition software.

"They are Sgt. David Styler and Sgt. Bradley Joseph" Ochi said looking at their personnel records on her screen.

Yuki looked down at the screen now standing beside Ochi reading, that both dead assassins were honorably discharged just months ago from Fort Bragg in North Carolina.

They were both documented as "Special Forces" Marines highly trained in weapons, hand to hand combat, explosives, and both were highly decorated; each serving three tours in Afghanistan.

"Why were two highly decorated Marines trying to kill a man they had NO connection too" Yuki asked, confused, looking at Ochi as she continued to read their profiles.

"It says here, that after Styler and Joseph both left the military they got jobs working for Allied Security Limited" Ochi said continuing to read the two dead men's profiles.

"Allied Security Limited, who are they?" Yuki asked watching Ochi type on her laptop.

"They are a highly trained contracted security firm that protects company CEO's, diplomats, and celebrities with offices all over the United States" Ochi said reading out loud.

"The firm is run by a Colonel Joseph Howler; but do you want to hear the interesting part?" she asked looking up at Yuki with a smile.

"Colonel Howler was dishonorably discharged from the Marines fifteen months ago, and both Styler & Joseph were under his command at the time" Ochi revealed to her friend.

"Why was Howler dishonorably discharged?" Yuki asked combing the tangles out of her almost dry hair.

"Insubordination unbecoming of an officer is all it says" Ochi replied. "Whatever it was, it happened in Afghanistan while the three of them were there" Ochi continued.

"How many ex-soldiers work for Howler; and where does he operate from?" Yuki asked curiously.

"Howler works out of Raleigh, North Carolina right now" Ochi responded. "He has about fifty men working for him there" she continued.

"Who is he contracted to in Raleigh?" Yuki asked as Ochi continued typing.

"It looks like Howler and his men are working for Covington Industries; a new up and coming smart phone company in Raleigh-Durham" Ochi said reading the company's promotional website.

"They are advertising a BIG announcement this week to the

media" she read from her screen. "They are owned by Evelyn and Nathanial Covington from Raleigh" she continued reading.

"Are they husband and wife?" Yuki asked curiously.

"No; mother and son actually" Ochi replied.

"OH MY GOD, this can't be right" Ochi said out loud causing Yuki to be concerned.

"WHAT'S WRONG, WHAT'S THE PROBLEM OCHI?" Yuki asked sternly to her assistant.

"THEY ALL WORK FOR, YOU" Ochi said with concern in her voice looking up at Yuki from her seat.

"WHAT?" Yuki asked with shock on her face dropping her brush on the hotel floor.

"I followed the money like you taught me" Ochi said continuing to stare at her computer screen. "Allied Security deposited $15 million dollars into their account this past Friday; the day BEFORE Admiral Cartwright's party" she continued.

"So how does that connect them to me?" Yuki asked confused by her statement a moment ago.

"I looked for any business that withdrew that kind of money the past few days and came up with five companies, including Amikura Electronics" Ochi replied with a stern look on her face.

"NOKI" Yuki said loudly knowing her cousin had the clearance to withdraw that kind of money from the business without a second look.

"It seems your cousin wants Max Mason dead as well, but doesn't want to get his hands dirty doing it" Ochi said to her friend who she could see was getting angry at how this situation was unfolding now.

"Do we have a location on my cousin; is he still in Japan?" Yuki asked watching Ochi type away to get her the information.

"Interesting enough, your cousin is in Raleigh as we speak" the young assistant replied back with a grin.

"Get us to Raleigh; and Ochi, lets do it quietly if we can" Yuki asked smiling at her friend, her smile turning to anger as she walked away knowing she was going to have to confront her cousin Noki about trying to kill her adopted father Max Mason.

"Let's go meet the Covington's and see what kind of southern hospitality they have since my cousin Noki has been lying to them all this time" Yuki said watching Ochi type away on her laptop.

CHAPTER THREE

About three-hundred miles south of the Nations Capitol, the Secret Service, Northern Virginia, AND Max Mason; lies the beautifully wooded state of North Carolina.

Full of rustic slow paced charm, poverty, backwoods' cultures, golf courses, down-home friendly people, and of course pork barbecue; these are just a few of the things the cities of North Carolina have to offer anyone wanting to visit or stay.

One of these cities; Raleigh, with its population of just under a half a million people; pride themselves on bringing big businesses to their city, especially telecommunication companies who bring millions of dollars of revenue and jobs everyday into their fair state.

Covington Industries is a world-wide conglomerate in the telecommunications and satellite market; a family run company, established over thirty years ago; with a somewhat new subsidiary in Raleigh, established here just five years ago.

The company is a "smart phone" application business that designs "phone apps" to allow technology to help people in their everyday lives with such things as shopping, dining, home improvements, transportation, entertainment, and much more; right from their cell phones.

Covington Industries was about to present the world with their most ambitious application yet; an "App" that paid the person to use it. For a one time fee to purchase the application; every time the person used the "App" they would receive 1.5% cash back from their purchases after the first month.

The company was raved upon for putting money back into the consumers pocket and strengthening the world's economy. Covington's simple and straight forward marketing strategy covered everything around the world, from social media, television, radio, print, to the internet.

Everyone was talking about them; from Presidents of foreign countries, to the grocery store bag boy in downtown Raleigh.

The countdown to the digital satellite launch, and up-link to everyone's phone; flashed outside the Covington's main building.

The Covington's digital billboard; right outside Raleigh's North Carolina state government district, as of eight AM Monday morning reading 16-hours, 00-minutes, 00-seconds until launch; or tonight, Wednesday at midnight.

But, Covington Industries wasn't without its demons. The company had lost countless millions of dollars the past couple of years on flimsy breakable products, bad tech support, social media complaints, and legal bills for an investigation by the Stock Exchange Commission for "corporate corruption & insider trading". The "SEC" believed Covington Industries' Board of Directors were arrogant, corrupt, abused their employees, and continue to believe THEY were above the law.

Wealthy matriarch Evelyn Covington and her only son Nathaniel, owned Covington Industries for over thirty years. Evelyn inherited the company from her husband Phillip after he died from a car accident the night after she brought their son home from the hospital twenty-eight years ago. Evelyn raised him not wanting anything or anyone; except her, and her guidance.

She also ran Covington Industries with an iron fist, not allowing anyone to stand in her or her son's way with the business. She was ruthless, something she learned from her husband before he died; passing it on to her son.

When Nathaniel turned twenty-one years old Evelyn Covington turned the company over to him to run, with her as a silent partner. She noticed he had a knack for the business just like her deceased husband and could see a dark, ruthless side in him that she admired and encouraged.

On this particular Wednesday morning Nathaniel Covington stood in the middle of the large martial arts studio his mother had built in their house for him, as the morning sun shined through the large windows Nathaniel wore a white karate gee uniform with a black belt surrounded by three other men all dressed in black uniforms.

Nathaniel stood about 6'-2" tall, muscular, and weighed about 245 pounds with short brown hair waiting for the three men circling around him to attack. Covington's valet and personal bodyguard Simon stood against the wall and watched holding a white towel.

The first man came at the twenty-eight year old millionaire with a straight right leg kick which Nathaniel blocked easily hitting the man hard with a left handed backhand across the face knocking him to the matted floor.

The second man attacked immediately throwing a right handed punch to Nathaniel's face that he quickly blocked turning the man's back to him, allowing Nathaniel to kick him in the back hard causing him to sprawl across the floor face first.

Just as the third man attacked, the door to the large room opened and a tall man dressed in black military fatigues walked in; distracting Nathaniel for a split second, just as he took a hard right hand punch to his mouth. He looked at the man that walked in and smiled at him as he wiped the blood from his busted lip with the sleeve of his white uniform.

Covington gave the military dressed man a sinister grin then looked at the man that hit him and motioned with his hand for him to come at him again.

Covington waited for his attack, blocking the kick that came towards his head pushing the man back hard with a straight palm thrust to his chest causing him to stagger backwards holding his chest in pain.

Covington looked over again at the man that just came in and gave him a smile and a wink, seeing the man roll his eyes at him.

Still holding his chest in pain the man dressed in black swung carelessly at Nathaniel with his right fist who quickly ducked under his swing coming back up to hit him hard in his left ribs, again staggering him backwards in more pain now.

The other two men that Nathaniel defeated stood watching as their colleague tried to kick him, in which Nathaniel grabbed his leg and came down hard on the bone with his elbow breaking the leg with a loud crack then tossing his leg out to watch the man crumble to the floor in extreme pain.

Nathaniel Covington stood there watching the other two men pick the third up and carry him out the door still hearing his sobs and groans of pain as Simon approached and handed him the towel.

"What can I do for you Colonel Howler?" Covington asked drying his arms off with the towel looking at the man dressed in military fatigues.

"Do you feel better?" Colonel Howler asked watching Covington smile as he wiped the remaining blood from his mouth then handing the blood stained towel back to Simon.

"Yeah, actually I do" Nathaniel Covington replied laughing.

"We may have a slight problem" Howler said looking Covington in the eyes with a serious look on his face.

"My mother and I pay you A LOT of money so there aren't any problems Colonel" Covington said with concern in his voice.

Dishonorably discharged former Army Colonel Joseph Howler served the U.S. Army for over fifteen years as a Special Forces commander in Afghanistan and Iraq with thirty-five confirmed insurgent kills to his record.

He commanded an elite squad that went through villages to capture Taliban and Red Guard insurgents for interrogation. Upon capture he himself would interrogate the prisoners, most times to the Army's dislike ending in their deaths.

Howler's methods were finally challenged by a General whom Howler attacked during the proceeding, sending him to the brig and a court-martial for insubordination and striking an officer.

After his dishonorable discharge, Howler returned to the states and started his security company Allied Security Limited after his short six month stint in Kansas's Leavenworth military prison; hiring former military and law enforcement who didn't have issues going the extra mile to achieve their objective, of making money; and lots of it.

Allied Security Limited had grown to include over thirty locations across the United States, including Raleigh N.C. where their primary service was protecting CEO's, politicians, and wealthy individuals who could afford them like Evelyn and Nathaniel Covington.

"My tech analyst says that a piece of code was emailed to an outside source earlier this morning" Howler said knowing this would upset Covington.

Covington looked at Howler with rage in his eyes and asked angrily "Do we fucking know who sent it out, and who they sent it too".

"My guy hasn't broke down the firewalls they used yet, but he's working on it as we speak" Howler told Covington as he stood at the bottom of the stairs watching Covington walk up the stairs.

Covington stopped halfway up the stairs, stood there for a moment then turned around and looked down at Colonel Howler saying "Find them Colonel, or someone will be looking for YOU; and you won't like where they find you" then he smiled and turned back climbing the remaining stairs and going into an open room with Simon following close behind.

Simon was hired by Phillip Covington twenty-eight years ago to help protect his wife and newborn son.

After her husband's death Evelyn Covington kept him on as her son's bodyguard and companion, as well as HER occasional sexual partner and confidant when her need arose. He was hired because of his highly trained skills in martial arts to protect the family and train

Nathaniel "to become a man" one day as Evelyn put it. Nathaniel Covington became his best student surpassing even his skills in the fighting arts.

Howler left the Covington house and drove back to Covington Industries. The large mansion-like house and the business were on the same property just outside the Raleigh city limits so it only took him two minutes to get back to his office.

Howler pulled into the parking lot, got out and looked up at the countdown timer above the entrance doors stating 13-hours, 45-minutes, and 34-seconds; shaking his head thinking how stupid the thing looked when no one could see it out here other than him and the Covington's.

Just as Howler walked into the lobby of the building his phone buzzed in his pocket, he pulled it out and spoke into it "Howler" he said.

Colonel Howler listened to the guard at the front gate then replied "Send him up, Mr. Covington is expecting him" then he hung up and put his phone back in his pocket. Howler smiled and thought to himself "I guess someone other than us will actually see that stupid sign now".

The long black limousine pulled up to the house where two young, well dressed Asian men got out of the car and looked around the perimeter to see several heavily armed men positioned around the expensive house.

They understood the situation was controlled as they both opened their jackets to reveal handguns in holsters; and that they were expected, to several guards standing there with their machine-guns pointed at them.

One of the men went to the back door of the limo and opened it for another well dressed young Asian man, who got out stood there and looked around, then proceeded to walk towards the stairs up to the front door of the house.

Simon stood in the room as Nathaniel Covington got dressed

then looked at his phone that buzzed in his pocket. "Your guest has arrived sir" he said placing the phone back in his pocket.

Covington put on his suit jacket and smiled at Simon and said "Please show him into the dining room" then followed Simon out the door and down the stairs.

Simon opened the door and stepped aside allowing the three Asian men to enter into the foyer then said "Mr. Covington is waiting for you in the dining room sir" slowly walking ahead of the three men towards the closed dining room doors.

Simon slid the two doors open as the three Asian men walked in to see Evelyn Covington sitting at the table with a glass of red wine in her hand. Nathaniel Covington was standing at the far end of the table next to his mother smiling at the three men that entered.

Evelyn Covington was a handsome, yet petite woman, about 5'-4" tall, in her mid -fifties, dressed in a bright blue pants suit with a white blouse smiling at the Asian man as she continued to sip her wine.

Two of the Asian men stopped and stood at the door opening as the third one stepped forward and bowed to the Covington's who returned his bow.

Nathaniel Covington walked slowly around the table extending his hand out to the Asian gentleman saying "Welcome to our home Mr. Amikura" shaking the man's hand vigorously.

Nathaniel stepped aside and directed Noki Amikura to sit across from his mother as the two men sat down at the table together. Noki Amikura smiled at Evelyn Covington and expressed "It is a pleasure to finally meet you Mrs. Covington" as Simon poured him a glass of wine.

Noki Amikura was the nephew of Nabu Amikura, raised by his uncle along with his cousin Yuki. He was trained in the "ways of the ninja" and taught the family electronics business. When his uncle died he expected to become the company's CEO having run the business most of his life, but instead his uncle willed the entire company to his cousin Yuki; a WOMAN.

"I understand in your culture a woman doing business is unheard of and disrespectful" Evelyn said with a smile taking a sip of her wine having done her homework on the young Asian businessman.

"How can WE set your mind at ease that your money is being well spent" she asked the young Asian industrialist.

"Mrs. Covington; Amikura Electronics has been in business of making money for over fifty years" Noki Amikura said to her with a smile.

"We ONLY loan money to those companies we feel will benefit US" Amikura said taking a sip of his wine continuing to smile at her then looking at Nathaniel with a stern look.

"We understand your purpose is to control the smart phone market around the world; too enslave the people to their cell phones" Amikura said seeing the smiles on both Covington faces.

"Its much more than that Sir" Nathaniel replied smiling at his mother. "We want YOU to help us enslave the world through their cell phones" Nathaniel continued with a big grin. "We already have orders from cellular companies for ten million apps" Covington said laughing.

"What are you asking for Mr. Covington?" Amikura asked looking over at his two men standing by the door.

"Another $10 million dollars to boost our security for tonight's big satellite launch" Nathaniel asked smiling at both his mother and Amikura.

"We have sunk all the money you gave use into the servers, technical support, and government bribes, but we believe our competitors may try to stop our application launch which calls for a little more security around the building" Nathaniel explained to the young well dressed Asian.

Noki Amikura put his wine glass down and slowly stood up, straightening his tie and buttoning his jacket. He looked at Nathaniel and Evelyn Covington and smiled nodding in agreement to what they were asking for.

He bowed to the Covington's, receiving one in return from them; then turned and walked out of the dining room towards the front door, his two guards leading the way.

Noki Amikura slowly descended the front steps leading down to his car; stopped at the open car door and looked up to Nathaniel and Evelyn Covington standing on the front porch saying "You'll have your money by this afternoon's close of business" with a stern look towards Nathaniel.

"You won't be disappointed" Nathaniel said as Amikura's security guard stood by the opened car door waiting for his boss to get in.

Evelyn Covington smiled at the young Asian businessman as he stood at the car door looking up at her and listened to her say "We are having a little get together tonight to celebrate the launching, as well as a "special" charity auction; I do hope you will attend Mr. Amikura". She asked as they both watched as Amikura smiled back at her and nodded in acceptance.

"Wonderful" she said down to him as Simon took a gold envelope and descended down the stairs to hand it to the young Asian man. Amikura nodded again after accepting the invitation; got in the car and the door was closed.

Amikura's limousine pulled up to the security entrance gate to leave the compound when Colonel Howler stepped out of the guard's booth rapping his knuckles on the back passenger's bullet-proof glass window, watching as it lowered slowly.

Howler looked at Noki Amikura peering through the open window smiled and asked the annoyed Asian business man "Do the Covington's know about your "other business" here?"

"NO; you were supposed to kill Max Mason before they found out" Amikura said with anger.

"How was I supposed to know one of YOUR guys would be there to kill him" Howler asked confused about what Amikura said.

"WE didn't send anyone" Amikura said with anger in his voice.

"We didn't want any of this leading back to me, or Amikura Electronics; that's why I hired you and paid you cash to get it done Colonel" Amikura continued as he stared at a confused Colonel Howler from inside the car window.

"You swore your soldiers could take care of Mason and frame the Covington's for it all; but you didn't, now did you?" Amikura said angry knowing that Max Mason was still alive.

"You need to keep YOUR men in check; that ninja killed one of my best men" Howler replied leaning on the car door.

"GET IT DONE COLONEL" Noki Amikura screamed as he slowly rolled up the car window.

Amikura's car left the gate and headed down the highway back towards the city of Raleigh as he stared out the closed window thinking. Amikura turned to the guard sitting across from him and asked "Find out where my cousin was Saturday night, and do it quietly". The guard bowed his head acknowledging his boss's request.

Monday mornings were always hectic for Max Mason since he took the Domestic Terrorism Director's job last year. Agent meetings, phone calls, and networking with the other agencies making up most of his work day; but today was different, today was ALL about HIM.

He carefully went over each page of the report sent to him by the FBI and Secret Service crime scene tech's of Saturday night's murder attempts on his life by two dead assassins.

He read all the witness accounts, the ballistic reports on both guns used by the assassins, and Karen Tyler's shotgun cane; the autopsies of each dead man, and the casualties that occurred that night.

As Max continued to read the eye witness reports of a "white ninja" he thought about how his adopted "ninja" daughter Yuki Amikura saved his life by killing one of the assassins, then disappeared; only to show up at his home later that night wanting to kill him; after being missing from his family's life for over ten years.

He started going over the two assassins criminal, personal, and military profiles when he made a discovery and picked up the phone on his desk calling his assistant. "Jamie, have Agent Tyler join me in my office please" he asked continuing to read the page he had in his hand then hanging up the phone.

A few minutes passed and Karen Tyler knocked gently on Max's office door seeing he was engrossed with the report he was reading not seeing her standing at the door. "I guess I don't light up the room for you anymore" she asked laughing as he sat behind his desk.

Max looked up from the file folders and multiple pages on his desk and smiled at her saying "Darlin' you light up the WORLD for me and you know it".

"I found our connection between both assassins" Max said to Tyler as she came into the office and sat down in the chair across from Max's desk.

"I found something too" Tyler replied holding a file folder of her own in her hand.

"Ladies always first" Max said with a grin admiring how beautiful she looked this morning.

"Okay; they both worked for Allied Security Limited based out of Lubbock, Texas; they were basically paid mercenaries to protect dignitaries and rich people" Tyler read from the report she had.

"That lines up with what I have" Max replied. "They were both decorated ex-military; they were both honorably discharged, once under the command of Colonel Joseph Howler" Max said smiling at her.

"Wanna hear the fun part?" Max asked smiling. "Colonel Howler is the CEO of Allied Security, and he's personally contracted to Covington Industries in Raleigh, North Carolina." Max explained with a grin.

"I know this asshole Howler; we met once in Iraq; he enjoyed torturing prisoners for information over in the sandbox, literally got off on it" Max continued telling Tyler knowing she understood his reference to "the sandbox" as being in the Middle East and Afghanistan.

"I guess it looks like we're headed to Raleigh" Tyler replied with a grin. "I'll call dispatch and get us fixed up with a vehicle when we arrive, and a chopper to get us down there" she said getting out of her chair and looking down at Max.

"I've got a police connection in Raleigh; I'll give HER a call to let her know we're coming; she can meet us at the airport" Max said with a big smile on his face.

"Are we reconnecting with an old girlfriend from your past Mr. Mason?" Tyler asked with a sly smile.

"Something like that" Max replied laughing seeing Tyler a little bit jealous.

Max thought for a moment as Tyler started to walk out of his office and said "Do me a favor and double up on the armament that we normally take with us; I'll grab a couple of things from the back of my car as well" smiling at Tyler as she stopped and looked at him with confusion on her face.

"Are you expecting trouble down there Director?" Tyler asked knowing that Max's intuition usually was dead on when it came to criminal minds and how they worked.

"Lets just say, we can't go to a BIG party under dressed" Max replied laughing seeing Tyler smile then turn and leave his office.

Max sat back in his chair and thought to himself with a smile "It'll be fun seeing you AGAIN Colonel".

Colonel Howler walked into his office at Covington Industries and sat down in the chair behind his desk thinking about what Noki Amikura said to him just as one of his men approached his open door and saluted him.

"What do you have Lieutenant Hanson?" Howler asked annoyed for being disturbed as he opened a file folder on his desk.

"We believe we found the computer code leak Colonel" the tall man wearing a black tactical uniform and handgun replied holding a file folder in his hand.

"Who is it Lieutenant?" Howler asked as he dropped the file folder and stood up behind his desk.

"His name is Jonah Singh; he works for the tech support division of the R&D department on the 3rd floor Sir; but he called in sick this morning" Hanson replied reading from the file he had in his hand. "He's single, no family, and lives alone Sir" the Lieutenant continued.

"Send a team over to his house, hold him till I get there; confiscate all of his electronic devices" Howler replied with a smirk on his face. "We need to know if he sent the code out to anyone" Howler explained as Lieutenant Hanson saluted then turned and walked out of his office.

Jonah Singh was a young twenty-something computer genius from Bangladesh, India; having graduated from Cornell University with a degree in computer programming.

He worked as a tech support consultant for Covington Industries going on four years now, making a good life for himself on a six figure salary.

Jonah Singh was one of two, twenty-four hour on-call techs for Covington Industries. Because of the high quantity of servers the company used for their world-wide communication applications he had to be available 24/7; getting a call from one of the analysts Sunday night that the digital software wasn't keeping the application locked in to those using it. In fixing the problem he found out more information than he wanted too.

Jonah Singh quickly moved around his apartment as the mid-morning sunlight shined through his living room window. He was putting things in a duffle bag when he got a knock at his door. The young tech looked through the peephole to see a delivery man with a package standing there.

He remembered he had ordered some computer parts for his

laptop online and without thinking opened the front door. As soon as he did the delivery man hit him with a high-voltage taser sending him into convulsions and causing him to lose consciousness as he fell to the floor inside his apartment.

Jonah Singh's eyes slowly opened realizing that his arms and legs were tied to one of his kitchen chairs with zip-tie plastic straps; and a piece of duct tape over his mouth. He looked around his apartment to see it completely ransacked by the two men standing there with him, obviously they were looking for something. He vigorously tried to move but couldn't, finally stopping when he heard a knock on his door.

One of the men looked through the peephole then opened the door allowing Colonel Howler to come in.

Howler walked into the living room where Singh was sitting and smiled at the confined young man and said "Mr. Singh, I understand you gave away something that belongs to me" as he rips the piece of duct tape off of his mouth painfully.

"I don't have anything of yours" Singh replied with fear in his voice.

Howler backhanded Singh hard across the face not liking the response he got. "AGAIN, Mr. Singh; who did you send the email to with the code in it?" Howler asked angrily.

"I don't know what you're talking about" Singh replied tears coming down his face.

This annoyed Howler who reached his hand out to one of his men and was given a large combat knife that he immediately plunged deep into Singh's left thigh as the other mercenary standing behind him put his hand over Singh's mouth to muffle his screams of pain.

Howler pulled the knife out of Singh's leg smiling at him as he watched the blood ooze out of the hole in his jeans watching Singh crying in pain with his man's hand over his mouth.

Howler nodded to his man to take his hand away from his mouth as Singh sobbed uncontrollably begging him "Please don't kill me, please don't kill me".

"Tell me who you sent the email too and all of this goes away" Howler said wiping the blood off the knife on Singh's shirt giving his two men a sinister look.

"JAKE, I sent it to Jake; Jake Mason has it" Singh said his leg searing in pain from the knife wound.

"See, now that wasn't so hard" Howler said seeing Singh start to calm down thinking he was going to be okay now.

Howler smiled at Singh placed his hand on his shoulder then plunged the long blade of his knife into his chest looking into his eyes as the young technician slowly died, the blood flowing fast out of his mouth.

Howler looked at the two men then back at the dead body of Jonah Singh and said "Make it look like a home robbery, then go find this Jake Mason".

Max Mason and Karen Tyler's helicopter landed at Raleigh-Durham International Airport at just about 1pm, it was a quick hour flight from DC so they both felt refreshed and ready to go when they stepped out of the chopper seeing a young blonde woman wearing a police uniform standing beside a squad car and a black SUV.

Tyler saw the female police officer and wondered if this was Max's connection in Raleigh he spoke about before they left. The young attractive officer smiled at Max and walked up to him and hugged him hard making Tyler give her an evil look.

"Hi dad" Tyler heard the young officer say kissing him on the cheek.

"Hi sweetheart, how are my boys?" Max asked smiling over at Tyler who had a confused look on her face.

"Jake and Parker are fine; now introduce me, I've been waiting for this for a long time" the young police officer said sternly to Max.

"Special Agent Karen Tyler, this is Lieutenant Linda Mason of the Wake County Police Department here in Raleigh; my very special daughter-in-law, and the mother of my five year old grandson Parker" Max said beaming with pride and smiling at Tyler knowing what she was thinking before.

Tyler reached her hand out to shake Linda's hand instead got a big hug from her saying "We've heard so much about you from Stacy, it's wonderful to finally meet you; sorry its not on better circumstances" Linda said smiling.

The helicopter pilot put Max and Tyler's bags in the SUV along with the several weapon cases they brought with them and shut the door. He nodded to Max who returned his own nod as he watched the pilot get back in and fly the chopper away.

"Nathaniel Covington and his mother Evelyn are waiting for us in his office" Linda said to Max and Tyler.

"Can you leave your patrol car here and ride with us?" Max asked Linda with a smile hoping she would say yes so she could get to know Tyler better.

"Yes; let me tell my dispatch where I'm going first" Linda said as she walked over to her car and pulled the radio handset out.

"You let me believe she was an old girlfriend you snake" Tyler said smiling at Max who laughed at what she said.

Linda Mason came back over to Max and Tyler and acknowledged that her dispatcher knew she was riding with Federal investigators and the three of them got into the large black SUV.

Linda gave Tyler the address to Covington Industries and she programmed the SUV's on-board GPS and they left the airport security lot towards the highway.

Linda sat in the backseat fastening her seatbelt when she looked at Max smiling at her in the rear view mirror and asked "Max, you know Covington is Jake's boss; right?" seeing a confused look on his face.

"I thought he worked for Syntech Software" Max asked surprised to hear that Jacob was working for a possible sociopath that wanted his father dead.

"Syntech was bought out by Covington Industries almost a year ago; they took over the building last year" she said continuing to look at Max in the mirror. "Jake is one of their primary tech support guys; he keeps the place running" Linda said proud of what her husband did.

As Max drove to Covington Industries he and Tyler filled Linda in on the information they had concerning the two assassins trying to kill him Saturday night, and the connection they both had to Covington Industries, Allied Security Limited; and Colonel Howler.

"Is Jacob, and my son in danger Max?" Linda asked a bit concerned now.

Max didn't want to worry her but looked over at Tyler with a look and said "I'm sure he's fine sweetheart, we just have to be through in our investigation".

Tyler quickly changed the subject asking "Tell me about Parker?" turning and smiling at Linda behind her.

"He's incredible; smart and funny just like his father" Linda said with a proud smile. "And he loves his grandpa" she said excited looking at Max smile in the mirror.

"He loves skyping with you every Thursday night, you know that" Linda said as she looked out the window to see they were coming up to the turnoff to Covington Industries.

Max smiled at Linda from the mirror thinking how much he loved talking to his young grandson any chance he got. Jake, Linda, and Max set up a scheduled "skype" or computer video conference as Max preferred to call it; every Thursday night at 7pm with Parker. Max was amazed & proud at how smart, and articulate the young five year old was with him, able to talk to him about everything from animals, his favorite cartoons, foods he liked, to his favorite superheroes. Max knew he would cherished these conversations for the rest of his life.

"Did Max tell you what he sent him for Christmas this past year?"

Linda asked Tyler with a disapproving grin to her father-in-law as he continued to smile at her in the mirror.

"He sent him a red Ferrari convertible" Linda said smiling at Tyler knowing Max could hear her. "A Ferrari" she repeated to Tyler.

Tyler didn't understand what they were saying only that she thought all little boys liked to play with cars especially at Parker's age and asked "Sounds like you didn't approve of the car Max sent him".

"It was a FULL SIZE Ferrari that Parker could sit in and Jake could control with a remote control; basically a giant remote control car for adults to put their kids in and play with in the parking lot" Linda said laughing.

"I don't know who loves it more; Parker or Jake" Linda said continuing to laugh.

"I wanted my grandson to understand that his grandpa bought him a Ferrari when he grows up; I get to say I bought him his first car" Max said looking at both women and smiling proudly.

They had arrived at Covington Industries as Max pulled up to the security gate. He rolled down his window as the guard came out of the booth and said "Secret Service Special Agent's Mason & Tyler; accompanied by Officer Linda Mason of the Wake County police department to see Nathaniel and Evelyn Covington".

Max noticed the guard's black military style dress and hardware including an AR-15 machine gun, 9mm handgun, a large military issued K-bar knife, and wearing a tactical vest with flash bang grenades. Max thought it was a lot of firepower just to guard a computer software company.

The guard came back out after making a phone call and opened the gate for the SUV; informing Max to park in the visitor's parking lot up the driveway and present their ID's to the guard at the lobby desk.

Max parked the SUV in the visitor's parking lot just like the guard requested. The three of them got out and walked towards the lobby of the large five-story building. Max noticed before they went in several very large satellite transmitter dishes up on the roof wondering why they needed so many.

Max looked at the large digital screen above the entrance way as they approached the glass entry doors noticing the numerical countdown was now at 10-hours, 55-minutes and continuing to count down.

He snickered at the sight of it wondering who was seeing it all the way out here in the middle of nowhere as he opened the lobby door.

The three of them walked over and presented their Federal, and Police ID's to the desk guard who looked them over, handed them back and instructed them that Covington's office was on the top floor, pointing to where the elevators were.

Again, Max noticed how arrogant and heavily armed the guards were for being a so called "simple" software company. He looked around the room to see two more heavily armed guards observing them closely as they stepped into the elevator.

The elevator opened and the three of them walked out into a large open office. Standing just outside the open elevator door they could see an attractive older woman sitting on a plush white sofa sipping a glass of white wine smiling as they came in, and a tall young man standing behind a glass topped desk.

The room was spacious with large plants, expensive furniture, and floor to ceiling windows wrapping around the room that allowed the natural light to come in throughout the office. Max noticed there were two guards standing inside the room both holding AR-15 machine-guns.

"Mr. and Mrs. Covington, thank you for seeing us; I'm Officer Linda Mason with the Raleigh Police department, and these are Special agents Max Mason & Karen Tyler with the Secret Service; we'd like to ask you a few questions about two employees of yours for a joint ongoing investigation" Linda asked politely knowing they were Jake's employers and extremely connected wealthy upper-class residents of Raleigh.

Nathaniel Covington was dressed in a white suit, wearing a bright blue shirt without a tie looking like he was about to do a model cover shoot for GQ magazine. His mother Evelyn was wearing her bright blue pants suit, with a very expensive string of pearls around her neck continuing to sip from her wine glass as they both stared at the three visitors standing in front of them.

Max jumped in on the questioning right away looking around the room at both Covington's and asked "Why would two of your employees want to go to DC and kill a high ranking federal official then leave a very easy trail back to you two and this company?" he asked continuing to stare at Nathaniel Covington who couldn't take his eyes off of Linda.

Nathaniel Covington seemed fixated on Linda; walking slowly around his desk to stand just a few feet away from her asking with a big smile "Don't we know each other?"

"Yes Sir, we met at the company picnic this past summer; my husband Jacob Mason works for you in the R&D department" Linda replied with a smile.

"You have a darling little boy I remember; Parker, I believe his name was" Covington said looking at Max and smiling who returned a stern stare at the man. Covington put out his hand and shook Linda's then moved over to Tyler standing in front of her with a big smile.

"And who are you again?" Covington asked Tyler reaching out his hand to shake hers, but she refused.

"I'm Special Agent Karen Tyler of the Secret Service Mr. Covington, I'd appreciate it if you would answer the question my colleague just asked you Sir" Tyler said giving him a firm stare knowing he was avoiding the question.

Evelyn Covington still sitting on the sofa spoke up before her son could say anything, smiling at Max then giving Tyler an evil look for disrespecting her son. Tyler stared back at her knowing she knew something about these men trying to kill Max listening to what she was saying.

"My son and I heard about the issue that happened Saturday night just this morning; we didn't know either of them personally only that they both worked for the security company we have contracted to protect our building, our personal home, and of course our employees" Evelyn Covington explained still smiling at Max Mason.

"Why all the heavy security for a cell phone software company?" Max asked. "What's so special about this place?" he said smiling back at Evelyn Covington in a condescending grin.

Nathaniel Covington stepped in front of Max and said "Our new "Dragon" phone application will revolutionize the cell phone business forever; already millions have pre-ordered our "App" for their phones that goes online tonight at midnight" Covington declared beaming at his mother.

Max looked at Tyler and whispered "Dragon" understanding they both knew the word was written on the other side of Max's picture each assassin had in his pocket when they tried to kill him.

Max looked at Tyler again as he had another thought about Covington's product name, he would give her his thought when they left.

"Why use the name Dragon?" Max asked looking at Tyler and Linda.

"Because the application will "breathe fire" into everyone's phone" Nathaniel Covington replied laughing. "The countdown is on" he said walking over to his mother leaning down and kissing her on the cheek as she touched his cheek.

CHAPTER FOUR

Colonel Howler had just walked into Covington Industries from his productive visit with the now dead Jonah Singh when his tech specialist rushed up to him and said "Sir, the good news is I have the information you asked for on Jacob "Jake" Mason".

"And the bad news Sergeant?" Howler asked walking towards his office as the young man followed him.

"There's a lot of bad news sir; Jacob Mason is the son of Secret Service Director Maxwell "Max" Mason a former Navy SEAL Captain; his wife is Raeligh police officer Linda Mason, a former Army criminal investigating officer & MP; he also has a sister Stacy Mason, who is also a Navy SEAL stationed at Norfolk Naval Base; and Jacob Mason himself is a former mountain Army Ranger" the young Sergeant explained looking at the large file he had in his hands.

"This day just keeps getting better" Howler said out loud sarcastically starring at the young Sergeant.

"It's about to get worst Sir" the young tech replied. "Max Mason and Officer Mason are up in the Covington's office as we speak; asking questions about Styler and Joseph" he said as he could see the worry on his commanding officers face now.

Howler pulled out his cell phone and made a call just as the elevator doors opened to take him up to the Covington office.

The elevator doors opened on the 5th floor and Howler stepped out to see Max, Tyler, Linda, and the Covington's standing around staring at one another then they turned all their attention towards him smiling at everyone.

"Captain Max Mason; I haven't seen you since Afghanistan in 99'" Howler said extending his hand out to shake Max's.

"Actually; it's Admiral now" Max said avoiding Howler's handshake then looking over at Tyler and Linda smiling at him because they knew it was the first time he acknowledged his new rank in public to anyone.

"WOW; Admiral, that's impressive" Howler replied sarcastically. "What can we do for you ADMIRAL?" Howler asked with a slight bit of anger and sarcasm knowing Max Mason out ranked him now.

"We found out that Sergeant's David Styler and Bradley Joseph both worked for you Colonel; they tried to kill someone at a Federal party the other night and ended up dead themselves" Max said standing toe to toe with the Colonel. "Got any idea who gave them their orders Colonel?" Max asked with a grin already knowing the answer.

"I'm afraid not, I found some illegal discrepancies in their mission reports about a month ago and had to let them go; they haven't worked for Allied Security for a while now, so whatever they did they were acting on their own, I can show you the termination reports if you'd like" Colonel Howler replied to Max with a condescending smile of his own.

"We'd appreciate that Colonel; thank you for your time, if you can get those reports to us immediately we can eliminate yours and the Covington's company from our investigation" Tyler said grabbing Max's arm as he stared into the Colonel's arrogant eyes then turned to smile at both Nathaniel and Evelyn Covington as he walked toward the elevator with Tyler and Linda.

Nathaniel Covington reached into his opened desk drawer and pulled out two gold colored envelopes and walked back over to Max and Linda handing them each one saying "These are "special" invitations to tonight's launch party; I hope all of you will attend" he said smiling at everyone.

"Thank you, but we're not down here for a party Mr. Covington" Max said sternly staring into his eyes and handing the invitation back to him.

Tyler grabbed the invitation from Max's hand before Covington took it back smiled and said "We would love to come; of course if our time permits" seeing the smile on Covington's face.

Max stood inside the elevator beside both Tyler and Linda continuing to stare into Colonel Howler's eyes as the doors shut.

Max knew this smug asshole had something to do with the two dead assassins and him almost getting killed, and knew the two of them would be seeing each other again real soon.

Tyler could see how angry Max was and reached down and grabbed Max's hand to calm him down looking up at him saying "They'll get what's coming to them sweetheart; criminals like the three of them always fuck up" looking through the closing elevator door at the Covington's & Howler.

The elevator door closed and Nathaniel Covington lit into Colonel Howler aggressively "YOU LED A FUCKING FEDERAL INVESTIGATION TO OUR FRONT DOOR; WHY THE HELL WOULD YOU DO THAT COLONEL?" he asked angrily watching his mother stand up and throw her wine glass against one of the glass walls shattering it into small pieces, really pissed at Howler.

"The news I have isn't going to be any better" he started. "Mason's kid Jacob, is the one Singh emailed the software codes to last night; and he's out of the building with it right now" the worried look on Howler's face reflecting to the Covington's. "Those in his department assume he's at lunch down the road at Stoney's" Howler said knowing he was about to get brutally chastised for what he just told them.

"REALLY COLONEL; the one person who can destroy this entire company just happens to be the son of the most famous Secret Service agent in U.S. history, and you have NO CLUE where to find him?" Covington expressed looking at his mother disgusted with him.

"They have nothing to connect us with these two dead soldiers" Howler said looking at them both.

"The fact that they were here tells ALL of us we are connected to this; do you honestly believe a hard ass like Max Mason is going to let this go?" Covington asked.

"Just wait till he finds out that Amikura Electronics is our financial backer" Covington said holding his mother tightly in his arms to calm her down, her face bright red with anger.

"Kill them all" Evelyn Covington said to her son. "Kill the entire family, but bring the boy to me; after all he is about to become an orphan and will need a mother figure to help him in his time of grief" she said with an evil grin on her face as she stepped away from her son.

"I'm sure we can find a nice family for him to go to at tonight's auction; for the right price of course" Evelyn said then turned and headed towards the elevator.

Nathaniel Covington walked with his mother to the elevator and kissed her on the cheek as she got in watching the doors close. Looking back at Colonel Howler he said "Make it happen Colonel; NO MORE MISTAKES".

The elevator came back up and the doors opened as Howler walked by Covington who grabbed his arm and stopped him saying "Make sure they're dead Colonel or YOU will be" looking into Howler's eyes who nodded to him understanding.

Max, Tyler, and Linda all got back into their black SUV and backed slowly out of the space and headed towards the front security gate. Max looked at Tyler and smiled then said "It was way too easy getting out of there" as they drove through the open gate onto the four lane highway heading back to Raleigh.

"OH SHIT; something bad is about to happen isn't it Max?" Tyler asked knowing his annoying six-sense was always right.

Max looked into the mirror to see Linda and said to her as she looked back in the mirror to see him "Linda sweetheart, I need you to pull two AR-15's out of one of the black bags behind you and four or five magazines" Max said looking into his rear view mirror to see a lone black SUV about a mile behind them.

"Two, maybe three vehicles about a mile back in single formation" he said to Tyler smiling at her.

"Why are you smiling?" Tyler asked looking in the back seat watching Linda load two AR-15 machine-guns with fresh thirty round magazines.

"Well, it looks like we found out who's trying to kill me now" Max said with a chuckle just as Tyler swung and hit him in the arm out of frustration.

"Oh I like her Max" Linda said smiling knowing that they were about to engage in a firefight with highly trained mercenaries and Tyler wanted Max to know that he wasn't funny right now.

"OH MY GOD; JACOB AND PARKER" Linda yelled realizing that Colonel Howler would be going after them as well and they didn't know anything that was going on.

Max understood Linda was starting to freak out about her family being in danger but he also knew she was a soldier and understood that she needed to command the situation you are in first.

"Lieutenant; I need you to focus right now on what's happening with us, or we can't go help our boys" Max said looking into her eyes in the mirror.

Linda knew Max was right and replied "Yes Sir; but if they harm my baby I'll burn that place to the ground" she said, her eyes red with anger.

"Yes ma'am, copy that" Max said smiling at his brave daughter-in-law now pointing one of the AR-15's towards the back window.

"Ms. Tyler I would enjoy having your company back here if that's okay with you; I'm sure Parker would like it that his future grandmother helped protect his mom and dad" Linda said with a big smile to her sitting up in the front seat.

"I would be honored" Tyler said smiling at her as she started to climb into the backseat stopping along the way to smile and kiss Max knowing he heard Linda call her "grandmother" then told him "DRIVE IT LIKE YOU STOLE IT COWBOY".

"Yes ma'am" Max replied with a smile pressing down the accelerator pedal.

Linda handed Tyler the other loaded AR-15 and waited for Max to lower the back window. The extra magazines sat on the seat between them and they smiled at one another waiting for the Colonel and his men to make their move against them.

Finally the second SUV moved along side of the first one in a classic military split attack formation. Max watched from his side mirror that men were starting to climb outside the SUV's windows with machine-guns and lowered the back window. As soon as it was completely down Linda & Tyler took them by surprise by opening fire on them.

Bullets from Linda and Tyler's machine-guns hit the SUV's windshields and at least two of the black clad mercenaries, dropping them out of the car windows and unto the highway pavement.

Tyler took careful aim through the scope on her rifle and hit the front tire of one of the SUV's causing it to hit the other SUV beside it; rolling it over and crashing into the guardrail then bursting into flames quickly engulfing the entire SUV.

"WOW; who taught you that?" Linda asked seeing what Tyler did with a single shot as she reloaded a new magazine into her rifle.

"He did; you should see me bake a cake" Tyler replied laughing looking over at Max who smiled back from the mirror.

"Looks like the Covington's and Colonel Howler spared no expense for us" Max said as he could see another black SUV take the place of the one Tyler just blew up.

"There are a few toys in the bag Mikey made for me I've been saving for a rainy day" Max said looking up into the sky out his driver's window. "Not a cloud in the sky, but what the hell" he said laughing.

"Tyler grab the red box in the first bag while Linda lays down cover fire" Max said as a few bullets hit the back of their SUV, one of them hitting the windshield in front of him causing Max to swerve.

Linda opened fire spraying at both SUV's while Tyler quickly grabbed the large plastic red box and opened it. Looking inside she smiled seeing what was in it.

"I love that man's ingenuity" Tyler said out loud about Mikey Steven's ability to make anything a weapon. "He made you giant road spikes with explosives on them, didn't he?" Tyler said to Max laughing as Linda continued to fire at the two SUV's.

Tyler could see in the box that Mikey had taken about twenty Police road spikes that look like giant "jacks" from the children's game about the size of golf balls. They were used by police officers to blow out tires during a criminal pursuit, but these looked different because Mikey attached a very small cartridge to one of the six prongs on each of them with a plastic zip-tie.

"Toss them all over the road" Max replied, watching as Tyler scattered Mikey's giant size steel jacks out of the window and onto the highway in front of the remaining two black SUV's coming up rapidly behind them.

The driver's of both SUV's were paying more attention to avoiding Linda's bullets coming at them then they did Tyler dropping the steel objects on the road; running over the explosive spikes and blowing up on impact causing all four tires to blow out on both SUV's making them collide into one another then crash over the guardrail and down the embankment in a huge cloud of smoke and fire.

"WHAT THE HELL WAS IN THOSE THINGS?" Tyler yelled at Max from the back seat knowing they weren't ordinary explosives the way they took out both vehicles like that.

"Mikey calls them "impact caps" sorta like blasting caps only a bit more powerful, they're equivalent to an eighth of a stick of dynamite; he told me they go off with the slightest impact to them" Max said chuckling a bit.

"My question isn't how he made them; it's how the Hell did he test them to be used like this?" Tyler asked with a serious look on her face. Max looked at her from the mirror and smiled then laughed for a moment at what she said.

Max didn't care about stopping and checking for any survivors he was just happy no one that he loved and cared about got hurt this time; speeding away from the scene.

Max knew something else now; that the Covington's, Colonel Howler, and his Allied Security mercenaries worked for an "Amikura".

Max figured it was Noki Amikura, the spoiled rich playboy nephew of his beloved Sensei Yoshi Amikura. Noki Amikura loved "dragons" just like Tanaka did and as soon as he heard what the Covington's new "app" was called he knew it had something to do with the Amikura's. He knew it was a bit of a stretch, but knew his intuitions were never wrong.

A long, black stretch limousine stopped at the front gate of Covington Industries and the well dressed driver rolled down his window to address the guard standing there next to the small guardhouse saying "Ms. Yuki Amikura and her assistant from Amikura Electronics to see Nathaniel & Evelyn Covington".

The guard looked on his clipboard and replied "We don't have you on our list of meetings today with the Covington's" he said flipping through the pages. "The ONLY Amikura I have on my list is Noki Amikura and he was here this morning, and has already left" he said, continuing to see Noki Amikura's name on his page; watching as the passenger's window started to lower after what he said.

When the window completely opened the guard could see two young Asian women in the back of the limousine.

The one closest to him demanded "Get YOUR boss Colonel Howler on the phone and tell him to inform the Covington's that the REAL President & CEO of Amikura Electronics is here to speak with them" the young Asian woman said with authority.

They watched as the guard turned and grabbed the phone inside the guardhouse dialing quickly.

Colonel Howler picked up his phone from his desk answering it "Howler".

"Colonel; we have a couple of Asian women down here at the gate that claim to be President & CEO of Amikura Electronics wanting to see the Covington's without an appointment" the guard said as he looked at both Yuki Amikura's and Ochi Osaka's company ID's.

"Tell them I have to clear it with the Covington's; it might take a couple of minutes" Howler said to the guard nervously stalling for time.

"I'm going to put you on hold for a moment" he replied pushing the hold button then dialing Nathaniel Covington's direct phone line.

"What is it Colonel?" Covington hit the on-speaker button and answered seeing it was Howler on his caller ID.

"Yuki Amikura is at the front gate wanting to talk with you and Evelyn" Howler replied knowing this could be a problem for them all.

Nathaniel looked over at his mother sitting on the sofa drinking another glass of white wine and smiled knowing what she was going to say before she said it and that was to get rid of her, but his curiosity got the best of him and he said "Show her up Colonel".

Yuki and Ochi sat patiently in the back of the limousine waiting to hear back from Colonel Howler when Yuki had a thought and whispered over to Ochi "Check to see if there are any pending financial transactions with Covington Industries before we go in" she asked watching Ochi type fast on her laptop beside her.

"There is a $10 million dollar wire transfer pending for completion at 5pm today" Ochi said reading her computer screen.

"Can you override it and cancel it?" Yuki asked smiling at her young companion.

Ochi smiled back at Yuki and replied "Yes ma'am" as she furiously continued to type looking up finally and smiling at her friend saying "Done".

Yuki grabbed her friend's hand to say "well done" and turned back to the open car window just as the guard returned from hanging up his phone saying "The Covington's will see you now".

The gate slowly opened and the limousine drove up to the front of Covington Industries visitors entrance and parked. The driver got out and opened the door for the two Asian women who immediately looked up at the digital countdown clock seeing there was just over ten hours until the Covington's satellite launch; then walked through the double-glass doors and was greeted by Colonel Howler, who was standing there waiting for them.

"Good morning ladies, I'm Colonel John Howler; the Covington's head of security, they have asked me to escort you both to their offices" he said with a smile on his face. "Please follow me to the elevator" he continued, pointing down the hallway towards the elevator doors.

The three of them rode up to Covington's office floor and the doors opened; where a smiling Nathaniel Covington stood in front of them.

"This is an unexpected surprise Miss Amikura; what brings you to our beautiful state of North Carolina?" he asked looking over at his mother still sitting on the sofa smiling at the two young girls.

Yuki stepped forward staring at Nathaniel Covington knowing he and her cousin Noki had something to do with trying to kill Max Mason; as Ochi looked around the room keeping a watchful eye on Howler and Evelyn Covington.

"I'm here to discuss my cousin Noki's business dealings with your company Mr. Covington" she said sternly.

"We just had a wonderful business meeting over an hour ago with your cousin; he's a VERY honorable man" Nathaniel Covington said as he shook Yuki's hand.

"For the record, my cousin doesn't have the authority to make ANY financial deals without MY permission or signature, because it's MY company not his; and quite frankly I believe he has entered into a partnership that could ultimately be the demise of Amikura Electronics if we continue business together" Yuki said to him watching his smile turn slowly into anger.

"I'm sorry you feel that way, but your cousin and I have a contract that's going to make us all a lot of money" Covington said watching his mother stand up from the sofa she was sitting down on.

"I already have a lot of money, so I guess I'll see you both in court then" Yuki said turning to walk back towards the elevator doors.

"DON'T WALK AWAY FROM MY SON YOU STUPID BITCH" Evelyn Covington drunkenly yelled walking towards Yuki as Ochi moved to stand between them.

"WHAT ARE YOU GOING TO DO?" she asked Ochi who looked at Evelyn Covington and smiled.

"Hospital & breathing tube" Ochi said sternly which gave Evelyn Covington chills the way she said it as she stepped back away from the intense Asian girl.

"All of us need to calm down; it's just a misunderstanding mother, one that can be fixed" Nathaniel Covington said smiling at Yuki and then giving his mother an evil stare.

"Come to the launch party tonight; give me a chance to show you what our "app" can do for people" the young billionaire asked.

"If you still don't want to invest we simply have a drink and go our separate ways" Covington said walking back to his desk and opening a drawer causing Ochi to move the right side of her jacket back to expose a holstered pearl handled .380 caliber automatic pistol, placing her hand on the white grip in case Covington pulled his own gun out of the drawer.

"Easy now" Covington said with a grin to the young Asian assistant as he pulled out another gold colored envelope then walked back over to Yuki Amikura handing it to her slowly continuing to smile at her.

Yuki took the card from the gold envelope and saw it was an invitation to the launch party tonight reading that it was by invitation ONLY.

"I'm not sure if we'll come, but thank you for the invitation Mr. Covington" Yuki said bowing her head to Nathaniel then looking over at Ochi who was staring down Evelyn Covington.

Yuki turned just as the elevator doors opened looking back at

Nathaniel Covington and his mother saying "I will deal with my cousin OUR way; OH YEAH, and don't worry about that $10 million dollar wire transfer, it's been canceled" as she and Ochi got on the elevator and the doors slowly closed.

Nathaniel looked at his mother then at Howler and said angrily "KILL THEM BOTH".

"Yes Sir" Howler said with a grin as the elevator came back up and the doors opened for him to go back down.

The limo driver opened the back door as the two Asian women came out of the front door of Covington Industries and closed it behind them as they both got in back. He rolled the privacy window down to look back at the two women and asked "Where to ladies?"

Yuki looked at Ochi and smiled saying softly "You know they're going to try and kill us; right?" ignoring the driver's question for a moment.

"Yep, afraid so; we need to save him too you know" Ochi replied smiling at her friend then smiling at the cute limo driver.

"Head towards Raleigh, but don't take the interstate; I'll let you know when to stop" Yuki said smiling at the confused driver. "Head down NC Parkway, and listen to what I have to say VERY carefully; ALL our lives depend on it" Yuki said leaning into the privacy window to talk with the driver.

Colonel Howler was sitting at his desk when his phone rang and he picked it up. "Colonel, this is Stanton; we just found the limousine parked at a public rest stop on NC Parkway with no one in it Sir" he said waiting for Howler's response.

"WHAT THE FUCK DO YOU MEAN THERE'S NO ONE IN IT" Howler screamed into the phone. "THEY JUST LEFT HERE TEN MINUTES AGO" he yelled stopping to hear Stanton's reply.

"We searched the immediate area and found nothing Colonel; it's like they just vanished into thin air" Stanton said knowing Howler was about to scream at him again.

Instead of screaming at Stanton, Howler slammed the phone

down on the receiver over and over again screaming "FUCK, FUCK, FUCK" each time he hit it.

A black SUV pulled up to a plush hotel entrance and the two Asian women got out smiling at the driver. Yuki nodded and smiled at him as he handed her his card and said "Call me if you need anything" and closed the door walking towards the hotel's front door.

Both Yuki Amikura and Ochi Osaka understood before they left for North Carolina that if they challenged ANY one of them; the Covington's, Colonel Howler, or Yuki's cousin Noki Amikura that they were painting proverbial targets on their backs; but this was the way of the Ninja.

Yuki knew she had to confront the Covington's as well as her cousin, but also knew she had to have an escape plan; so she and Ochi devised one.

Ochi ordered the limousine the night before, which arrived to pick up Yuki in front of the hotel they were staying at that morning to take her to Covington Industries. Ochi also rented a black SUV from the hotel's private car rental office and followed the limousine down the NC Parkway to the public rest stop.

Yuki convinced the limo driver that she needed to use the ladies room at the rest stop before proceeding. After a few minutes in the ladies room Yuki came out with Ochi who had parked the SUV on the other side of the rest stop designated for large trucks.

The limo driver looked confused when the two Asian women got into the back of the limo together as he closed the door.

While driving down NC Parkway heading towards Covington Industries he asked a couple of times if Ms. Amikura was okay; still not understanding the situation.

After leaving the Covington's angry for cancelling the $10 million dollar wire transfer that her cousin Noki Amikura had promised them, both Yuki and Ochi tactically concluded that Nathaniel Covington would order Colonel Howler to send some of his mercenaries after them looking for the limousine, NOT the black SUV.

Yuki talked the limo driver into carrying out their plan simply by offering him a thousand dollars in cash that she had gotten from the hotel bank earlier that morning. She explained to him what he needed to do, and say, so he wouldn't be held responsible or get in trouble with his company.

He called his limo company and explained that the limo broke down at the rest stop and he had already sent for a tow truck to haul it back to the company garage.

He further explained to the limo dispatcher he had acquired a taxi cab to come from Raleigh at the client's request and expense; because she insisted upon it.

Yuki looked at Ochi and smiled as the limo driver drove away taking the SUV back to the rental lot of the hotel and said "I think he liked you" with a sheepish grin to her assistant & friend.

"Bring the other car around, and let's go say hello to my cousin" Yuki said with a stern look on her face as Ochi turned to head to the hotel's parking lot.

Noki Amikura arrived at his hotel in the rich North Hills section of Raleigh and stood quietly at the desk while one of his guards checked him in with the management.

"We have you booked into the "Presidental" suite Mr. Amikura" the manager said as Amikura looked at him with an arrogant blank stare.

Amikura's guards grabbed his bags and walked slightly behind him towards the elevator. Amikura was a bit tired after his discussions and confrontations with both the Covington's and Colonel Howler; needing to wash the smell of them off as well as get something to eat.

One of Amikura's guards opened the room door with the keycard and walked in to the completely dark room with the other guard to make sure it was safe.

Noki Amikura sensed something in the room and stood in the doorway as he heard a commotion happening inside the room.

"I'm not surprised you showed up cousin" Noki Amikura said into the dark as the curtains were suddenly drawn open to reveal the sunlit room and Yuki Amikura sitting in the chair dressed in a dark pants suit, her legs crossed starring angrily at her cousin standing in the still open doorway.

Noki Amikura walked into the room to see his two guards laying unconscious on the floor with a defiant Ochi Okasa standing over them both with two handguns she had taken from them; keeping them pointed at them in case they awaken from the beating she just gave them both.

"You have dishonored OUR name cousin" Yuki said knowing it was him that paid the men who tried to kill Max Mason in Washington D.C. Saturday night.

"You have stolen millions of dollars from the company to exact revenge on someone you have NO connection too" Yuki continued as Noki snickered at her statement.

"NO CONNECTION; your brother Tanaka was MY best friend, who do you think he came to for help after your father died" Noki replied with a defiant grin on his face.

"You mean after HE murdered OUR father; that still doesn't justify you taking millions of company funds to put out a contract on the one man who has treated me like family my entire life other than MY father" Yuki said standing up and looking her cousin in the eye.

"IT'S MY COMPANY; UNCLE NABU DIDN'T KNOW WHAT HE WAS DOING GIVING IT TO YOU; YOU DIDN'T EVEN WANT IT" Noki yelled causing Ochi to raise one of her guns at him.

Noki Amikura looked at Ochi Okasa defiantly and smiled saying "I should have put this orphaned mutt down before Uncle Nabu gave her to you as a pet".

Ochi took a step towards Noki only to see Yuki put her hand up for her to stay away from him. Yuki smiled at Ochi who smiled back and walked past Noki staring at him.

"Enjoy your few hours of rest cousin; be on the plane back to Japan by tonight" she said as she motioned to Ochi to leave; slowly following her.

"And if I don't cousin" Noki asked smiling arrogantly.

Yuki stopped at the doorway and looked back at her cousin and said "Then the next time we meet you should have a SWORD" as she smiled at him then walked just outside the room then turned and looked him in the eye again and said "By the way cousin; I informed the Covington's that the wire transfer was terminated, I hope that didn't cause an issue with your new friends" turning and walking away.

Yuki and Ochi walked to the elevator doors and looked at one another and both said to each other at the same time "He's staying" then got on the elevator.

Max continued driving down the highway towards Raleigh when he realized Howler was probably tracking them through their cell phones and abruptly pulled over to the side of the road raising dust in the air.

"We need to get off the grid to find Jacob; we need to do this old school" Max said to the two women in the back seat looking at Tyler.

"I'm afraid ladies I'm going to have to take your phones away from you for a bit" Max said to them with a grin on his face.

"That leaves us with no way to communicate with anyone; to warn Jake they're coming" Linda said not liking this idea of Max's.

Max pulled out his satellite phone Jordy had made, which was untraceable to any satellite communications system ever built and handed it to Linda. "Call Jacob on this one; he'll recognize the number as mine, it can't be traced" Max said as Tyler handed him her phone.

Seeing Tyler hand Max her phone showed Linda that Tyler trusted Max's instincts and she quickly handed him hers.

Tyler knew what Max meant about "going off the grid" they couldn't use credit cards ONLY cash, and they needed to get another car older than the year 2000 when the GPS chips weren't installed in cars yet.

No one, not even Howler with Covington's sophisticated communication equipment could find them this way. Tyler looked around the black duffle bag and found the black plastic box Max kept in there and got out of the SUV and back into the front passengers seat.

Tyler handed the small black plastic box to Max who quickly opened it to see a few stacks of $100 bills and asked "How much is there?"

Max smiled at her now sitting across from him again and replied "$10 thousand dollars".

Tyler smiled and said "Oh goody, looks like we're going shopping" to Max's big grin on his face.

Linda kept dialing and redialing Jacob's cell phone with no answer getting more frustrated after each time. Max could see the worry on her face and asked "Is there any place that you and Jacob would go that ONLY you two knew about".

"Why doesn't he pick up?" she asked with fear in her voice not paying any attention to what Max asked.

"There could be several reasons" Max said trying to reassure her that Jacob would be fine. "Where's Parker?" Max asked needing to know his grandson was going to be okay.

"He's at the daycare center next door to the police station; no one is stupid enough to go in there with all the cops around the building that know him" Linda said but still not sure, hearing what she said.

"We need to pick him up and get you two someplace safe until we can figure this out and find Jacob" Max said

Just as he said that, Linda's portable police radio came on saying "Dispatch this is Unit Twelve we have a homicide at Cascade Apartments on that 911 tip you received; according to his ID his name is Jonah Singh, we're going to need a CSI team and the coroner" the officer said.

"Copy that Unit Twelve, crime scene units in transit" the dispatcher replied over Linda's radio speaker.

"OH MY GOD" Linda yelled out. "Jonah works with Jake at Covington Industries, he was a computer technician like Jake" she explained. "He's been to our house for dinner several times" she said.

"Linda I need you to focus right now; where will Jacob go in an extreme emergency; you both should have a safe place designated that only the two of you know about" Max said getting a strange look from Tyler not understanding what he was asking her.

Linda smiled at Max and said "STONEY'S".

CHAPTER FIVE

As he looked out the window seeing the bright sun shining into Stoney's Coffee & Cafe from his corner table Jacob "Jake" Mason sipped his cup of coffee and typed on his laptop computer thinking to himself how lucky he was to have such an incredibly beautiful, supportive wife, an incredibly smart & precocious five year old son, and a great job that paid him well; he had the perfect life or so he thought.

As his friend and co-worker Jona Singh would always say to him "He was living the dream", drinking coffee and getting free Wi-Fi from Stoney's to use his laptop he normally brought in with him. Jake came to Stoney's almost every day at lunch time mostly because of the location being so close to Covington Industries.

The owner Stoney Madison made a mean Rueben sandwich, and a great cup of coffee; Jake would tell people, but most of all it's where he proposed to Linda after they both got out of the military close to seven years ago.

Jake looked back at his laptop screen after putting his coffee down and a confused look came over his face. He had logged into his personal email account and saw that Jona Singh had sent him an email message with a VERY large file attached to it. The confusing part was the title of the message "DANGER; DOWNLOAD IMMEDIATELY" it read.

Jake didn't hesitate; he knew that if Jona said it was important, it was important.

Jona Singh and Jacob had worked together as computer tech-support staff for nearly seven years together at Covington Industries and knew each others quirks and thoughts concerning computer software coding.

He grabbed two flash drives from his computer bag and plugged them both into the two USB ports on the side of his laptop then opened the email and proceeded to download the file to the portable drives.

Jake looked seriously concerned as he stared at the email message on his screen Jona had sent him this morning. The first line of the message read "They will KILL to get this back, send to FBI" which made Jake think that maybe he needed to send it quickly to his dad and the Secret Service up in Washington DC.

Jake watched patiently as the file download went a bit slowly seeing how large the file material was on it, when he saw the flashing download message at the bottom of the screen "GPS File Tracking Engaged".

Jake understood what Jona was telling him; that someone was coming for HIS laptop, and probably HIM as well because they had embedded a tracker code into the file program, enabling someone to find any digital device that was downloading it.

Jake didn't know how much time he had before someone or someone's showed up wanting what was on his laptop; but his curiosity got the best of him and he clicked on the file attachment, opening it. He starred at his screen with big eyes seeing there were hundred's of text files, picture files, and audio files downloading to the flash drives.

Jake looked at a few pages of text and a couple of pictures saying "Holy Shit" loud enough that several people enjoying their lunches looked over at him. He smiled as if to apologize watching the flash drives complete their download.

Jake continued looking at the text files when he noticed out the window a large black SUV pulling into Stoney's parking lot.

The SUV parked and four men dressed in black got out and stood in front of each other as if they were discussing what they were going to do.

Jake quickly picked up the piece of chewed bubble gum he had placed in a napkin when he first got there, he was going to throw it away with his trash after he had his lunch. Grabbing the two downloaded flash drives he placed one in his pants pocket, and the other he pressed into the used bubble gum, sticking it under the bottom of the table until it hardened a bit keeping the flash drive in place against the table's surface.

Jake quickly grabbed his phone and texted his dad's SAT cell phone with the message "85/19/Joe/17" and pressed "send". He figured his dad would understand the initial code he sent and be on his way to him. Jake watched as his text went through then got up placed his laptop in his bag and headed for the front door.

He dialed another number on his phone and said two words "Nightingale flew" into it then tossed his phone into the trash can. Jake could see the four men's faces through the front window from where he was standing and recognized one of the men as a hired security guard at Covington Industries.

Just as he was about to leave the coffee shop Jake saw through the glass door that the four men in black were coming towards it and quickly changed his direction towards the other exit near the back of Stoney's.

Jake walked towards the exit passing an assorted drink cooler; reaching up and placing the other flash drive on top of it thinking no one would look for it there. He managed to get out the back exit without being seen and ran to his car.

One of the large muscular men stationed himself at the front door entrance and barely got a glimpse of Jake jumping into his car and pull out of the parking lot. He motioned to the other three men inside that they needed to come back out, pointing that Jake had left the premises.

Jake quickly got on the interstate highway 85 heading towards Raleigh to try and put some distance between him and Stoney's, knowing the SUV would be closing in on him fast.

Jake was thinking what he saw on his computer screen and understood something like this was much to big to handle alone. He needed his dad, he needed Max Mason.

Max, Tyler, and Linda were heading towards Stoney's Café after getting away from the three black SUV's that tried to kill them. Linda believed Jake would go there for lunch at this time of day and hoped this was the case today.

Max felt the vibration of his cell phone in his jacket pocket and pulled it out to see a text message from Jacob's phone. "Jacob just texted me, but it looks like he may be in danger from all this" Max said to the two women in the car with concern on his face.

Max handed the phone to Tyler who looked at it and said "Another coded message from one of your kids; did they have any sense of a normal childhood growing up with you?" she asked looking at Max who had a smile on his face.

"So Stacy told you about our code system during the GBN fiasco, did she?" Max asked continuing to drive towards Stoney's.

"Yes she did, and it boggles my mind why you just can't say what you mean instead of having all this gibberish that someone; meaning YOU has to decipher" Tyler said in a condescending tone.

"85 means "family in danger" Max said out loud so Linda could hear him looking at her in the rear view mirror seeing the concern on her face for her husband and son.

"Howler is going after Parker, he must need leverage on Jake for some reason" Max said thinking out loud.

"We need to get to Parker's Day Care center; NOW" Max said loudly with anger in his voice.

Tyler looked at the phone and the rest of the message saying "19, Joe, and 17" looking at Linda who smiled back at Tyler.

"We NEED to go to Stoney's first Max" Linda said even though she knew that the bad guys were headed to kidnap her son.

"The rest of the message is for me" she continued. "19 means "he's okay, and looking for us" Linda said with a smile.

"Jake has called his coffee "Joe" since I met him, he even had the owner of Stoney's put the name on the menu; as for the number 17 it's the table number he's usually served at" Linda explained. "He proposed to me at that table" she said with a smile and tears running down her face.

Just as Linda finished explaining why the importance of Stoney's Café was to her and Jake, Max slowed down and pulled into their parking lot stopping the big SUV close to the front door.

He pulled his SA-XD handgun from his holster, checked the magazine, making sure a 9mm round was chambered ready to fire.

He placed the gun back in its holster then pulled his shirt down over it so it couldn't be seen. He looked at the two women then handed Tyler the keys smiling and said "I'll be right back, but if I don't; get the hell out of here; okay".

"I'm NOT leaving without you Max" Tyler said squeezing the hand he had given her the keys with.

"I'm just going to get a cup of Joe; trust me, I'll be right back" Max said smiling at Linda and returning the gentle squeeze to Tyler's hand leaning in to kiss her softly on the lips.

Max got out of the car closed the door and started walking towards the coffee shop's front entrance as Tyler and Linda looked on through the front windshield.

"I am so happy for you two" Linda said as she watched Tyler turn a bit red with embarrassment knowing Max and her let an emotional moment come out in front of someone, even though she was family.

"We're taking it slow; moving in with him while I was rehabbing my knee was a BIG step for him" Tyler replied smiling at what she said.

"He looks at you, like Jake looks at me" Linda said smiling from ear to ear. "He's crazy about you sweetie" she said smiling at Tyler turning their attention back to Max as he walked into Stoney's.

Max stood inside Stoney's and looked around the room seeing quite a few people enjoying their lunch and coffee's keeping his right hand on the butt of his concealed handgun in case someone from Howler's organization was posted there to intercept him or his son Jacob.

Max glanced at the menu up on the wall behind the register and smiled, because there in big letters was "A Cup of Joe" dedicated to his son Jake Mason. "A Cup of Joe" was simply a cup of black coffee with nothing else in it, no cream, no sugar; just straight black coffee.

Max knew that Jacob preferred to drink black coffee for the caffeine to get him going in the morning. He always thought cream and sugar killed the caffeine. Max continued to smile then laughed for a moment knowing that his son had a cup of coffee named after him here; thinking that was impressive.

The young twenty-something woman behind the counter asked if she could help him and Max immediately said "Three cups of Joe to go please" with a grin on his face knowing how silly that sounded to him.

Max continued to look around Stoney's dining room wondering if any of these people sitting here worked for Covington Industries; and if they did, do they know Jacob and if he'd been here this morning.

The young woman rang it up and asked Max for $17 for the three coffees. Max grinned and thought to himself as he handed the woman a $20 bill that his son had expensive taste in coffee.

She handed him his change and advised him he could pick his coffees up at the far end of the bar.

Max slowly moved down towards the far end of the coffee bar continuing to glance at the patrons enjoying their lunch when he noticed that all the tables had a number stamped on top of them like Linda said.

He looked around the room until he found table seventeen seeing that a couple was sitting there enjoying coffee and eating what looked like a large salad up against the large front window.

A young black man wearing an apron looked at Max who had his back to him continuing to look around the room and asked "Did you order three Cups of Joe to go sir?"

Max turned around and nodded to the young man behind the

counter who handed him a cardboard tray with three cups of coffee with lids secured on them.

Max said "Thank you" and took the tray over to the condiment bar where he picked up a couple of creamers and some packets of sugar for Tyler because he knew she didn't drink her coffee black.

He watched as the two young people sitting at table seventeen got up and put their lunch remains in the trash container next to the door and walked out into the parking lot.

Max immediately sat his tray of coffee on the now deserted table and sat down looking it over carefully. He looked at the top of the table to see if Jacob scratched a message into the wood, but didn't see anything. He looked out the window into the parking lot seeing Tyler and Linda in the black SUV parked right next to the door with bewildered looks on their faces.

Max thought about Jacob's message for a moment continuing to look at the table with "seventeen" stamped on it then smiled and nonchalantly reached UNDER the table to find a big glob of pink bubble gum stuck to the bottom of the table.

He felt around a little more to realize the bubble gum was holding a metal object in place under the table. Max grabbed the glob of bubble gum and yanked it off the wood and looked at it to see it had a silver flash drive attached to it.

Max cleaned the bubble gum off the flash drive and looked at it with a smile saying to himself "Well done son" then got up collected his coffee tray and walked out of the coffee shop back to the SUV where Tyler and Linda waited.

He opened the driver's door and handed Tyler the tray of coffee cups which she quickly took so he could climb into his seat.

As he settled in his seat Max looked at Tyler with a grin on his face and said "I taught him well" showing both her and Linda the flash drive in his hand that he had retrieved from Stoney's.

"Where's Jake?" Linda asked as Tyler handed her one of the cups of coffee.

"I don't know sweetheart, he wasn't inside; just this flash drive under table seventeen like he said" Max replied hoping to keep her calm.

"If he's not here, he's on his way to Parker" Linda said. "We need to go NOW" she said forcefully looking at Max staring at her in the rear view mirror.

Max started the car and backed up then floored the accelerator spinning his wheels in Stoney's gravel parking lot as they got on the highway towards Raleigh where Max's grandson Parker's day care was about thirty minutes away from them.

Colonel Howler's cell phone buzzed several times on his desk before he picked it up and looked at the caller ID. He put it on speaker and asked with stress in his voice "Do you have him Lieutenant?"

"Not yet Colonel" Lieutenant Hanson replied looking over at the large well armed muscular driver rolling his eyes knowing that Howler was about to lay into him.

"He saw us coming, and got out with his laptop before we had a chance to acquire him sir" Hanson continued.

"DO YOU KNOW WHERE THE FUCK HE IS LIEUTENANT?" Howler screamed into the phone pissed that Jacob Mason got away with his laptop still out in the open.

"Yes Sir, he's headed back into Raleigh; we can see him ahead of us now" Hanson said seeing Jake's car about a half a mile in front of them moving fast knowing someone was after him.

"I NEED him alive Lieutenant" Howler said firmly into his phone needing to know if Jake Mason gave Jona Singh's email download to anyone else; especially to Max Mason.

"Yes Sir, will contact you when we have acquired the target" the confident Lieutenant stated hanging up the phone.

The SUV's driver sped up until they were right behind Jake's car almost touching his back bumper. Jake nervously looked into his rear view mirror to see the two men staring at him.

Jake watched as one of the men, the one in the passenger's seat lowered his window and put his arm out pointing a gun at the back of Jake's car.

Jake swerved into the left lane just as he heard the loud gunshot in back of him. "OH SHIT" he yelled out to himself knowing that the first shot barely missed his car.

The black SUV quickly moved back behind Jake's car just as he heard the second gunshot ring out shattering his back window causing him to duck down in his seat feeling his seat belt tighten around his shoulders and waist.

The bullet went through the passenger's headrest and out the front windshield leaving a hole and a rather large spider-web crack in the glass.

Jake thought as he looked back at the black SUV; what if Linda or Parker were sitting there when that shot came through, one of them would be dead changing his fear into anger.

Jake continued to speed up as he moved back into the right lane ahead of the murderous SUV realizing to himself that this violent encounter definitely had something to do with Jona Singh sending him the email that he downloaded; that people were REALLY trying to kill him, and possibly his family for it.

Just as he had finished his thought Jake could see in his side mirror that the SUV was behind him again just as another shot rang out blowing out his back passenger side tire causing the car to start sliding towards the gravel emergency pull off area and the guard rail that was protecting vehicles from a ravine with a sharp incline.

Jake could see that he was losing control of the car and that it was only a matter of seconds before he and his car plummeted through the guard rail and down the ravine.

He quickly grabbed his laptop bag from the passengers seat then opened his door and jumped out hitting the pavement hard, and rolling with his momentum like his dad taught him; protecting the bag in his arms as he watched his car crash through the steel guard rail and down the ravine hitting a large rock and bursting into flames.

The black SUV came to a quick stop and Colonel Howler's four mercenaries jumped out their guns pointing at a battered and bruised Jake Mason still lying on the pavement. Hanson looked down at him smiling saying "The Colonel would like a word with you Mr. Mason".

With blood dripping down his forehead from a cut he sustained Jake looked up at the Lieutenant and smiled saying "You do know, this isn't going to end well for any of you; right?" thinking his dad was on his way; not knowing Max Mason was already in Raleigh looking for him.

Lieutenant Hanson bent down and grabbed Jake's arm to help lift him off the road looking him in the eye and smiling saying "You'll be dead within the hour" as his partner got out to direct on-coming traffic around them. Jake could hear the mercenary telling several cars that slowed down to offer help that "Everything was fine, it was a Police matter" showing them his security badge.

Jake was quickly handcuffed with his hands behind his back and his bag taken. The Lieutenant looked inside the bag and smiled seeing Jake's laptop inside. They quickly put him in the back of the SUV between two mercenaries, one of which placed a black cloth bag over his head and sped off watching the smoke from Jake's burning car bellowing up into the sky.

As they headed down the highway towards Raleigh the Lieutenant pulled out his cell phone and quickly dialed Colonel Howler's office phone, looking over at his driving partner and smiling.

"Do you have both packages secured Lieutenant?" Howler asked as he answered the phone.

"Affirmative Colonel; both packages are secured and we are

heading to Outpost Charlie as you requested" the young Lieutenant said proudly knowing he had succeeded in his mission for the Colonel.

"Well done Lieutenant Hanson, I will be there in fifteen minutes" Howler replied. "Have the package prepped by the time I get there" he advised.

"Affirmative Colonel" Hanson said into the phone then disconnecting and placing it back in his pocket.

"Turn yourselves in and I promise I won't kill any of you today" Jake Mason said through the bag over his head getting a sharp elbow in the ribs by one of the men sitting beside him for his obnoxious comment.

"We'll see who dies today" Hanson replied laughing looking over at his partner who gave him a grin.

"Okay, don't say I didn't give you a choice" Jake said through the bag again now in a little pain from the hard elbow to his side.

They continued driving down the highway towards Raleigh as Jake still couldn't see out of the black bag over his head, figuring they were heading towards Raleigh's massive warehouse district with its giant cargo containers and storage facilities; he knew Covington Industries had some buildings there, and it was a secure private area.

Howler smiled to himself then pulled out his handgun from its holster and checked to make sure there was a round in the chamber then placed it back securely.

He walked around his desk and picked up his military backpack and started to walk out of his office when Evelyn Covington walked up and stood in his office doorway blocking his exit, her graying blonde hair tied up in a pony tail.

"Colonel Howler, where are we on finding the missing laptop?" she asked with a smile on her face continuing to stand in the middle of Howler's doorway so he couldn't get out without talking to her.

"I'm kind of in a hurry Mrs. Covington, can we discuss this a bit later?" Howler asked seeing the smile leave her face.

"We have Federal Agents breathing down our necks right before the launch, and you want to discuss it later Colonel; I DON'T THINK SO" the matriarch replied with anger in her voice.

"My men have acquired the laptop; I'm on my way there now to retrieve it, and find out if Jake Mason gave the information to anyone else" Howler said finally giving in to Mrs. Covington's aggressive rant.

"Good, I'm coming with you" she said moving out of the doorway to allow Colonel Howler to lead the way out.

"Do you think that's such a good idea ma'am?" Howler asked as he walked past her into the hallway.

"If the young man and his wife are going to die today, he should at least be allowed to know they're child will be taken good care of; and I should be the one to tell him" Evelyn Covington said with an evil grin on her face.

"Not to mention, it gives us leverage against any of his other family that might want to oppose us" she said laughing.

"Okay, you're the boss" Howler replied thinking this was a VERY bad idea, that this could get messy and public.

He also knew that Max Mason would take this SERIOUSLY personal; kidnapping his grandson, and killing his son and daughter in law. He knew that Mason would hunt everyone down like a dog with a bone. In order to get out of this with his money and his life Howler knew Max Mason needed to die as well.

Howler knew he was going to have to collect his money from both the Covington's and Amikura quickly in order to get out of the country before the Fed's came for him. Howler thought $30 million dollars was a good retirement fund on a tropical island.

It was already too late to turn back; Howler had already sent several men to Parker Mason's day care center next to Linda Mason's Police Precinct and was waiting on a phone call to give them the order to proceed and collect the young boy at ANY cost.

The black SUV pulled up to a warehouse where one of the men sitting beside Jake Mason got out and raised the garage door watching as the SUV pulled into the lighted warehouse, then pulled the door back down sealing them inside.

The other mercenary pulled Jake out of the backseat, walked him over, and shoved him down on a chair that was sitting in the middle of the large room yanking his blindfold off his head.

Lieutenant Hanson grabbed Jake's already handcuffed arms and pulled them hard over the back of the chair.

He then un-cuffed one of his wrists and twisted the open cuff through the chair's metal bar and re-cuffed it to his wrist securing Jake to the chair.

Jake looked around the large room and said "I love what you've done with the place; I can see this place on the cover of "Scumbags & Assholes" real soon" he said laughing just as Hanson back handed him across the face with his open right hand splitting his lip.

"Wow, for an Army guy you sure hit like a squid" Jake said laughing spitting blood at the Lieutenant's feet.

Jake likes to tease his sister Stacy since she is in the Navy by calling her a "squid" even though she is a Navy SEAL. The term "squid" is not very enduring when said by other branches of the military other than the Navy.

"Go ahead and laugh" the Lieutenant said with a grin. "When the Colonel gets here you won't be laughing that much" he continued.

"I'm sure the Colonel is a funny guy" Jake replied condescendingly.

Hanson bent over and tried to tie Jake's ankles to the front legs of the chair but not before Jake kicked him hard in the face knocking him backwards on the floor.

The other mercenary hit Jake across the jaw with a right handed punch dazing him long enough for them to tie his ankles together with some thin rope; then proceeded to take his shoes and socks off.

Jake shook off the punch to his jaw and looked at the pissed off Lieutenant slowly getting up off the floor and said laughing "You had to know that was coming asshole".

Just as Hanson was about to hit Jake again his phone started buzzing in his pocket and he turned and looked at it saying to his partner "He's here, go open the door".

Jake continued smiling at him because he knew he kicked Hanson really hard seeing blood coming from his mouth saying "Oh goody, we have company" knowing that Colonel Howler had arrived; showing the young Lieutenant he wasn't afraid of any of them.

CHAPTER SIX

One of the mercenary's raised the garage door and another black SUV came through, parking next to the other one in the large empty warehouse.

Colonel Howler and Evelyn Covington got out of the SUV and walked towards Lieutenant Hanson and Jake Mason who they could see was cuffed and tied to the chair; as the other three mercenaries secured the room around them.

"Hey look, the Colonel brought a date" Jake said out loud laughing as Howler and Covington walked closer to him.

"Oh wait, he brought his mother" he said smiling sarcastically seeing it was an older blondish-gray haired woman.

"Wow, you have the same smart-ass mouth like your father" Howler said with a grin.

"Thank you" Jake said with a sarcastic smile to him knowing his father had a sharp tongue with assholes.

Jake smiled at the middle-aged gray haired woman and said "Sweetheart I think you can do better; he's going to be in jail soon so you might want to start looking for someone in YOUR own age group".

"You don't know who I am, do you Mr. Mason?" Evelyn Covington asked smiling.

"I'm afraid not; if you're hanging out with the Colonel here you can't be that impressive" Jake replied laughing.

"I'm Evelyn Covington" she said to a smiling Jake Mason.

"I guess this means I'm fired" Jake asked laughing, knowing now that she was the owner and matriarch of Covington Industries along with her son Nathanial where he worked. "Is this a bad time to ask for a raise" he asked smiling at the older woman.

"You have your father's sharp wit; and his eyes" she said to him brushing his hair out of his face.

"He told my son just this morning that he was going to find out what he was hiding; we're going to find out what you're hiding first young man" Covington said backing away from him continuing her evil grin to him.

"WAIT; MY father is in town?" Jake asked with a smile on his face seeing the looks on their faces confirming to him that he was.

Jake started laughing uncontrollably seeing the confused look on everyone's face. Evelyn Covington smacked him across the face and shouted "Your father, and that bitch he's with are just like you; DEAD" she said.

Jake started laughing again then asked "My father, AND Tyler are HERE in Raleigh?" smiling from ear to ear.

"You people are SOOOO fucked; whether you kill me or not" Jake said with a condescending grin. "The most dangerous man in the world, and the woman HE trained are here looking for HIS son; you are REALLY screwed Howler" he said continuing to smile seeing anger and fear come over the Colonel's face.

"You're not going to die yet Mr. Mason, we haven't asked our question yet" Covington said smiling at him as Lieutenant Hanson and one of the other mercenaries brought over a large metal washtub filled with water.

"Don't worry Mr. Mason, after Colonel Howler's men have killed your wife, along with your father, and Agent Tyler I will make sure young Parker goes to a good home; for the right price of course" Covington continued watching the smile come across Jake's face again.

"Let me make sure I understand all of this lady; MY SWAT trained police officer wife, is with MY Navy SEAL father, and his special tactics trained Secret Service girlfriend here in Raleigh and you expect to kill ALL three of them; THEN, sell our five year old son during some kind of child auction?" Jake asked with a smirk on his face.

Jake could see the confusion on both Covington's and Howler's face as Jake put everything in perspective with his family. "Good luck with that assholes, you're damn lucky MY Navy SEAL sister isn't here to help fuck you all up" he said with a grin.

"We've had your sister under surveillance for sometime now; her ship left Norfolk Naval Base for the Persian Gulf earlier this morning" Howler said with a grin. "She's halfway to England by now, so she won't be helping you anytime soon" Howler said looking at Hanson with a smile.

Evelyn Covington looked at Colonel Howler and smiled at what he said, then looked back at Jake saying "I hope you said goodbye to your family this morning Mr. Mason; because none of you will ever see each other again" she said with an evil smirk.

"You're forgetting one thing lady; the love a mother has for her child; my wife is going to fuck YOU up pretty hard for taking our boy" Jake said continuing his smile to her.

"I may be dead, but I'll be seeing most of you real soon" Jake said laughing at both Howler and Covington.

Covington let her emotions get the best of her and she screamed at Jake saying "NOTHING IS GOING TO STOP US FROM CONTROLLING THE ENTIRE WORLD'S COMMUNICATIONS MARKET; ESPECIALLY NO BACKWOODS RENT-A-COP" as her face turned bright red with anger.

"Lady, you're a stupid old woman that's going to die violently at the hand of my wife; I'd shut up if I were you" Jake said laughing.

Evelyn Covington smiled at what he said knowing Howler's men were going to torture him to death as she watched the young Lieutenant prep Jake Mason.

Jake continued to smile as he thought neither Covington nor Howler had a clue about what his wife Linda was capable of when it came to those she loved; remembering the first time he saw her.

Linda was a young, strong eighteen year old U.S. Army military police woman (MP) working for the Criminal Investigative Division stationed in Kabul, Afghanistan; seven years ago. She was the youngest woman to achieve the rank of Lieutenant in less than a year in ALL of Armed Forces history.

On this particular night her MP unit got a call from a popular dance club that U.S. servicemen frequented about a disturbance called in by the owner; when she arrived with two other military police officers a large fight had broken out among some local Afghan young adults and several Army personnel outside of the club.

Jake Mason along with his two best friends were walking down the street towards the foray when he observed the young, attractive blonde-haired woman taking on three Afghan assailants alone; kicking their asses badly. She punched hard like a mule and kicked with precision that led Jake to believe she had extensive martial arts training which impressed the hell out of him.

One of her attackers grabbed her collapsible baton from her gun belt, extended it then tried hitting her in the head with it.

She was faster then he was and disarmed him quickly throwing him to the ground causing the baton to roll on the sidewalk towards Jake and his two friends continuing to watch.

The local Afghan thugs battered and bruised figured they were getting their asses kicked and decided to take off down the street. Linda stood there looking around to make sure there wasn't another threat then looked around for her fallen baton only to have Jake walk up to her and say "This looks like it belongs to you" handing her the steel black baton with a goofy smile on his face.

Linda smiled at Jake looking him up and down thinking he was cute then said "Thank you", putting her baton away.

She could tell he was U.S. military either Army or Marines but wasn't sure of his rank because he was wearing civilian clothes.

Her partner called out to her from their vehicle "Lieutenant, we have another call".

Jake watched as she walked back to the black SUV then turned and looked back at him and smiled, got back into the heavily armored SUV and left before Jake could get her name.

"I think I just met my future wife" he said to his two friends who laughed hard at what the smitten young man said grabbing him by the arms and walking him down the street to the restaurant they were heading to before all the commotion happened in front of them.

Jake's mind came back to Covington and Howler standing in front of him smiling as his feet, now untied; sat soaking in the washtub full of water.

Jake knew what this torture technique was about as he watched the other mercenary roll up a portable automobile battery charger he had gotten from the back of the SUV.

He sarcastically asked anyway "Can I get some ruby red polish on my toenails after my foot bath; I think that would look real sexy" smiling as Howler walked up to him and ripped his shirt open to expose his bare chest.

Jake looked up smiling at Howler asking "Shouldn't you buy me dinner first Colonel?" looking down at his naked chest. Jake watched as the mercenary placed large yellow sponges into the battery clips then soaked them in the washtub full of water standing there awaiting for Howler's order to proceed.

"We'll see if you're smart mouth still works after two or three hours of shock therapy" Howler said laughing.

"Who did you give the download to?" Howler asked smiling at a defiant Jacob Mason.

"Officer Mason, this is dispatch; do you copy?" a familiar voice came over Linda's police radio.

"Officer Mason here; OVER" Linda replied into her radio as she sat in the back seat of Max's SUV heading back to Raleigh starring at Tyler who turned around when she heard the call.

"Linda we have a report of a vehicle crashing through the guard rail and catching fire on interstate 85, right before the city limits" the female voice said through the radio's speaker for everyone in the SUV to hear.

"We're about five minutes out from that location on I-85 dispatch; OVER" Linda said looking at Max in his rear view mirror with concern on her face.

"The officer on the scene ran the burning car's plates and found out it belongs to your husband Jake" she said over the speaker. "Officer Murphy is on the scene; over" she continued hearing Linda Mason reply "Copy that".

Linda looked at Tyler in the front seat and turned white as a ghost knowing that Jake's car was sitting in a ravine engulfed in flames, wondering if he was still inside of it or lay injured or dead outside of it.

"Is he...?" Linda asked nervously as Tyler reached back to hold her hand.

"Officer Murphy found no one at the scene; witnesses say four heavily armed men dressed in black placed an injured man in the back of their black SUV and left the scene quickly; we're assuming the injured man was Jake" the woman said over the speaker.

Max could see ahead of them that he had to start slowing down because of the heavy traffic and continuous red brake lights in front of them. He started looking for a way around everyone, understanding that traffic was slowing down because someone from Linda's police unit was investigating the burning car they just found out was Jacob's.

"HOWLER'S MEN HAVE JAKE, AND THEY'RE GOING AFTER OUR SON" Linda yelled from the back seat seriously upset that her family was in danger.

Max flipped on the SUV's flashing red & blue lights and quickly swerved over to the right side avoiding stopped traffic driving straight down the emergency side road. He looked at Linda in the rear view mirror seeing her distraught and scared then looked over at Tyler with concern on his face.

"Lieutenant you need to calm down and look at the big picture" Max said hoping she would understand what he was saying.

"WHAT THE HELL MAX; THE BIG PICTURE IS THAT I'M GOING TO KILL HOWLER AND ANYONE ELSE THAT HARMS MY FAMILY" Linda said her face turning bright red with anger.

"I can appreciate that sweetheart, I'm with you on that" Max said still looking at her in the mirror.

"Howler won't kill either of them, he needs them both alive for leverage against ME" Max said smiling at Tyler knowing Howler was an egomaniac and couldn't stand NOT being in control of everything, and EVERYONE; including Max Mason.

Linda seemed to accept Max's explanation because he could see she was calming down when she said "We still need to get to Parker's day care, like NOW".

Max slowed down when he came up on the lone police car sitting in the emergency lane. They could all see a bellowing cloud of black & white smoke coming from the other side of the guard rail. They could also see the police officer standing at his car writing out a report when Max stopped and both he and Linda rolled down their windows.

Linda recognized the officer right away and called out to him "MURPHY" she yelled seeing that he saw and recognized her hanging her head out of the back of the SUV and walked towards them.

"Linda are you alright?" the young officer asked as he looked at her through the open window.

"Yes, this is my father-in-law Max Mason and his partner Karen Tyler with the Secret Service" she replied as both Max and Tyler showed him their government ID's.

"This is Officer James Murphy, he's one of the good ones at the station" Linda said introducing the young policeman to Max and Tyler.

Officer James Murphy was about 6'-4" tall, weighed around 220 pounds but it looked like it was all muscle. He was a twenty-three year old reserved local boy; born and raised in Raleigh who was only six months out of the North Carolina State Police Academy.

Linda quickly took him under her wing seeing his potential as a great police officer; always calling in for him to back her up on certain cases.

Murphy reached in and shook Max's hand then turned to Linda with a concerned look on his face saying "Its Jake's car down the hill burning" he said. "A couple of witnesses said they saw four men with guns dressed in all black pick a man up off the pavement, put him in cuffs, then into the back of their black SUV and drive off down the highway" Murphy said looking at his note pad then looking back at Linda through the window.

"We need to make sure our son Parker is okay" Linda replied, more concerned about her son because she knew her husband Jake could take care of himself in any hostile situation.

"Isn't his day care right next to the station?" Murphy asked seeing the worry on the young mom's face as he stood there continuing to look at her through the open window.

Murphy pulled his radio off his belt and spoke into it "Dispatch, this is Officer Murphy with Officer Mason copy?" he asked releasing the transmitter button.

The young officer's radio crackled and hissed several times before Murphy brought it to his lips again asking "Dispatch, do you copy, come in dispatch; over?"

"Max I need to call Parker's daycare, something's not right" Linda stated knowing that their dispatcher has NEVER taken this long to get back to an officer in the field.

Max didn't hesitate handing his SAT phone to Linda who quickly dialed the daycare's office number she knew by heart only to get the dreaded recorded message "The number you have dialed is NOT in service at this time".

Max could tell by Linda's facial expression she was terrified of what she heard on the phone which prompted him to say "We gotta go" as the three of them quickly left Officer Murphy standing there wondering what was happening.

"Who did you give the flash drive to?" Howler asked sternly standing over Jake then looking over at Hanson wearing rubber gloves holding the car charging cables, with the wet sponges attached; letting him know what he was going to do to him if he didn't tell him.

"I haven't a clue what you're talking about Colonel" Jake said with a smile on his face knowing what was coming next.

Howler nodded to Hanson who placed the electrically charged sponges on Jake's bare chest sending five-thousand volts of electricity into him causing his body to convulse and shake as he sat in the chair.

Jake gritted his teeth as Hanson held the electrified sponges on his chest looking at Howler, refusing to give him the satisfaction of screaming in pain.

After about twenty seconds Howler nodded to Hanson to stop, who stepped back as Howler leaned in and smiled at Jake asking "Who did you give the flash drive to?"

Jake's heart was racing from the electric charge Hanson gave him causing his over stimulated brain to remember the first time he asked Linda out over in Afghanistan. His heart raced the same way that first time.

He had walked into the base MP station seeing no one in the office. He thought he might be crazy looking for a blonde "Lieutenant" he had no clue what her name was, only that he had a brief encounter with her last night outside a bar.

The young blonde, blue-eyed Lieutenant came from the back office carrying some files to find Jake standing there at the front desk smiling at her and smiled back asking "Can I help you soldier?" recognizing him as the guy who gave her baton back to her after last nights fight at the bar.

"I wanted to make sure you were okay after last night" Jake replied his smile never leaving his face.

"I'm fine, thank you for asking" she said just as another MP came into the office and promptly stood at attention and saluted.

The young Lieutenant couldn't take her eyes off of the young attractive soldier standing at the desk in front of her smiling, only glancing over to her partner for a moment to ask "Why are you saluting me Todd, we're the same rank?"

"I'm not saluting you Linda; I'm saluting Captain Mason" the Lieutenant said to her continuing to salute Jake.

"At ease Lieutenant" Jake said continuing to smile at her seeing the look on her face as he saluted her colleague. Linda stood at attention and saluted Jake immediately embarrassed that she didn't know who he was.

"Would this be a bad time to ask you to dinner?" Jake asked smiling seeing her lightly red face as he returned her salute.

"WHERE'S THE GOD DAMN FLASH DRIVE MASON?" Howler screamed as Jake came back to reality his body convulsing and shaking from the electrical charge searing through his body for the second time.

Lieutenant Hanson continued to shock him a bit longer this time until Jake closed his eyes and slumped over. Howler walked over and lifted his head up to see Jake was unconscious, smiled at him and walked back to Evelyn Covington's side; who was enjoying the show.

Howler smiled at Covington then looked over at Hanson and said "I already know who he gave the flash drive to; Max Mason" as he turned with Covington to walk back to the black SUV near the garage door.

"We'll see if he has the balls to sacrifice his grandson for it" Howler said laughing as Hanson put down the sponges and handed Howler Jake's laptop.

"Hey Colonel, if you go near my son I WILL kill you VERY

painfully" Jake Mason said raising his head up to look Howler in the eyes.

Hanson walked over to Jake and was about to hit him in the face when Howler shouted "STOP" walking up beside Hanson smiling at Jake.

"WOW kid, you are as tough as your old man" Howler said smiling. "It's a shame I have to kill you, you would have made a great soldier in my company" the Colonel said waiting for a snappy response from his battered and bruised prisoner.

Jake looked at him as not to disappoint saying "I don't work for assholes" then looked over at Evelyn Covington and smiled saying "Oh wait; I already do" watching as her smile turned to contempt at what he said.

"Kill him Colonel and be rid of him" Evelyn Covington said to Howler tired of toying with the arrogant young man they knew wouldn't break.

Howler reached into his pocket and pulled out his now vibrating phone and answered it. The voice on the other end said "We are in position, and communications are being jammed Colonel; do we proceed with the mission sir?"

Howler looked at Jake smiling saying "Your mission is a go Sergeant" then turned off his phone and placed it back in his pants pocket.

"Looks like I have to leave you in Lieutenant Hanson's capable hands" Howler said then looked over at Evelyn Covington with a grin saying "We have a young guest to get ready for" knowing this will antagonize Jake.

Jake looked up at Howler and said "Remember my promise Colonel; and it WILL be painful" as he continued to stare and smile into Howler's eyes.

Howler looked at Hanson saying "Give this asshole a couple more jolts, then kill him and leave the body just like it is" Howler ordered.

"I want to send a message to his old man" Howler said seeing Jake's smile turn to anger.

Howler walked back over to Evelyn Covington then looked at the two mercenaries guarding the door ordering "You two with me, back to the compound" as the four of them got into the SUV.

Hanson's partner opened the garage door and the SUV slowly backed out, then he pulled the heavy steel door back down again and went back to standing against the lone SUV about fifteen feet away from Jake and the Lieutenant.

"I have nowhere to be, so I can do this all day" Hanson said as he turned the battery charger back on and shocked Jake again with the wet sponge cables.

Jake's body shook and convulsed dangerously close to having his heart explode inside his chest. Hanson pulled the cables off his chest and looked over at his partner laughing who had placed his AR-15 machine-gun up against the SUV leaning it against it and now looking at his phone bored at what Hanson was doing to Jake.

Hanson turned to give Jake another jolt when Jake grabbed his two gloved hands and pushed the wet electrical sponges against Hanson's chest causing him to convulse and shake rendering him unconscious.

Just as Hanson was falling to the ground Jake dropped the cables and grabbed Hanson's handgun out of his holster and fired two shots hitting the mercenary against the car in the chest with both rounds. The mercenary slumped to the ground blood pouring out of his chest and mouth, his eyes looking at Jake as he slowly died.

Hanson slowly started to wake up realizing he was now in the chair tied to it, his boots and socks removed and his feet soaking in the bucket of cold water.

Hanson's bare chest was now exposed his shirt ripped opened as he looked up at a frazzled and smiling Jake Mason holding the wet sponge cables in front of him.

"Well hello there sleepyhead, did you have a nice nap?" Jake asked Hanson sarcastically.

"You've been out for about ten minutes; I was getting a bit worried I might have zapped you to much and we wouldn't be able to have our little talk" Jake said smiling as he watched Hanson look over at his dead partner sitting against the SUV with bullet holes in his chest and start to struggle to get out of his cuffs rocking the chair some.

"HOW THE HELL DID YOU GET OUT OF YOUR CUFFS?" Hanson yelled continuing to struggle knowing he was about to be tortured by the guy he was torturing, and had orders to kill.

"Something my dad taught me and my sister when we first went into the military; and that's to always carry an extra handcuff key & mini box cutter in a secret pocket of your tactical pants in case you're captured" Jake said showing Hanson his handcuff key and smiling.

"Now I know you weren't expecting that first jolt; kind of took you by surprise, but I want you to know this isn't business; its COMPLETELY personal" Jake said smiling as he placed the highly electrified sponges on Hanson's bare chest causing him to shake, convulse, and scream in pain as the electricity coarse through his body.

Jake pulled the sponges away and watched as Hanson calmed down but continuing to breathe hard. "I need you to tell me where they are taking my son?" Jake asked stepping back to look him in the eyes.

"KISS MY ASS" Hanson screamed defiantly at Jake.

"Really, that's your snappy comeback; kiss my ass" Jake asked placing the wet sponges on Hanson's chest again watching as his body shook harder this time.

Jake pulled back the sponges from Hanson's chest and asked the young Lieutenant again forcefully "WHERE ARE THEY TAKING MY SON?".

Just as Jake was ready to shock him again Hanson yelled "ENOUGH, I'll tell you what you want to know".

Hanson went on to tell Jake everything; where Evelyn Covington was taking his son Parker, what they were going to do with him, about the satellite launching, and how Howler was working with Noki Amikura to kill his father Max Mason.

Hanson also informed Jake WHY Nathaniel & Evelyn Covington wanted this satellite in space so bad for their so called new "phone app". Finally telling Jake about the secret Howler and he found out about the Covington family.

"So now you'll let me go?" Hanson asked watching Jake flip the button to the off position on the battery charger then come back over to look at him.

"I never said I would let you go; I just said I wasn't going to kill you" Jake said as he dropped the sponge cables into the bucket of water on top of Hanson's bare feet knowing they were turned off watching Hanson jump thinking it was still charged up.

Jake picked up Hanson's phone, the keys to the SUV, and his handgun and turned away from Hanson to head to the SUV only to stop and turn around smiling at him.

"Howler implied that I was exactly like my old man; but I'm nothing like him, you want to know why?" Jake asked Hanson who was listening intently.

"My father; he NEVER lies" Jake said walking up to the battery charger and flipping the switch back on, watching Hanson shake and convulse while the battery cables bounce around in the water at his feet until he slumps over dead the smell of burning flesh rising from his now charred body.

Jake looks at him with a serious face and says to the dead Lieutenant "I'll tell the Colonel you're waiting for him in Hell" then he turns and walks over, opening the garage door then climbs into the black SUV.

He sat in the SUV for a moment to collect his thoughts then pulls out Hanson's phone and dials a number then asks "What's your status?"

After listening for a moment Jake looks at the time on the phone seeing it's a bit after 2pm and replies "Romeo Echo 1900" then tosses the phone on the passengers' seat backing the SUV slowly out of the warehouse looking at the two dead mercenaries one last time before he heads to his son's daycare center where Colonel Howler's men were sent.

Max, Tyler, and Linda arrive in downtown Raleigh pulling up to a police roadblock about a block away from Linda's Police Precinct and Parker's daycare center. They can see several police cars on fire from their position, the black smoke rising into the North Carolina sky. They watched as emergency vehicles flashing lights could be seen from the roadblock as medical personnel worked feverishly on what seemed to be wounded police officers in front of the station and daycare center.

Linda jumps out of the SUV and is quickly detained by two officers standing guard at the roadblock as she tries to force her way in. Max and Tyler get out and walk up to Linda who is screaming at one of the officers "LET ME GO MY SON IS IN THERE".

Max looks around at the chaotic scene then looks at the visibly upset police officer holding Linda who shakes his head slightly hoping Linda won't see, giving Max the impression that his grandson; HER son was taken with serious casualties.

Tyler holds Linda who is crying uncontrollably as Max asks the officer "What happened here?" showing the two officers his Secret Service ID.

"I can answer that" a tall elderly man with gray hair and a mustache said walking up to them wearing a bullet-proof vest over his police uniform.

Linda heard the man's voice and stood at attention immediately wiping her tears from her face as the other officer handed the man Max's ID.

"Captain Hargrove" Linda addressed the man still standing at attention seeing the solemn look on her commanding officers face.

The man smiled at Linda then turned back to Max and extended his hand "I'm Captain Andrew Hargrove, I've heard so much about you Director Mason" he said shaking Max's hand.

"What happened here Captain?" Max asked with concern as Linda and Tyler listened carefully.

"Several men wearing masks; possibly as many as six to eight, all military trained, and heavily armed ran into the daycare center killing two teachers and taking Linda's son Parker" the Captain replied.

"When they came out several of my officers were coming back from lunch; seeing them must have spooked them because they engaged them wounding three of them and blowing up two cruisers to mask their getaway" Hargrove explained with a solemn look to Linda.

"I'm so sorry about your son Linda; we will get him back I promise" the Captain said seeing Linda getting more and more upset at what had happened.

"Permission to be dismissed sir" Linda asked her Captain looking at Max with a scowl on her face.

"We'll keep you and Jake updated, forensics' is going over the scene as we speak; we'll find out who did this" Hargrove said hoping what he said would help her cope with the situation at hand.

"Where is your husband?" Hargrove asked not seeing Jake here with Linda or his father.

"I'M RIGHT HERE CAPTAIN" a voice behind them shouted over the sirens of the ambulances that were leaving.

"JAKE" Linda yelled running to her husband and wrapping her arms around him putting her head on his shoulder with tears coming down her face.

"Easy baby" Jake said as she squeezed him hard still feeling the effects of the painful electrocution from Lieutenant Hanson.

Linda pulled away from him giving him a long concerned stare saying "Oh my god, what happened to you".

"I had a long lunch with some friends" he said smiling at her seeing that Captain Hargrove was listening to they're conversation.

Max walked up to his son and gently hugged him recognizing the burn marks partially covered up on his chest by his torn shirt whispering in his ear "Are you okay son?"

"Yeah Pop, I'm good" Jake replied. "We ALL need to go somewhere and talk" he said to his father with a smile.

"Howler knows you have the flash drive" Jake whispered in his father's ear then kissed him on the cheek so Captain Hargrove wouldn't get suspicious of what they were about to get into.

Max looked at Hargrove and extended his hand saying "I'm going to take them both home; please call us at their house if something on Parker comes up" he asked shaking his hand then turning with Tyler and walking slowly to the SUV behind Linda and his son.

Just as they were getting into Max's SUV the phone Jake took off of Lieutenant Hanson started ringing. Jake stuck it in his pocket when he got out of the mercenary's SUV and now pulled it out knowing it was Colonel Howler wondering if the Lieutenant had killed him.

Jake turned the phone on speaker as the four of them listened and Howler asked "Why haven't you returned to base Lieutenant?"

"Sorry Colonel; I'm afraid Lieutenant Hanson won't be joining you anytime soon, in fact; EVER" Jake said with a smile to his dad who returned a glaring stern look to his son knowing he was baiting Howler.

"So how do we do this Howler?" Max asked, surprising Howler he was there with his suppose to be dead son.

"WOW, this does throw a wrench in the mix doesn't it Admiral" Howler said laughing through the speaker.

"You want the flash drive, WE want my grandson" Max said

sternly to the phone in Jake's hand. "A simple exchange Colonel" Max said knowing what Howler's response would be.

"How do you know I won't kill you and your family once I have the flash drive Mason?" Howler asked continuing to laugh over the phone speaker.

"Lets call it professional courtesy Colonel; we both know when a mission has gone south, you need to abort to save lives, and face" Max replied looking at Jacob, Linda, and Tyler.

There was silence for a few seconds then Howler came back saying "Okay Mason, we'll try it your way; the boy dies if you try anything stupid" he declared. "Be at Umstead State Park outside of Raleigh at 1800 hours; just YOU and your asshole son" Howler said knowing that would piss them both off.

"Hey Colonel, if you fuck this up and hurt my son I will kill you like I promised back in the warehouse" Jake stated as his father gave him a disapproving yet understanding look.

"1800 hours, NO tricks Howler" Max said then hanging up the phone and handing it back to Jake.

"You know he's going to try to kill us Pop" Jake said with a grin.

"Yeah I know, the man is predictable if anything" Max replied with a grin. "I have a plan but I need to make a phone call" he said looking at Tyler with a grin.

"I already made mine" Jake said to his dad looking at his wife Linda with a big smile on her face knowing who Jake called.

CHAPTER SEVEN

As they all walked back to the parked SUV Max pulled out his SAT phone from his pocket but hesitated for a moment before making his call, seeing the extreme worry on his daughter-in-law Linda's face concerning her son; HIS grandson Parker's kidnapping by Colonel Howler and the Covington's yet Jacob showed he was VERY calm and in control of this situation.

Max grabbed Jake's arm and pulled him aside as both Tyler and Linda got into the SUV and closed their doors. "What's going on son?" Max asked wondering why his son was so cool and collected knowing HIS son was in the hands of a psychotic homicidal Colonel, with an army of mercenaries at his command.

"What's SO valuable to Howler and Covington on this flash drive that they would be so desperate to kidnap a little boy for it?" Max asked holding the drive in front of his son's face awaiting an answer.

"First, I got a brief look at the open file before I realized it had a GPS transponder embedded in the software code" Jake said looking at his dad.

"That's why they took me and tortured me; to find out whom I gave it to or if I read it" he continued as his dad listened.

"Howler automatically figured I gave it to you, and gave Hanson the order to kill me; as you can see he didn't, thanks to your handcuff key in the pants trick" Jake said with a grin.

Max smiled knowing his son actually listened to him when he was over in Afghanistan; something that saved his life today.

Max taught both him and Stacy that 90% of anyone captured by hostile forces have their hands "usually" tied or cuffed behind their backs, giving them a disadvantage in trying to escape their captors.

Max showed Jacob & Stacy that in that situation if you sewed a small piece of cloth in the back waist band of your tactical pants you could use it as a pocket to store a handcuff key and a small folding box cutter to escape handcuffs, rope, or plastic zip ties. Max smiled thinking some of the knowledge he taught Jacob & Stacy may have actually stuck with them.

"And to think I almost wore dress pants this morning" Jake said to Max with a laugh, glad he wore a pair of his khaki military tactical pants instead.

"So what did you see on the flash drive son? Max asked looking his son in the eye then glancing back over at Tyler and Linda who were watching the two of them from the car windows.

"It's a blackmail list" Jake said looking at his dad. "It has names of congressmen, local politicians, judges, celebrities, and financial figures all over the world" Jake explained to his dad.

"That's not even the worst part" Jake said giving his dad a worried and angry look.

"I looked at the software code that my friend Jona Singh found" Jake said with pain in his voice as he continued.

"I'm afraid your friend is dead son; they found him in his apartment this morning from an apparent robbery gone wrong" Max replied seeing that Jake had no idea he was dead.

"HOWLER; that son of a bitch" Jake said with sadness in his voice hearing about his friend.

"The Covington's are going to use their new phone "app" that launches tonight using the technology to record audio and video of everything anyone does or say's without their knowledge; continuing their blackmail opportunities" Jake said to Max.

"How many people are we talking about having this "app"?" Max asked concerned with what his son has told him so far.

"Anyone or everyone; from President Bradshaw to Parker's preschool teacher Mrs. Elias, everybody wants the app because of the cash back guarantee the Covington's have promised if they use it" Jake continues explaining to his dad. "Millions of people have already pre-paid for the application that launches at midnight" Jake said looking over at Linda in the back of the SUV.

"That's why Howler and the Covington's took Parker, to keep you and I from screwing up their deal; NO flash drive, no evidence, NO Federal injunction to stop the satellite launch" Max said understanding the gravity of the situation now.

"Actually; Evelyn Covington took Parker for another reason" Jake started. "She's running some kind of child auction ring; selling children to the highest bidder coming in from overseas" he continued.

"Covington told me she would make sure he went to a good family at a good price" Jake said, his father hearing the anger in his voice. "Hanson told me she was having one of those auctions tonight celebrating the satellite launch" he said looking at his dad who was starting to get angry himself.

"Pop, you understand that the meeting at the park is a trap to kill us all and take the flash drive, right; it has NOTHING to do with Parker, he's not even going to be there" Jake said as his dad just smiled at him.

"Oh yeah, I know" Max said continuing to smile at his son already forming a plan in his head.

"Howler wants to kill you dad, REAL bad for some reason" Jake said a bit worried his dad wasn't taking this serious enough.

"I know, and I know why" Max replied smiling grabbing his son by the back of his neck and bending him down so he could kiss him on the fore head.

"I'm EXTREMELY proud of you son" Max said smiling into his son's eyes releasing his grip on his neck.

"Thanks Pop" Jake replied smiling then looking over at Linda looking at him from the car window giving him a smile herself seeing the special moment he and Max were having.

"I need to take a look at those files before Howler gets a hold of them" Max said to his son knowing he was the only one around that could open the flash drive for him.

"That's going to be the problem; the moment I open the files the GPS tracker will kick in giving Howler and his computer freaks our exact location" Jake replied.

"You know Howler will be coming" he said looking at his dad's playful evil grin.

"I need to see how desperate Howler is to kill me" Max said grinning. "HOWEVER, we need to get to a safer, unpopulated area so there's no more civilian casualties when Howler and his goon squad comes calling" Max said looking around at the wounded officers being taken care of, the burning & smoking patrol cars, police investigators, media, distraught parents, emergency response people, and observers around the police station and daycare center that was just attacked to grab his grandson Parker.

Max looked over at Tyler sitting in the front seat of the SUV and smiled hoping she wouldn't see the worry in his eyes; seeing her smile back at him through the car's front windshield.

He looked back at Jake and said "You need to talk to Linda and tell her about Parker so she knows he's not in harm's way; we all need to be focused and have our heads on straight to go get him back" Max said putting his hand on Jake's shoulder then watching him turn and head for Linda's car door.

Max dialed his SAT phone and spoke into it "We have a situation that I need your help on".

Max stood by Tyler's open window smiling at her as he talked on his phone for about twenty minutes or so. Tyler listened as Max explained his plan on meeting Howler to the mysterious person on the phone; looking back every now and then at Jake and Linda in the backseat of the car.

Jake and Linda were having their own conversation concerning their son Parker, Evelyn Covington, the obvious trap at the park, and how they were going to get him back unharmed.

"I'll KILL that psychotic bitch if she hurts our son" was Linda's ONLY response to everything Jake had to say about the situation.

"Yes ma'am, I copy that" Jake said reaching over and hugging his worried wife lovingly.

Max put his phone back into his pants pocket leaned in Tyler's window and kissed her with a grin then looked at both Jake and Linda smiling knowing they heard most of his conversation on the phone.

Max came around to his driver side and got into the SUV looking into the rear view mirror at his son asking "We need a secure place outside the city limits to open the file folder; any idea's son?" as he started driving down the interstate to put distance between them and the towns people of Raleigh.

Jake looked at Linda and smiled saying "Yeah I got an idea; there's a small secluded area right outside of town that would give us the tactical advantage of seeing them coming" he said seeing Linda's face start to turn red.

Both Max and Tyler noticed Linda's bright red face as she gave Jake a stern look; and looked at one another with grins when Max asked "A special place for you two?".

"You might say that" Jake said, continuing to smile at his wife; who playfully smacked him on the arm with her open hand grinning at him.

"We go there to make out and have sex sometimes" Linda said out loud surprising Jake with what she said to everyone.

Jake smiled at her and she playfully stuck her tongue out at her husband who laughed "Well, we're married; we're not dead" she said laughing with her husband not embarrassed anymore.

Tyler smiled at Linda, her curiosity overtaking her and she asked "When was the last time you two were there?"

Linda smiled at Tyler then sheepishly, and shyly said "This past Saturday night".

Max looked at Jake again from the mirror and smiled at his son who shrugged his shoulders and smiled at his dad with an "It's what we do" grin.

Tyler looked over at Max and smiled saying "Remember what she said; married, NOT dead" giggling after she said it.

"Can we get back to Howler trying to kill us all, and put the discussion of OUR sex life on hold for later" Jake asked sarcastically looking over at Linda smiling.

"How long will it take you to disable the GPS tracking in the file?" Max asked looking again at Jake in the rear-view mirror as they continued driving down the highway.

"I'm assuming there's a Government issued laptop in one of these bags back here" Jake asked seeing all the large black duffle bags behind his seat. Howler took his, but he could use any laptop with the flash drive as he started looking in the back of the SUV; opening up the closest duffle bag sitting there.

"Tyler's laptop is in the second bag; it's charged up and ready to go" Max said seeing his son turn and start digging through the black duffle bag from his mirror.

"Once I open the file it will take me about twelve to fifteen minutes to disable it Pop" Jake said as he turned back to look at Max in the mirror now holding Tyler's laptop computer.

"So we need to keep them busy for about fifteen minutes you're saying?" Max asked with a smile to his son in the mirror.

"I'm afraid so; they encrypted the tracking code deep in the software, it's going to take a few minutes" Jake replied turning on Tyler's computer.

"We're coming up on the spot Max" Linda said leaning up into the front of the car between him and Tyler and pointing to a hidden gravel entry way.

Jake was right Max thought, looking around and seeing that it was a good tactical location. They would be able to see who was coming from either direction without any surprise or being seen themselves.

Trees would hide the large SUV easily he thought pulling onto the coarsely gravel road behind a few tall trees and dense shrubbery parking the SUV.

Everyone got out and followed Max to the back of the car where he opened the back door and pulled out the large black duffle bags and placed them on the ground at everyone's feet. Max thought they were a bit heavier than usual but then remembered he asked Tyler to "double up" on the tactical armament they normally bring on a mission.

Two of the bags were already opened, one showing the AR-15 machine- guns the girls had used earlier, as well as two tactical 12-gauge pump shotguns laying underneath them.

The other opened bag was where Jake got Tyler's laptop from, and everyone could see it held a couple of bullet-proof vests, and special tech equipment that Jordy Alexander had built for the team's use in the field including night vision equipment.

Max bent down, putting his right knee on the ground and opened the other two zippered bags; pulling out three SA-XD handguns with holsters & ammo belts, handing one to both Tyler and Jake; then placing an empty gun belt on the ground beside him for his handgun already on him.

Max handed a dark blue Kevlar vest to both Tyler and Jake watching them pull them over their heads and secure the Velcro sides. Tyler looked at Max with confusion on her face as she finished securing her own vest knowing that she only brought two vests and that Max had given Jake his to wear.

Tyler was about to say something to Max about not having a vest when Max smiled at her and shook his head as if to say "Don't say anything"

Linda was already wearing a vest under her uniform as well as her service weapon when she reported to work this morning.

She saw the looks Max and Tyler gave each other and understood that Max had given the last vest they had to Jake; putting his son's safety ahead of his own.

Linda smiled at Max and nodded in appreciation seeing that Jake was too preoccupied with the laptop and the Covington's sinister file to even notice what was going on.

Everyone checked their guns making sure there were fresh, fully loaded magazines in them and that there was a round in the chamber. Max loaded red slug 12-gauge shotgun shells into both shotguns and leaned them both against the SUV after he chambered a round in each.

Linda grabbed Jake's handgun sitting beside him as he sat on the back of the SUV typing furiously on the computer sitting on his lap. She checked his magazine, and chambered the first round then sat the loaded gun back down next to him.

Jake looked up from the screen and smiled at his dad saying "You know we'll have about five minutes before Howler & his men come for us, once I click on the file to open it" he said grinning at Max.

Then he looked at his wife Linda smiling, then quickly looked back at his father and said "Your grandson is waiting for all of us to bring him home Pop; lets do this" Jake said leaning over to kiss Linda on the forehead.

"They're going to lock onto the laptop; so distract them for a moment and we can get the fuck out of here" Jake said out loud knowing everyone could hear him as he continued typing software code in preparation of opening the file.

Max looked at his son Jacob and his wife Linda smiling and said "DO IT" then grabbed Tyler's hand and squeezed it continuing to smile at her. He gently let go of her hand turned and walked away from everyone heading to his front line position waiting for Howler's men to show up, the ONLY one NOT wearing a bullet-proof vest.

Jake clicked on the file that got Jona Singh tortured & killed and watched as it opened seeing the flashing GPS transponder message being sent back to Covington Industries and Colonel Howler over the internet.

KILLS OF THE FATHER

Colonel Howler's desk phone rang and he picked it up and said "Howler" into it, hearing a loud beeping noise over the phone in the background. He pulled the phone away from his ear and looked at it strangely then put it back to his ear again.

"Colonel, this is Carl Sullivan in charge of IT Surveillance up on the 3rd floor; you wanted me to inform you when the "package" had been opened again sir, well; it just opened" he said nervously.

"SHIT; I'm on my way up" Howler said slamming the phone back down on his desk then grabbing his gun belt and buckling it on as he headed out of his office towards the elevator.

The elevator door opened to the 3rd floor and Howler walked out between two heavily armed guards standing at the elevator doors seeing several large video screen monitors on the walls around the room, about ten people sitting at desks typing on computers, and a glass enclosed room to his right that housed several lab-coated people working on several drone stations; and hearing a continued loud beeping noise coming from the overhead speakers in the room.

A tall young man dressed in a black suit, light blue shirt, and a bright blue tie; looking like a magazine model approached Howler and extended his hand to the Colonel who arrogantly ignored him, continuing to be fascinated by what was going on in the room in front of him, but starting to get annoyed with the loud beeping going on around them.

"I'm Carl Sullivan, head of the IT department here at Covington Industries Colonel" he said to Howler who didn't seem too impressed with him.

"WHAT THE HELL IS ALL THIS SHIT?" Howler yelled over the piercing sound of the beeping coming from the speakers as he walked into the glass enclosed room housing Covington's communications control room; where he knew the satellite launch would take place.

Sullivan looked over at one of the people sitting at the computer and motioned with his hand across his throat to kill the beeping audio that was blaring over the huge speakers above their heads. He typed on his keyboard for a few seconds then the beeping noise stopped. Sullivan smiled at the technician then turned back to Colonel Howler smiling.

"We are Mr. Covington's IT surveillance team" Sullivan said to the beleaguered Colonel. "Our jobs here are to collect all the personal data from the satellite, siphon through it with audio word association, and speech algorithms".

"We can use video/face recognition as well, then the Covington's can decide what to do with it" the young supervisor said to the Colonel.

"You said that the file folder that Max Mason got from his son has been opened?" Howler asked seeing the smile on the man's face.

"Yes Sir, they opened it three minutes ago; we have its location locked in" Sullivan replied looking over at one of his tech's nearby video screen that was showing a blinking red dot on a map.

Howler looked up at the large digital clock on the wall and saw that it was just after 2pm thinking to himself if he couldn't retrieve the flash drive; he needed to get rid of it, destroy it so no one else could read it; or if anyone did read it kill them; NO WITNESSES.

Sullivan turned and looked at Howler proudly saying "Colonel we have their location, do you want to dispatch a team to retrieve the data file?" looking back at the computer screen in front of them then back to Howler. "We can have a team there in thirty minutes Colonel" Sullivan said.

Howler totally ignored him, walking silently past Sullivan to the open glass doorway in the far corner where several tech personnel were working diligently on four highly-sophisticated aerial drones sitting on their special launch podiums.

Howler stood in the doorway watching as some people used their computers, while a couple of others were using small screw drivers, and wrenches to adjust and calibrate the drone's mechanical parts.

Howler stepped into the room and asked loudly "WHO'S IN

CHARGE HERE?" standing next to one of the drones and admiring its complexity.

Everyone in the room turned around and surprisingly looked at Howler, then at Sullivan through the glass window as if wondering what they should say to this menacing armed man.

"Technically, I'm in charge Colonel" Sullivan said as the confused tech's turned around and continued their work on the drones knowing that Sullivan was handling Howler.

"Okay pretty boy, are these toys weaponized?" Howler asked continuing to admire the drone in front of him.

"Yes, they each carry twin 5.56 caliber machine-guns with two fifty-round magazines; so they only carry a hundred rounds at full capacity" Sullivan said wondering where this was going with Howler.

"I can see they have video cameras built into them, can they transmit images they receive, back here?" Howler asked with a smile.

"Yes sir, they can" Sullivan replied with a confused look on his face.

"How many of these are fully loaded and charged up?" Howler asked out loud so everyone in the room could hear him in case Sullivan didn't know the answer, because he knew someone in the room did.

Hearing what Howler asked, one of the technician's looked at Sullivan and held up one finger letting him know that ONLY one drone was fully armed and charged for use at the present time.

"How fast can it get to the GPS location from here?" Howler asked.

Sullivan looked at one of his technician's who answered "About ten minutes" then he turned back to his video screen.

"Send it out to where the file location is and kill everyone out there" Howler said thinking the Mason's would see a "special op's" team coming from the road; but not a heavily armed drone from the air.

The technician who told Sullivan they had one drone available stood beside him and said something to him softly so not to anger the Colonel. Howler could see from Sullivan's facial expression that he wasn't going to like what he said.

"We can send the drone out like you want Colonel; but its targeting software hasn't been updated" Sullivan said seeing confusion on Howler's face. "What we mean is, that the automated self-targeting software hasn't been uploaded to them yet; we will have to shoot manually at the target from here" Sullivan said.

"DO IT" Howler ordered watching Sullivan nod to one of the technician's who pushed the rolling podium the large 3-foot x 3-foot square, 4-propeller drone sat on slowly through a side door to the outside where their launching pad was for testing.

Sullivan escorted Howler over to the drone's technician station and the two of them watched as the drone rose into the air from the window, the young technician sitting at the controls maneuvering the drone towards the data files location, and Max Mason.

Jake Mason looked around from the back of the SUV seeing his police officer wife Linda, his dad Max, and his Secret Service partner/girlfriend Karen Tyler positioned behind several trees their rifles trained on the road in front of them waiting for Howler's men to come for the data file flash drive they had.

Jake continued to type furiously on Tyler's laptop trying to disengage the GPS tracking software before Howler's men showed up to try and take it from them; and kill all of them in the process.

Jake noticed how beautifully landscaped, peaceful, and quiet it was there; seeing it in the daylight for the first time as he turned back to the laptop he was typing on.

He thought to himself that he & Linda never got out of the car to appreciate the outside with a sheepish smirk on his face.

Jake continued decoding the data files to disengage the tracking software when he noticed a buzzing noise, like a small swarm of bee's over head; coming towards the trees. He glanced up thinking there was a bee hive in one of the trees above him when he saw the shiny silver metal of the drone hovering just above the front end of the SUV about twenty feet in the air.

"DAD; ABOVE US" Jake yelled seeing the drone coming towards him as he moved quickly from the tailgate of his dad's SUV. The drone's twin machine guns opened fire spraying bullets into the SUV's raised door shattering the window glass and putting holes into the metal tailgate.

Jake managed to get behind two large oak trees as the bullets rained down on him protecting the laptop then watching the drone re-position itself in front of the trees he was hiding behind.

"HOWLER IS TRYING TO DESTROY THE DATA FILE WITH THE DRONE" Jake yelled knowing everyone could hear him.

Max walked out from his position and aimed his shotgun at the drone pulling the trigger, only to see the slug bounce off of its bullet-proof metal body. He pumped quickly to fire another round only to get the same result.

The drone turned towards Max after the second slug from his shotgun bounced harmlessly off of it, looking away from Jake behind the trees.

"MASON" Howler screamed seeing Max's face on the video monitor in front of him from the drone's camera as he stood behind the technician operating the drone that hovered above Max Mason.

"Kill Mason, Kill him NOW" Howler ordered the drone operator, grabbing the back of his shirt collar.

Sullivan moved next to Howler giving the nervous technician a smile letting him know he would handle the situation.

"Colonel, shouldn't we be concentrating on destroying the data file right now?" Sullivan asked with a smile seeing Max Mason move out of the drone's camera sight on the monitor.

Without hesitation Howler pulled his handgun from his holster and fired a single .45 caliber round into a shocked and stunned Carl Sullivan's chest looking into the man's dying eyes and smiling.

Sullivan fell to the floor his blood oozing out of his chest onto the floor beneath Howler's and the drone technician's feet.

Howler looked at the scared drone technician and smiled glancing down at the dead body of Carl Sullivan and asked him "Would you please kill Max Mason" as he placed his smoking gun back in his holster.

The now scared technician moved the control stick slightly to his left to move the drone away from Jake Mason who was hiding behind the trees continuing to work on getting rid of the tracker on the data file; instead turning the homicidal drone towards Max Mason as he came back into the drone's camera sight.

Max dodged the drone's bullets as they splintered the trees around him moving quickly from tree to tree as the drone continued firing it's machine-guns at him. He finally got behind a large pine tree and yelled out to Tyler and Linda "SHOOT AT THE TWO BACK PROPELLERS" he said sticking his head out from behind the tree.

Tyler and Linda opened fire with their AR-15 machine-guns aiming at the propellers behind the machine-guns that kept the drone level and elevated hoping Max knew what he was talking about.

Max figured that Howler wanted him dead so badly in order to collect his money from Noki Amikura that he completely discarded the idea of retrieving the data file. HE was the target now, NOT Jacob; or the blackmail file.

Max stuck his head out from behind the tree and smiled flipping the drone's camera his middle finger to say "FUCK YOU HOWLER" as the bullets ripped into the tree protecting him.

Howler could see Max's condescending grin and flipping him off on the monitor and screamed "KILL THIS ASSHOLE NOW" pulling his gun from his holster again and pointing it at the young drone technician's head.

The drone technician continued to fire bullets into the trees that surrounded Max Mason hoping one would find its mark as Tyler and Linda continued firing their own rifles at the drone's vulnerable propellers.

Jake continued typing on the laptop hearing the drone's bullets hitting the trees hoping his dad was okay. He glanced over at his wife Linda standing beside Tyler shooting at the drone then looked back at his video screen to see he had completed his hack disabling the GPS tracker Howler and the Covington's put into the data file.

"IT'S FINISHED; CAN WE GET THE FUCK OUT OF HERE NOW" Jake screamed so everyone could hear him over the loud sounds of machine-gun fire and shattering trees.

Just as Jake finished yelling both Tyler and Linda's bullets hit the drone's two large metallic propellers behind the machine-guns causing them to spark and move the malfunctioning drone up and down erratically.

The drone's bullets went up and down into the trees above Max's head as it wobbled up and down finally empting its magazines.

It continued to make clicking noises above their heads as the firing mechanism continued firing but emptied of bullets.

Tyler and Linda continued firing their AR-15 rifles into the drone's propellers finally bringing it crashing down to the ground.

Howler could see on the monitor that the drone was now useless lying on the ground, realizing the Mason's had shot it down. He also knew now that the data file was gone and he had to tell the Covington's and Amikura he had failed; AGAIN.

Everyone slowly surrounded the downed, and now harmless drone as Max reached down and grabbed it with both hands picking it up and looking into the camera as the emptied machine-guns continued to click in his face.

"Can he hear me?" Max asked Jake looking over at his son smiling as he held the bulky disabled drone in his hands.

Jake moved next to his dad to take a closer look at the drone giving it a good inspection, then giving Max a disappointed look saying "No, it's just a video feed transmitting back to the control source" he said looking into the video camera and smiling to show everyone at Covington Industries that both he and his dad were still alive.

Colonel Howler stood there behind the technician and stared in disbelieve at the video monitor as Max Mason smiled then flipped his middle finger at the camera one more time to say "FUCK YOU HOWLER" then handing the drone over to his son who smiled & waved mischievously himself.

Howler lowered his head defeated and pissed off, taking a step towards the doorway only to quickly turn around to raise his gun and fire a single shot into the technician's head splattering his blood and brain matter all over the large video monitor in front of him as he slumped over his computer keyboard.

The young technician's blood started dripping to the floor making a puddle beneath his feet as Howler stood there and watched.

As he slowly walked towards the open door Howler looked at another lab technician standing there stunned; stopped, and looked at him smiling smugly saying "You might want to have that cleaned up before tonight's launch" then proceeded to walk out the door heading towards the elevator and the two guards.

As Howler stood waiting for the elevator door to open he pulled out his cell phone from his pants pocket and dialed a number saying aggressively "Get me Stone".

Max exhaled as he walked towards Tyler and Linda standing by the SUV reloading their AR-15 rifles looking at the broken killer drone Jake was holding one more time.

"Note to self, remind Jordy to keep his toys away from me" Max said to Tyler with a laughing grin as he walked up to her and hugged her.

Max looked at the writing on the side of the drone and started laughing uncontrollably looking at Jake and saying "You've got to be fucking kidding me; they named it FRED" seeing the bold first letter of each word on the drone F.R.E.D. remembering that "SARAH" was the name of Jordy's surveillance drone.

Jake looked at the drone and saw that it had printed on its body "Fortified Reconnaissance Engagement Drone" or FRED, manufactured by Covington Industries; then looked at Max strangely not understanding his humor as his wife Linda walked up to him and hugged him.

"We need to get out of here Pop" Jake said kissing his wife Linda on the forehead knowing she was still concerned for their son Parker.

"There's a cheap touristy type motel just off the interstate, right before Umstead Park that we can recharge and refocus at" Linda stated looking at the three of them.

"Excellent idea sweetheart" Max said as he and Jake placed the loaded duffle bags back into the SUV after placing the AR-15's and shotguns back inside them.

"I NEED to see what is on this flash drive" Max said to his son as they all got back into the SUV and put their seat belts on.

Max started up the car looking at the broken, short-circuited drone lying on the ground in front of them one last time from his driver's window and backed slowly out of the wooded area back onto Interstate 85.

They drove north as Tyler researched the motel from the internet on Max's phone. "It's called the Star Gazer Motel" she said scrolling down the phone. "It's out of the way and close to the park" Tyler continued.

"Tactically it has several entry & exit points that we can monitor from most of the rooms" she said looking over at Max who flashed her smile.

CHAPTER EIGHT

The elevator doors opened and Colonel Howler walked into the large glass office to find Nathaniel Covington sitting behind his glass topped desk looking at some papers, while his mother Evelyn sat at the antique wood conference table on the other side of the office with a young boy who was eating a bowl of vanilla ice cream.

Howler looked at Nathaniel Covington who gave him a glance and rolled his eyes then went back to his paperwork. Howler watched Mrs. Covington get up from the table smiling seeing he had concern on his face looking back at the little boy enjoying his ice cream saying to him "Colonel Howler, this is Parker Mason he's staying with us until his parents come to get him" she said to him with an evil grin then looking over at Parker and smiling at him.

Parker Mason was like any other precocious 5-year old little boy who enjoyed eating ice cream, playing on the playground, or watching cartoons with his dad; but he was polite and respectful to other adults because that's how he was raised. His parents taught him the difference between right and wrong, saying "Yes Sir & No Ma'am", not talking with his mouth full, brushing your teeth at night before bed, saying your prayers, and most importantly respecting the LAW and the BADGE.

Earlier that afternoon, right after his lunch Parker was told by two mercenaries that came to his classroom that they were there to pick him up for his mom; that they were her police friends and would take him to her because she, and his dad were going to have to work late and wouldn't be able to come get him before the daycare closed.

Seeing they both had large badges on their uniforms; even though he didn't understand that they said "Security" and not "Police" knowing that his mom was also a police officer with a badge Parker easily left with them feeling safe not knowing they had killed the school administrator and a teacher on their way in to get him.

The little boy was brought to Covington Industries where Evelyn Covington waited for him in the lobby. She introduced herself to the young sandy-haired boy as one of his mother's dearest friends and politely took his hand and led him up to her son's office on the elevator.

She quickly got him settled into Nathaniel's office by offering him a bowl of ice cream which he accepted and enjoyed when Howler came into the office.

"Yeah, about that" Howler replied looking at the boy then watching the matriarch's smile turn to an evil stare with her back to the young boy looking over at Nathaniel now standing up from behind his desk.

"Mother, perhaps the young lad would enjoy some television in the other room while us grown-ups talk" her son said to her seeing the anger on her face for Howler right now.

Evelyn Covington turned and smiled at the little boy saying "Parker would you like to watch some cartoons until your mom & dad arrives?"

Parker smiled and shook his head yes then asked "Can I take my ice cream please?"

"Of course you can, aren't you such a polite young man for asking" Evelyn Covington said smiling bending over to brush the hair out of the boy's face then looking over at the machine-gun toting mercenary standing behind Howler at the elevator door.

She motioned for the guard to escort the little boy out of the office and into the adjoining room where a television was set up.

As soon as the door closed behind them Evelyn Covington screamed at Colonel Howler as her son Nathaniel slowly made his way from behind his desk.

"WHY AREN'T THEY ALL DEAD YET COLONEL?" she

yelled seeing the guilt on his face when he came in, knowing that they weren't.

"The four of them together are better than good; they're even better than MY men" Howler replied knowing how that sounded.

"What do you mean the FOUR of them Colonel?" Evelyn Covington asked getting angrier at Howler's incompetence by each excuse.

"Jake Mason is still alive, and he's disengaged the GPS tracker from the data file" Howler replied slowly putting his hand on the butt of his holstered handgun just in case the Covington's tried to kill him right there where he stood.

"THE FILE IS OUT IN THE OPEN COLONEL?" Nathaniel Covington screamed quickly drawing & pointing his own handgun at Howler's head and cocking the hammer back before he had the chance to do the same.

"Give me one good reason why I shouldn't get new carpeting tomorrow Colonel?" Covington asked knowing if he shot Howler his blood would stain his beautiful beige shag carpeting in his office.

"I sent for someone; someone who knows everything about the Mason's, if ANYONE can get the file back it's HIM" Howler replied starting to sweat from having the hard steel barrel of Covington's 1911 handgun pressed against his head now.

Nathaniel looked at his mother who nodded in agreement with him and he slowly lowered his gun from the side of Howler's head de-cocking the hammer saying "Get rid of them Colonel, and get OUR data file back; NO more excuses or WE will kill YOU".

"We're going to need the boy as bait" Howler said looking at Evelyn Covington who smiled at him.

"I think something can be arranged Colonel" she replied with another evil grin.

Max, Tyler, Jake, and Linda pulled into the Star Gazer Motel and parked the SUV right outside the manager's office door. Tyler turned in her seat looking at everyone thinking they could all use a little rest without bullets flying at them; even if it was for only an hour or two.

"I'll go get us a room" Tyler said as Max handed her a couple of $100 bills.

Tyler smiled at Max as she took the money and got out of the car. She walked into the office coming back out about five minutes later with a room key dangling in her hand. She smiled at Max through the window got back in the car and pointed to the far end of the motel saying "We're in the last room on the end; wanted to make sure we had a tactical escape route away from possible civilian casualties" she said as Max backed the car out and drove down to the far end of the building parking in front of the last door.

Everyone got out and went to the back of the SUV, each grabbing a duffle bag from the back and following Tyler through the motel room door she just opened. They all put they're bags on the floor next to the two queen-size beds.

Being the last one in; Max stood in the doorway and looked around the perimeter of the motel to see if any of Howler's men had followed them; not seeing anyone before closing the door behind him.

Jake put Tyler's laptop on the desk that was near the window as he watched Tyler pull the curtains closed, and booted it up again so Max could take a look at the Covington's blackmail list.

"We need to charge the computer's battery Pop; I drained quiet a bit out of it while I was playing with the GPS tracker" Jake said to his dad seeing it had about 25% battery power left in it.

Max reached into the tech bag and grabbed the power cord for the laptop and handed it to Jake who plugged it into the electrical outlet in the wall next to the desk. The laptop started charging immediately and Max sat at the desk in front of it to look at the data file the Covington's are willing to kill for.

"Why don't you ladies freshen up a bit then we can go over the plan I already have in motion to get our boy back" Max said smiling at both Linda and Tyler.

Linda volunteered to go first giving Jake a kiss and a hard hug before going into the bathroom and closing the door. She started sobbing uncontrollably knowing everyone in the other room could hear her through the thin walls. She looked in the mirror staring at herself for a moment understanding she needed to get herself together for Parker's sake then turned on the facet and splashed some water on her face quickly drying it with one of the towels sitting nicely folded above the toilet.

Max and Tyler looked over at the bathroom door then at Jake who said to them both with a determined look "She'll be okay, she knows what she has to do" as Tyler grabbed his hand to reassure him they were bringing Parker home. Jake smiled back at Tyler appreciating the support.

Jake leaned over his dad now sitting at the desk staring at the computer screen and opened the data file for him while Tyler looked over Max's shoulder now standing behind him. Jake moved next to Tyler as the three of them started reading the names associated with the various file folders in the large data storage file.

There were hundred's of names on the file's root directory with audio, video, documents, and picture attachments for each; a lot of the names they recognized as they looked at several with shock on they're faces.

Congressmen, high-ranking military figures, local politicians, Presidential cabinet members, state governors, sports stars, movie stars, famous recording artists, and yes; Presidents, of a few countries we're all part of this blackmail list that the Covington's wanted back so badly.

Max could see why this flash drive was so valuable now, probably worth billions to the Covington's in blackmail money, and political favors; valuable enough to kidnap and KILL for.

Max clicked on several files to understand why the names on

the directory were being blackmailed; for everything from bribery, indulging in male & female prostitutes, gambling, drug trafficking, child pornography, money laundering, contract murder, criminal cover-ups, human trafficking, and corporate corruption & espionage.

Linda came out of the bathroom still drying her face off with a towel, her hair now in a ponytail standing beside Jake and looking down at the laptop's video screen asking "Is that who I think it is?" recognizing the person in the picture they were all looking at.

"Yeah, it is" Max answered out loud knowing they all knew the person in the picture.

"We need to keep this to ourselves for right now" he said scrolling down to another name he recognized.

Max opened the file to see a black & white picture of current Texas Congressman Harold Jenkins accepting illegal campaign money from Evelyn & Nathaniel Covington; remembering his son Thomas nearly got him and Tyler killed in the hospital takeover just a few months ago because he wanted to play FBI agent.

Max clicked on the next page to see that Jenkins was on the recent congressional committee convened to discuss, and vote on allowing the Covington's to launch their communication satellite.

Max was now completely fixated on knowing what the elderly congressman was doing illegally; and WHY he was so adamant about dismantling his agency.

He continued scrolling through several of Congressman Jenkins private files; finally realizing the Congressman was the final and deciding vote for the Covington's satellite launch; AND, that the recently approved Department of Domestic Terrorism was HIS idea many years ago according to a memo in the file. Watching Max Mason fulfill his idea has festered into hate, and revenge; blaming Max for all of it.

"Gotcha asshole" Max said smiling at the computer screen knowing now that Jenkins was blackmailed and paid off by the

Covington's; so technically Jenkins was as much to blame for Parker's kidnapping as they were.

Max picked up his SAT phone he had placed on the table beside the computer and dialed, positioning the phone to his ear saying "We need to talk about what we found on the computer file".

Max put his hand over the phone to muffle what he was about to say, then looked at his watch and said to the three of them "We have about two hours before all Hell breaks loose; I need all of you rested and ready to go in an hour" he said smiling at Tyler and watching Jake & Linda lay on one of the queen size bed's cuddling with each other.

Max stepped outside to continue his phone call; coming back inside after about ten minutes to see Jake & Linda sound asleep and Tyler scrolling down the names continuing to study the data file. As Max walked over to her, Tyler looked up at him from the video screen with concern on her face as Max said to her "It's being looked into; quietly".

Max sat on the other bed with his back & head against the headboard and closed his eyes as Tyler diligently combed through the names on the list recognizing quite a few. She decided that knowing their names were on this blackmail list was just as bad, as knowing what they did to get on it, so she made a conscious decision not to open their files, it was the right thing to do she thought.

Linda couldn't sleep knowing her son was with cold-blooded murderers even if she knew they wouldn't harm him, and got up and stood next to Tyler gazing into the computer screen.

"I need to know if anyone from my precinct is involved with this damn list" Linda asked as Tyler looked up at her with a solemn face.

"Your Captain, Andrew Hargrove" Tyler replied seeing his name earlier on the list.

"ARE YOU FUCKING KIDDING ME" Linda yelled waking both Max and Jake up abruptly.

Max got off the bed and asked "What's going on with you two?"

"I found Linda's Captain Hargrove on the Covington's list'

Tyler started. "He's been taking money to look the other way from the Covington's heavy handed dealings the past ten months" she continued seeing the anger on Linda's face turning into rage.

"That son of a bitch looked me in the eye with a straight face concerned for my family, when all along he was getting paid to help kidnap my son and try to kill us all" Linda replied looking at Jake. "His OWN men, some of them MY friends almost got killed because of his fucking greed" Linda stated with anger and contempt in her voice.

Max stood in front of Linda and sternly replied "We can go after Hargrove later Lieutenant; right now we have to focus on Howler and getting Parker back".

"I've been thinking Pop, it's a crazy idea but if it works would answer a lot of questions about what's going on at Covington Industries" Jake said seeing a smile come over his dad's face.

Jake started typing on his computer as he explained to everyone what he was doing. Max, Tyler, and Linda listened carefully as Jake's laptop came alive from his nimble keystrokes. When he finished he sat back and put his hands behind his head admiring his work smiling at everyone in the room.

Max smiled at his son realizing how special he was with a computer saying "Very nice son, we can use a little razzmatazz on them" Max said with a grin seeing everyone's smile.

Colonel Howler went back down to his office and sat behind his desk staring at the wall when he suddenly exploded with anger shoving everything on his desk to the floor and flipping his desk over. He had just been reamed out by the Covington's for losing the highly sought after data file, and not being able to kill the Mason's. He stood there calming down when he caught a glimpse of someone standing in his doorway.

"I love what you've done with the place Colonel" a tall, young, muscular man said sarcastically standing at the door smiling at Howler.

"Captain Eric Stone" Howler said with an evil grin.

"I'm no longer in the military Colonel, I'm just a guy who likes to get paid" Stone said laughing.

"I have a $5 million dollar contract for you; are you interested?" Howler asked with a smile.

"WOW, $5 million dollars is a lot of money Colonel; who the Hell is the target?" Stone asked curiously.

"Max and Jake Mason" Howler said seeing the anger start to show on Stone's face. "I thought that might peak your interest" he said moving around the messy office to stand in front of the young man.

"Jake Mason left me in an Afghan prison to rot for three years, I'll kill him for free" Stone replied seeing Howler smile at him.

"However; Max Mason and the flash drive will cost you $10 million dollars; I know who HE is Colonel, and who he works for; he won't be easy to kill" Stone continued, a big smile on his face seeing the surprise on Howler's face.

"$7 million dollars for Mason and the drive, and I give you the men you need" Howler counter-proposed to Stone who smiled at the Colonel's offer.

"DEAL; I'm going to need at least six good men fully tacted-up" Stone replied looking at his watch.

"You said over the phone that the meet is at 1800 hours at Umstead State Park; it's now 1630 hours, I need your men assembled for an operation briefing right now" Stone ordered watching Howler pull his phone out of his pocket and make a call.

"I want to be set-up at the park by 1730 hours" Stone said as Howler finished his phone call.

"They'll meet you in the armory in ten minutes" Howler replied placing his phone back into his pants pocket.

Stone smiled at Howler and moved out of the doorway saying "I'm following you Colonel" as the two men headed to the elevator for the 2nd floor.

Captain Eric Stone was a highly-trained CIA commander of a

search & destroy unit that worked out of Afghanistan looking for Taliban leaders, drug warlords, and rebel forces to eliminate under orders from his country.

He was ruthless, power-mad, and arrogant; the definition of a true sociopath, but he was considered a tactical genius by his CIA superiors.

Stone's history with Jake Mason started when they crossed paths several times in Afghanistan when they were both Captains, commanding their own teams.

High in the Afghan mountains Stone had several run-ins with then, Captain Jake Mason and his Army Mountain Ranger team who captured several high ranking Taliban leaders before Stone could torture & kill them; turning them over to proper authorities for debriefing enraging Stone and his CIA contacts.

One of Stone's operations to kill a Taliban leader was thwarted by Jake and his team, only to be thrown into a fire fight that resulted in several of Stone's men being killed and Eric Stone being captured and imprisoned for almost three years in a Taliban prison until he finally escaped.

To say Eric Stone had a vendetta against Jake Mason was an understatement; he's thinking now he can exact his long festering revenge for the years that he lost by killing him.

Colonel Howler and Eric Stone walked into the 2nd floor security armory to find six large, black uniformed muscular mercenaries standing around a black table that sat in the middle of the room surrounded by machine-guns, handguns, shotguns, and other tactical equipment & body armor on all four walls of the room.

Howler looked around the table at each one of them then looked at Stone acknowledging him and said "This is Captain Eric Stone; he is in charge of this operation, you WILL listen to him".

Stone stepped up to the table hearing what Howler said to them and smiled looking at the six men around the large planning and preparation table politely saying "I know everything about Jake

Mason; understand that I'm the ONLY one that gets to kill him" Stone relayed to the heavily armed men around the table. "Let's get started shall we".

Tyler and Linda checked their AR-15 rifles; making sure they were loaded with a new fully-loaded magazine, securing silencers to the end of each barrel, attaching high-powered scopes, and tripods to turn them into "sniper' rifles. They were both instrumental in Max's plan working.

"Whatever we do, we don't give them the flash drive; it's our ONLY copy to put Howler and the Covington's away" Max said looking at everyone ready to head out of the motel to the SUV.

Jake looked at everyone, smiled, and sheepishly said to his dad "That's not exactly true".

"You made a copy, didn't you Jacob?" Max asked looking at his son with a grin on his face. "I thought they could detect if you made another copy?" Max asked facing his son.

"They could if I made one copy after another; but if you "ghost" the drive together they think you only made ONE copy, not two" Jake said proud of his ingenuity.

"Where's the other copy?' Max asked standing there looking at his son continuing his proud smile to him.

"On top of Stoney's drink cooler near the back exit" Jake replied smiling.

"Very cool; it should be safe there for now, so let's go get my grandson back and put these assholes away" Max said opening the motel door and grabbing the full black duffle bag filled with weapons and walking to the back of the SUV with Tyler, Linda, and Jake following out the door behind him.

Max drove his black SUV to the entrance of Umstead State Park; pulled over and parked waiting for Howler's call to give Max the precise location to make the exchange.

They didn't have to wait long because Jake pulled out the now dead

Lieutenant Hanson's buzzing phone from his pocket and put the caller on speaker. Max asked immediately "Where's my grandson Colonel?".

"I have him with me, he's a VERY polite little boy; WHERE'S my flash drive Mason?" Howler asked with a chuckle in his voice.

"I have it; now give me my grandson" Max said looking at the phone Jake was holding. Linda was about to say something when Max put his finger in the air to stop her.

Max understood she was at her breaking point with Howler but he needed Howler to believe he was in control or none of them would get out of the park alive, especially Parker; IF he was there.

"Easy Admiral, we wouldn't want to do something foolish where no one gets anything; now would we" Howler replied over the speaker.

"Where are we making the exchange Colonel?" Max asked trying to move the situation forward so he could initiate his plan.

"Piedmont Beech visitors center, a few miles inside the park; it's closed during the winter; follow the signs" Howler replied giving Max and his family a location where Parker would be.

"Leave Agent Tyler & Officer Mason at the entrance; ONLY you and your son Jacob comes to us, any confusion and I WILL kill the boy" Howler said.

"I believe the boy's mother might be a bit less rational seeing her son tied up with a hood over his head" Howler continued hoping to get a response out of Linda Mason who he knew was sitting there listening, but didn't bite.

"We'll be right there; and Howler, you best have my grandson there or I promise you I'll let my son have you" Max said knowing Jake wanted to kill Howler for taking his son.

Everyone heard the phone hang up and got out of the SUV closing their doors. Max walked around the front of the car smiling at Tyler who gave him a big hug and said snickering in his ear "You know this isn't going to be good for my bad knee".

"Yeah I know, sorry about that sweetheart" Max replied smiling at her as she hugged him hard then kissed him passionately on the lips.

Jake hugged Linda who had her arms wrapped around him kissing her on top of her head saying "He's going to be fine, I promise; we're not going to let anything happen to him okay" believing Max's plan would work.

Linda looked up at her husband and smiled saying "I love you, bring our son home; but I swear to God I will kill Evelyn Covington if she harms my boy in any way".

"Yes ma'am, I love you too" Jake replied leaning down to kiss his wife breaking her embrace to climb back into the SUV where his dad was already sitting behind the wheel waiting for him.

Max backed the SUV up and smiled at both Linda and Tyler standing on the side of the road, leaving them their fully equipped sniper rifles to protect them.

He saw the sign with directions to Piedmont Beech as he and Jake headed into the park seeing it wasn't more than a mile away from where they just were.

They drove for about five minutes following the two signs they came across then drove up to a rustic cabin with a large "Visitor's Center" sign in front of it. Max parked the SUV on the side of the building and both he and Jake got out walking back to the front of the building to wait for Howler and Parker.

Max noticed how beautiful the log-cabin style visitor's center looked with its vaulted ceiling, floor to roof windows, towering stone fireplace, and the high arcing roof top and thought what a nice vacation home it would make for a couple. He could see across the meadow the hill top that looked down on where they stood, watching as the sun was starting to go down behind it.

Max started to wonder where Howler was, looking at his watch and seeing it was after 6pm knowing he was more punctual then this. They didn't have to wait much longer as a black SUV pulled up on the other side of the entrance and stopped.

The SUV sat there for about a minute before two black-clad, fully armed mercenaries got out and stood by the back passenger's door of the large car; quickly pointing their AR-15 machine-guns at both Max & Jake yelling at them both to get on their knees.

Max and Jake stood there with their hands on top of their heads smiling at one another as two more mercenaries came up from behind them pushing them both to the ground on their hands & knees standing there looking down their guns pointed at each of their heads. They searched both Max and Jake finding only a pair of handguns on them taking them and tossing them about ten feet into the high grass.

Max looked up at the two large mercenaries and said "REALLY" hating that someone tossed his SA-XD handgun on the ground, AGAIN.

The driver's door opened, and Max & Jake watched a tall man get out and open the passenger's side door and roughly pull out a young boy by his arm and stand him between the two mercenaries by the car. They both could see that the boy was no older than six years old, his hands tied in front of him, and his head covered with a black cloth bag. Max figured he had duct tape over his mouth because he could hear muffled crying coming from inside the hood over the boy's head.

"Captain Jacob Mason, Army Mountain Rangers division" the man said looking at Jake as he walked towards him and his dad.

"Captain Eric Stone; murderer, torturer, and all around asshole" Jake said looking at Stone grinning.

Jake leaned over to his dad and whispered "That's NOT Parker, he hates anything the color green" he said as they both could see the young boy was wearing bright green sneakers on his feet.

"And WHO do we have here?" the man asked as he now stood in front of Max. "Rear Admiral Maxwell Mason; Director of Domestic Terrorism for the Secret Service, and Jake's father" he said looking down at Max and smiling.

Max looked up at the man smiling and said "Captain Eric Stone, Army Intelligence for the C.I.A., and from what I hear a REAL scumbag; what's up buttercup?" looking over at his son snickering at what he said.

"So you DO know who I am?" Stone asked smiling looking around at his men who were smiling as well.

"NOPE; never heard of you, I just know an asshole when I see one" Max said with a grin looking over at Jake who snickered again at his dad.

"It's been a long time Jake, how are your boys; I remember one of them bought it in Degak" Stone asked trying to get an emotional response from Jake.

"It's a shame what happened to him" Stone said snickering as he looked around at his four mercenaries standing with him.

Jake gave him a hard look remembering that one of his men Sergeant James "Fireplug" Jones died in a fire fight in the Balkh mountain region of Afghanistan called the "Degak Mountains" he had stepped on a land mine placed there by Stone and his men to kill a ruthless Afghan drug warlord.

In the final debriefing it came out that Stone had placed the mine where it killed Jones under orders of the C.I.A., but that didn't stop Jake from beating the shit out of Stone outside of the command tent that same day which landed Stone in the infirmary and Jake in the brig for three days.

"You're still an asshole Stone, you would think taking it up the ass the past three years in prison would mellow you out some" Jake said looking at his dad with a smirk.

Stone smiled at Jake, then back handed him across the mouth knocking him down watching him spit blood on the ground at Stone's feet. The mercenary standing next to him grabbed Jake's arm and straightened him up to his knees again.

Jake looked at his dad with blood dripping down his mouth and said "I guess that's a "sore-ass' subject with him" he said snickering making Max laugh.

Max got serious looking at Stone and asked "Where's Howler and my grandson; errand boy?" knowing the little boy they were holding near the car wasn't Parker.

Stone looked over at the young boy and smiled as Max said "Nice try asshole, where's my grandson?" now knowing that Parker wasn't there.

Stone knew he didn't have any leverage with either Max or Jake now and yelled at the two mercenaries standing beside them "Search them both, find me the flash drive" he said watching one of the mercenaries search them as the other covered them.

They searched Max and Jake one at a time, finally finding the flash drive in Max's front pants pocket; handing it to Stone who held it up showing it to both Max & Jake as he smiled at the two proud mercenaries that found it.

One of the mercenaries came up with a laptop as Stone handed him the flash drive. After a few seconds the mercenary nodded to Stone that the flash drive was the real one, pulled it from the computer and handed it back to the Captain.

"I'm afraid Howler and the Covington's have other plans for your grandson this evening" Stone replied placing the flash drive inside his pants pocket. "I understand he'll be well taken care of the rest of his life; knowledge the whole Mason family can take to they're graves" Stone said chuckling looking at Jake, then Max.

"You can surrender now, and I'll put in a good word for you not to get the needle; or MY son & I can kill you all right here and now" Max said smiling at Stone.

Jake leaned over to his dad again and said "Nice speech" loud enough for Stone to hear him, smiling at his dad.

"I thought so; Tyler say's I should be more open to giving people a chance to be good, but we both know what they're going to do" Max replied smiling then looking around at the four mercenaries and Eric Stone who were laughing at what he said.

"He's not really all that good at this whole kidnapping and ransom thing is he?" Max asked his son sarcastically in front of Stone. Jake smiled at his dad and shook his head in agreement.

Eric Stone's radio on his belt crackled loudly and he grabbed it and brought it to his mouth pushing the transmitter button asking "Do you have them Team One; over?"

Max looked at Jake smiling and said "I love the cute code names they have for one another, don't you?".

"Makes you feel warm and fuzzy, don't they?" Jake said snickering to his dad.

"You honestly didn't believe I would let the lovely & honorable, Lieutenant Linda Mason walk away from here without saying Hi, did you?" Stone asked looking at Jake hoping to get a response from him.

"I remember how sexy she was back in the day, shame she has to die for YOUR stupidity" Stone said to Jake who smiled at the arrogant Captain.

"We'll see dude; and for the record she's STILL sexy" Jake said grinning.

A voice came over Stone's radio saying "We have BOTH of them Captain; we're about a quarter of a mile south of you, above the ridge line" the voice said over Stone's radio speaker loud enough that both Max and Jake could hear.

"That must be Special Agent Karen Tyler of the Secret Service with the Lieutenant" Stone said smiling at Max knowing she was his partner, then turning and looking up at the ridge line where the sun was going down behind it.

"That's a pretty ambitious long-range shot for a couple of women Admiral" Stone said chauvinistically then he put the radio to his lips and said "KILL THEM BOTH, and make it loud so we can all hear it from down here; do you copy?".

"Copy that Captain" came back over the radio as they all waited to hear the gun shots.

CHAPTER NINE

Special Agent Karen Tyler, and Raleigh police officer Linda Mason laid prone on the ground looking through their sniper scopes one last time to see smiles on both Max & Jacob Mason's faces as they kneeled in front of Colonel Howler's mercenary "enforcer" Eric Stone; because they both knew they were being watched by them.

The sun started going down behind them on the southern ridge of the Umstead State Park as they both were about a quarter of a mile away from the visitor's center when they heard "Don't move ladies" from behind them, as well as the racking of a round from two AR-15 machine guns.

Both Tyler and Linda slowly looked over their shoulders putting their arms out away from their rifles to see two large heavily armed men in full black tactical gear pointing their rifles down at them. One lowered his rifle as the other kept the two defenseless women covered and grabbed his radio as they all heard from the speaker "Do you have them Team One; over?"

"We have BOTH of them Captain; we're about a quarter of a mile south of you, just above the ridge line" the mercenary replied looking down at Tyler and smiling.

They could all hear Stone's response "KILL THEM BOTH, and make it loud so we can all hear it from down here; do you copy?"

"Copy that Captain" the mercenary replied then putting his radio back on his gun belt.

"Use your handgun, it makes a louder sound then a rifle shot" the mercenary with the radio advised his colleague knowing the gunshots would be heard almost everywhere in the large park especially down by the visitor's center where Stone was.

"You two are pussy's; shooting two defenseless women because some asshole told you too" Tyler said looking up at the two men now pointing their 1911 handguns at them both.

"Why don't you give me a gun and let's mark off twenty paces, see which one of us ends up dead that way asshole" Tyler said looking at the mercenary in charge.

"Sorry lady, only following orders" he replied laughing with his partner at what she said then cocking the hammer back on his gun pointing it at Tyler's head as the other did the same standing above Linda Mason.

Tyler grabbed Linda's hand and smiled acknowledging to her that it was nice to meet her and work with her, just as both mercenaries dropped to the ground behind them at the same time.

Tyler grabbed her gun and quickly got to her feet pointing her AR-15 sniper rifle at the two men laying face down in the grass realizing they weren't moving. Linda got up and grabbed her rifle kicking the feet of the mercenary near her seeing he wasn't moving either.

Tyler and Linda quickly rolled the two mercenaries over on their backs to see a single bullet hole in each of their foreheads with blood oozing out running down their dead faces, their eyes staring up at the sky.

"Quick grab his gun" Tyler said to Linda looking at the mercenary lying at her feet.

"What for, he's dead" Linda replied confused at what Tyler was asking.

"Stone is expecting to hear two shots from these assholes" Tyler explained seeing the understanding look on Linda's face now.

Tyler shot once into the ground, then watched Linda shoot her gun into the dead mercenary that was about to kill her.

Linda looked at a surprised Tyler and said "WHAT?; he didn't feel it, and it makes me feel better" she said smiling at Tyler.

"I can live with that sweetie" Tyler replied with a grin grabbing hold of Linda's hand and squeezing it.

The two shots rang out loud from way up the hill as Max and Jake continued to kneel in front of Eric Stone, his four mercenaries, and the little boy in front of the log cabin style visitor's center.

"That has to be a bit disheartening knowing that you're two loved ones won't be around for Thanksgiving dinner this year" Stone said grinning to a solemn Max and Jake as he looked at all his men with a grin.

"Turkey is SOOO overrated, don't you think?" Max asked Jake with a smile.

"I actually like turkey; Linda does this recipe with chicken gravy makes it VERY moist" Jake replied smiling back at his dad then looking at Eric Stone who was getting angry at their banter with one another.

"I'll have to try that, as long as it comes with a side of sweet potatoes with those little marshmallows on them" Max said continuing to smile at his son.

"You could come to our house this year, and bring Tyler; Linda would love cooking for everyone" Jake said seriously to his father.

"I'm not sure what she wants to do yet, this whole relationship thing is new to both of us right now, but I can ask her later about it" Max replied with a smile then looking back at Stone who he could tell was getting annoyed with their holiday conversation.

"Sorry dude, you're not invited" Max said with a grin to Stone.

"YOU TWO ASSHOLES THINK THIS IS A JOKE, I JUST KILLED YOUR WOMEN AND ALL YOU TWO CAN DO IS LAUGH ABOUT IT" Stone yelled at the two of them looking around at his mercenaries with a big smile.

"We'll see Stone" Max replied with a sheepish grin looking over at Jake.

Stone put his radio back to his lips and said "Snipers put a little dust on these two assholes show them how seriously dedicated we are here".

As soon as Stone finished two shots hit the ground beside both

Max and Jake causing Max to look out into the field with a scowl on his face thinking the shots were a little too close for his taste.

"The Covington's and the Colonel must be paying you quite a bit of money to kill a couple of federal agents and a cop" Max asked looking up at Stone knowing he would get the death penalty in North Carolina for murdering either a cop, or a federal agent; definitely for killing all three.

"I'm getting $7 million dollars for you from Howler and some Japanese guy; as for your son, I'm going to kill him for free; for leaving me in that hell-hole for three years" Stone replied to Max as he leaned in and spoke softly so only the three of them could hear what he said.

"Do we need to hug it out you and me?" Jake asked with a grin to Stone; then looking over at his dad and smiling.

Stone reached back and hit Jake hard in the left jaw knocking him up against his dad who caught him before he hit the grassy ground under them.

"Can I PLEASE kick his ass now Pop?" Jake asked wiping the blood from the corner of his mouth.

Eric Stone pulled his handgun from his holster pointing it at Jake's head saying "I may go and kill that little brat of yours after you're dead, what do you think about that asshole" pulling the hammer back on his gun.

Max started laughing hysterically looking at Jake, then all of a sudden stopped; looking at Stone with anger in his eyes saying "You fucked up Stone, I wasn't going to let him touch you, was just going to put you back in a cage where you belong; but you went and threatened to kill his son, MY grandson; so I only think its fair that he get a shot at you now" looking over at Jake with a grin.

"Oh, and by the way; haven't you learned by now that every good military tactician ALWAYS has a "Plan B" up his sleeve" Max said with a big grin.

Stone looked at Max and laughed at what he said then noticed he had a flesh colored ear bud in his right ear and yelled "WHAT THE

FUCK" turning to look over at his two mercenaries standing beside the car with the little boy.

"NOW" Max yelled as the two mercenaries standing behind him and Jake fell to the ground blood oozing out of the bullet hole in each of their heads. Max and Jake watched as two snipers fell from two trees in front of them hitting the ground hard with a thud presuming they were both dead.

Stone yelled "KILL THEM BOTH" just as a bright blue clad figure came up behind the two remaining mercenaries killing them swiftly with a long samurai sword slashing their throats open as the blood sprayed all over them. They both grabbed their throats with both hands trying to stop the blood from pouring out falling to their knees then face down into the grass.

The blue ninja pushed the little boy to the ground so he wouldn't be harmed and quickly grabbed Stone by the hair pushing him down to the ground on his knees.

The shiny steel blade of their sword up against his throat, a bead of blood trickling down his neck.

"DON'T KILL HIM" Max yelled quickly before the ninja stroked the blade across Stone's throat, watching as another bead of blood trickled down his neck from a small cut already made by the ninja's blade.

The ninja heard what Max said and stopped before bringing the razor sharp blade across Stone's exposed neck, kicking his handgun from his hand then slowly removing the bright blue mask and hood from they're face to reveal Yuki Amikura under it.

Eric Stone watched as both Max Mason and his son Jake got up off of their knees smiling at the young female ninja when he screamed "WHO THE FUCK IS THIS WOMAN?" still feeling the sharp blade pressed against his throat.

Max looked at Jake, who looked back at his dad; then at the blue clad Yuki Amikura saying together loudly "SHE'S FAMILY" both seeing the big smile on her face and the confusion on Stone's after they said it.

Yuki kept the blade of her sword on Stone's shoulder the sharp edge still touching his tender neck as she motioned to Max with a grin to look up on the roof of the visitor center.

Max, Jake, and Stone looked up on the roof of the visitor's center to see a black clad figure stand up near the fireplace chimney holding a large sniper rifle, then a second figure stood up on the other side of the roof holding an identical rifle as well. Eric Stone looked around seeing all of his dead mercenaries lying in the grass then turned to watch the two figures slowly climb down from the roof then walk towards them.

They were both wearing identical black ski masks and pointing a SA-17, .308 caliber sniper rifle with high-powered night vision scopes and silencers at him as they walked up to Max and Jake standing in front of the visitor center.

The closest one pulled their mask off to show a smiling Stacy Mason who quickly said excitedly "Hi daddy; I brought back up" brushing her hair to the side and seeing how stunned Eric Stone was seeing Max Mason's daughter standing there.

Max smiled at his little girl and replied "I see that sweetheart".

Stacy looked at Jake and grinned saying "Hey big brother" giving him a high five slap above their heads.

"Hey there sis" Jake replied still staring and smiling at Yuki Amikura.

"I WAS TOLD YOU LEFT, YOU SHOULD BE HALF WAY TO ENGLAND BY NOW" the frustrated and confused Eric Stone screamed to Stacy.

"You bad guys are all the same; arrogant and PREDICTABLE" Stacy said giggling at Stone.

Max smiled at Stacy then smirked at Stone saying "Admiral Cartwright owed me a favor, so he pulled a few strings to get my daughter here; she's the real sniper in the family" he said proud of his baby girl.

"I called my sister to see if she would help, imagine my surprise finding out she was already here in Raleigh with her own family issue" Stacy said to Max smiling at Yuki who still had her sword against Stone's neck.

Max looked back at Yuki smiling saying "Thank you for coming sweetheart; by the way, I like the blue on you better" seeing Yuki look over at Stacy grinning.

"See, I told you" Stacy said smiling at her big sister knowing she told her she would look good in a blue uniform.

"Who have we here?" Max asked as the other person who continued to keep they're rifle pointed at Stone slowly took her mask off to reveal a young Asian woman.

"She's MY family" Yuki said smiling at Ochi Okasa who returned the smile to her childhood friend.

"Then she's OUR family too" Max replied smiling at Yuki, then at Ochi Okasa who was smiling as well. "Thank you young lady" Max said continuing his smiling to Ochi.

Everyone heard a noise behind Yuki and Stone, as Stacy and Ochi quickly turned to aim their rifles at Karen Tyler & Linda Mason who had walked from the hillside their rifles over their shoulders.

"You cut that a bit close didn't you sweetie?" Tyler asked Stacy with a grin.

"I saw a cute little bunny behind you" Stacy said with a grin looking over at Ochi who shook her head with a smile agreeing with what Stacy said. "I wanted to make sure he was clear first" she said grinning.

"This family reunion bullshit is so sweet" Stone said to everyone sarcastically putting his hands on top of his head.

Stacy walked up to Stone and put her rifle barrel against his head saying "I'm the rational one, and I WANT to kill you for taking my

nephew; imagine what my brother wants to do with you asshole"
pressing the barrel into his head painfully.

Jake hugged his wife Linda seeing she was okay, pressing his
forehead against hers and both closing their eyes to take a moment
together.

Linda broke off their embrace and walked over to Eric Stone and
looked at him with his smug smile on his face and asked "Where's my
son Eric?" remembering him from their military service.

"I already did the threatening thing sis, he wouldn't budge" Stacy
said continuing to point her rifle at Stone as Linda stood there.

"He just hasn't heard it from an angry mother" Linda said as she
hit Stone quickly on the side of his head with the butt of her rifle
knocking him down watching his face hit the dirt.

Stone rolled over slowly getting back to his knees, spitting blood
out of his mouth and laughing then looked up at Linda saying "Is that
anyway to treat an old friend sweetheart?".

"You were NEVER a friend asshole; NOW WHERE IS MY
SON?" Linda screamed grabbing Stone by his jacket collar.

Max came over to Linda and grabbed her hand to calm her down
saying "We know where he is, and we're going to go get him; okay?"
"I think Tyler could use a little motherly help right now" Max said
seeing tears coming down Linda's face.

Linda looked at Tyler who had walked over to the little boy sitting
on the ground next to the black SUV Stone and his men drove up
in, slowly taking the black hood off of his head and smiling at him
talking softly to calm him down knowing he was scared.

Yuki looked at Stacy and smiled seeing her head nod to go talk
to her dad, THEY'RE dad. Stacy smiled at her sister acknowledging
that she would keep her rifle on Stone as Yuki took her sword blade
away from his throat and slowly returned it to its scabbard slung
behind her back.

Yuki approached Max who was attentively watching Tyler with
the young boy, standing in front of her step-father saying "I'm SO

sorry for trying to kill you Max Mason, I feel so ashamed" bowing her head in the traditional Japanese way, but avoiding Max's smiling eyes.

"Nothing to be ashamed of, or apologize for sweetheart; all that matters is that you are here, and you are safe" Max said being the father he's always wanted to be to her seeing tears coming down the young Asian girl's face. Max reached out his arms to her and she put her head against his chest crying uncontrollably as he kissed her on the forehead saying over and over "It's okay, It's okay".

Ochi watched Yuki release all the frustrations and emotions she had over not having Max Mason in her life and she couldn't help but wipe away the tears coming down her own face as well.

Yuki rose up from Max's chest and looked over at Jake and smiled as he asked "Where have you been big sister, we've missed you?" watching Yuki continue to smile at everyone.

"This is all so touching Jake, but you do understand your son is still being shipped off tonight by the Covington's and there's NOTHING any of you can do about it" Stone said with a smirk on his face.

"Really; are you sure about that?" Max asked looking down at Stone.

"Aren't you even a bit curious at how everything you set up here fell apart; how the Mason family made you and your men look like a bunch of amateurs?" Max asked grinning, seeing the anger start to show on Stone's face.

"Howler and the Covington's should have never came after the one man who could turn the whole situation back on them" Max continued, seeing the confusion on Stone's face looking at Jake proudly.

Max went on to tell Stone how Jake had used his computer skills back at the motel to turn Howler's own cell phone into a transmitter, that when Stone & Howler were discussing their park plan in the armory; Max and his team heard every word and detail of it and countered with their own plan.

"Like I said before Captain; always have a Plan B" Max said smiling.

Stone looked over at Yuki Amikura knowing who she was now and the deal Howler made with her cousin to kill Max Mason and smiled saying "Your cousin Noki will be waiting for you at Covington Industries this evening; I understand he has plans of taking over the family business" he said laughing.

"I guess you could call it a hostile & violent takeover" Stone said continuing to laugh.

"Now can I Pop?" Jake asked angrily looking over at his dad standing beside Yuki.

"Sure; why not, he deserves it" Max said to his son who walked over to Eric Stone pushing his sister's rifle away from the arrogant mercenary's head.

"Get up asshole" Jake said looking down at Stone still on his knees.

Stone slowly got up surprising Jake with a right handed punch to Jake's jaw before he stood all the way up, knocking Jake backwards a few feet.

"I've waited three years for this" Stone said with a smile now standing straight up and seeing Jake rub his painful jaw.

"You're going to be painfully disappointed then" Jake replied quickly spin kicking Stone upside the head knocking him to one knee.

"You still hit like a computer geek" Stone said smiling then throwing a left handed punch to Jake's ribs, then quickly hitting him again in the jaw with his right fist knocking Jake to the ground causing him to roll a few feet away.

Both Yuki and Stacy who were standing beside Max took a step towards Stone seeing they're brother lying on the ground; but Max put his arms out to tell them "He's got this" as they watched Jake get up slowly.

Yuki and Stacy looked at one another and stepped back to let their brother finish HIS fight; his way.

"You always had a big mouth Stone, it will serve you well in prison" Jake said ducking under Stone's spin kick and hitting him hard in the stomach bending him over then quickly hitting him under the chin with a hard right upper cut thrusting Stone upwards and back down to the ground knocking the wind out of him.

Stone rolled back and forth on the ground for a moment to catch his breath realizing Jake had turned his back on him. Stone reached into his boot and pulled out a steel throwing knife and reared back to throw it at a defenseless Jake Mason's back.

Tyler and Linda were still attending to the young boy shielding him from the fight that was going on behind them between Jake and Eric Stone when Tyler glanced back over at Eric Stone lying on the ground with a throwing knife in his hand.

Tyler screamed "JAKE LOOK OUT" as Stone reared back his arm to throw.

Jake had his back to Stone as he walked away thinking the fight was over when a shiny steel ninja throwing star whirled passed him hitting Stone in the forehead right between his eyes killing him instantly dropping the blade from his hand.

Everyone looked at the now lifeless body of Eric Stone seeing the steel blade fall out of his hand, his lifeless eyes staring at everyone; then they all looked over at Ochi Okasa who threw the ninja star at him shocked and relieved at what she had done.

Jake walked up to Ochi and smiled saying "Thanks sis" putting his hand on her shoulder as he walked by her towards his wife bringing a big smile to her face as she looked over at Yuki who also smiled with approval.

Max walked over to Stone bent down and checked his pulse to confirm he was dead when he heard the buzzing of a phone in his tactical pants pocket.

Retrieving the phone he could see the caller ID had Howler's name on it so he signaled everyone to keep quiet and he answered it.

"Are they dead Captain?" Howler asked not knowing he was on speaker phone or that he wasn't talking to Eric Stone.

Jake smiled at his dad and motioned with his head if he could answer. Max smiled and gave him a "Why not" look as he winked at Tyler still holding on to the little boy beside Linda, Stacy, Yuki, and Ochi Okasa.

"I'm afraid Captain Stone can't come to the phone right now Colonel, kinda because he's dead" Jake said with an evil grin.

"Jake Mason; I take it your old man is standing there next to you?" Howler asked surprised to hear his voice.

"Present and alive Colonel" Max said with a laugh.

"Seems you're running out of mercenaries, might want to try doing the job yourself" Jake said smiling at his dad and then looking over at Linda.

"Remember what I told you Colonel; I'll see you shortly, I'm on my way" Jake said reminding Howler of what he said to him when he was being tortured, that if he took his son he would kill him.

Everyone knew that Howler delivered Parker to the Covington's and that they STILL had plans to sell him off to someone tonight, so killing Howler was high on Jake's priority list this evening.

"You'll never get through the front gate you little prick, I have men everywhere guarding this compound" Howler said to Jake knowing everyone could hear him on the speaker.

"Who said anything about coming through the front gate?" Jake said laughing then abruptly hanging up and tossing the phone on the ground stomping on it destroying it into little pieces.

Max looked around at everyone seeing that they were all okay and said "We all need to get out of here before that asshole brings more men here".

He pulled out his phone from his pants pocket and jokingly spoke into it "Clean up on aisle seven sir" looking at everyone with a sheepish grin on his face.

Max had called Admiral Cartwright explaining everything that took place at the park, requesting a Federal CSI team to close off the park, and secure all of the dead bodies they had left. The Admiral agreed with everything Max asked for, then asked to address everyone on speaker.

"I have some good news and some bad news for you all" Cartwright said knowing that Max and everyone with him could hear him over the speaker phone now.

"NASA can't stop the launch of the Covington Industries satellite at Goddard Space Center because it is now less than six hours before launch and we've been locked out; it's flight controls have been turned over to Covington Industries now" the Admiral continued.

"HOWEVER; there is an ABORT code that will destroy the rocket before it releases the satellite if you can get to it in time, as well as a secondary satellite self-destruct code" Cartwright explained.

"Do we know the "codes" Admiral?" Max asked looking over at Jake who was now the official computer expert on this mission.

"No; it's something ONLY the Covington's know" Cartwright replied.

"Looks like this is on you son" Max said to Jake with a grin as he watched his son roll his eyes at him.

"Covington Industries is heavily fortified, the President doesn't want a blood bath sending in federal agents" Admiral Cartwright said.

"I'm afraid this one is ALL on you Max" Cartwright said.

"I know you've said your grandson is being held by the Covington's Max, but President Bradshaw has sanctioned that we need you to destroy that satellite with extreme prejudice" Cartwright ordered.

"I sent you a care package; THEY should be arriving soon" the Admiral said with a chuckle.

"Good luck Max; bring your loved ones home safe" Admiral Cartwright said then hung up the phone with a loud click.

Max placed his phone back in his pocket then looked around at everyone with a worried look on his face knowing he was going to have to ask them to go into a hornet's nest of ruthless mercenaries, a ninja bent on revenge, a maniacal Colonel, and a mother & son's bid for power & world domination through technology and blackmail; in other words just another normal day in the life of Max Mason.

Tyler could see the stress in Max's eyes as she came up beside him taking his hand in hers smiling, saying so everyone could hear "I'm in boss; what are we doing?"

Max smiled at her then looked around at everyone again realizing what a brave and beautiful family he had standing before him.

"I have nothing to do until Saturday when I have to catch a plane back to my ship; so let's go get my nephew, and fuck up the Covington's evening" Stacy said smiling at her brother and father.

"I made a promise to always protect my father, little sisters, my brother, and Lady Tyler; I go where you go Max Mason" Yuki said seeing everyone smile at her statement.

"I will deal with my cousin when the time comes" Yuki said looking at Ochi who nodded in agreement with her.

"I go where she goes" Ochi said with a grin to Yuki.

Jake and Linda looked around at everyone as the sun finally went down over the ridge watching as the outside security lights came on from the visitor center. They both knew and appreciated that they were all going to risk their lives for their son who was nothing more than a pawn in all of this.

Jake smiled at everyone and said "We need everyone to understand how much we love and appreciate what all of you are doing for our family; but everyone needs to know that we plan on hurting some people real bad tonight for what they've done to our son".

Linda looked around at everyone shaking her head up and down, agreeing with her husband holding his hand and arm tightly at what he said to everyone.

"I can live with that" Max said knowing that getting Parker back was the most important thing to him, and his mom & dad now; and he didn't care how violent he had to get with Howler, his men, or the Covington's to do it.

Getting this little boy back safely, that they all loved so much was more important than Max & Jake's agenda of revenge; thinking that the kills of the father's wasn't that important anymore.

Max looked around at everyone then looked at his watch seeing it was just about 7pm, now dark with a full moon in the sky. It wasn't daylight savings time yet, but the sun went down early in North Carolina now that it was November.

"We have darkness on our side; that's a major thing" Max said to everyone forming a plan in his head. "We could use a few more guns though" he continued, snickering at what he said.

Stacy smiled and looked at her dad with a sinister grin saying "We could break into a gun store, seems that's what everyone is doing these days" looking around at everyone giggling knowing Max was going to scold her for what she said.

"Or, you could just come with us" Jake said to his dad looking over at his wife Linda who was sheepishly smiling at him like a cat who ate a canary.

Where are we going son?" Max asked, looking over at Tyler still holding on to the little boy; then shrugging her shoulders at him as if to say "Okay".

"Trust us Pop" Jake said with a grin. "But I suggest we get the Hell out of here before either the Colonel's, or the Admiral's men show up" he said knowing they would either end up in another fire fight, or have to stick around answering a lot of questions for the good guys; taking away time to rescue his son.

Max looked over at Tyler seeing the little boy cling tightly to her leg still scared from what was going on around him and asked her "What do we do about him?"

Max glanced down at the now dead Eric Stone, and his four dead mercenaries lying on the ground a few feet away now completely lit up by the security spotlights hanging from the visitor's center roof shaking his head; knowing all this bloodshed could have been avoided.

"I know someone who can help us with that" Linda said replying to Max's question concerning the little boy they rescued. Linda grabbed her radio from her belt and smiled at the boy as he looked up at her still afraid and in shock.

Linda spoke into the radio "Dispatch, patch me through to Officer Murphy on a secure line; copy?" she asked knowing that the police communication system was back online at the station. Linda smiled at Tyler and the little boy standing there in front of her as she waited to hear back from her dispatcher.

"Copy that Linda" the young female voice replied over the radio.

"Go for Murphy; everything okay with you and Jake, lieutenant?" Murphy asked over the radio not caring if anyone else could hear them or not.

"I need a BIG favor; meet us at the entrance of Umstead State Park in the next fifteen minutes" Linda asked over her radio.

"Copy that; Captain has me down the road from there directing traffic to the Covington Industries party, can be there in ten" James Murphy said through the radio speaker.

"10-4; thanks Murphy" Linda quickly replied turning off her radio and clipping it back to her gun belt behind her back.

CHAPTER TEN

"We gotta go" Max said to everyone walking towards the SUV after he and Jake picked up their handguns from the grass. They moved quickly towards the SUV parked beside the visitor's center, looking back one last time at the dead bodies scattered on the ground thinking to himself that death is such a waste; even for Eric Stone.

Jake, Linda, Tyler, and the young five year old boy still holding Tyler's hand tightly with both of his, followed Max to the car and everyone got in. Max stood outside his driver's side door once he placed Tyler's & Linda's sniper rifles in the back of the SUV.

He watched Stacy, Yuki, and Ochi smile at him as the three of them went into the woods behind the Piedmont Beech visitor's center to rendezvous with their own car they had hidden on the other side of the hill to avoid being detected by Stone or his men.

Max watched until the three young women disappeared into the darkness of the black forest then he got into the car and looked around at everyone. Max stared at Jake from the rear-view mirror and asked "Where to son?" with a bit of confusion on his face as Jake just continued to smile at him from the backseat.

Jake looked at Linda sitting in the front seat as he sat next to Tyler and the little boy; smiled at his wife, then replied to his dad "Raleigh Storage on Rosemont; Linda can GPS it for you" he said reaching from the backseat to squeeze Linda's hand who had reached back to grab his, giving him a big smile.

Max slowly backed up the SUV trying not to run over any of the dead bodies scattered in the grass and on the driveway, finally making it out to the main road and heading towards the park's entrance where they were to meet Officer Murphy.

Max came up on the park's entrance and could see a blue & white

Wake County police car parked in the bright beams of his headlights with Officer James Murphy standing beside it.

"Let me talk to him alone, or he's going to want to come with us Max" Linda said as Max pulled up near him and parked.

Linda knew Murphy was a good cop and would want to help, but this was about her family and she didn't want anyone else to be in danger from Howler or the Covington's.

Linda got out with the little boy and walked over to Murphy seeing the concern on his face. "I need you to do all of us a favor and take this little boy somewhere safe" Linda said looking up at the tall police officer.

"What's going on Lieutenant?" Murphy asked seeing the fear on the little boys face and the desperation in Linda's voice.

Linda went on to explain to Murphy everything; about Jake & Jona Singh, Howler, the Covington's, the Amikura's, the blackmail list, the satellite launch, her son Parker being kidnapped and what Evelyn Covington was planning to do with him, as well as Eric Stone dead at the park, and about Captain Hargrove and his part in all this.

Murphy stood there stunned, confused, angry, and betrayed thinking about the people that got injured at the station earlier today, now knowing that his Captain was partially responsible for it.

"What do you need me to do ma'am?" Murphy asked looking over at Max who nodded to him with respect from his now rolled down window.

"I need to know this little boy is safe; I need for you to leave the Captain to me, and I need to know you are safe as well James" Linda replied grabbing the young man's elbow for reassurance.

"I've been assigned to inspect the vehicles going into the Covington Industries party tonight; the Captain is expecting me to be there at the front gate helping Howler's security; I just can't NOT show up Lieutenant" Murphy said just as Max walked up to them both.

"He's right, he needs to be there" Max said to them both seeing

Linda start to get agitated at what he said and James Murphy smiling back at him.

"Howler and his men are already on high alert for us, if he see's anything different it could change how we get to them" Max explained seeing that Linda was starting to understand his logic.

Max turned to Murphy reaching out his hand to shake his and said "We need you to take this boy to social services; tell them someone will be there to explain everything in the morning, and get back to Covington Industries as fast as you can so you don't draw any suspicion from any of Howler's men; okay?" shaking Murphy's hand firmly.

"I can do that Director" Murphy replied as Tyler walked around the car towards him with the little boy in tow.

Murphy squatted down to the boy's level and said smiling "Hey slugger, have you ever been for a ride in a police car before?'

The boy still hadn't spoken but managed a smile shaking his head "no" to Murphy's question feeling safe with the young police officer.

"Thank you Officer Murphy; he didn't deserve this" Tyler said to the young policeman with a smile.

Tyler bent down to give the boy a hug whispering in his ear "Don't worry he's one of the good guys" then watched as the young boy grabbed Murphy's hand who quickly lead him to the passenger seat of his patrol car.

Murphy made sure the boy's seat belt was secure then closed the door continuing to smile at the young lad through the car window. Murphy walked to the front of his car and stood there in front of Jake & Linda Mason who shook his hand and said "Thank you" as he smiled and got into his car; slowly driving out of the parking area and onto the highway.

As they all watched Murphy's car drive down the highway Stacy, Yuki, and Ochi pulled up in the black SUV Stacy Mason was driving. Stacy rolled down the driver's window and asked "Where to big brother?" with a big smile to her brother Jake standing beside Linda and the parked SUV Max was driving.

"Follow us" Jake replied to his sister with a grin as he got into the backseat with Linda.

Max and Tyler got back into the car, as he started the ignition Max could see the worry on Tyler's face so he grabbed her hand and squeezed it tight saying to her "He'll be okay, we'll find his family; it's what WE do" this made Tyler smile and squeeze Max's hand as well, knowing the little boy would be safe and protected.

The two SUV's got on the highway as Max listened to the talking GPS's directions occasionally glancing out the side mirror to see Stacy continuing to follow close behind. As they drove a few minutes they could see a slew of government vehicles with their flashing lights on the other side of the median heading towards Umstead Park.

They drove for about ten minutes more when they came to the gated entrance of the Raleigh Storage Company. It was a public use storage facility that allowed people to store their belongings, furniture, even cars that they didn't have room for in their homes for a monthly fee.

The company rented several different size containers from 16'x 8' for furniture & boxes, to 32'x 16' which a large car or van could be stored. They all had personal locks on the containers as well as everyone needing a security code to get inside the gates.

"1006" Jake said to Max as he rolled down his window next to the security code keypad. Max pushed the numbers one at a time then hit the entry button and the high steel security gate in front of them started sliding to the right of them.

As soon as the gate slid all the way from in front of the SUV Max drove it onto the lot looking back at his son with a grin.

Stacy followed her dad close behind so she could get through the gate without having to use the security code again making it seem like only one car went through.

"Pull up to units 2001 & 2002" Jake said pointing down the long row of units that Max slowly drove past.

"Stop at those last two on the end, over on the left-hand side" Jake said to his dad then looked at his watch seeing it was exactly 1900 hours, or 7pm.

Max could see that there was only one security light at the end of the building where Jake's two storage units were and parked the SUV on the side of the building so no one could see it just sitting there this late in the evening.

Stacy saw where her dad had parked and followed his example by parking her SUV behind the end of the building on the right-hand side, directly across from her dad's car.

Everyone got out of the two SUV's and converged on Jake & Linda's two storage units just a few feet away; one small, the other large. Max could see a combination lock on both units hoping that one or both of them remembered the numbered combination to get them off.

Just as Jake had grabbed the small unit's lock to open it bright headlights lit up the group of seven standing there, pulling up to them as they all drew handguns except for Jake, and Yuki Amikura who drew her ninja sword thinking they may be part of Howler's men still looking for them.

Jake dropped the lock hearing it clang against the steel door and shouted to everyone "DON'T SHOOT; THEY'RE WITH US" watching as two figures got out of the car and slowly walked towards them with everyone's guns still trained on them both through the blinding headlights.

Both men recognized Max Mason immediately and came to attention saluting the confused Admiral standing in front of them. Max smiled finally recognizing one of the men and saluted them both proceeded by an "At ease gentlemen".

Max walked up and said "Detective Martin; nice to see you again" extending his hand out bringing a confused look from both Jake & Linda.

"You to Director" replied Detective Jose Martin who shook Max's hand vigorously and smiled.

"You two know each other?" Jake asked the two of them standing there smiling at each other.

"I guess you could say; we worked a case together a while back" Max said to his son looking over at Tyler, then smiled back at Martin who chuckled at what he said.

"This handsome young man is…" Martin started to introduce his colleague when Max interrupted him.

"Master-Sergeant Lamar "Crusher" Davis" Max replied knowing who the muscular young man was with admiration in his voice and a big smile on his face.

"I watched you play against Navy your senior year" Max said grinning.

"You had three sacks, a fumble recovery, and a 60 yard interception for a touchdown that game" Max said to the tall, muscular, and handsome African-American young man standing in front of him.

"Your quarterback was slow that day sir" Davis said with a grin.

"Yes he was" Max replied laughing.

"You were the most gifted middle-linebacker that ever played college football" Max said with admiration.

"You gave up quite a lucrative career to stay in the Army with these two knuckleheads" Max said to Davis with a grin looking over at his son Jake & Jose Martin standing there beside Linda and Tyler.

Max noticed that Davis was respectfully talking to him but he couldn't take his eyes off of Yuki Amikura, and the feeling was mutual it seemed.

Lamar "Crusher" Davis was a high school football phenomenon in his hometown of Murfreesboro, Tennessee. Making first team

All-State all four years of high school, he was the most sought after football player by major colleges & universities across the country.

Lamar Davis was 6'-6" tall, short black curly hair, muscular, shy, intense when it came to protecting his friends & family, and compassionate; who wanted nothing more than to help others before himself. He was always volunteering at soup kitchens and homeless shelters around his hometown every weekend; which is why he chose to go to West Point to study social science and join the U.S. Army.

At the end of his senior year Lamar "Crusher" Davis was awarded the coveted "Heisman Trophy" given to the outstanding college football player that year.

He was also drafted #1 in the professional football draft by his own home state team the Tennessee Titans.

He was awarded the rank of Master-Sergeant upon graduation, but because of his mandatory seven years of military service for his college education at West Point, Davis had to decline a multi-million dollar contract to play pro football upon his release from his military obligation. He believed being a social worker and taking care of the homeless was more rewarding, and decided those were his plans after the Army; not football.

Davis was recruited into joining the Army Mountain Rangers by Jake Mason after Jake watched him rescue several people from a burning building next to the bar he, Jose Martin, and James Jones were drinking in just outside of Kandahar.

The four of them became great friends and worked well together on missions always watching each others backs. Davis was considered the weapons & demolition expert of the team, highly trained in both as well as mountain climbing.

After the death of James Jones the three of them were reassigned out of Kandahar after Jake was released from the brig for assaulting Captain Eric Stone.

The three of them together were a highly successful "search & apprehend" team for the Army the rest of their time in Afghanistan.

Upon their release into the Army reserves they were sent back to the United States where Davis got a job with the Tennessee state government as their Director of Social Services. He always made it for their team reunion every year, and his reserve weekends with Jake & Jose.

The bright car headlights continued to light up the area as Max reached out and shook Davis's hand glancing over to see Linda hugging Jose Martin who stood there rigidly and uncomfortable looking at him.

"You look like you have something on your mind Detective" Max asked wondering why he was so official to his friends and colleagues.

"I have an email on my phone addressed to you from Defense Secretary Cartwright that you need to read Sir" Martin said pulling out his cell phone from his back pocket.

Jake looked at Jose and asked "What's going on dude?"

"Better let the Admiral explain Captain" Jose replied standing at attention again along with Davis.

Max quietly scrolled up and down the email on Jose Martin's phone then looked at him and asked "Has this been confirmed Lieutenant?"

"Yes Sir; Secretary Cartwright called us both right after he sent it to each of our phones" Jose replied seeing confused looks on both Jake & Linda Mason's faces.

Max snickered then looked at his son and daughter-in-law with a sly grin saying "You've both been activated".

"ARE YOU SHITTING ME?" Jake asked looking at his wife in disbelief while his sister Stacy snickered putting her hand over her mouth quickly when her dad gave her an evil look; then a grin.

"Seems you're back in the Army Captain; you as well Lieutenant" Max said looking over at Linda then handing Jose's cell phone to his son so he could read for himself the Admiral's email reactivating their reserve status for this particular mission to avoid any legal ramifications to any of them.

KILLS OF THE FATHER

"Can he do that?" Jake asked Max with a scowl on his face.

"Yeah, actually he can; if there is a domestic problem he believes state and federal law enforcement could be over their heads with" Max explained to his son.

"He can reactivate the closest military reserve unit to take care of the problem without any legal problems; I'm afraid that would be you four" Max replied seeing Jose Martin & Crusher Davis still standing at attention in front of him.

"It doesn't change anything for us ADMIRAL" Jake said sarcastically looking over at Linda who moved closer to her husband to agree with him.

"I know son" Max replied knowing how they both felt seeing the anger in both Jake & Linda's eyes over their son being kidnapped by Howler & the Covington's.

"Does this mean I can order Stacy to go get me coffee" Jake asked his dad laughing seeing Stacy stick her tongue out at her big brother now trying to lighten the situation they were walking into.

"Just tell us why we're all standing here?" Max asked giving his two children that look they've seen so many times before when they pick on one another and he wants them to stop.

Jake smiles and walks over to the small storage unit door and unlocks the combination lock. Taking it off, he drops it to the ground beside the big orange doorway.

Just as he was about to raise the door up a police car pulled up behind their SUV's with flashing blue lights. They all trained their guns on the large figure walking towards them in the bright headlights.

"You should turn your radio off if you don't want anyone to follow you Lieutenant" James Murphy said as everyone could see him standing in front of them. Murphy turned the flashing lights off and closed the car door walking towards everyone.

"Murphy, I told you this wasn't your fight; to stay out of it and be safe" Linda said seeing her friend there wanting to help.

"You and Jake are my friends, it's not right what the Captain has done; I want to help" Murphy replied seeing the smiles on everyone's faces.

Murphy looked over at Stacy and couldn't stop staring, thinking how beautiful she was; totally forgetting about everyone else. Murphy walked up to Stacy and smiled introducing himself "I'm James Murphy, and YOU are?".

"I'm Lieutenant Stacy Mason, Navy SEALS; and that growling old guy over there is my father" she said giggling looking over at Max who had a sour look on his face.

"Really daddy; I'm 22 yrs old and kill bad guys for a living, I'm too old for you to screen who I date now" Stacy said looking over at Tyler and Yuki smiling liking this young police officer standing in front of her not caring who her father was at the moment.

Jake ignored what was going on with his sister and raised the orange storage container door reaching in to turn on the light switch on the wall. The lights came on overhead and everyone could finally see what was so special inside.

"What the Hell" Max said confused as he looked into the now well lit storage unit to see racks of machine-guns, handguns, shotguns, and a variety of long-range sniper rifles along the unit's walls.

"Where did all this firepower come from Jacob?" Max asked as he stood in the middle of the storage unit admiring the variety of weapons, ammunition, explosives, tactical gear, and electronics that was being stored inside.

"Last year Admiral Cartwright ordered a weapons & tactical gear storage facility in every area of a major military training base like Fort Bragg, just in case something like this happened" Jake replied grinning at all the toys in the unit.

"He asked Linda & I to set it up, buy everything a Special Forces unit would need in a hostile crisis, and send the bills to him" Jake continued.

"This isn't even my favorite part of all this" Jake said smiling as he walked to the larger storage unit next door having already unlocked the combination padlock and tossed it on the ground when Martin & Davis showed up.

Jake raised the door overhead and flipped the light switch on the wall to reveal a black over-sized SUV van inside.

"I got to build this from the wheels on up; it took me almost a year" Jake explained grabbing the keys from the wall they were hanging from and rubbing the hood of the shiny SUV as if it was a pet.

"Admiral Cartwright said I can keep the prototype as long as I made blueprints to have others like it mass produced; how ironic that I just finished and tested it two weeks ago" Jake continued looking over at his sister with a smile.

"Stacy and Uncle Jordy helped me design the electronic interior" Jake said with pride looking over at his baby sister as he pushed the button on the key remote.

Twin doors slowly slid apart in the middle of the SUV to show everyone the rather sophisticated electronics inside and two command chairs in front of the console.

"Its completely bullet-proof, and can withstand a direct hit from a RPG" he stated with a grin. Jake knew most cars & SUV's were made out of the standard-type steel, so he decided to replace it with armor plating that could withstand almost anything; even "rocket propelled grenades".

"It has slide down bullet-proof wheel wells, retractable console-aimed .50 caliber mini guns on all four sides, remote smoke screen in the rear, twin 60mm cannons in the front grill; AND, can climb a hill like a frickin' mountain goat" Jake said bragging about his new toy.

Max walked around and stuck his head inside the SUV looking at his son & daughter with a smile of pride at what the two of them had accomplished.

"Remind me to smack Jordy in the back of the head when I see him" Max said laughing and looking at Tyler thinking that Jordy must have been keeping this secret from him for awhile.

"Can you build me a red Mustang convertible like this?" Max asked his son laughing.

"You want a fire engine red Mustang convertible with machine guns popping out of it?" Jake asked with a snicker.

"Doesn't everyone?" Max replied watching his son shake his head amusingly.

"Tell me what this machine can do for us tonight" Max asked looking over at Stacy.

Stacy smiled at Murphy gently brushing her hand against his as she walked up to the SUV next to her father.

"It has infra-red & heat signature recognition, night vision, X-ray video cameras, frequency jamming capabilities, vocal tracking software, and world-wide secured internet & satellite communications" Stacy said pointing to each switch on the lit up console.

"And the entire project is powered by continuous charging solar panels up on the roof" Stacy explained smiling at both her father and brother.

"So basically, it's a weaponized armored surveillance vehicle" Max asked his two children who nodded in agreement, seeing their dad smile at their new toy.

"Does it have a cute name like everything else these days?" Max asked sarcastically as he continued looking around the large SUV knowing that Jordy calls his drone "SARAH" and that the drone that tried to kill them earlier by Covington Industries was named "FRED".

Jake laughed and looked at Stacy who smiled then turned back to his dad and said "Bruno".

Max laughed at the name then asked "Does BRUNO stand for anything?".

"Nope; just Bruno" Jake replied grinning at his dad.

"Okay, very cool son" Max said smiling back at Jake.

"We need to get back to the motel and formulate a plan; Howler & the Covington's know we're coming and we have NO idea what we're going into or what we're up against" Max said to everyone still admiring the SUV his son built.

Yuki stepped forward shyly smiling at Crusher Davis who returned her smile then she looked at Max and said "I have an idea Max Mason that may get us everything that we need".

Colonel Howler was sitting behind his desk looking at his computer screen when his phone rang. Picking it up he yelled "HOWLER" angry that the Mason's were still alive and heading to Covington Industries.

"Sir; I have Noki Amikura here at the gate to see Mr. Covington" the security gate guard said into the phone.

"Send him up" Howler replied slamming his phone down on the desk.

There were parking attendants directing where the limousines would be parked at the entrance for tonight's party as Amikura's limo pulled up to the front door of Covington Industries.

Amikura's driver, one of his ninja guards; could see where they were being parked as he stopped to let his boss out of the car.

The other guard got out and came around to open Amikura's door. As Noki Amikura stepped out he stood at the driver's window waiting for it to roll down.

"Go to my cousin's hotel and text me when she has left" Amikura ordered looking at the young ninja who nodded back to his master in agreement.

Amikura and his lone ninja guard walked up the sidewalk towards the entrance as his limousine headed back out towards the front gate.

The black suit & tie dressed ninja guard opened the glass door and they both walked into the lobby seeing Nathaniel & Evelyn Covington walking towards them from the elevator across the hallway.

Waiters & waitresses were moving quickly around the giant open first floor lobby where the party was to take place. Dozens of tables with chairs sporting blue table clothes were being dressed with flower arrangements on top; and over in the corner was a champagne fountain with dozens of high quality champagne bottles sitting on the table ready to be poured into it.

Noki Amikura bowed to the Covington's then said "I have come to discuss our arrangement concerning my cousin; she is on her way here".

"I know; I invited her and her cute little sidekick earlier this morning" Nathaniel Covington replied with a grin.

"I will need someplace away from your party guests to discuss my business dealings with my cousin if that is acceptable" Amikura said bowing again in appreciation to his request.

"You mean kill her; don't you?" Covington asked with an evil grin looking at his mother who was smiling at the young Asian business man.

"The 4th floor conference room is at your disposal Mr. Amikura" Covington said returning his bow.

"Now if you'll excuse me I have to get ready for my guests; the Mason family will be here soon" Nathaniel Covington said grinning seeing the anger on the Asian man's face that Max Mason was still alive and coming to the party.

Yuki looked around at everyone still standing in the bright glow of Stacy's & Jake's modified SUV and shyly spoke "It seems they know were coming, but they believe were coming over the walls" she said looking at Max.

"What if we went in through the front gate as party guests; the Covington's or Colonel Howler wouldn't expect that" Yuki continued looking over at Crusher Davis again smiling. Ochi elbowed her gently to stay focused with what she was saying.

Max looked over at Tyler & Linda who were smiling when Tyler said "We do have invitations".

Max thought for a moment looking at Jake, Jose Martin, and Crusher Davis then replied "Us guys have nothing to wear" snickering at how that sounded.

"We can fix that" Ochi said smiling at Max with a confused look on his face.

"We have a professional tailor at our hotel that rents and alters men's suits & tuxedos; we're sure he can help the four of you" Ochi said grabbing Yuki's arm giggling.

"What about you ladies?" Max asked knowing it was a foolish question.

"There's a high-end Shopping Mall across the street from the hotel; I'm sure we can all find something to wear" Ochi said with a grin.

"We can rent a couple of limousines to blend in with the others going in as well" Ochi said looking at Yuki who had a big grin on her face knowing where that idea was going; remembering the limo driver they had that afternoon that Ochi had a slight crush on.

Max looked at Ochi & Yuki with a confused look on his face as the two young giddy Asian women spoke loudly together "WE KNOW A GUY".

Tyler stepped forward and said "Let's load up what were EACH going to need for tonight, then we can drop the boys off and go shopping ladies" smiling at Max who grinned back at her.

"Looks like we're going to another party" Max said to everyone laughing.

"Two parties in the same week, you sure do know how to show a girl a good time Mason" Tyler replied smiling at Max.

"Only the best for you sweetheart" Max replied laughing seeing everyone load bags of weapons and gear into large duffle bags; glancing over at Stacy & Jake as they powered up the "killer SUV" to make sure everything was charged up when they came back for it.

CHAPTER ELEVEN

If a "six star" instead of the normal "five star" quality rating for a hotel could be given to an extraordinary, old-fashioned, classy hotel in the south; the Raleigh Renaissance Hotel would be that one.

Located in the middle of the banking & financial district near "Old Town" Raleigh; the Raleigh Renaissance Hotel welcomed the financially elite to it's seventeen stories of luxury rooms, penthouse suites with private elevators, special amenities & services, world-renown dining, top shelf wine & alcohol, valet service, and much more.

The two SUV's pulled up to the front of the hotel and everyone got out looking around as the two valets took their keys and left the nine of them standing there looking around and up, seeing how tall the hotel stood.

"We'll have to go through the lobby to get to our elevator" Ochi Okasa said to everyone now staring at both her and Yuki stunned at where they were staying.

"We have about three hours before the satellite launch at midnight" Max said to everyone as they all walked through the sliding glass doors of the hotel; now standing in the lobby.

"WOW" Stacy said out loud knowing everyone in the group could hear her thought about the place as she walked in.

Officer James Murphy walked up joining the group standing there on the sidewalk admiring the front of the hotel.

Not wanting a valet to park his squad car he parked in the underground garage and caught up to them just as they were about to go inside the luxury hotel.

The hotel lobby was beautifully designed with mahogany wood walls & pillars, crystal chandeliers, white marble floors, brass fixtures, crushed-velvet chairs and sofas, and fresh-cut flowers everywhere.

The check-in desk was made of brightly polished wood with three nicely dressed hotel attendants standing behind it to greet guests and help settle them into their rooms. One of them walked from behind the desk towards the small group standing there in the middle of the lobby.

Everyone stayed back behind Yuki & Ochi as a tall well dressed man wearing a black suit and tie approached the two of them smiling, reaching out his hand to shake Yuki's saying "How wonderful to have you & your assistant stay with us Miss Amikura" he stated.

The well dressed man smiled at Yuki Amikura then casually looked around at everyone standing with her in his lobby.

"I'm Travis Hawthorne the hotel manager; we hope your stay here at Raleigh Renaissance will be a pleasant one" he said vigorously shaking her hand continuing to look at everyone standing behind her, especially the two uniformed police officers; curious why they were among them.

Yuki and Ochi bowed to the gentleman as he released Yuki's delicate, but hard hand.

Yuki smiled and said "Thank you Mr. Hawthorne, your hotel is magnificent; now if you'll excuse us" she said abruptly, but politely walking away from him towards the west end elevator with everyone following behind.

"If there's anything you need; please call the front desk, I'm sure we can accommodate anything you might need" Hawthorne replied as the group headed towards the elevators.

As they all headed towards the elevator Max noticed a young Asian man in a suit & tie sitting with his legs crossed in one of the plush chairs reading the sports page of today's newspaper.

He also noticed that the man glanced at Yuki Amikura a couple of times as she walked ahead of him, then watched him go back to his reading; thinking he was there to keep an eye on her for Noki Amikura.

They all stood in front of the elevator door as Ochi pulled a chain from around her neck and inserted the key that was hanging from it into the private elevator keyhole. Turning the key the elevator doors opened immediately and everyone got in.

The elevator stopped on the 17th floor penthouse suite and the doors opened to a huge room with wrap around glass windows, expensive furniture, incredibly bright art work on the walls, marble floors, chandeliers, and a fully-stocked bar.

Everyone looked at one another as they continued to look around the large living room wondering who these two women were; being able to afford something like this.

Max looked over at Stacy with a smile and asked quietly "This is what you meant when you said she would be okay; isn't it?"

Stacy Mason smiled at her dad then at her big sister who smiled back at her. Yuki winked at Stacy then looked at Max with a smile and said "You could say I have a dollar or two Max Mason".

"If anyone needs to freshen up before we go back out, there is a bathroom in each of the two bedrooms" Ochi said looking at everyone still admiring the room.

Ochi walked up to Max then glanced over at Yuki who was chatting with Stacy and said "She has more than a couple of dollars; she didn't want to tell you because she thought you might think she was shallow and power crazy like her brother & cousin; I told her you wouldn't think this way but she still wanted to keep the money situation quiet from you, only Stacy knew".

"She should never have to think about any of that with me" Max replied to the young Asian assistant who he now trusted with his life.

"I need to call down to the tailor shop and give him your suit, shirt, and shoe sizes if anyone knows them" Ochi asked out loud so all the men could hear her as she took a pen and notepad out of the desk drawer to write the sizes down.

"I'm a forty regular, seventeen neck, and size ten shoe" Jose Martin replied first, looking out the sliding glass door where he could see the private pool now glistening in the moonlight.

"Jake is also a forty regular, seventeen neck size, and a size ten shoe" Linda said knowing her husband's sizes because she buys some of his clothes for him sometimes.

"Thanks honey" Jake said with a grin to his wife who was standing next to Stacy.

Crusher Davis smiled at Yuki then looked over at Ochi with a sheepish grin saying "I'm kind of a big guy; I wear a forty-four wide suit, nineteen neck size, and size thirteen shoes" he said seeing Yuki return his smile shyly.

"And what about you; Max Mason?" Ochi asked looking at Max who was still amazed at the luxury penthouse they were staying in.

"I'm a forty-two regular, eighteen shirt size, and I also wear a size ten shoe" Max replied as he looked out the large window to see all the lights of Raleigh starting to light up around the city.

Ochi Okasa walked into one of the bedrooms and sat down on the bed and picked up the phone on the nightstand calling the hotel operator who connected her to the hotel's tailor shop. She proceeded to tell the person on the other end of the phone the four different size men they needed clothing for.

Ochi hung up the phone and returned to the living room looking at everyone saying "The tailor and his assistant will be up in forty-five minutes; the front desk will call when they are ready to come up" Ochi said looking at the four men standing around the room.

"Stacy, I need to talk to you before you go" Max said looking at his daughter with a solemn look on his face.

"I'm not going to the party, am I?" Stacy asked with a look of disappointment to her dad knowing what he was going to say to her.

"You and Jacob are the only two that know how everything works on that van sweetheart; I can't ask Jacob to do it, it's his son were going after" Max said putting his hand on her cheek knowing she was disappointed not being able to go to the Covington's party to rescue Parker with everyone.

"I have to let him and Linda go in to find Parker; you understand that don't you?" Max asked feeling guilty she couldn't go in to help find her nephew.

"I'll stay with her if that's okay sir" Murphy asked looking at Stacy with a smile then back to Max who had a concerned looked on his face.

"That's fine Officer Murphy; NO screw ups, we all need to stay focused understand" Max said to the young police officer forcefully then looked over at Stacy and winked at her, who gave her father a big grin.

"Can she still go shopping with us Max Mason?" Yuki asked after hearing that Stacy wasn't going to be inside the party, instead she would be tech & recon support outside the Covington Industries building on this mission.

"Sure sweetheart; I know my princess loves a good shopping spree" Max replied smiling at his two daughters then looking over at Tyler who had an approving smile on her own face.

Yuki looked at Stacy and smiled saying "I still owe you a new leather jacket little sister" getting a smile from Stacy.

Tyler walked over and stood in the middle of the large living room and said out loud "Let's saddle up ladies, we have two hours before we need to leave here dressed & pressed for the Covington's" she said.

"We need to do this quickly" Tyler continued as she started walking towards the elevator stopping in front of Max to kiss him before she left.

Linda did the same to Jake and the five women walked to the now open elevator and waved to the men as the door closed in front of them.

As soon as the elevator doors closed Jake got up from the sofa and grabbed his laptop surprising Max and the rest who gave his son a "What are you doing?" kind of look.

"I have to know" Jake said to everyone typing quickly on his keyboard and staring at the screen.

"Know what?" Jose Martin asked not knowing what his Captain was up to.

Jake ignored his Lieutenant's question as he continued to read from his laptop screen. Max could see Jake's eyes getting bigger and bigger as he continued to read finally hearing him yell "HOLY SHIT"

"Dad; Yuki's worth over $100 billion dollars, not a $100 million dollars, a $100 BILLION dollars" Jake said stunned turning the laptop screen towards his dad.

"She's the third richest person in the WORLD according to Financial World Magazine" Jake continued as his dad slowly read the profile on his adopted daughter.

Max continued to read what Jake had looked up on Yuki Amikura's financial records. She was the majority stockholder for Amikura Electronics; the third largest electronics producing company in the world.

After her Uncle Nabu Amikura died and left her the company in his will five years ago she became the face of the company while her cousin stood in her shadow.

He continued to read that her cousin Noki Amikura was Nabu's second in command, but was written out of the will because of several questionable business deals within the Japanese crime world, including giving millions of dollars to his cousin Tanaka Amikura's "Dragon Breath" terrorist organization.

"Now this whole Howler trying to kill me thing makes more sense" Max said as he turned Jake's laptop back around to him.

The phone on the desk started ringing next to Max and he picked it up listening, then saying "Send them up" placing the phone back on the desk.

Looking at the other four men in the room Max said "That was the front desk; their sending up the tailor now" as he could see everyone anticipating the elevator door opening now.

Max stood up just as the elevator door opened to show a skinny, short gray-haired man with glasses standing in front of them.

Max figured him to be in his late sixty's, wearing a suit & tie with a long cloth yellow measuring tape hanging around his neck.

"Good evening gentlemen, my name is Teddy; I'm the Raleigh's resident tailor" he said as he stood just inside the open elevator in front of several racks of suits and shirts.

Max could see the assistant the tailor brought up with him standing behind the clothing racks trying to avoid eye contact with everyone, finally recognizing the man as the young Asian he saw in the hotel's lobby earlier.

The young Asian was dressed in a hotel uniform, but something seemed off to Max as he watched him push the clothing racks from the elevator into the large living room following closely behind the elderly tailor.

Max looked over at Jose Martin & Crusher Davis who were both keeping a close eye on the two men now standing in the room and walked over to his son Jake and placed his hand on his shoulder leaning in to whisper "Take the tailor to the bedroom son".

Jake smiled at his dad knowing what was about to happen and walked up to the elderly tailor and asked "Mr. Teddy would one of these bedrooms do as a dressing room?" gently guiding him towards the bedroom to inspect for its use.

"James can you help me push these racks into the bedroom for Teddy?" Jake asked James Murphy as he watched the Asian assistant remove something shiny from under one of the racks.

Murphy was pushing the largest clothing rack through the bedroom doorway when Jake leaned in and whispered to him "Don't let the old man out of the room, keep him occupied" as Murphy looked back at Max Mason who nodded to him in agreement with what his son just told him.

Jake turned back to his dad as he got the tailor and the clothing racks into the bedroom letting him know he was now safe. Jake looked over at his two friends saying "Hey guys, how about coming over here and joining me with the tailor for a moment" watching his dad slowly approach the tailor's Asian assistant.

"Howler or Amikura; which one of those assholes sent you?" Max asked looking the Asian man in the eye who slowly came from behind the clothing racks with two katana half swords one in each of his hands and an evil grin on his face.

"My Master sent me here to observe his disrespectful cousin and I find the traitor Max Mason here with her; imagine my good fortune" the young Asian replied going into a fighting stance.

"You were considered the greatest ninja warrior of our clan, yet you disrespected our code and left to pursue the law; a fruitless endeavor" the Asian ninja said swinging his sword at Max as he quickly jumped back to avoid it.

Jose Martin and Crusher Davis looked at one another and said together "Ninja warrior?" then looked at Jake with confusion on their faces as they all stood at the bedroom door blocking the tailor from seeing the fight that was happening with Max Mason.

"Your dad's a ninja?" Jose asked Jake as he continued to watch what was unfolding with his dad and the ninja.

"Yeah; it's kind of a long, funny story" Jake replied, grinning at his two friends. Jake pulled out his XD handgun from behind his back and pointed it at the ninja standing there ready to attack his dad again.

"Can I shoot him Pop?" Jake asked with a smile on his face as he watched his dad duck under another swipe from the ninja's sword.

"Nah, he came here for a fight; let him have one" Max replied laughing. "But I could use my baton's" he said looking over at Jake who had his dad's bag sitting on the floor beside him.

Jake reached into his dad's tactical bag and pulled out one of his steel combat baton's and extended it with a sharp swing then yelling at his dad "Here you go Pop".

Max dodged another swing of the ninja's sword then moved

behind him smacking him hard in the back of the head with his right fist causing him to stumble forward.

Max grabbed the baton out of the air Jake had tossed him then looked at his son confused, who had a big grin on his face

"Really; only one?" Max asked out loud moving quickly to his left as the ninja came at him again swinging both swords at him together.

"You want to make it a fair fight don't you?" Jake asked his dad looking over at Jose & Crusher grinning knowing his dad could easily defeat the ninja with both of his kenpo baton's; that his dad was an expert at using them.

"Smart-ass kid" Max said out loud smiling at his son as the ninja swung his two swords back and forth at him barely missing him as he bobbed and weaved away from the razor-sharp steel blades.

Max skillfully blocked each swing with his lone baton hearing the loud "CLANGS" as they hit one another finally kicking the young Asian in the chest knocking him to the marble floor.

"Your dad's pretty good" Jose said leaning over and whispering to Jake as he watched Max intently.

"Yeah, my Uncle Yoshi was a great teacher" Jake replied watching his dad swing his baton at each sword swing from the ninja.

Jake remembered when he was seven years old Sensei Yoshi Amikura trained him in martial-arts; while his dad was trained using various weapons, including swords and his batons. Sensei Amikura was a ninjitsu master highly respected in the Philippines' and they both loved him as a friend and a teacher.

Max was getting bored fighting the ninja, blocking his two swords being pushed towards his throat. He looked the ninja in the eye and smiled bringing his right knee up hard into his adversary's groin seeing the intense pain in his eyes.

The ninja backed away from Max who said "I've enjoyed this, but I have to get ready for the party" smiling at his prey.

"I will kill the great Max Mason for my Master, then I will kill all of your friends" the angry young ninja said raising one sword above his head while he placed the second at his side.

"Great?" Jose whispered to Jake hearing what the ninja said about Max.

"You could say my dad's kind of a big deal in the Philippines' and Japan; in the so-called ninja world" Jake replied grinning at his friend.

As Jake, Jose Martin, and Crusher Davis continued to watch Max fight the ninja and stand in front of the bedroom doorway to keep the hotel's tailor safe they could hear the elderly gentleman inside say "I'll be ready in just a moment" continuing to place shirts, suit jackets, and shoes on the large king size bed in the room, completely oblivious of what's going on in the other room.

The ninja swung his swords at Max as he stepped back to avoid them, but this time he managed to cut Max on the chest slicing his shirt open with a small slit. Max stepped back and looked down at his torn shirt seeing a small cut with blood slowly coming out of it then looked at the ninja with a scowl on his face a bit pissed off now.

The ninja attacked again as Max blocked his swords again and again hearing the loud "clang" each time the blade hit his steel baton. Max ducked under the blades moved quickly behind him jumped up in the air hitting the ninja hard in the head with the baton knocking him to the floor seeing both of his swords slide across the slick marble floor.

The ninja didn't move, continuing to lay face down on the cold floor. Max bent down on one knee beside him and rolled him over to see the ninja was completely unconscious with a big bleeding gash on the side of his head where his baton hit him.

Max checked his pulse to see if he killed him; and found he was still alive. He then grabbed him by the wrist and dragged him across the floor to one of the chairs in the beautifully decorated dining room, lifting him up and placing him in one.

"Handcuffs and duct tape that's in the bag" Max said looking at Jake who started rummaging through the bags sitting on the floor.

Jake walked over and handed his dad a pair of handcuffs which he quickly used pulling the ninja's arms behind the chair clicking them on both wrists. Max reached his hand out to Jake for the silver duct tape that they always brought with them on missions, and promptly started taping the ninja in the chair wrapping the tape around and around the ninja's chest and the chair. Then he placed a large piece across the young Asian's mouth to keep him quiet when he awoke.

"Who wants to go first?" Teddy asked as the elderly tailor walked out of the bedroom past Murphy, Jose Martin, and Crusher Davis to see the young Asian man who helped bring the clothes racks up from his tailor shop; bloody and duct taped to a dining room chair.

"Oh my, I hope you know I don't make prison uniforms" Teddy said looking at Max with a big grin seeing the bloody cut on the front of his shirt.

Max pulled out his Secret Service ID and showed it to the tailor who wasn't all that impressed grabbing Jose Martin by the arm and leading him into the bedroom saying "I have a deadline; you can be first" closing the door behind the two of them.

One by one, the tailor dressed Jose, Jake, Crusher, and finally Max in very nice fitting tuxedos with matching bow-ties & shoes looking at all four of them standing there with Officer Murphy admiring his work.

"My work here is done gentlemen" Teddy said as he started wheeling out one of the clothing racks from the bedroom towards the suite's elevator.

"I'll have the front desk call Miss Amikura in the morning to pick up the other rack" the elderly tailor said to Max as the elevator door opened and he pushed the clothing rack inside.

"You'll have to deal with him on your own" he said giving Max a smile as he glanced over at the Asian man taped to the chair once more.

"Good luck gentlemen, enjoy your party this evening" Teddy said as the door slowly closed in front of him.

Max looked at everyone smiling and said "We all look like a bunch of well-dressed penguins" watching everyone smile and snicker at what he said.

A few minutes later the elevator door reopened again and Max, Jose, and Crusher all pulled their handguns out and pointed it at the open elevator as Tyler, Linda, Stacy, Yuki, and Ochi stood there stunned carrying assorted shopping bags and garment bags.

Tyler walked into the living area looking over at the unconscious Asian man duct taped to the chair with blood on his forehead and seeing his two swords on the floor and said "You boys have been busy since we left" smiling over at Max thinking how handsome he looked in his tuxedo.

Yuki & Ochi walked over to the confined Asian then looked at Max and Tyler with concern on their faces. "He's one of Noki's ninja guards" Ochi said seeing the anger in Yuki's eyes knowing her cousin tried to kill Max again; in HER own hotel room.

"We know; he and I had an interesting chat about your cousin while you were gone" Max replied looking at Yuki with a grin.

Tyler looked at her watch and saw they needed to be dressed and ready to go in an hour saying "Ladies, our men look incredible; let's go play dress up for them" she said looking at Max with a seductive grin.

"I need to make a phone call; so Yuki and I will take one bedroom and you two take the other" Ochi said looking at Linda and Tyler.

Stacy sat down on the sofa next to Murphy wearing a new black leather jacket as her dad sat across from them on one of the plush chairs.

He smiled and asked "How much did that cost her?" knowing that Yuki bought it for her because she messed up Stacy's other jacket just a couple of nights ago in a fight between the two of them.

"$1,500 dollars" Stacy said a bit embarrassed knowing her ruined jacket only cost Max about $100 dollars a few years ago.

"Stacy Marie; sweetheart, isn't that taking advantage of your sister's generosity?" Max asked a bit put out that she would allow Yuki to spend that kind of money on her.

"I tried to tell her daddy that I didn't need something that expensive but she grabbed it and bought it anyway" Stacy said feeling a little ashamed.

"That's not the worst of it" Stacy said looking at her dad with an evil grin.

"What do you mean Princess?" Max asked adjusting the tie around his neck which was starting to irritate him.

"Everything we bought came to just over $10,000 dollars; she didn't even blink just pulled out her credit card and swiped it" Stacy said with a grin. "I've never seen anyone do that before, then again all my friends are poor" she said laughing.

"Yeah, I found out from your brother she has a dollar or two in the bank" Max replied looking over at Jacob and hearing him say "filthy rich" to his sister who smiled at her big brother.

"Your sister is back in our lives, we need to be thankful for that" Max said to his two children who nodded in agreement with him.

"And she's not trying to kill you anymore; could have been awkward at family reunions" Stacy said laughing and getting a snicker from James Murphy sitting next to her.

"Smart ass" Max replied laughing with her.

About forty minutes had past when Tyler walked out of the bedroom wearing a bright red evening gown with spaghetti straps, and a slit up the thigh all the way to her hip. She was wearing 4 inch red heels which now made her taller than Max. Her hair and makeup looked stunning on her.

Max couldn't take his eyes off of her, and both Stacy & Jake noticed that; smiling at one another seeing their dad was finally happy with someone.

"WOW" was all Max could say while he continued to smile as Tyler slowly walked up to him with a big smile on her own face.

"You clean up pretty nice yourself cowboy" Tyler said grinning at the clean shaven and well dressed Max Mason standing in front of her who kept looking her up and down.

Linda Mason walked out behind Tyler wearing a full length black halter evening gown that sparkled whenever the light hit it a certain way. She looked at her husband Jake smiling and blushing at the same time.

"Not really practical to fight in, but it will get me through the front door" Linda said to Jake with a laugh.

"You look incredible sweetheart" Jake said with a smile looking over at his dad who smiled at Linda and nodded in agreement with what Jake said to her.

Linda started straightening Jake's tie looking into his loving eyes then saying "You look very handsome sweetie; Parker would think you were a dressed up waiter or something" she said with a giggle, her eyes getting misty thinking about her son.

"A WAITER; that's it" Jake said out loud kissing Linda hard on the lips then looking over at his dad.

"The Covington's & Howler is expecting all of us together knowing we're coming for Parker; what if the three of us go in the backdoor as catering wait staff, while dad uses the ladies as eye candy going through the front door?" Jake asked out loud looking over at Jose Martin and Crusher Davis.

Jose Martin stepped forward and asked his commanding officer "Isn't a Hispanic/Portugese & Black waiter a bit of a cliché Captain?" looking at Jake with a grin.

"Maybe, but they don't know who you two are; and they expect me to be at my wife's side to find our son" Jake replied looking over at his dad for approval of his plan.

"I'm not so sure of this plan" Martin replied giving his commanding officer a stern look.

Max looked at Tyler who smiled and shrugged her bare shoulders thinking Jake's plan had merit listening to Max say "It's a good idea son, providing that the three of you can get in quickly and blend in with the rest of the waiters before someone like the Covington's or Howler finally recognizes you".

"Piece of cake Pop" Jake said with a laugh looking at Jose & Crusher who were shaking their heads back and forth knowing some of Jake's wacky scheme's never quite worked out well for any of them, thinking this may be one of those plans.

Ochi Okasa walked out from the other bedroom looking around at everyone wondering what she interrupted. She was dressed in a black oriental silk pants suit, wearing an orange silk blouse, and a matching jacket. She felt uncomfortable knowing everyone was staring at her when Stacy spoke up saying "That's really cute on you Ochi" who turned a bit red smiling at Stacy thanking her for her reassurance.

"The limousines will arrive in about ten minutes; the front desk will give us a call when they are here" Ochi said looking directly at Max Mason who smiled back at her approvingly.

As Crusher Davis stood beside Jose Martin waiting, suddenly his eyes got real big as Yuki Amikura stepped out of the bedroom. Jose chuckled and waved his hand several times in front of Crusher's eyes continuing to stare at the beautifully dressed Asian woman.

"This can't be good" Jose said with a laugh to Jake after he nudged him about Crusher's catatonic state as Yuki walked into the living room.

"Our boy may be leaving the nest soon" Jake said giggling to Jose knowing Crusher could hear them teasing him. They both abruptly stopped when Crusher gave them both a very evil look, then went back to stare more at how beautiful Yuki looked.

Yuki was dressed in a low cut, full length, bright royal blue evening gown. The top half was covered in sequins, with spaghetti straps that hung over her bare shoulders, and a slit up the side that seemed to go higher than the one Tyler was wearing. Her long silky Asian black hair was let down over her shoulders and curled up on the ends; something no one has ever seen except for Ochi.

Crusher brushed past Jose & Jake almost knocking them out of the way walking up to Yuki smiling at her as she returned the smile back then lowered her head shyly to avoid more eye contact.

"You look so incredibly beautiful" he said as he slowly took her hand and kissed the top of it seeing her turn a bit red with embarrassment understanding that she never got this kind of attention from a man before.

"Thank you Mr. Crusher" Yuki said looking back up into his smiling face not caring that everyone was staring at the two of them.

"Please, call me Lamar" Crusher replied not able to take his eyes off of her. Yuki smiled and nodded in acceptance of his name then looked back at Ochi with a big grin to her companion.

Linda leaned over and whispered to Tyler "This is serious; he never lets anyone call him Lamar" she said with a big grin.

The phone rang a couple of times and Ochi picked it up and said "Hello" then "Thank you, we'll be right down" hanging up the phone and looking at everyone.

"The two limousines are outside the hotel lobby waiting for us; what is the plan Max Mason?" Ochi said as everyone turned to Max to listen what he had to say.

"First we have to commandeer the two limos; Tyler and I will take care of that" Max said. "Crusher, you drive the front limo, Detective Martin the other" Max said looking at Jake's two men.

"Jake you ride with Stacy to get Bruno and the weapons, then meet us at the rest stop" Max continued seeing his son's face in agreement with what he was saying so far.

"I can take her; it's right on my way to Covington Industries" Murphy said to Max smiling at Stacy Mason.

"I can ride up front with Jose; Stacy knows what to do with

Bruno" Jake responded to his father seeing Stacy's infatuation with James Murphy.

"Okay; get to the rest stop rendezvous point with Bruno, and the gear as fast as you can sweetheart" Max said looking at Stacy.

"Okay daddy" Stacy replied pulling on her new black leather jacket and heading towards the elevator door with James Murphy close behind her.

Tyler, Linda, and Yuki grabbed colored shawls that they wrapped around themselves just as the elevator door opened.

Everyone got inside as Jake picked up the two bags they brought with them and slid them both on the floor next to him.

Max turned and smiled at everyone seeing how wonderfully dressed, they all were and said "Looks like its party time" as the elevator doors closed.

CHAPTER TWELVE

The private elevator doors opened on the hotel lobby floor and everyone got off standing just outside the door, waiting for Jake and Jose to grab the two large black duffle bags they had brought down with them.

Travis Hawthorne, the hotel manager was standing at the registration desk when he saw everyone get off the elevator and approached the group looking at Yuki Amikura asking her "Are we headed to the Covington party this evening Miss Amikura?"

"Yes we are Mr. Hawthorne" Yuki replied smiling at the older gentleman.

"Your two limousines are waiting outside; we hope you and your friends have a wonderful evening" Hawthorne said to the young Asian woman, then giving Max and unexpected stare.

"Thank you so much" Max replied to Hawthorne with a sheepish arrogant grin thinking Hawthorne was being paid by Covington to keep an eye on them, and that as soon as they left he would be on the phone to Nathaniel Covington letting him know they were on their way to him.

They all walked out of the hotel's front door to see two black "stretch" limousines parked in front with two nicely dressed drivers standing at the passenger door of each car. Max glanced back inside the hotel's large glass doors to see Hawthorne go directly to the front desk and pick up the phone, as he expected.

Max and Jose approached one driver, while Tyler and Crusher approached the other. Both Max & Tyler informed the drivers they were commandeering the two limo's in the name of "National Security" showing their Secret Service credentials to each of them.

The driver who helped Yuki & Ochi earlier that morning looked at Ochi and asked a bit angry "Is this ALL you needed from me?"

Ochi feeling a bit guilty having used the young driver's affection for her, walked past Yuki and stood in front of him; then grabbed his jacket lapels and kissed him hard and long pulling back saying "That is what I need from you; and now I need you to trust me" she said with a smile handing him a card with her cell phone number printed on it.

The driver smiled at her seeing her name and number on the card and said "I'm good with that; my name is Joey".

"Thank you Joey; will you call me tomorrow?" Ochi asked smiling at Yuki who returned one of her own to her best friend.

"Yes ma'am" Joey said squeezing her hand.

Joey turned and looked at Max saying "Sir, my cars are at your service; please don't let them get shot up" he said with a grin knowing Max was a federal agent.

"We'll try and bring them back in one piece young man" Max said looking over at Tyler with a grin as he watched Crusher take the keys from Joey and climb into the front seat to drive.

Joey opened the back passengers' door and smiled at Yuki as she got in and slid over. Ochi stood at the doorway continuing to smile at Joey placing her hand on his cheek and leaning in to kiss him again softly this time, saying "Thank you" then getting into the car as he closed the door behind her.

Jake put the two black duffle bags of weapons his dad had brought with him from DC in the trunk of Crusher Davis's limo; as Max, Tyler, and Linda got into the back of the other car.

Jose Martin climbed into the driver's seat as Jake opened the door and sat down next to him in the passengers' seat giving him a grin saying "Climb or Fall Hard Lieutenant, Climb or Fall Hard" referring to the Army Mountain Ranger "mantra" they would say to one another in Afghanistan before a mission; reaching over to give Jose a fist bump.

"Climb or Fall Hard sir" Jose said with a grin bumping Jake's fist as he slowly drove out of the hotel parking lot with Crusher following closely behind them.

The two limousines drove out of Raleigh and headed to the NC Parkway where they would meet up with Stacy at the rest stop not to far from the Covington Industries compound.

After driving about thirty minutes on the NC Parkway the two limo's pulled into the rest stop parking lot where Stacy was alone and waiting for them; standing beside Bruno, the heavily armored surveillance & tactical vehicle that Jake, Jordy, and she had built and playfully named.

Stacy stood outside waiting, wearing her hair in a ponytail tucked inside a black baseball cap in full tactical gear along with her twin XD handgun rig; understanding that Howler's mercenaries could come after her while she was alone sitting inside the van helping the others.

Both limousines came to a stop and everyone got out and walked over to Stacy who was holding a gray molded plastic box standing in front of the open doorway to Bruno's communication console.

They all stood there discussing the next part of Yuki & Max's plan to infiltrate the party to find Parker and destroy the satellite launch.

Stacy opened the box and handed her dad the first flesh tone colored ear bud communicator and watched him place it in his ear.

She climbed into the van and did some quick typing on the computer keyboard then said "Done" giving her father a smile.

"Say something daddy" Stacy asked to get an audio reading from his communicator.

"Test, test, test" Max said seeing his daughter smile and give him a thumbs up.

She next handed Tyler her ear bud turned back and typed again on her keyboard, quickly turning back to Tyler saying "Done".

Tyler knew she needed a audio test so she quickly said "1, 2, 3" with another thumbs up from Stacy.

Stacy continued to do this for Jake, Linda, Jose, Crusher, Yuki, and Ochi who ALL confirmed they could hear each other and be heard by her.

Max looked inside the van to see the large video screen behind

Stacy had several different colored dots on it bunched up together and asked her "What are the dots for sweetheart?" trying to keep the situation calm for his baby girl.

Stacy smiled at her dad and turned to point to the dots on the screen saying "Each of you have been given a designated color through your com's" she said looking at everyone paying close attention to her.

"All of your com's have built in GPS locators, so not only can we communicate with one another I can keep track of everyone's whereabouts in case there is separation" she said.

"As long as everyone has their com's in place I will know where everyone is, and we can all get out of here alive; and together" she said smiling at everyone.

Max smiled and kissed Stacy on the forehead as she smiled back knowing he was proud of her, and her technical skills.

"Lets load up, we have a party to attend" Max said with a grin to everyone nodding to Crusher Davis and Jose Martin, who nodded back grabbing the extra weapons bags they had packed earlier from the back of Bruno; placing them ALL in the back of the limo Crusher was driving.

They all climbed into the back of the limousines as Jose & Crusher got into the drivers seats.

Jake closed the door behind his wife and leaned into the open passenger window to kiss Linda whispering "We're going to get him back; trust family" smiling at her then turning and getting into the passenger seat next to Jose Martin.

Jose & Crusher pulled out of the roadside rest stop and headed down the NC Parkway towards Covington Industries with Stacy Mason close behind driving Bruno.

After driving about ten minutes they pulled off the parkway onto the large signed entrance way for Covington Industries almost instantly to bright red limousine break lights backed up in a line to get through the security gate of Covington Industries.

As the two limo's stood in line for the security check Stacy Mason drove past the gate nonchalantly seeing Officer James Murphy standing at the security gate helping to inspect the cars as they entered the gated compound.

Stacy said "Murphy's on site" knowing her dad would understand that James Murphy was now in position to help them at the front gate.

Max replied "Copy that Eagle" giving Tyler a smile.

Max thought Stacy should have a cool code name since she was going to be stuck inside the communications van during this mission.

Max knew that an "Eagle" would soar above its prey watching & calculating its next move before striking. That's what Stacy was for all of them; she was their eyes and ears inside the party; she WAS they're Eagle.

Police officer James Murphy smiled as he saw Stacy Mason drive past the main gate knowing where she was going to position Bruno to help her dad and his team. He would meet up with her as soon as he helped Max and the others get through the gate in the two confiscated limousines.

Having been assigned by Captain Hargrove to help with the Covington Industries launch party security, Murphy was still dressed in his patrol uniform outside the closed front gate; assisting one of Colonel Howler's heavily armed security guards.

The two of them inspected each limousine as it drove up to the gate; looking into the passenger, driver, and trunk compartments; making sure there wasn't anything dangerous or explosive inside before allowing it to enter the compound.

Murphy could see that Max's two limousines were next in line and knew he needed a distraction to get the guard away from inspecting the trunks. Seeing that the guard was drinking a cup of coffee to stay warm in the brisk November air he purposely walked into the tall, muscular guard spilling his hot cup of coffee all over the front of his tactical gear he was wearing.

"You stupid son of a bitch, look what the fuck you did" he said angrily to Murphy looking at his tactical vest and seeing the coffee spilled onto his extra ammunition magazines for his AR-15 rifle he was holding.

"Sorry, I didn't see you standing so close" Murphy said to the soaking wet guard.

"Why don't I take the next couple of cars by myself while you go clean that off your vest" Murphy said sounding sincerely apologetic seeing the guard continue to brush beads of coffee off of his chest.

The guard looked pissed at Murphy but decided his idea of cleaning off his vest was a good one and started walking through the open gate as the next limousine cleared inspection.

Crusher Davis pulled his car up to the front gate and rolled down his window and smiled at Murphy, who then stuck his head inside the opened passenger window to see Yuki Amikura & Ochi Osaka sitting in the backseat smiling back at him.

Yuki handed Murphy her gold invitation as he glanced back at the other guard who controlled the opening of the gate knowing he was watching him as he looked it over and quickly handed it back to her.

Crusher popped the trunk open from inside and Murphy did a quick open & close knowing there were several bags of weapons sitting inside, then waving to the guard inside the guardhouse that the inspection was complete and it was okay to open the gate.

Yuki smiled from the open window and whispered to Murphy "You & Stacy be careful" slowly rolling up the window again.

Crusher watched as the gate opened, driving the limo through seeing the Covington's building lit up like a Christmas tree with different bright colored spotlights shining up & down the side of the five story building.

Jose Martin drove up as the gate slowly closed, rolling down his window to smile and wink at Murphy who looked inside so the guard wouldn't become suspicious seeing Jake sitting beside Jose.

Max lowered the back window and handed Murphy the invitation; who glanced at it and gave it back to him.

Murphy could see Linda & Tyler sitting across from Max as he looked inside the window and smiled at the two beautifully dressed ladies.

"Get back to MY daughter as soon as you can" Max said to Murphy who nodded in agreement with him. "I have a feeling this is all going to go bad REAL soon" Max informed Murphy who agreed with him.

"Stacy knows to send me a fake dispatch call as soon as everyone is inside the compound" Murphy relayed to Max. "That will get me out of here and back to her" Murphy continued.

Linda looked at her friend and colleague through the window and said "Be careful James".

"Yes ma'am" Murphy replied with a smile back to his partner.

Seeing that the guard he spilled coffee on was returning Murphy had to ask Max since the guard could hear him "Could you pop the trunk for me sir?" knowing the bags of weapons were already inside the compound in Crusher's limousine, and to keep his cover from being blown.

Jose Martin opened the trunk from inside the car watching in the side mirror as the guard and Murphy walked around to the back as the trunk lid popped open. Murphy and the guard looked it over for a moment seeing it was completely clean & empty inside.

Murphy closed the trunk and smiled at Max saying "Enjoy the party" motioning to the guardhouse to open the gate.

The security gate slowly slid across the driveway allowing Jose Martin to drive through and pull up next to Crusher Davis's limousine already parked on the less visible side of the building.

"All available units, we've got a 211 in progress at Stoney's Café; does anyone copy?" the voice said from Murphy's radio on his belt.

Murphy pulled the radio off his belt and spoke into it "This is Officer Murphy; I'm close by I can take it, requesting backup; copy" he said looking at the guard standing next to him.

"Roger that Officer Murphy, backup in route" the female voice replied back over his radio.

Murphy clipped his radio back to his gun belt looked at the guard and smiled knowing it was Stacy Mason calling him from the armored vehicle saying "Duty calls", then turned and headed to his patrol car sitting on the side of the road near the front gate.

Everyone got out and stood in front of the two limousines situating their attire before they went in. Max pulled his XD handgun out of his shoulder holster from inside his tuxedo jacket, checked the magazine and put it back inside so no one could see it.

Crusher, Jake, Jose, and Ochi did the same with the guns they were carrying inside their jackets then looked over at Tyler, Linda, and Yuki standing in front of them wondering where they were going to put guns; seeing they were all three wearing full length evening gowns to the party.

Max and Jake just smiled when they saw Tyler and Linda hike up their dresses to each pull a small .380 automatic pistol from thigh holsters they were both wearing.

They each checked the magazines then re-holstered them pulling their dresses back down over their long sexy legs, without hesitation or embarrassment.

Yuki Amikura stood there watching Tyler & Linda pull their dresses back down over their handguns seeing Jose Martin & Crusher Davis raise an eyebrow to what the two brazen women just did, thinking she would be to shy to do something like that in front of men she really didn't know all that well.

Max knew that the plan was for Jake, Jose, and Crusher to go in as waiters so they could move around the building more freely, but his maternal instincts kicked in realizing he didn't like the idea that his two "other daughters" Yuki & Ochi were going in without any backup other than each other.

"I'm making a small change to the plan" Max said getting everyone's attention.

"Crusher will go in with Yuki & Ochi as part of Yuki Amikura, the electronic tycoon's protection detail" Max said to the group.

Yuri looked at Max turning a bit red in the face with embarrassment knowing Max knew how rich she was now seeing him smile then say to her "That's okay sweetheart, we all have our own reasons for doing things" he said trying to make her feel better.

"Let's move out; find Parker, destroy this damn satellite, and kick Howler & the Covington's asses" Max said watching everyone nod in agreement with him.

Max grabbed Jake by the arm as he was walking past and looked at his son saying "Don't let the kills of YOUR father define you son; listen to your gut when you take on Howler tonight".

Jake smiled and said "I love you pop" giving him a big hug knowing he was torn between his pacifist ways and wanting to kill Howler for kidnapping his son.

"REALLY; you two are going to hug it out while my little nephew is in there scared to death" Stacy said boldly over their com's hearing everything everyone said sitting in the surveillance van outside the perimeter of Covington's high security fence.

"Looks like our eagle has a sharp beak" Max said to Jake with a laugh.

"Move out Admiral" Stacy ordered ignoring what her dad said as she watched the colored dots start moving to the front of the building.

Jake and Jose Martin headed the other way from the group slowly and stealthily moving towards the back entrance.

They both stood behind a large oak tree observing waiters & waitresses going in and out of a catering truck carrying trays they both assumed were full of food for the party guests.

Two waiters were hanging outside the open back door next to the white van with "Raleigh Catering" on the side panels smoking cigarettes and chatting with each other. They were both wearing black trousers, white long sleeved dress shirts, black button down vests, and bright red neck ties.

"Looks like were going to have to make friends" Jake said to Jose with a grin.

"Don't you mean knock their punk asses out and take their clothes" Jose asked rolling his eyes to his Captain.

"Well yeah, but if it makes you feel any better we only have to take their vests & ties" Jake said with a sheepish grin.

"Oh, is that all?" Jose replied a bit annoyed seeing the grin on Jake's face.

"You DO get it from your father" Jose said cryptically seeing Jake playfully smile and shrug his shoulders agreeing with his insinuation that he and his father Max have the same sarcastic attitude when it comes to dealing with bad guys.

They slowly moved behind the two waiters and put them both in choke holds pulling them away from the doorway; dragging them both behind the catering truck, squeezing their necks tightly as they both struggled a bit finally losing consciousness.

They carefully lowered the two unconscious men behind some bushes along the building wall to hide their bodies, quickly removing their vests and ties.

Jake patted both unconscious men on the head saying "Just be thankful neither of you are around when the shooting starts" smiling over at Jose who just shook his head.

Both Jake and Jose were already wearing black trousers, and long sleeved white dress shirts from the suits they both got from the tailor back at Yuki's hotel, so they only needed the black vest & red tie to make them fit in with the wait staff hired by the Covington's.

They put on the vests and ties, leaving their jackets with the two unconscious waiters and nonchalantly walked over to the back of the van. They each picked up a tray that they both could now see had different types of hor d'vores on them made special for the Covington party tonight and went inside the building.

Max, Tyler, and Linda Mason walked up to the front entrance and presented their invitation to the well dressed security guard standing there.

The guard looked at it carefully then opened the door for them saying "Enjoy the party" as the three of them walked slowly into the main lobby of the building.

Max took Tyler's hand and slowly walked with her through the door, with Linda following to the left of them so they could observe and surmise the entire room before doing anything.

They noticed that the Covington's had gone all out for this party; that they spared no expense; from the long stem crystal champagne glasses, the huge open bar in the corner, the well dressed waiters & waitresses bringing around trays of champagne & hor'dvores, and the small four piece orchestra playing on the other side of the room gave the large lobby the pomp & circumstance of a high class luxury event.

The room was decorated with Nathaniel & Evelyn Covington's many profile pictures of their achievements with Covington Industries over the years depicting them as the perfect mother & son entrepreneurs.

Max, Tyler, and Linda were offered a glass of champagne by one of the waiters, each taking a glass noticing the bright lights all around the room making the glasses sparkle. They started walking around and mingling with the fifty or sixty well dressed guests looking at the various pictures on the walls as they all three took small sips of the champagne to blend in with everyone else in the room.

Max thought it was a bit arrogant seeing Nathaniel's picture of him receiving his World Karate Association championship belt, but then he took a closer look and noticed someone in the picture's background; Tanaka Amikura. Covington had a connection to the Amikura's for years it seemed to Max, knowing this picture was taken just three years ago because of the date on the description caption under the picture.

Max knew Yuki could hear him in her ear com and said as he stood beside Tyler & Linda looking closely at the picture "Seeing what I'm seeing; looks like the Covington's had a hand in helping Tanaka finance his GBN attack last year".

Just as he finished his statement he heard someone behind him say "It's a shame you don't compete, it would have been interesting for you & I to go against one another".

Max recognized the voice to be Nathaniel Covington's and he smiled at Tyler who gave him a stern look knowing he was about to "poke the bear in the cage" as he loved to put it.

Max turned around to see both Nathaniel & Evelyn Covington and their bodyguard Simon standing right behind the three of them smiling from ear to ear.

Nathaniel Covington was smartly dressed in a solid white suit, bright red shirt, a white tie, and white shoes. Max could see the amusement he had in his eyes as he stared at him.

Max thought for a moment as he looked Evelyn Covington up and down, that she actually looked lovely in her bright red, sequined, full length evening dress then realized who she really was; a kidnapping, human trafficking sociopath who preyed on little children for money.

The Covington's bodyguard Simon looked like he came from the "70's disco era" Max thought with a snicker giving the large man a condescending grin.

He was wearing a light brown Na'rew jacket that buttoned up at the collar, with large sleeves, matching bell-bottom trousers, and brown high heeled boots that zipped up the side.

Max smiled at Nathaniel as Tyler gently squeezed his arm to remind him to stay cool as he said "I only fight when I have too; but I do make exceptions for arrogant little pricks who hide behind their mommies; and bully others" he said with a grin to Nathaniel Covington staring him in the eyes.

Evelyn Covington could see Max Mason was getting to her son and spoke quickly before either Max or her son could say anything else to one another.

She looked at Linda Mason and asked with a smile "Where is your husband Jacob tonight?" seeing Linda with Max and Tyler, knowing she saw him earlier being tortured by Howler & his men.

Linda could see the protective look both Max & Tyler gave her as she said "Jake had other plans with a couple of friends tonight".

"I hope he's taking good care of that charming little boy of yours while mommy is out on the town" Evelyn Covington said with an evil grin.

Tyler could see Linda was getting pissed at what Evelyn Covington said and knew Max needed them all to stay focused on the mission, but she knew the woman needed to be put in her place.

Tyler stepped in front of Linda grinning at Nathaniel Covington, then looked his mother in the eyes and said with a stern voice "You're lucky I don't break that scrawny little chicken neck of yours right here and now old woman; if you know what's good for you you'll give the boy to his mother before SHE kills you".

"Ladies, ladies it's a party; no need for hostilities tonight we're having a celebration" Nathaniel Covington said with a smile to everyone grabbing his mother's arm and walking her away because he could see the anger in her eyes at what Tyler had just said to her.

Nathaniel Covington started walking towards the other guests with his mother but turned and gave Max a arrogant grin before turning to talk to another guest.

Yuki Amikura, Ochi Osaka, and Crusher Davis had just walked into the building when Yuki heard over her com what Max said about her dead brother Tanaka.

Yuki felt a bit sick to her stomach knowing that the Covington's, along with her cousin Noki helped fund the terrorism plots that her older brother designed; that killed a lot of innocent people over the past few years.

She grabbed Crusher's arm to steady herself looking at Ochi who looked concerned for her friend. Crusher grabbed her hand and held it tight looking into her sad, guilt ridden eyes saying "Don't worry pretty lady I won't let you go" he said with a smile to her.

Just as Yuki settled herself finding comfort with what Crusher

Davis said, Nathaniel & Evelyn Covington walked up to the three of them and smiled.

"Miss Amikura, how delightful you were able to come tonight" Nathaniel said with a big smile then bowing to her in the Japanese custom.

Yuki bowed back to Covington even though she knew he was a terrorist along with her brother & cousin but did not wish to disrespect her Japanese upbringing.

"And who might this VERY large, handsome, and menacing gentleman be?" Covington asked looking up at Crusher Davis who was a good 8" inches taller then he was.

"This is my private security specialist Lamar Davis" Yuki said looking Covington sternly in the eye.

"There has been some idol talk of a corporate takeover by my competitors; you wouldn't know anything about that would you Mr. Covington, after all YOU are one of my competitors are you not?" Yuki continued seeing Ochi smile with approval at what she said to Nathaniel Covington.

"Your cousin Noki and I have done a little business over the past couple of years but nothing that you should worry about" Covington said looking at his mother and smiling.

"That business ends tonight Mr. Covington" Yuki said sternly staring Nathaniel Covington in the face.

"You might want to discuss that with your cousin; you can find him up in the 4th floor conference room" Covington said with a smile as he turned to meet more guests with his mother under his arm.

Yuki looked at both Ochi and Crusher with anger in her eyes knowing her cousin Noki was already here waiting for her.

The Covington's walked a couple of feet towards the crowd of guests then Nathaniel Covington stopped, turned, and smiled at Yuki saying "Your cousin wanted me to remind you that you should have a sword when you meet him tonight; because he'll have one".

Ochi Osaka took a step towards Nathaniel with anger on her face,

214

but was gently grabbed by the arm by Yuki who smiled at her and said "We both knew it was going to come to this" trying to make Ochi understand that her cousin Noki wanted her dead so he could take over the company she never really wanted, but understood why her uncle gave it to her and not him.

Just as Yuki finished talking to Ochi a familiar voice behind them asked "Would you folks like some champagne?"

The three of them turned to see Jose Martin standing in front of them smiling, wearing a waiter's outfit and holding a tray of champagne glasses filled with the bubbly alcohol.

Yuki & Ochi quickly smirked thinking Jose looked good as a waiter, then they each took a glass from his tray.

They both kind of stared at Jose & Crusher looking at one another wondering what was going to happen next with the two friends.

Jose looked at Crusher who had a big grin on his face and quickly said "If you tell ANYONE about this, I'll make sure you have enough parking tickets to pay for years; do we understand each other Sergeant?" Jose said playfully embarrassed he was waiting on his large muscular friend.

"Yes Sir Lieutenant" Crusher said with a smile taking the last glass of champagne off his tray, and reaching into his pants pocket to pull out a one dollar bill placing the small tip on the tray Jose was still holding giving him a small chuckle.

"Really, a dollar that's all you got; you and me are going to have a long conversation about this if we get out of here alive" Jose said with a grin to his friend and trusted colleague.

"Copy that sir" Crusher replied smiling.

Max thought all this witty banter had gone on long enough and spoke up knowing everyone could hear him in their com's "Time to focus everyone, who's got eyes on the Covington's?" he asked.

"I do" Jake Mason said having kept a low profile until now.

Just as Jake spoke he turned to stand face to face with Colonel Howler and two of his mercenaries as one stuck the barrel of his handgun into Jake's ribs keeping it well hidden from the rest of the guests.

"Hey there Colonel, what took you so long?" Jake asked with a sheepish grin.

"You're so predictable Jake, I knew you'd show up here eventually; never thought you'd be working the party though" Howler said laughing, standing in front of Jake Mason wearing a dark suit, white shirt, and black tie.

"I'm just here to ask you one more time for my son Colonel; no one has to die tonight" Jake said looking at Howler hoping to see some compassion for his little boy.

"Your son's leaving HERE with a good family; something you won't have to worry about because you'll be dead" Howler replied looking at his two companions and laughing at Jake who stood there smiling at him.

"What are you smiling about asshole?" Howler asked Jake who leaned in to whisper something to him.

"You fucked up Colonel; you should know better than to give up your "asset" to your enemy; now I know my son is here in the building" Jake replied still smiling.

"I may not be around to burn this place to the ground looking for my son, but my wife & my dad will" Jake said with a grin knowing his dad Max Mason heard every word he and Howler said.

Howler was about to say something to Jake when one of his guards whispered in his ear "Sir, we're getting several different radio signals from outside the perimeter fence; we believe someone is outside monitoring our frequencies here inside" he said quietly so Jake couldn't hear.

"Send out an assault team and neutralize the problem" Howler said looking at the guard sternly.

"Yes sir" the guard replied turning and leaving through the crowded lobby.

Everyone heard what Howler said through Jake's com

understanding Howler was sending a mercenary kill team out to Stacy sitting alone in the armored surveillance van.

"Eagle, looks like the jig is up sweetheart; time to see how well built Bruno is" Max said in front of Tyler & Linda with a big grin believing in his children's tech skills.

"Aye aye Admiral" Stacy said with a giggle in her voice so everyone knew not to worry about her. "Just go get my nephew" she said to her dad.

"Copy that Eagle" Linda replied knowing that Stacy needed to hear from Parker's mom knowing her brother Jake was being held at gunpoint by Howler and his men.

"Everyone move out on their targets; remember recon ONLY until we have eyes on Parker" Max said loudly enough that everyone could hear clearly in their com's.

"Jose, on Jake" Max said knowing Jose & Jake could hear him.

"Yes sir Admiral" Jose replied" "I got you Captain" Jose said in Jake's ear com listening to Stacy give him directions towards him & Howler.

Jake continued to smile at Howler and his two mercenaries holding him with the gun still in his ribs knowing Jose was on his way to them.

"Take him out back and put a bullet in his head" Howler said to the two men holding Jake who continued to smile at him without fear.

"You can't say I didn't give you a fair enough chance Colonel" Jake said as Howler turned to walk away from him.

"Trust me Colonel, you WON'T like what happens tonight if I walk out that door without my son" Jake said sternly, now giving Howler the evil look of a father protecting his family.

Howler started laughing uncontrollably at Jake Mason then turned and walked away as the two men dragged Jake towards the back entrance of the building.

CHAPTER THIRTEEN

Stacy Mason sat patiently monitoring the computer video screen in front of her, listening to her team and other guests through their sensitive ear com's. She watched each of them move slowly throughout the 1st floor of the Covington Industries building mingling with the large crowd when she was startled by the loud beeping sound of the "proximity" motion alarm now going off inside the van.

She quickly switched the video screen from her team's GPS locations to Bruno's outside cameras to see four heavily armed men approach from each side; on four separate screens on her monitor, quietly surrounding the van.

Stacy smiled as all four men opened fire with machine-guns on the heavily armored van knowing it was completely bullet-proof.

She watched as the bullets bounced off ricocheting back towards each of them seeing them dive to the ground so not to get hit by one of their own stray rounds.

"Looks like I've got company" Stacy said out loud with a giggle knowing everyone could hear her in their com's.

"Eagle, are you compromised; copy?" Max asked looking around, then at Tyler and Linda with concern.

"I'm good daddy, Bruno is doing great" Stacy said smiling, looking at all four video screens watching the mercenaries get up off the ground and reload their weapons.

Stacy grabbed the firing-control stick on her console, and flicked the safety switch off on the side to expose the trigger, arming each .50 caliber mini-machine-gun on all four sides of the van. She flipped another switch that exposed and extended out the barrels from behind sliding panels on each side of the van.

One by one she slowly moved the stick back and forth to lock onto each of the deadly mercenaries she could see creeping up on the vehicle a second time; pulling the trigger, watching the screen as the bullets riddled each of their bodies. She continued to move each camera back and forth around the perimeter of the van seeing that there were no more threats, re-engaging the safety back on the guns.

"It's like playing video games" Stacy said with a snicker seeing the four dead bodies lying on the ground.

"Let's stay focused Lieutenant" Max said into her headphones, but feeling a bit less anxious knowing she was alright; giving Tyler and Linda a proud smile.

"Yes sir" Stacy replied with a grin knowing her father was worried about her.

Just as Stacy switched back to the screen monitoring her team's com's and locations the motion alarm sounded off again, beeping loudly that someone else was approaching the armored van.

She switched back to the four outside cameras to see a smiling James Murphy standing outside the van's entry door with his gun in his hand looking directly into the camera.

Murphy had hurried back to Stacy's location from the Covington's front gate after she sent the fake dispatch call to his radio. He parked his patrol car on a nearby dirt road when he heard both sets of machine-gun fire as he left the car.

He walked cautiously up to where the van was parked, carefully moving around it seeing the four dead bodies lying on the ground all with multiple gunshots to their torsos, their last bit of body heat rising through their wounds up into the cold North Carolina darkness.

He stood looking around, not seeing anyone else then stood in front of the van's large secured door looking up again at the video camera.

Stacy was happy to see the young handsome police officer jumping out of her chair to open the van door so he could join her inside. She stood and smiled at Murphy as the door slid back revealing her inside.

She stepped back so he could climb into the van when several loud close range shots rang out hitting Murphy in the back knocking him forward and on top of her pinning Stacy to the floor of the van.

Stacy could hear footsteps in the grass coming towards the open door way of the van as the cold November air filled her lungs realizing Murphy was not conscious; his weight pinned her to the floor of the van his 1911 handgun still in his hand.

"Targets have been neutralized; perimeter secured Colonel, copy" the voice outside the van said as Stacy could see that James Murphy wasn't moving and seeing blood coming from his mouth continuing to lay on top of her.

The crack of a twig on the ground outside the van told Stacy that the assailant was coming towards the van to check on the bodies lying inside.

She could see that Murphy was still unconscious but now breathing. His bulletproof vest saved their lives and she knew she had to do something or they both would be dead for sure this time.

She grabbed Murphy's 1911 handgun that was still in his left hand and quickly rolled his body partially over firing four rounds directly outside the door at the lone mercenary standing there just inches from the doorway using Murphy and his vest as a human shield.

The bullets riddled the surprised mercenary knocking him to the ground. Stacy quickly rolled Murphy's heavy body off of her and stood up looking at the mercenary from the doorway with Murphy's gun still trained on him. She could see he wasn't much older than she was, as she watched him take his last breath.

"Stacy are you okay, copy" Max said over the van's console speakers having listened to what took place outside the van with Howler's man.

Just as Stacy was about to confirm that she & James Murphy were okay Murphy rolled over and looked up at Stacy asking "Are YOU okay?"

Stacy smiled hearing what Murphy said and leaned down and kissed him hard and long knowing he was more concerned for her well being then his own.

"Stacy, come in NOW" Max bellowed over the loud speaker in the van.

Stacy smiled at Murphy as she got up hearing her dad and pushed the talk back button replying "Really dad, can't a girl show a little appreciation to someone for saving her life without you interrupting; it's like I'm in high school again" she said laughing as she watched Murphy get up and remove his jacket, shirt, and vest to reveal multiple black & blue bruises on his back where the bullets hit him.

"That's gotta hurt" Stacy said to Murphy seeing the discoloration practically covering his entire back, yet smiled at his chiseled muscular physic.

"Feels like my Aunt Edna's mule that kicked me when I was 10; I didn't like that either" Murphy replied with a big country boy grin as he wiped the blood from his cut lip on his shirt sleeve before putting it back on.

"Are you okay Officer Murphy?" Max asked rolling his eyes seeing the evil look Tyler was giving him to be a little more compassionate and appreciative to the young man that just saved his daughter's life.

"Yes Sir, we're both good" Murphy replied looking at Stacy Mason sitting back down at the console and smiling as he put his Kevlar vest back on over his uniform shirt.

Just as Max was about to reply back to Stacy & Murphy a loud voice came over the speaker system in the building saying "Welcome ladies & gentlemen; my mother and I would like to thank you all for coming to witness history tonight".

Max, Tyler, and Linda looked at one another with contempt because they knew what the Covington's were really doing tonight.

They looked towards the large decorated stage seeing Nathaniel & Evelyn Covington standing there in front of a microphone stand smiling at everyone.

"In exactly fifteen minutes, Covington Industries will change how the world sees cell phone technology; bringing in a new era of personal communication" Nathaniel Covington said as he pointed to the countdown clock over the elevator door.

He looked at Max from across the room and smiled seeing the scowl on his face. He leaned down and kissed his mother Evelyn on the cheek then spoke again into the microphone "We will countdown the last minute together" he said continuing to stare at Max Mason.

"Looks like our boy believes his insane plan is going to work, how about we do our best to fuck it up for him" Max said with a grin returning Nathaniel's stare from the back of the room knowing everyone could hear him in their com's.

Colonel Howler's two men dragged Jake Mason quietly through the crowd of guests and out the back door throwing him hard to the cold ground in front of the catering truck. They each took their guns and tightened silencers on the muzzles as Jake got to his feet.

The back door opened and Howler's men could see a waiter walking out yelling back into the doorway "I'm taking a smoke break, I'll be right back" making the two armed mercenaries put their guns behind their backs to hide them from him.

"I see you guys had the same idea I did" he said to the three men as he closed the door behind him, pulling a pack of cigarettes from his back pocket. He smiled at the three of them then offered the pack to the closest guard to him.

The waiter came out of the shadows into the moonlight so everyone could finally see his face as he lit a cigarette hanging from his lips with a Zippo lighter.

Jake rolled his eyes at the waiter now seeing it was Jose Martin as the young security guard plucked a cigarette out of the paper pack.

One of the men moved closer to Jake his gun still behind his back. Jake Mason had a grin on his face as the other mercenary said to Jose "Those things will kill you".

Jose smiled then nodded to Jake, just as he was about to light the guard's cigarette. Jose turned quickly and hit the unsuspecting guard hard in the face with his right fist knocking the guard backwards against the catering truck.

"Yep, they sure will" he said watching Jake turn and hit the guard next to him upside the jaw with his fist, then quickly give him a hard right forearm to his face knocking the young guard out cold dropping him to the cold ground.

Jose Martin turned back to the guard he hit who had collected himself after hitting the side of the truck turning his handgun on Jose. Jose reacted quickly with a spin kick to the guard's gun hand knocking the bullet off course as the shot exploded from the barrel hitting the concrete building across from them.

Jose's foot impact sent the handgun flying towards the building surprising the guard who stood there watching it fly from his hand, hitting the wall, and falling to the ground. Jose hit the guard three times rapidly, twice in the face and once in the throat causing him to slump to his knees grabbing his throat with both hands having a hard time breathing.

Jose Martin leaned down and hit him in the jaw one more time to watch him fall face first into the cold grass unconscious then looked over at Jake with a grin.

"Cutting it kind of close weren't you Lieutenant?" Jake asked Jose with a grin on his face looking down at the two incapacitated guards Howler assigned to kill him.

"I HAD to serve Crusher champagne, making you sweat a little was the least I could do Captain" Jose said with a smirk on his face.

Jose touched his com in his ear making sure it hadn't dislodged and said "I have Jake" even though he knew their conversation with Howler's men could be heard by everyone.

"Since the two of you are outside already, grab the bags from the limo and bring them inside" Max said figuring they could find some secluded place to hide them in this large room without security detecting them.

Max, Tyler, and Linda slowly moved closer to the stage gently moving past guests smiling and watching as guards stood beside the closed elevator doors.

They continued to listen to Nathaniel Covington's boring speech of cellular world domination from the stage then heard him say "Thank you so much for coming, enjoy the champagne" as they watched both he and his mother walk down the stage stairs. They hugged each other and kissed one another on the cheek then parted ways walking in opposite directions.

Evelyn Covington walked to the elevator pushed the button, and walked in with both guards that were standing there when the doors opened then closed behind them.

"I guess you ladies are up" Max said with a grin to Tyler & Linda watching the elevator door close with Evelyn Covington inside from across the room.

"I can't promise this will go quietly as planned Max" Linda said looking at her father-in-law knowing that Evelyn Covington had her son somewhere in the building.

"I know sweetheart; focus on getting Parker back" Max replied.

"I really don't care how loud it gets as long as my grandson is safe; probably going to make a bit of noise myself" Max said with a chuckle smiling at Linda then hugging her tight looking over at Tyler with a grin.

"Everyone knows their assignments, stick to the plan" Max said knowing everyone including Stacy & Murphy could hear him.

"Jake on me" Max said seeing his son and Jose Martin coming from the side entrance with their weapons bags in hand.

"I see you were able to make it tonight Admiral" Max heard behind him glancing over his shoulder to see Howler smiling with two of his men, standing in back of him.

Max turned to face the three men seeing Colonel Howler was nicely dressed in a suit & tie, while both of his men were dressed in tactical uniforms and wearing side arms.

"Wouldn't have missed it for the world" Max replied with a sheepish grin.

Howler watched as Tyler and Linda both gave him an evil stare slowly walking towards the elevator saying out loud "I hope it wasn't something I said; OR did" smiling at Max knowing HE was the reason they both left because of the several attempts on their lives.

"Nah, they wanted to go powder their noses before all the fun started; WE never gave you a second thought Colonel" Max replied chuckling with a grin seeing he was getting to Covington's so-called head of security by the angry scowl on his face.

The elevator door slowly opened and Evelyn Covington casually walked into a huge communications control room, the two guards that followed her standing behind the elderly matriarch.

The room was big with two rows of five rather large video screens hanging on the wall above the control room's electronic consoles. There were four audio/video technicians sitting behind the complicated consoles filled with buttons & switches managing the controls.

"Is everyone online?" Evelyn Covington asked as she stood behind one of the technicians then looked up at the video screens to see ten different faces staring back at her.

"Yes ma'am" the young male tech replied looking up at her.

"Then let's begin, shall we" she said with a smile.

Tyler and Linda stood at the door waiting for the elevator wondering why it was taking so long when Linda with a confused look on her face wondered out loud to Tyler "Something's weird; where did she go?"

"What do you mean?" Tyler replied seeing the look Linda was giving her.

"The three of us watched her get in the elevator, but I didn't see her getting off on any of the floors above" Linda said pointing at the floor indicator above the door still seeing a bright red "one".

A waiter carrying a tray of champagne slowly walked by the two women still waiting on the elevator when Linda gently grabbed his arm and asked "Where's the ladies room?" with a smile.

"It's on the 2nd floor ma'am" the polite young man replied offering them both another glass of bubbly.

The waiter walked away after they said "No thank you" causing both Linda & Tyler to suspect that Evelyn Covington left the elevator by some other means.

Tyler thought about what Linda said, lowered her head and asked "Stacy, is there another floor in this building that we don't know about?"

Stacy Mason and Officer James Murphy looked at each other strangely at what Tyler asked as they continued to monitor everyone's com's from the van outside the Covington compound.

Stacy diligently typed on her computer keyboard as she and Murphy scanned the screen for what Tyler asked about.

"Nice call mom" Stacy replied with a giggle in her voice knowing calling her mom made Tyler smile.

"The Covington building was built on top of an old basement. The house burned down many years ago, some say suspiciously" she replied.

"There's also an underground tunnel that runs all the way to the stables on the other side of their home; behind the large building you're in now" Stacy said continuing to read the blueprints on her computer screen.

"That's why the elevator didn't move up, it was going down" Tyler said smiling at Linda

"The Covington's must have bought off the building inspector because there's no building permits, or documented plans registered with the county's zoning office" Stacy replied smiling at Murphy.

"Nice work sweetie" Tyler said to Stacy as she smiled at Linda standing beside her.

"You two be careful, that woman is a snake" Stacy replied referring to Evelyn Covington.

"Copy that eagle" Linda said with a grin to Tyler.

Max was listening to the entire conversation between his three girls thinking how lucky he was to have such brilliant, and brave women in his life as he continued to keep an eye on Nathaniel Covington now standing with Simon, and Howler across the room.

Max quickly glanced around the large room to see Jose Martin and his son Jake kneeling at the far end of the table near the champagne station.

He could see they both had their protective vests on and were pulling out AR-15 rifles from the large black duffle bags they brought in.

Jake looked over at his dad and smiled playfully saying "What's up pop?" as he pulled the slide back to chamber the first round in his rifle.

Max smiled and rolled his eyes at his boy knowing he was about to do what HE normally did in these situations "poke the bear in the cage".

Max noticed that the elevator door opened and watched as both Tyler and Linda walked in. They quickly turned to face the crowd seeing everyone having a good time.

Tyler smiled at him from across the room and said out loud "I love you" knowing Max could hear her.

"I love you too; but we need to have a serious talk about your earlier gung-ho attitude young lady" Max replied laughing remembering what she said to Evelyn Covington, calling her out about kidnapping Parker.

"Hon, the lady's a psychopathic bitch" Tyler said with a grin as the elevator doors closed in front of her and Linda Mason.

"Can we get back to saving MY nephew, and not having any of

my family get killed" Stacy said over everyone's com's telling everyone to focus in her own loving way.

"Copy that eagle" both Linda & Tyler said as they both raised their dresses to grab their concealed handguns from their garter holsters.

Tyler looked at the elevator floor buttons near the door and saw a small keypad just below them figuring they needed a security code to go down to the secret basement the Covington's were trying to hide from everyone.

"Eagle we need access to a keypad security code" Tyler said hoping Stacy could still hear her being closed inside the elevator.

Stacy furiously typed on her keyboard looking at her video screen, rewriting the security software code on the elevator keypad.

A few seconds later the red light on the keypad turned green and the elevator slowly started moving downward startling both Tyler and Linda for a moment.

"We're heading down, good luck everyone" Tyler said with concern on her face as she looked at Linda who smiled at her.

"Love you Jacob Mason" Linda said hoping her husband could still hear her as she checked to make sure there was a round chambered in her gun.

"Love you too baby" Jake replied getting smiles from both Linda & Tyler.

"Let's go get OUR boy" Jake said knowing everyone could hear him.

Jake smiled at his dad and slowly stood up from behind the champagne table while Jose continued to load the weapons from the bag as several women screamed seeing Jake standing there holding a machine-gun. Scared seeing the gunman, they moved quickly towards the building's exit.

Howler looked over at the screaming guests to see Jake Mason smiling at him, and fully armed now. He pulled his gun from inside his jacket and started firing at him making Jake duck down behind the table again beside a visibly pissed off Jose Martin.

"What?" Jake asked his friend with a smile as the bullets from Howler's gun hit the wall multiple times just above their heads.

Jake quickly looked up over the table that protected him and Jose to see Crusher Davis, Yuki Amikura, and Ochi Osaka running towards the east end emergency exit on their side of the building, but he could also see that Howler's armed mercenaries were coming through the other emergency exit across the room now.

Jose handed Jake a large black duffle bag which he quickly flung towards their three friends sliding it across the floor yelling "CRUSHER" to get his attention.

Crusher Davis smiled at his commanding officer and grabbed the bag by the handles as it stopped sliding next to the exit doorway. Yuki and Ochi were already through the door as he ran into the stairwell to join them. Bullets from the mercenary's machine-guns riddled up the steel & concrete wall into the door just as he got inside.

The panic stricken guests all started running towards the front entrance like a cattle stampede as Max watched from behind the pillar near the front of the building his XD handgun in his hand.

He could see Nathaniel Covington and his bodyguard Simon run towards the west end emergency stairwell using Howler's mercenaries as shields as they came through the doorway.

Covington saw Max standing behind the pillar and stopped at the doorway to give him an arrogant smile. Simon sneered at Max and pushed his boss through the exit door past two armed mercenaries now securing the door as they both headed up the stairs.

Jose Martin raised up from behind the table and fired his AR-15 machine-gun in a short burst; the bullets hitting two mercenaries standing just a few feet away from them, watching them both drop to the floor their guns sliding away from them.

He could see that neither of them were moving any longer, as blood started flowing on the floor underneath them. He quickly ducked back down behind the steel table as another barrage of bullets hit the wall above his head.

Jake Mason smiled at Jose as they both crouched down behind the large steel table they had flipped over earlier hearing the loud clanging noise the bullets made as they hit the hardened steel on the other side.

Jake turned to Jose grinning then said " I hope the girls are having a better time then we are" as Jake peeked over the top of the table to see Howler and his men heading towards the emergency exit door themselves following after Covington.

He looked back at Jose now seeing Howler heading towards the exit door asking "Was it something I said?" laughing as his friend just stared at him.

"Hey Colonel; you're not leaving before we have our little chat; are you?" Jake yelled standing straight up from behind the table smiling at Howler, seeing the contempt & anger in his eyes as he stood behind a couple of his mercenaries going through the doorway.

Howler's mercenaries pushed him towards the exit door to keep him safe seeing several of their comrades lying on the floor dead. Howler stopped for a moment just inside the doorway to look at both Jake & Max Mason through the small window in the door, across the room with a scowl on his face; pissed off that they weren't dead, then headed up the stairs as his four remaining men barricaded the door behind them.

Max smiled as he could see Howler through the door window one last time before he turned to face Jake and Jose Martin.

"Secure the perimeter; get the rest of these people out of the building, then lock this place down" Max said seeing that the room was filled with dead and wounded bodies lying on the floor both hostile and civilian.

"Yes sir Admiral" Jose said laying one of the black duffle bags at Max's feet.

Jake and Jose went back and forth helping the wounded guests out the front door sitting them down on the curb just as the first emergency medical vehicle came through the gate with the North Carolina State Police.

"Looks like we're going to have company REAL soon Pop" Jake said to Max as he watched his dad walk over to the large glass entrance door and stare at Police Captain Hargrove who was coordinating with the state police to help rescue the Covington's inside.

Hargrove stood on the sidewalk outside the entrance door and gave Max Mason an evil grin, knowing Max had figured out that he had something to do with helping Howler and the Covington's kidnap his grandson Parker; who was still inside the building.

Max smiled at Hargrove then turned to Jake & Jose saying "Let's go to work boys" as he opened the gun bag and pulled his protective vest, guns, and batons out.

Jake glanced out the doorway at Hargrove and smiled with a chuckle saying out loud "Linda's gonna kick his ass" looking over at his dad who smiled in agreement.

CHAPTER FOURTEEN

"Good evening ladies & gentlemen" Evelyn Covington said with a smile standing in front of the large video screens full of faces smiling back at her.

She continued smiling up at the screens saying "We are completely honored to have all of you here with us this evening" not knowing that at the same moment on the floor above her all Hell had broken loose with her son, Howler, and the Mason's.

"We have three beautiful offerings available tonight for your consideration; including a well raised five year old boy" she said moving elegantly in front of the communication consoles and technicians so her video guests could see her completely now.

Mrs. Covington looked at the technician closest to her and gave him a nod as he flipped a switch on his console then looked over at a steel door sliding open with a grin.

A tall, bald, well dressed man walked out with a sandy-haired little boy dressed in dark trousers, white short-sleeve shirt, and a black bow-tie. The young boy was calm and smiling at Mrs. Covington when he saw her. He looked around the room curiously seeing all the video screens thinking they looked cool.

Evelyn Covington motioned to the two guards that had accompanied her down the elevator smiling at them both ordering "Head down to the helicopter and have it ready to go in case of an emergency" as she watched them both nod in acknowledgment then walked through the door opening the young boy just came through. The door quickly closed as the two men went through.

Evelyn Covington walked over to the little boy and put her arm around him the two of them looking at one another smiling.

They both watched as the bald man walked over and stood in the corner of the room keeping watch over the proceedings.

"Everyone, this is Parker" she said looking up at the screens.

Looking back down at the young boy Mrs. Covington asked in a calm loving tone "How old are you Parker?"

"I'm five, almost six" the little boy replied smiling so everyone could see.

Evelyn Covington smiled at Parker Mason's polite response then motioned to the man in the corner who came forward bringing the little boy back to stand with him in the corner of the room.

"We will start the bidding for this adorable little boy at $1 million dollars" she said smiling; looking at everyone on the video screens.

Yuki Amikura, Ochi Osaka, and Crusher Davis with the weapons bag in hand made it up the emergency stairwell to the 4th floor exit door knowing Yuki's cousin Noki Amikura was waiting for her in the conference room.

The three of them stopped at the doorway cracking the door slightly to see if there were any hostiles in the hallway. Not seeing anyone Crusher pushed the door closed then went down to a knee on the concrete step opening the black duffle bag tossing his tuxedo jacket & tie on the steps below them.

He pulled out Yuki's white samurai sword, handing it to her as she stood there in her beautiful evening gown giving her a smile and a wink.

Yuki smiled back at Crusher then pulled the sword from it's scabbard, slowly sliding it back together seeing Ochi had sharpened the blade razor-sharp.

Crusher continued to pull out "ninja style" weapons out of the bag including Ochi's dual katana swords, steel shuriken throwing stars, and her matching 9mm handguns with shoulder-holsters.

He pulled out a small black protective vest, a black sports bra, bright blue calf-high boots, and a matching blue ninja uniform from the bottom of the bag looking at them a bit confused who they belonged too. He watched as Ochi checked her guns, and both of her blades still a bit bewildered about the clothes he was holding.

"Those are for me" Yuki said smiling as she undid the side of her evening gown stepping out of it without hesitation after it had fallen around her feet.

Yuki Amikura blushed a little as she stood there standing in front of Crusher Davis wearing only her high heels and her black lace panties. Her breasts stood high, her nipples erect because of the coolness of the stairwell as she reached her hand out to Crusher for her things.

Crusher hesitated, not being able to take his eyes off of her beautiful naked body with those long legs when he heard Ochi clear her throat; he lowered his eyes embarrassed that he stared for so long handing Yuki her clothes.

Yuki quickly pulled the sports bra and bullet-proof vest on over her head covering her exposed breasts; securing the sides then pulled her flared pants up over her panties and well curved buttocks tying them at her slim waist.

She pulled the ninja "hoodie" over her head situating it around her neck and waist.

She tossed her high heels into the bag and pulled on the ninja fighting boots; lacing them tightly, then slung her white samurai sword behind her back.

Yuki pulled the bright blue mask over her face then immediately pulled it back down leaning into Crusher to kiss him long and hard; their tongues dancing together in each other's mouths, surprising him.

Crusher Davis stood there smiling as she broke off the long erotic kiss and simply said "Yes ma'am" knowing that she wanted this to be more than just this one night with him.

Yuki looked at Ochi and smiled, then pulled her mask up over her face as she took several throwing stars from her best friend hearing her say "It's about time girl" placing the sharp blades inside the hidden pockets of her ninja jacket.

Crusher grabbed the AR-15 machine-gun out of the bag and loaded it, then checked his handgun from the shoulder holster he was wearing and replaced it looking at the two heavily armed women smiling.

"Let's go fire my cousin" Yuki said to her two companions who smiled at her attempt to make a joke.

She understood that her cousin was there to kill her and take over the family business for his own criminal enterprises.

Yuki already knew Noki had aligned himself with the Covington's & Colonel Howler, as well as financing her dead brother Tanaka's terrorist endeavors; ALL behind her back.

Max turned away from staring at Captain Hargrove through the glass entrance door now seeing the flashing lights of police cars & emergency vehicles surrounding Covington Industries corporate office building.

He evaluated the large party room seeing at least eight of Howler's mercenaries lying dead on the floor as well as a few dead civilians.

Max stood there shaking his head thinking this carnage should never have happened; he knew this was ALL on Howler & the Covington's.

Jake could see his dad was seriously pissed as he walked over and picked up the weapons bag after Max got everything out that belonged to him.

He knew not to say anything sarcastic or snide when he was this way, instead he quietly walked back to the steel table he & Jose hid behind when all the shooting started and placed the bag safely behind it on the floor in case Linda & Tyler needed it.

Max looked at his son with anger in his eyes "Lock this place down; make it hard for anyone to get in or out" he said giving his son a stern look. "I want Covington" he said angrily looking at a dead young woman lying on the floor a few feet away from them.

"Yes sir" Jake replied opening up his laptop seeing that the loss of innocent life really pissed his dad off.

Max took off his tuxedo jacket tossing it to the floor then grabbed his Kevlar vest from the bag and pulled it over his head securing the Velcro sides. He wrapped his tactical gun belt around his waist buckling it, pulling his twin batons out of their holsters and spinning them both around in his hands wanting to hit someone with them; especially Nathaniel Covington.

"Huh, dad" Stacy Mason said hesitantly into her father's ear.

"Not now sweetheart" Max replied not wanting to be abrupt with his daughter who understood what was going on inside the building.

"Admiral Cartwright is on a secure line wanting to speak to you" she said with apprehension in her voice.

"Patch him through Lieutenant" Max replied shaking his head and snickering as he looked out the window to see a couple of TV news trucks now sitting outside in the parking lot behind the police barricade.

"Hello Admiral" Max said starting the conversation as he smiled at Jake diligently typing on his computer keyboard.

"How's the party Max?" Cartwright asked knowing he was about to get a sarcastic answer from him.

"Not bad; shrimp puffs could use a little more seasoning" Max said with a snicker looking over and nodding at Jose Martin who was keeping the emergency stairwells secured in case any of Howler's men doubled back.

"How's your family enjoying the party?" the Admiral asked cryptically, in case they were being monitored inside the building.

Admiral Cartwright understood that Stacy, Jake, Linda, and Tyler were all there to help rescue Max's grandson Parker and to destroy the Covington's satellite sanctioned by him and the president, but he couldn't ask the question directly.

"They're ALL enjoying it at the moment sir" he replied looking over at the entry door having heard the magnetic door locks clamp down with a loud click.

Max looked over at Jake who smiled and gave him a thumb's up on securing all the outside doors in the building. "Time to go make friends Admiral" he said with a smirk in his voice watching his son pack up his computer and sling the bag over his shoulder.

"I've had a long talk with OUR friend and he swears nothing happened to warrant an investigation" Cartwright said waiting for a response.

"Do you believe him sir?" Max asked hesitantly.

"I've known the man for awhile, its possible he was set up by Covington" Cartwright replied with a sigh in his voice.

Max didn't comment on what the Admiral said instead he grabbed his AR-15 machine-gun and loaded it with a fresh magazine, then attached it to the sling he was wearing nodding to both Jake & Jose Martin he was ready to head up to the satellite control room up on the 3rd floor.

"When you see Agent Tyler tell her I sent those medical files she requested to Lieutenant Mason's "present" duty station" Cartwright said not sure why Tyler wanted them but knew they must be important because someone tried to erase them almost thirty years ago.

"Copy that Admiral" Max replied pulling the slide back on his rifle then releasing it as the bullet slid into the firing chamber.

"Good luck Max" Admiral Cartwright said understanding Max's silence meant he was open-minded to learning more about their friend's problem with Nathaniel Covington, not wanting to make a quick judgment.

"Copy that Admiral" Max replied hearing the click of the Admiral's phone disconnecting.

"Did you get all that Lieutenant?" Max asked waiting for his daughter's response.

"Yes sir, looking at the files now" Stacy replied staring at her computer screen as James Murphy sat next to her looking on as well.

"I've been trying to contact Tyler and Linda ever since they went below ground but they're not responding" Stacy said a bit concerned continuing to look for something in the medical files that Tyler thought was so important.

"I'm sure they're both fine; Jake & I would have felt something was wrong" Max replied knowing he had a special connection to Karen Tyler like Jake had with his wife Linda.

"Cross reference everyone's name in that file; see if there are ANY connections to the Covington's or to Howler" Max requested knowing if there was something to be found Stacy could find it.

"HOLY SHIT" Stacy declared out loud seeing the results of her speedy search pop up on the screen in front of her as she looked at Murphy with confusion on her face.

"Easy Lieutenant" Max replied with a snicker understanding his daughter's enthusiasm in doing her job.

"These files are hospital records from the day Evelyn Covington gave birth to her son Nathaniel almost thirty years ago" Stacy said out loud knowing her dad and everyone else could hear the information.

"Anything stand out to you as being weird or strange about that day" Max asked looking at both Jake & Jose standing at the east side emergency stairwell door.

Stacy continued to scroll through the hospital information doing her best speed reading then replied "Nothing really Admiral; basic recording procedures time of birth, weight, mother was fine, baby was fine" she said.

"WAIT A MINUTE" Stacy said as her eyes got real big reading the page in front of her.

"Evelyn Covington was committed to the hospital's psychiatric ward by her husband three days after Nathaniel was born for almost killing a doctor and nurse" Stacy said intrigued by what she was saying to her dad.

"How long was she committed?" Max asked with a confused look on his face.

"Her husband checked her out of the psych ward a week later against doctors orders when they took Nathaniel home" Stacy replied curious about why her husband had changed his mind about his wife.

Evelyn Covington stood elegantly in her underground communications room below Covington Industries smiling at all the faces up on the video screens in front of her asking "Who will start the bidding for this adorable little boy?" looking over at Parker Mason standing beside the large bald bodyguard in the corner.

"$1.5 million dollars" a Middle Eastern man said from one of the screens.

"I have $1.5 million dollars from the man in Armenia, who will give me $2 million?" she asked smiling at all the faces.

"$2 million" an older woman said out loud smiling at Evelyn.

"Well done Sofia" Covington addressed the woman making the bid with a smile.

"I now have $2 million dollars to the lady in Spain, do I hear $3 million?" she asked with enthusiasm in her voice.

"How about I take him off your hands for free and I won't kill you" a familiar voice asked from the shadows near the elevator door.

Linda Mason slowly came out of the small shadow her gun pointed at Evelyn Covington's head smiling finally seeing her son standing there in front of her.

"MOMMY" Parker yelled as he tried to run to her but was caught and picked up by the bodyguard and used as a shield as the little boy struggled to get away.

All of the video screens suddenly went dark displaying the message "online video disabled" on all of them as the buyers disconnected to protect themselves, causing Evelyn Covington to scream out her anger towards Linda for messing up her auction.

"Take another step and my man will snap his little neck like a twig" Covington said with an evil grin her face still red with anger watching as her bodyguard put his hand around young Parker's neck.

"Do that and you BOTH die after; and I'm pretty sure SHE's going to make your death slow and painful" Tyler replied coming out of the shadow her gun pointed at the bodyguard's head and seeing the intensity in Linda's eyes as she stared down the elderly Covington.

Tyler looked over at the four console technicians and ordered "All of you put your hands on top of your heads, or so help me God I will put a bullet in each of you" she said pissed that they were involved with Covington in the human trafficking of little children.

"Look what you went and did; ruined a really good adoption to a wonderful couple, who would have loved and adored your son for the rest of his life" Evelyn said continuing to smile at Linda.

"He already has a family, you crazy bitch" Linda replied angrily cocking the hammer back on her handgun and taking a step towards the elderly woman.

Having no fear of either women Evelyn Covington walked slowly over to Parker and her bodyguard knowing neither of them would put the young boy in harm's way. She motioned to her bodyguard to place his feet on the floor then smiled at them, their guns trained on her and the bodyguard.

She continued smiling, and then nodded to one of the technicians who dropped his hands and hit a switch on the console to open the steel sliding door behind Covington, Parker, and the bodyguard; where he and Parker had come in from at the start of the auction.

Evelyn Covington grabbed Parker by the arm and pushed the bodyguard towards Tyler, as she and the young boy went through the doorway. The door immediately closed behind them separating Linda & Tyler from them both.

Linda backhanded the technician in the face with her gun barrel knocking him out of his chair and onto the floor. She looked down at him her gun pointed at his head with hate in her eyes as blood started oozing out of the large cut on his forehead. He looked up at her scared for his life knowing he may have just gotten himself killed for a paycheck.

The bodyguard threw a right handed punch at Tyler who hit his fist with her gun causing him to shake it vigorously from the pain. Tyler stood there waiting for his next move as he tried to hit her again this time with his left fist.

She moved quickly out of his reach, rolled her eyes at him then shot him in the back of the left knee knowing it wouldn't kill him, not having the time to spar with him because Parker still wasn't safe in his mother's arms.

Tyler smiled at the stunned technicians watching Evelyn Covington's bodyguard roll around on the floor screaming in pain saying "Never fuck with a pissed off grandma".

"Open the fucking door; DO IT NOW" Linda ordered placing the barrel of her gun against the wounded technician's head as he slowly got back up into his seat.

"Where does that door lead?" Tyler asked the injured technician watching Linda nervously pushing the barrel harder against his head to get him to answer her.

"It's an escape tunnel that comes up into the stables, right outside the Covington Industries helicopter pad" the scared tech said to her.

"She's making a run for it" Tyler said looking at Linda.

"Get this door open; NOW" she said getting angrier seeing Linda starting to get anxious to get to her son, and Evelyn Covington.

The technician worked feverishly on his keyboard as the blood from his head wound started running down the side of his face.

Tyler made the other three technicians get up waving her gun at the three of them. They walked over and sat down on the floor with their hands on top of their heads next to the wounded bodyguard who had finally stopped screaming.

Tyler could see the blood flowing from his wound seeing a pool forming under his leg. She pulled the first-aid kit that was hanging on the wall next to the elevator and threw it on the floor next to him saying "You're lucky I'm in a caring mood asshole".

"OPEN THE GOD DAMN DOOR" Linda Mason screamed pushing her gun barrel harder into the back of the technicians head.

"I'M TRYING" the scared and bleeding tech said. "She must have broken the electronic lock on the other side of the door somehow" he said not wanting to get hurt again.

Evelyn Covington in fact did just that. She took the fire extinguisher off the wall outside the door and cracked it over the digital keypad shattering it. Sparks flew from the casing as the lock engaged and the smell of burnt plastic could be smelled at the door.

She grabbed Parker by the wrist and started dragging him down the tunnel as the young boy yelled and fought to get away from the angry woman.

Covington stopped and looked at the scared little boy with angry eyes and yelled "If you ever want to see your mommy again you'll behave young man" calming him down as they continued their walk down the tunnel.

Tyler quickly sat down in one of the empty technician chairs next to the bleeding technician and furiously typed on the keyboard in front of her realizing the tech was telling them the truth, that the door couldn't be opened from their side.

Understanding that she was wasting her time trying to get through the steel door Linda Mason ran towards the elevator as Tyler continued typing not seeing that she left.

"Stacy, do you copy?" Tyler asked speaking into the small microphone on the console in front of her.

Waiting for an answer she stood up and waved her gun at the wounded technician indicating to him to sit with the others with his hands on top of his bleeding head.

Tyler & Linda knew their com's weren't working when they got out of the elevator figuring it had something to do with them being underground, but she needed to let everyone know they were okay.

She sat back down keeping an eye on the tech's, and the wounded bodyguard who had stopped his bleeding on the floor using the first-aid kit.

Tyler smiled at them and said sarcastically "The good news is you're not going to die down here, the bad news is you're ALL going to prison for kidnapping".

"Tyler, do you copy?" she heard Stacy Mason say over the small speaker on the console smiling that she remembered the com frequency.

"Hey sweetie, it's good to hear your voice" Tyler said into the small microphone.

"We lost your com's when you went below ground; are you & Linda okay, copy?" Stacy asked.

Just as she asked Tyler if they were okay Linda's GPS indicator popped back on her computer screen and she heard Linda's voice say "I'm okay Stacy, but I need a way out of the building towards the stables".

Everyone could hear Linda's anxious voice in their ears as Jake asked "Baby did you find Parker?"

"Yes, he's with that bitch Covington" she replied feeling a bit relieved that her husband was okay at the moment.

"Have you found Howler & her son yet?" she asked as she walked out of the elevator to find dead bodies on the floor.

"Looks like we missed all the fun" she said stepping over Howler's dead mercenaries.

"We're on our way sweetheart, please be careful Howler & Hargrove's men are all over the grounds" Jake replied looking at his dad with concern on his face.

"Linda, you and Tyler need to know what I found in Evelyn Covington's medical file" Stacy said over their com's.

Stacy proceeded to recalibrate the frequency to both their com's so they would now work underground telling everyone about Nathaniel

Covington's birth, Evelyn's mental issues, and the day they took Nathaniel home from the hospital.

"Are you serious; that does explain a lot" Tyler replied hearing everything Stacy had to say about the Covington's.

"I need you to download all the files from this computer frequency I'm on Stacy" Tyler asked knowing she could do it remotely from her communication van.

Tyler watched the screen in front of her as Stacy downloaded all the files from Evelyn Covington's kidnapping/adoption ring hoping to use the information to get back the children she took and sold.

When the download finished Tyler got up and fired several rounds into the four computers rendering them all useless, reloaded a new magazine she retrieved from her garter holster and walked over to the still bleeding technician sitting on the floor with the others pointing the barrel at his head once again.

"Where are the other children being kept?" she asked cocking the hammer back on her gun and pressing the hard steel barrel against his skull.

"Listen lady, I don't want to die" he replied visibly shaking. "She kept them on the 2nd floor; that's all we know" he said grimacing at the sight of her gun pointed at him.

Tyler stood up and touched her ear com saying "Well boys, looks like I'm headed to my own party".

"You always take me to the swankiest places Mr. Mason" Tyler replied with a giggle.

"Nothing but the best for my girl" he said to her, smiling at his son & Jose seeing them both roll their eyes at him, then looking down the hallway outside the 3rd floor stairwell.

"Crusher, what's your twenty?" Max asked wondering where he and the two "ninja girls" were.

CHAPTER FIFTEEN

Crusher Davis, Yuki Amikura, and Ochi Osaka cautiously walked out of the 4th floor emergency stairwell with guns drawn when Crusher heard Max Mason asked where they were in his ear.

They stood together in the large receiving lobby looking around the plush, nicely furnished room when Crusher replied "4th floor lobby, just outside the conference room Admiral".

"Copy that Master Sergeant, keep your heads on a swivel" Max said knowing only he could hear his concerns since Yuki & Ochi refused to wear ear com's not wanting to be distracted with voices in their ears. Max wanted Crusher to remind the two deadly Asian girls to keep their eyes on everything around them.

Max's concerns quickly became reality when several of Howler's heavily armed mercenaries came from the conference room and down the long hallway.

Seeing the three intruders they opened fire causing Crusher to grab Yuki by her long ninja gee sleeve and pull her behind the long crushed-velvet red couch for cover. He could see Ochi on the other side of the room lowered behind a large chair of the same color staring over at the two of them.

"What the Hell are you doing?" Yuki screamed at Crusher as bullets continue to hit the upper part of the couch causing the stuffing material to fly out over their heads.

"Saving your life" Crusher replied seeing how angry the young Asian woman was as she lowered herself to the floor to avoid the bullets that were ripping through the couch.

"I don't need ANY man to protect me" she yelled seeing the confusion on the young soldier's face.

Just as she finished her statement one of Howler's mercenaries came through an office door behind them, surprising them both.

Yuki quickly pulled a steel throwing star from her gee and flung it at the armed man; the sharp blade hitting him square in the forehead killing him instantly.

"See, I don't need your help" Yuki said to a surprised Crusher Davis understanding she just saved his life as he continued to stare at the mercenary's lifeless body a few feet away from them.

"Yes ma'am" Crusher said to her with a smile appreciating what she just did reaching over and grabbing her hand affectionately. Yuki looked at him and smiled in return under her ninja mask.

"If you two don't mind, can you stop your chirping at one another for just a moment and help me with these assholes" Ochi said staring at Yuki & Crusher with a scowl on her face then rising up from behind her chair with her twin CZ handguns blazing, hitting two of the mercenaries coming down the hallway killing them.

Ochi quickly ducked back down behind the chair as more bullets flew over her head into the office walls directly behind her.

The two remaining mercenaries emptied their handguns into both the couch and the chair. When Crusher heard the "click" of the empty guns he rose up and fired two short bursts from his AR-15 machine-gun into them both; riddling them with bullets, watching their bodies convulse as the molten hot lead hit them over & over again.

Crusher sat back down on the floor next to Yuki after evaluating that the mercenary threat was over for the moment replacing his spent rifle magazine.

The three of them sat silently behind the couch and chair glancing at one another waiting for Howler's next attack when they heard a loud voice say "Come fulfill your destiny cousin".

Both Yuki and Ochi looked at one another with a bit of fear and anger recognizing the voice coming from the end of the hallway to be that of Noki Amikura.

Crusher Davis and the two young Asian women stood up looking down the hallway towards the conference room where Noki Amikura was waiting. Four black clad ninja's all with samurai swords in defensive poses stood there at the conference room door waiting for the two "ninja girls" to try and get to their Master who was calling them both out.

Crusher aimed his rifle at the ninja's down the hallway ready to fire when Yuki grabbed the barrel with her right hand and lowered it towards the floor saying "This is OUR fight; it has been coming for a VERY long time" she said with a smile looking over at Ochi who understood what she was saying to the brave soldier.

"You don't have to do this alone" Crusher replied looking into her beautiful blue eyes worried this may be the last time he sees her.

"I've NEVER been alone" she said smiling at Crusher thinking how handsome he was, then looked over at Ochi giving her a smile. The two Asian women looked down the hallway at the waiting ninja's grabbing each others hand affectionately as they smiled at Crusher Davis together.

Stacy Mason was monitoring all the conversations hearing what her big sister was saying asking Crusher "Give her your com for a moment please Crusher".

"Lieutenant Mason would like to talk with you" he said as he took his communication ear bud out and handed it to Yuki. Yuki smiled taking it, placing it in her ear.

"Listen up sis, you don't get to die today; understand" "No martyr shit, we just got you back" Stacy said angrily, a tear coming down her face as she continued to keep an eye on everyone through their GPS on her computer screen still sitting next to James Murphy in the van.

Yuki gave a big smile hearing what Stacy said looking over at both Ochi & Crusher Davis knowing they couldn't hear the conversation.

"Let's hope that's not an option little sister" she replied with a giggle.

"I do however have a confession to make to you" Yuki said looking at Ochi with a sad smile.

"That you've been keeping an eye on me for the past three years" Stacy said boldly hearing her sister's silent breathing over her speaker.

"When did you know?" Yuki asked turning a bit red with embarrassment.

"That day in the mall on my eighteenth birthday; you looked me right in the eye and smiled then disappeared" Stacy said knowing her dad could hear their conversation choosing to say nothing.

"You looked so beautiful that day" Yuki replied tears coming down her face as Ochi squeezed her hand tightly.

"Why didn't you tell Max Mason that you saw me?" Yuki asked confused that she never said anything to anyone.

"He had just gotten his life back together after the bombing; he would have NEVER stopped looking for you if I told him".

"You seemed to want to stay hidden so I let you" Stacy said hoping she didn't upset her father who was listening intently.

"Ladies, not wanting to interrupt this emotional conversation that you're having but we have ninja's that are tired of waiting for us coming down the hallway" Crusher said seeing two of the ninja's approaching the three of them as the other two stayed back guarding the conference door.

"We'll talk later little sister" Yuki said with a laugh pulling her sword from its scabbard and swinging it out from behind her back.

"Here, hold these" Ochi said handing Crusher her twin handguns in their shoulder holsters, then pulling out her twin katana swords from behind her back.

Crusher looked at the guns holding the holsters leather straps then looked at Ochi swords thinking "Everything works out better with a gun" backing up to aim his machine-gun at the advancing ninja's.

Yuki softly touched Crusher's cheek and asked with a smile "Promise me you will stay here and not get in the way" she said feeling him place his hand on hers moving to kiss the top of it.

"I'm ALWAYS getting in the way, just ask Jose & Jake" Crusher replied with a laugh as he put his ear com back in after she wiped it off and handed it back to him.

"This is about family honor; about destiny" she said knowing that it was possible that her cousin Noki could kill her and she would never get to see Crusher again.

"I want to explore these feelings with you" "You have to trust that I know what I'm doing with my cousin" Yuki said as she pulled her bright blue mask up over her face.

"Roger that ma'am" Crusher replied with a grin melting into her bright blue eyes.

Yuki and Ochi moved in front of Crusher who stayed crouching behind the couch his machine-gun laying on top of the elegant piece of furniture pointed down the hallway.

Yuki looked back at him and smiled through her ninja mask. She looked at Ochi and said "Let's do this already" with a grin from her best friend.

Ochi smiled then looked back at Crusher saying "He is kinda cute; you could do worst" giving him a big grin.

Yuki glanced back at him his head just visible from the back of the couch aiming his rifle, smiled at him saying to Ochi "He is, isn't he" with a giggle.

"You both know I can hear you, right?" Crusher said grinning from ear to ear.

Yuki looked at Ochi and laughed as they both said in unison "Yep" walking towards the two ninja assassin's almost upon them.

Max Mason, his son Jake, and Detective Jose Martin slowly came out of the 3rd floor emergency stairwell crossing the hallway putting their backs against the wall so they could evaluate the situation.

The three men stood next to the men's room door parallel to several different hallways on both sides of them.

Max quickly looked around the corner seeing a large furnished lobby area in front of a glass wall from floor to ceiling. The glass double-doors in the middle of the room shined with bright colored lights burning behind them.

Max quickly glanced around the corner again to see about a half dozen heavily armed mercenaries standing guard in front of the glass doors. He figured out this must be the Master Control "launch room" for the rocket taking the satellite into space.

He could see that there were several technical & computer people moving around inside the room including Nathaniel Covington, and his bodyguard Simon.

There were also a couple of armed mercenaries inside the room standing watch as Covington paid close attention to one of the video screens, waiting for the final ten minutes; as the tech's continued preparing for the launch.

Max motioned to Jake to take a look pointing his two fingers at his eyes then to the glass room telling Jake & Jose they needed to keep radio silence at the time. Jake looked through the glass walls seeing dozens of tall racks of computer servers, video screens, and control consoles with technician's manning them inside the see-through room.

Jake also noticed the digital magnetic locks on the large glass doors knowing if those locks were engaged they would NEVER be able to get inside.

Jake whispered to his dad "We need to get inside that room before Covington locks it down" he said looking at both Max & Jose with confusion on their faces.

"If he locks that room down before we can secure it, there is NO WAY we can stop the satellite in time from positioning itself in space" Jake continued, glancing down the hallway again.

"The rocket's self-destruct program can ONLY be accessed from inside that room" Jake continued as he looked back down the hallway.

Just as Jake glanced back down the hallway towards the control room again he saw Colonel Howler walk up to a couple of his men.

"HOWLER" he said in a loud voice looking at his dad who rolled his eyes at him.

Jake knew he fucked up because Howler heard him and saw him duck back against the wall.

"MASON" Howler screamed not caring which one it was pulling his gun from his holster and firing it several times towards the wall the three men were standing against barely missing them.

Max swept his AR-15 machine-gun around the corner firing two short five round bursts, hitting two mercenaries in front of the doors noticing that the glass was bullet-proof after hitting it several times.

Nathaniel Covington looked up from the launch screen he was staring at to see the guards in front of the large control room had their guns drawn figuring it was a threat and hit the lock-down button just as Howler was trying to get inside.

Covington smiled at Howler and raised his hands as if to say "Oops" as the heavy magnetic locks clanged inside the doors locking them.

"Covington, you asshole" Howler screamed knowing he wasn't getting in. Now that the locks were engaged the control room was impregnable and he knew it. He knew he was on his own against the Mason's now.

Howler angrily stood there for a moment and stared into the glass flipping Nathaniel Covington the "fuck you" finger seeing the young billionaire laugh and smile at his meaningless gesture from the other side of the impenetrable glass. He could hear Howler scream at him "He's coming for you next asshole".

Howler figured the only thing he could do now was run or fight because he knew the Mason's wouldn't stop until he was either dead or caught.

He ordered his four mercenaries to continue firing on Max, Jake, and Jose as he ran towards the elevator.

"Stacy; shutdown ALL the elevators in the building quickly, copy" Max said out loud seeing Howler heading to it.

"Copy that Admiral" Stacy replied working feverishly on her computer keyboard on her dad's request staring at the digital code on her screen.

The words "Elevator Locked Down" came across Stacy's screen as she switched to the building's 3rd floor video camera in front of the elevator watching as Colonel Howler continued to push the button calling for it. Stacy giggled smiling at Murphy continuing to look at Howler on the screen saying "He's SO fucked".

"Elevator's down Admiral, copy" she said with a smile still watching a frantic & frustrated Howler pushing the buttons.

"Roger that Lieutenant" Max replied looking at both Jake & Jose Martin crouched down returning fire towards the mercenaries Howler left behind.

"Stay here Detective to cover our escape, while the two of us go settle our family issues with the good Colonel and Covington" Max said looking at his son Jake with a grin then returning his attention back to Jose Martin.

"Yes sir Director" Jose replied understanding what his orders were smiling at the two Mason men.

"Jacob; on me" Max said taking two flash bang grenades from the back of his belt pulling the safety pins but still holding on to the charging handles.

Max tossed the two non-lethal grenades down the hallway about ten feet away from Howler's remaining four mercenaries watching the charging handles fly in the air.

Max, Jake, and Jose all covered their ears with their hands as the loud explosion of sound and light knocked down the mercenaries as they stood firing from the corner of the hallway.

Max & Jake quickly moved down the hallway to the adjoining one and quickly hid around the corner getting closer to the control room and the remaining armed mercenaries outside the control room doors.

Jose Martin peeked around the corner to see his two colleagues safe against the wall and started emptying his machine-gun at the mercenaries keeping them pinned down so they didn't know the two of them were right next to them.

Just as he released the spent magazine from his rifle to put a fresh one in, one of Howler's mercenary's came in through the stairwell door surprising him.

Jose saw the large muscular mercenary's handgun in his hand slowly rising to shoot him. Swinging his rifle like a baseball bat he knocked it out of his hand as a shot went off into the nearby wall. Jose kicked him harshly in the chest causing him to fall back through the opened stairwell door.

Jose quickly went through the door to find the man just getting up from the concrete. Grabbing the man Jose threw him against the wall and hit him several times with right hand punches to his face.

Bleeding from his mouth, the mercenary brought his knee up hard into Jose's ribs causing him to cringe in pain letting go of his grip. The mercenary quickly hit the young police detective hard in the chest with his right fist making Jose move backwards against the metal railing.

He grabbed Jose around the throat with both hands choking him, bending his back over the railing to throw him over. Jose struggled to breathe glancing over his shoulder to see it was a long drop from there. He brought his knee up with serious force into the mercenary's groin causing him to loosen his grip around his throat.

Jose quickly slid to the side grabbing the mercenary by the shoulder straps on his vest and throwing him over the railing. He looked down through the stairwell watching the blood ooze out unto the 1st floor from under the mercenary's shattered skull.

"Are you finished Detective" Jose heard in his com breathing hard and bent over still in the stairwell.

"Yeah, I am" he said realizing Max and Jake listened in on his fight.

"Who's buying dinner after all this?" Jose asked slowly walking back inside picking his AR-15 rifle up off the floor and reloading it rubbing his painful chest.

Max, Jake, and Jose all thought for a split second then the three of them said at the same time "CRUSHER" snickering at one another that they all thought the same thing.

"I don't think so Sirs" they all heard; hearing Crusher Davis's voice in their ears.

"We have less then ten minutes to get into that control room and destroy that satellite" Max said looking at Jose Martin pointing his machine gun again at the remaining four mercenaries starting to make a move towards them down the hallway.

Just as the mercenaries were about to turn the corner Max & Jake watched as Howler looked them both in the eyes and ran into an adjoining office.

Jake looked at his dad with anger thinking Howler was going to get away when Max grinned at his son and said "Make it fast".

"Yes sir" Jake replied moving in front of Max to go after Howler.

Max put his hand on his son's shoulder knowing how pissed he was at the man who kidnapped his son and put his entire family in danger saying "Remember son, you have choices".

"I know Pop" Jake replied understanding what his father was trying to tell him nodding affectionately to him with a smile, then carefully heading down the hallway to where Howler was now hiding.

Jake quickly went down the abandoned hallway and stood against the wall next to the office door they saw Howler run into.

Thinking this was going to be a close-quarters combat situation Jake placed his AR rifle against the wall and took out his SA-XD handgun raising it to his chest in a shooter's aim position.

"Want to come out and surrender Colonel?" Jake asked sarcastically snickering to himself standing against the wall just to the right of the closed door knowing the response he would get.

"Fuck you Mason" Howler screamed inside the office as the loud sound of gunfire & bullets flew through the door.

"I'll take that as a definite maybe" Jake replied laughing, watching the bullets impale the other side of the wall in front of the door.

Howler continued to shoot at the door when suddenly Jake heard the clicking of an empty gun. He paused for a moment then reached over with his left hand and turned the doorknob.

Opening it just a bit he pushed it completely open to see if Howler would fire on him if he walked in. Not hearing any gunfire he slowly moved around into the open doorway to see Howler standing behind the desk with his hands empty having tossed his empty gun on the floor.

"So I guess you're going to be like your old man and kill me?" Howler asked a smiling Jake Mason standing there with a gun in his hand.

"Fortunately for you I'm not like my father; and to set the record straight, my father ONLY killed when his life; or innocent lives were in danger" Jake replied starting to get pissed at the arrogant Colonel.

"So, to answer your question Colonel; NO I'm not going to kill you, but I'm going to enjoy beating the shit out of you for what you did to my son & family" Jake said with a big smile dropping the magazine from his gun, ejecting the round from the chamber, and tossing the handgun on the floor making it a fair fight.

The two mercenaries continued to fire on both Max & Jose Martin from the control room lobby when they both had to stop and reload.

"Stay here Lieutenant" Max said to Jose giving him a wink and a smile.

Hearing they needed to reload gave Max the time he needed, running up to the two burly men and hitting them hard each in the face.

Max kicked one in the chest, which had enough force on it to knock him into the other making them both fall to the floor next to each other.

He quickly leaned over and punched them both in the jaw again, dazing them as he flipped them over and secured their hands behind their backs with the plastic cuffs he was carrying. He did the same with their ankles so neither could get up.

Max got up off the floor as the two mercenaries tried aggressively to get out of their captured predicament, playfully slapping them both in the back of the head telling them "Calm your asses down."

He looked over into the glass control room to see Nathaniel Covington smile and clap his hands at what he witnessed Max do.

Covington reached over on the nearest console flicking a toggle switch then said "Nicely done Mr. Mason" through a loudspeaker in the ceiling above Max.

Looking up at the ceiling and figuring it was a two-way receiver Max said out loud "Why don't you come out here so we can discuss sending you & your charming mother to prison" smiling at Covington & Simon.

"In eight minutes my mother & I will be the two richest people in the world; no one can touch us" Covington said arrogantly.

"There's nothing you or anyone else can do to stop us; this room is impenetrable now, it's like a safe on a time-lock" he said smiling, placing his hand on Simon's shoulder and laughing at Max Mason.

Max remembered what Jake said about not being able to get into the room once the magnetic locks engaged, but he also knew that a "ninja" could get into any place if he had ingenuity & patience.

Max carefully looked around the inside of the control room, looking at every inch to see if there was any possible breach.

He knew both he and Jake had only a few minutes to get inside and download the destruct codes to the rocket's onboard computer to activate its self-destruct sequence before it escaped the earth's atmosphere.

Nathaniel Covington continued smiling at Max from inside the control room when a big grin came over Max's face as he continued to stare into the glass enclosure.

Max turned around and walked a few feet away with his back towards Covington touching his com saying "Sweetheart I need your help with something, copy."

"What's up daddy?" Stacy asked playfully knowing her father just called her "sweetheart".

CHAPTER SIXTEEN

Linda Mason quickly stepped over the dead mercenaries & guests lying on the lobby floor as she headed towards the champagne fountain in the far corner of the room.

She moved the bullet dented steel table out of the way to find the black weapons bag Max, and her husband Jake had left for her and Tyler; sitting there on the floor next to the exit door.

She knew before she opened the large duffle bag that her police uniform and gear was inside. She quickly unzipped the back of her black party dress and let it fall to the floor below her, then kicking off her black hi-heels. She grabbed her uniform from the plastic bag she had placed it in back at Yuki's hotel, her boots, gun belt, and her Kevlar vest; and hurried to get dressed.

"Stacy I need a diversion to get around all these cops outside; any ideas?" Linda asked pulling the slide back on her Sig Sauer handgun to chamber its first round.

"Roger that; I can kill the lights and open the magnetic doors at the same time for about ten seconds before the auxiliary power kicks back in" Stacy explained to her sister-in-law.

"That will give me enough time to blend in with the rest of the cops out there" Linda replied smiling realizing how smart Stacy was with a computer; just like her big brother Jake.

Linda grabbed the MP-5 machine-gun from the bag, loaded it and grabbed two extra magazines; sliding them under her gun belt. She tied her hair up in a long blonde ponytail, and pulled it through a baseball cap with "POLICE" embroidered on it.

"Ready to go Lieutenant" she said to Stacy standing at the exit door.

"Be careful, go on my mark; three, two, one, GO" Stacy said as she hit the button on her console.

All the lights went out, both inside & outside the Covington Industries building. Linda heard the "click" of the door lock disengaging and quickly pushed it open seeing it was pitch black outside around the edges of the tall building.

The young officer & mother moved quickly to the other side of the catering truck that was still sitting there, then ran into the trees heading towards the stables where she knew Evelyn Covington was headed with her son Parker.

The lights came back on surprising the two advancing black robed ninja's, because now Yuki & Ochi were standing right in front of them hitting them both hard in the face with right hand punches staggering the stunned ninja's backwards.

"I thought my cousin wanted to kill me himself" Yuki asked the two deadly assassins as Ochi stood there in her fighting stance.

"Our Master has given that privilege to us" one of them said going back into a fighting stance raising his sword above his head and starring down Ochi.

"SO YOUR MASTER'S A COWARD WITHOUT HONOR" Yuki yelled knowing her cousin Noki could hear her from inside the conference room down the hallway.

"Killing you both will be an honor for our Master" he continued, swinging his sword down at Yuki Amikura.

Yuki brought her sword up quickly to stop the ninja's blade from striking her, hearing the "clang" of steel as they struck each other's swords. They moved around each other continuing to touch blades pushing against each other when Yuki kicked the ninja in the chest knocking him backwards.

"Then it should be an honor to die for your cowardly Master" Yuki replied seeing the ninja against the wall.

Ochi Osaka smiled at the other ninja who saw and heard what Yuki did, and said to his partner; then swung at him with both of her katana swords catching him completely off guard. He blocked each swing she had coming towards him but finally getting cut on his right arm. He grabbed his arm in pain and stepped back from Ochi's offensive attack.

The ninja fighting Yuki straightened up from her kick and angrily swung his sword back and forth as the young "ninja girl" continued to block his swings one right after the other; hearing the continued "clang" of the steel blades hitting each other.

Angrily, the injured ninja ran towards Ochi swinging his sword putting her on the defensive. She tried to block each swing of his razor sharp blade but finally one got through cutting a deep slice into her lower abdomen.

Ochi felt the searing pain and grabbed her side seeing the blood on her hand. She staggered backwards leaning against the wall knowing her wound was deep. She had never been wounded in a fight until now and she didn't like it.

Yuki could see Ochi was wounded and understood she needed to end this game of Noki's quickly. The ninja attacked again swinging his sword just above her head as she slid on her knees towards him swinging her sword towards his chest cutting into his clothes, and his flesh.

She jumped back up and turned around quickly to bring another swing of her blade down onto his shoulder cutting through the bone dropping him to his knees. She pulled her sword out of him and pushed him to the floor with her right foot watching the blood spill out onto the floor under him as he convulsed in pain.

Ochi stood up smiling at the ninja that cut her bringing her blood stained finger to her lips to taste her blood and taunt him then angrily ran towards him swinging both of her swords at him.

He did his best to block most of her strikes, but she spun around him and sliced deeply into his back severing his spinal cord killing him instantly dropping him to his knees then on to the floor face down.

Ochi stood over the dead ninja, his blood pouring onto the hallway floor when she suddenly became dizzy; doubling over in pain from her wound. She staggered backwards against the wall and slowly dropped to the floor.

Crusher Davis watched Ochi fall to the floor from behind the couch and raised up to go help his new friend when the office door behind him burst open and a visibly wounded mercenary came running towards him with a large military k-bar knife in his hand.

Crusher turned and blocked the large blade coming towards his head with his rifle. The mercenary continued to push down the knife as Crusher pushed back trying to keep the blade from stabbing him in the head.

He quickly sent his knee into the mercenary's ribs several times as the assailant feeling the pain took a step back grabbing Crusher's rifle and tossing it against the wall away from them both.

The mercenary grabbed Crusher by the vest and toppled on top of him as they both hit the floor hard, the knife still pointed at the Master-Sergeants face.

Continuing to hold off the blade from reaching his face with his right hand, Crusher hit the mercenary in the ribs several times with his left fist as the point of the blade got closer to his eye.

"OCHI" Yuki screamed seeing her best friend fall to the floor as the last two ninja's ran towards them both. Ochi smiles hearing her best friend, then closes her eyes.

"CRUSHER I NEED YOU" Yuki screams turning her head in his direction seeing him rolling on the floor with one of Colonel Howler's mercenary's.

Crusher heard Yuki scream for him slowly rolling the injured mercenary over sitting on top of him now pointing the knife down in his direction.

Crusher slowly pushed the large blade into the mercenary's chest, looking over at Yuki now sitting on the floor holding Ochi. Suddenly, he took the palm of his left hand and slammed the hilt of the knife

KILLS OF THE FATHER

hard into his chest watching as the blood quickly flowed from his mouth and hearing him stop breathing.

Crusher Davis quickly rolled off of the dead mercenary grabbed his rifle from the floor and ran down the hallway to Yuki Amikura seeing an unconscious Ochi Okasa lying in her arms.

He raises his AR-15 rifle towards the two remaining ninja assassins, but is suddenly stopped by Yuki who puts her delicate hand on his rifle lowering it towards the floor again.

"We are an honorable society, we do not kill our fellow ninja with bullets" she said softly with a smile to the confused soldier.

Now standing up, he watches Yuki as she suddenly spins and throws two steel bladed throwing stars at the two ninja's rapidly coming towards them impaling them both in the head right through their eye sockets and into their brains killing them instantly and dropping them to the floor.

She looks back down at the still unconscious, and bleeding Ochi then to Crusher and says "I need you to take care of her" as she places her hand on his cheek with a smile.

Yuki leaned down, lowered her mask, and kissed Ochi on the forehead saying "I love you little sister" then rose up kissing Crusher one more time on the cheek straightening up her uniform.

"You don't have to do this alone, you know?" Crusher says grabbing the young Asian woman's hand.

"I've ALWAYS had to do THIS alone" Yuki said smiling, glancing down at Ochi one more time knowing this showdown with her cousin Noki has been coming for a VERY long time.

She smiled and squeezed Crusher's hand turned and walked towards the unguarded conference room door replacing the mask over her face. She stopped at one of the dead ninja's lying on the floor and bent over to pull her throwing star from his eye, then the other. She wiped the blood from the blades on her uniform jacket then put them back in her concealed pocket.

Crusher grabbed the small medical kit from his gun belt then raised Ochi's shirt to see the blood slowly gushing from her wound.

He broke the seal on a small tube of antiseptic powder the military used for emergency medical treatment and poured it into Ochi's gaping wound causing her to wake up suddenly from the intense pain, yet she still didn't make a sound.

He held her down as gently as he could looking her in the eyes saying "I need to stop the bleeding, I need for you not to move" hoping that she understood what he was saying. He took out a tube of "super glue" adhesive and ran it down the length of her wound knowing it would help stop the bleeding as it sealed up.

Crusher quickly and carefully used gauze pads to soak up the blood seeing the medication powder was starting to help with the clotting. He took a large medical bandage and placed it completely over the wound and taped all four sides, securing it.

He could see how tough Ochi Osaka was having more concern for others than herself asking "Where's Yuki, where's MY sister?"

Crusher motioned down the hallway towards the conference room to show Ochi where her childhood friend was. He slowly helped her off the floor watching her smile at Yuki as she stood at the conference room door looking back at them, understanding what she must do.

Yuki stared at her two friends for a moment knowing now that Ochi was going to be okay then disappeared through the conference room door.

Agent Karen Tyler took the elevator back up to the 1st floor after she & Stacy Mason secured the hard drive from the underground computer system Evelyn Covington was using for her kidnapping & adoption scheme.

She could see the dead bodies all over the lobby floor thinking Max must have been put in a really bad situation by Howler & his mercenaries for all these dead bodies to occur.

She quickly ran over to the champagne fountain finding the gun bag Max had left for her and Linda Mason. Opening it she could see Linda had already been there seeing her black party dress inside.

She quickly unzipped her red dress and dropped it to the floor. She pulled out the plastic bag of clothes brought for her and got dressed pulling her Kevlar vest on over her t-shirt then tying her boots up.

Tyler grabbed her gun belt securing it around her waist then pulled her XD handgun out making sure she had a full twenty round magazine loaded; placed it back in the holster and grabbed the last AR-15 rifle in the bag loading it with a fresh thirty round mag.

She was headed up to the 2nd floor where the scared technician said that the two remaining kidnapped children were being kept. She pushed the up button on the elevator and the door opened immediately.

Tyler stood at the open elevator door for a moment looking over at the dead mercenaries thinking "What the Hell were they thinking" drawing down on Max Mason and his friends. She pushed the 2nd floor button and the doors closed.

The elevator door slowly opened on the 2nd floor to a hail of machine-gun fire, as bullets riddled every wall in the car. Two mercenaries stood there at the open door emptying they're guns into the elevator finally hearing the clicking of emptied magazines.

"Is that any way to treat a lady" Tyler asked as she stood in the emergency stairwell doorway surprising the two men who immediately dropped they're emptied machine-guns, and reached for their holstered handguns.

Tyler seeing them both reach for their guns fired a long burst of her own machine-gun into Howler's hired mercenaries killing them both as their bodies hit the wall violently and fell to the floor.

She started opening doors down the hallway, kicking in those she found locked looking for the two other children Evelyn Covington was going to auction off to her overseas contacts.

Finally, she came to the door at the end of the hallway and kicked it in to find a little brown haired boy and a blonde haired girl huddling together scared in the far corner of the room. She noticed there wasn't a bathroom, or furniture in the room; just a couple of old mattresses lying on the floor with some old dusty blankets on them.

"Hi, I'm Karen" she said going down on one knee seeing how scared they both were. "I promise I'm not going to hurt you" she said softly watching as the little girl turned and looked at her.

Tyler figured they were either six or seven years old, wearing expensive, clean clothes; thinking Evelyn had them dressed to present them properly to the video contacts she saw in the basement.

"What's your name sweetheart?" Tyler asked the little girl seeing she wasn't afraid to look at her.

"Abby, Abby Ashton; can I go home to my mom & dad?" she asked shyly.

Tyler smiled at the little blonde haired girl saying "Yes you can Abby; you both can". She watched the little boy slowly turn to look at her hearing that he could go home too.

She continued to smile at the two scared kids asking the boy "What's your name sweetheart?" seeing that they were both starting to trust her.

"Patrick, Patrick Taylor" he said hesitantly looking at his blonde companion who smiled at him and held his hand.

"Nice to meet you both, what do you say we get out of this place and go find your families" Tyler asked seeing the big smiles on both their little faces.

She stood up and touched her com and asked "Stacy, did you get all that? Copy"

"Yes ma'am, I'm on it" Stacy replied in Tyler's ear typing furiously on her computer keyboard.

"There are local "AMBER ALERTS" out for both of them; both have been missing for over a week, copy" Stacy said to Tyler.

"Contact their parents directly and get them down here, copy" Tyler replied holding Abby's hand, seeing that Patrick was holding the little girl's other hand tightly.

Tyler had to walk the children by the two dead mercenaries she killed in order to get to the emergency stairwell looking at them smiling "Don't worry the bad people won't hurt you anymore" she said leading them both through the door to the stairs.

"Stacy, I need to get these kids outside and get to the stables to back up Linda; can you turn the lights out again?" "Do you copy?" Tyler asked knowing Stacy Mason could do anything if she put her mind to it.

"The old "now you see me, now you don't" trick just reversed, copy" Stacy said with a laugh.

"Exactly, copy" Tyler replied with a grin finally getting down the stairs & standing behind the door waiting for the lights to go out so the children could move through the lobby without seeing all the dead bodies on the floor.

"You'll only have about ten seconds to get them out before the lights come back on outside; copy" Stacy said worried Tyler might get caught by the authorities now surrounding the Covington building because the front has very little cover to hide behind.

"Copy that sweetie" Tyler replied smiling down at the two children as she tried to formulate a plan.

Tyler went down to one knee to talk with the two young ones smiling at them both. "I need you two to be brave and help me do something; can you do that for me please?" she asked, watching them both nod yes to her.

"Stacy, on my mark" Tyler said ready to push the stairwell door open not wanting the two children to see all of the dead bodies lying on the floor.

"NOW" she said opening the door and running with the two children towards the front door of the building.

The lights outside & inside went off again as Tyler rushed the two kids to the sidewalk in front of the building. She stood them there then pulled the pins on two flash-bang grenades and threw them as far as she could underhanded to the right side of the building, as she ran towards the left.

The lights came back on just as the two grenades exploded making a loud "BANG" and flashing brightly.

Abby screamed at the loud sound drawing everyone's attention to her and Patrick standing there completely alone in front of the building.

Police, and EMT's slowly approached the two scared children not seeing anyone else in the area wrapping them both up in blankets and rushing them to their ambulances.

Tyler looked back at the two little kids through the dark bushes smiling & saying out loud "Nicely done sweetheart" as she headed towards the stables to help Linda rescue her son Parker from Evelyn Covington.

Jake heard the conversation Tyler had with his sister just as she turned the lights out again putting both he and Howler in the dark for just a moment. When the lights came back on Jake was standing in the office doorway looking at Howler thinking he might try to escape.

"Wasn't that fun; my sister can do amazing things with a computer" Jake said with a proud arrogant grin.

"Enough of this family bullshit" Howler said walking up to him and throwing a right-handed punch towards Jake's face.

Jake blocked his punch with his left arm then backhanded Howler across the jaw with his right knocking the arrogant Colonel backwards.

Howler rubbed his jaw grinning at Jake, "You hit like your old man; soft" he said.

"I hit nothing like my father, because if he hit you you'd be picking yourself up off the floor right now" Jake replied with a grin.

Howler moved quickly catching Jake by surprise with a roundhouse spin kick to his head staggering him backwards into the long oak conference table.

Jake grabbed the table so he wouldn't fall to the floor realizing the kick dazed him just a bit really pissing him off now.

"I guess you're a little out of practice Captain" Howler said laughing as he watched Jake slowly stand up straight again.

Howler tried to kick Jake again but he was waiting for it this time, grabbing the Colonel's foot in mid-air flipping it over sideways and dropping Howler to the floor hard, hitting the back of his head.

"I catch up pretty quick Colonel" Jake replied grinning at his "out of practice" comment.

He looked down at Howler lying on the conference room floor and watched as he took a large folding knife out of his pocket then slowly got back on his feet again.

"Really Colonel, this is what you want to do?" Jake asked seeing Howler stand up now with a knife in his hand.

Howler looked up at the clock on the wall causing Jake to turn and look at it as well. Howler pointed the knife at Jake and stood in a fighting stance ready to strike.

"Your wife is probably dead by now; your son now on his way to some rich third world family; Amikura probably killed his cousin; and you & your father have just over five minutes to stop Covington from taking over the world, and as for me I'm going to be VERY rich" Howler said with a maniacal laugh.

"Sounds like a Wednesday for us Mason's" Jake replied with a chuckle.

Howler charged toward Jake with the knife, slashing at him as Jake moved away from each swing. Howler stopped for a moment seeing Jake look at his empty gun on the floor saying "That's not going to help you now son".

Howler lunged at Jake with both his hands on the hilt knocking them both to the floor on top of each other.

Howler was on top trying to force the knife blade into Jake's eye when he smiled and said "Your father kills for a living, you killed under orders, that means your son will grow up to be a killer just like you both" seeing Jake's face turn red with anger.

"The kills of the father doesn't define us to our children asshole" Jake replied remembering what his father told him as he strained to push the sharp blade away from his eye.

"It makes us STRONGER; makes us FAMILY" he said staring up into Howler's eyes slowly turning the knife away from his face and in towards Howler's upper chest.

Jake smiled at Howler seeing fear in his eyes. He then suddenly let go his right hand from the knife and quickly grabbed the back of the Colonel's neck and forcibly pulled him down onto the blade sliding it up into his chest and heart.

Howler stared into Jake's eyes as he took his last breath. Jake rolled him off onto the floor grabbed his gun & magazine reloaded it and turned to go find his dad.

Looking back at the lifeless body of Colonel John Howler; Jake thought about what he said, believing everyone was a killer when they had to be; even a good father such as himself.

Jake continued thinking about Parker knowing the only reason he was forced to kill was to protect his son's future from a now dead madman; having faith in his wife, believing Linda would get him back from Evelyn Covington.

CHAPTER SEVENTEEN

Linda Mason made her way to the stables under the cover of darkness, looking up into the sky to see the full moon and stars shining brightly; knowing Evelyn Covington was trying to escape from the underground bunker with her son Parker.

She stayed hidden in the bushes continuing to recon the immediate area around the stables. From her perch up on the hill she could see the white helicopter with the "Covington Industries" logo written on the side in bold black lettering sitting there on a circular helipad with bright red flashing lights all around it on the ground.

The large, wooden fenced in horse corral was to her right of the helipad brightly lit with several tall lamp posts around its wooden rails. Just a few yards away from the helicopter on the other side of the fence was a large silver oblong fuel tank she figured was for refueling the helicopter; lit up by a separate street light.

The large red colored barn with white trim looked like it could house up to ten or more horses inside its closed wooden double doors. Bright security lights lit up the area around the front of the stable enabling her to see if anyone came out.

Linda thought the entire area was a security nightmare having no cover whatsoever, but she didn't see anyone hanging around from her vantage point; with no guards in sight she decided to head towards the barn door.

As she passed the helicopter with her gun drawn, she glanced inside it, and figured she needed to disable it somehow so Covington couldn't leave with her boy.

She came up on the fuel tank when she had an idea but her mind snapped back to reality when she heard the click of a hammer being pulled back on a handgun.

"You should have left well enough alone Lieutenant" a voice said from behind her; hidden from her by the shadows of the fuel tank.

Linda recognized the voice immediately and replied "And you should have never kidnapped my son Captain" understanding her boss, police Captain Andrew Hargrove was now holding a gun on her.

"He's going to go to a good family; I promise" Hargrove said trying to reassure Linda her son would be safe.

"He's already got a family asshole" she said turning to look the elderly Captain in the eye with contempt.

"I don't want to kill you Linda; so very slowly take your guns and toss them away" he said as he watched her toss the handgun as far as she could. She did the same thing with her MP-5 machine-gun she had hanging from a sling staring at him in anger.

"You use to be a good man; how did the Covington's get their hooks into you?" she asked looking around and behind the armed Captain.

"The money to look the other way was just too good to turn down" he said smiling at the pissed off mother.

"They didn't start hurting anyone until that asshole Howler & his mercenaries got involved with them" Hargrove continued.

"Evelyn Covington wouldn't let anything happen to the kids; she adored them" he said pointing his gun at Linda's chest. "Nathaniel was a different story; he's a lunatic, a hard ass" Hargrove explained to her, who listened with deaf ears.

"So you think that makes you less responsible?" Linda asked angrily. "You were involved with kidnapping & selling children; CHILDREN".

"You're all going to rot in a prison cell for taking my son and trying to kill my family; you might as well cuff yourself to that corral now" Linda said sternly pointing to the wooden fence behind him.

"Move to your left" Linda heard in her ear com knowing it was Tyler's voice.

Linda not knowing what Tyler was up too nonchalantly moved

a couple of steps to her left when she heard her say in her ear "Your OTHER left sweetie" with a slight giggle.

Linda sighed and rolled her eyes; then moved back over a couple of steps hoping not to give Hargrove any idea she was being talked to by Karen Tyler.

Just as she moved, a bullet hit Hargrove in his right shoulder causing blood to spray out from the wound making him drop his gun on the ground.

Tyler had come upon the two of them heading towards the stables. She could see Hargrove holding Linda at gunpoint from the top of the hill; she laid down in the bushes, flipped down her tripod on her AR rifle, looked through her night-vision scope and took the shot; hitting the police Captain right where she knew he would drop his gun.

Tyler could have killed the elderly Captain but knew Linda wanted to take him alive to pay for his part in helping the Covington's kidnap Parker; and the wounding of her fellow officers back at the precinct.

Hargrove screamed in pain as Linda picked his handgun up from the ground in front of her, pointing it at the now distressed Captain bleeding from his wound. She looked up towards where Tyler was hiding and smiled.

Linda quickly walked up to the now wounded man standing there holding his hand against his blood soaked police uniform, hitting him across the face with his own gun knocking him to the ground. "That's for my son asshole" she said pissed off, watching the elderly man spit blood out of his mouth and stare back at her with anger.

Dazing him, she grabbed the elderly Captain by his other arm and dragged him over to the wooden-fenced corral pulling out her cuffs and securing him to a steel ring bolted to the corral gate used to pull the large gate open.

"Where's the pilot?" Linda asked grabbing the Captain by the face seeing he was in extreme pain from his bullet wound.

"I'm the pilot; Evelyn called me to meet her and the boy here, just as Hell broke loose inside" Hargrove said wincing and grimacing in pain.

Linda touched her com in her ear and asked "Stacy look up Captain Andrew Hargrove, see if he has a chopper pilot license; copy".

"Copy that Lieutenant" Stacy replied typing away on her keyboard again as Murphy continued to watch at her side. Stacy knew that every helicopter pilot had to be licensed & registered with the Federal Aviation Administration; so she knew exactly where to look.

"Affirmative on the chopper license Linda; copy" Stacy came back almost immediately. "He flew Apache helicopters in Desert Storm back in the 90's; copy" she continued. "The FAA say's he just renewed it a couple of weeks ago" Stacy finished saying.

"Roger that, thanks sweetie" Linda replied looking down at Hargrove still bleeding from his shoulder with a big grin.

"Looks like you can tell the truth under extreme duress Captain" she said bending down to look him in the eye.

Linda stood up and asked "Hey Stacy, just for giggles look up Evelyn Covington with the FAA".

Stacy heard her sister in law and continued looking at the FAA pilot's registrar when she figured out what Linda was asking for.

"Nice call sis" Stacy said reading from her computer screen the findings she had.

"Evelyn Covington has a chopper license as well; AND, interesting enough she has a charted flight plan to Hartsfield-Jackson International Airport in Atlanta, Georgia at midnight; then a nonstop flight on their private jet to Seville Spain upon arrival" she said knowing Linda was listening intently and taking it all in.

Linda looked down at Hargrove and put her boot on his shoulder wound and pushed down on it slowly; making him scream louder from the extreme pain she was now causing.

"You're not the pilot asshole, Evelyn is" she said grinning at the captured police Captain, blood still oozing out of his shoulder and seeing her bloody boot print on his tan uniform shirt.

She turned and started staring over at the helicopter again sitting in the moonlight then looked over her shoulder at Hargrove saying "Don't go away now" sarcastically, picking her handgun off the ground and re-holstering it.

There was a steel bucket sitting beside the filled up water trough the horses drank out of and Linda was quick to pick it up and walk over to the fuel tank.

She filled the bucket with fuel; she figured it was a mix of oil & gasoline and carefully carried it over to the helicopter.

She proceeded to douse the entire helicopter both inside & out with the bucket of fuel. After she was finished she searched her pockets realizing she didn't have anything to ignite it with.

All of a sudden a big smile came over her face and she went back to get another bucket of fuel. She carefully poured the fuel in a straight line down the path back to the front of the stable. She stopped and put the empty bucket on the ground and looked down at Hargrove smiling at him.

"You got a light big fella" she asked playfully laughing, knowing Hargrove was a chain smoker and kept a pack of cigarettes & matches in his pocket at all times.

She reached down and searched his pockets finding a half empty pack of menthol cigarettes and a small box of wooden matches.

"These things will kill you" she said grinning as she threw the cigarette pack to the ground stepping on them and grounding them into the dirt opening the box of matches.

She pulled out a match and struck it along the side of the small wooden box igniting it into flame, then dropping the lit match on the ground into the wet fuel lighting it up.

Linda Mason & Captain Hargrove watched as the trail of flame quickly ran all the way up to the helicopter setting it a blaze about a hundred feet away. It was now completely on fire inside & out and they both knew what was about to come next.

The loud sound of the wooden stable door started sliding open causing Linda to turn and see Evelyn Covington standing there with her son Parker, holding him aggressively by his little wrist.

Just as Linda started to take a step towards the older woman a massive explosion and roar came from behind her as the helicopter exploded into hundred's of pieces.

Linda didn't even see or hear what happened behind her; she didn't even flinch because she was only focused on getting her son away from the evil woman standing in front of her.

Fiery pieces of metal continued to rain down all around Linda as she stood there unafraid staring into the eyes of Evelyn Covington holding her son tightly by his wrist; the night sky now lit up by fire from the destroyed helicopter.

Max Mason sat on the metal edge of the air duct looking down into the control room through the vented grate knowing this was his best & only way of getting into the room to stop Nathaniel Covington's rocket launch and destroying his illegal "blackmailing" communication satellite.

In order to get here, Max with help from Stacy's computer figured that the only way to get into the control room other than walking through the magnetically locked door was crawling through the air ventilation ducts above the ceilings.

Stacy found that the building permits called for oversized 36"x 36" sheet metal duct work in order to accommodate the air ventilation system of the five story building and its large amount of employees.

The floor plans also called for "vertical" ducting to be used in the ceiling of each room, especially in the computer labs; instead of the normal "horizontal" vents built into the walls above the rooms.

Max found an empty office a short distance down the hall from the control room. He secured his gear then proceeded to stand on top of the desk taking several ceiling tiles out and tossing them on the floor.

Looking into the ceiling he could see the large ventilation duct above his head.

He stuck his head into the ceiling looking all around; evaluating what he was about to do. Using his flashlight he could see the duct work going all the way down the hallway over top of the communications control room and beyond.

Max noticed that the duct work was well put together by Phillips-head screws; grabbed his universal tool from his gun belt and started unscrewing several sections of the metal ventilation. After each section was removed he slowly & quietly lowered them to the desk so he wouldn't give away his position, or what he was about to do.

He knew that time was running out so he had to quickly climb into the open section of the aluminum duct and crawl towards the control room.

He barely fit inside the closed in metal walls but was determined to stop Covington from launching his satellite. Max crawled inside the metal boxing as fast as he could finally coming to the control room vent.

Now sitting on the edge Max could see he was about ten feet from the floor of the control room. His feet dangled down towards the vent as Max whispered "Stacy I need eyes on any armed bogeys inside the control room; copy?"

"Roger that Admiral" Stacy replied switching her GPS visual on her computer screen to the security cameras inside the Covington building.

"Admiral; they have NO security cameras inside the communication control room" Stacy Mason said to her father with concern in her voice.

"But I can zoom inside through the glass with the two cameras they have OUTSIDE the control room lobby, and can see two bogeys at ten & two o'clock from your position sir; do you copy?" she asked seeing the two armed mercenaries standing inside close to Nathaniel Covington, and his bodyguard Simon.

"Roger that Lieutenant, nice work sweetheart" Max said holding his gun in his right hand as he was about to jump into the metal duct leading to the launch control room floor.

Nathaniel Covington watched patiently as the launch technicians sat at their stations looking over their data for the launch & flight of the rocket with his communication satellite onboard.

He intently watched the overhead video screen to see the rocket on its launch pad almost 400 miles away in Maryland. He knew NASA and the F.B.I. were monitoring the launch of his telecommunications satellite suspecting it was for nefarious uses.

Covington looked at Simon standing next to him and smiled at his protector, knowing Max Mason and his son was causing havoc with Colonel Howler & his men inside his building; but knew they couldn't get through the control room door in time to stop him.

Covington heard behind him & Simon a loud crash of metal hitting one of the technicians control station turning to see Max Mason standing there with his gun drawn aiming at the two armed mercenaries in the room.

"WHAT THE FUCK?" Covington yelled as he watched Max fire twice hitting both mercenaries in the forehead killing them instantly before they even had a chance to raise their weapons at him.

The technician that was sitting close to Max when he came out of the ventilation duct quickly got out of his chair and tackled Max, knocking him and his gun to the floor. Max looked over at Nathaniel now in a panic while the tech hit him in the ribs a couple of times.

Max could see Simon pulling Covington towards him as they both moved towards a now open doorway a few feet away from them. Nathaniel grabbed a computer tablet from one of the technicians moving quickly inside the small opening with Simon right behind him.

From under the technician Max could see stairs inside the door heading up figuring it was Covington's secret escape route out of the room if it was compromised.

Max hit the tech hard in the face with a right elbow blow glancing over at a staring Nathaniel Covington grinning at him as the door slowly closed.

He rolled the male tech over sitting on top of him and hit him hard in the jaw dazing the man. Max got up and quickly picked his gun off the floor pointing it at the tech, who raised his hands in the air still lying on his back.

Max looked out into the lobby area to see Jake come running around the corner and yelled at the remaining seated technician's, waving his handgun at them "OPEN THE DOOR; NOW".

He quickly looked up at the timer on the wall to see they had less than four minutes to abort the satellite being deployed.

The glass door's magnetic locks clicked loudly as they disengaged allowing Jake to quickly get inside just as his dad ordered "EVERYONE OUT; NOW".

The four technician's, even the one that Max fought got up and ran out the door without being told a second time, leaving Max & Jake alone as the timer continued to countdown to the launch.

"You have about three minutes left son, can you stop this damn thing?" "NO pressure" Max asked with a smile on his face.

"Yeah, I'm pretty sure I can Pop" Jake said already plugged in to the main control server typing away on his laptop and glancing up at his dad.

"I'm going after Covington & Simon; blow this thing up and get out of here before the Fed's come in; then go help your wife get your son back" Max said checking his handgun then placing it back in the holster nodding to his boy.

"Cool, Pop" Jake replied giving his dad a big grin then going back to his hacking of the control room server.

"Don't forget to lock the door" Max said laughing knowing he must of said that to Jake more than 10,000 times when he and Stacy were growing up because he would always leave the back door unlocked when he came in.

"Really Pop?" Jake responded grinning at his dad as he left through the doorway.

Max stopped after the door closed behind him looking at his son who smiled and hit a button on the console in front of him locking the door with a loud click.

Jake watched his dad run to the emergency stairwell door and disappear inside it, heading to the 5th floor to confront Nathaniel Covington.

Jake furiously typed on his computer trying to get into the control room server starting to feel the pressure as he continuously looked at the timer counting down to the rocket's launch.

Seeing he only had seconds before the launch he had a "Plan B" already formulated in his head for getting the rocket to abort its mission and destroy itself but his dad wasn't going to like it; AT ALL.

Jake watched the video screen over his head to see the rocket launch from Goddard Space Center quickly rising into the dark moonlit sky.

"I guess "Plan B" it is then" he said out loud knowing no one else was in the room to hear him.

Jake knew that ALL satellites are released in what's called "low earth orbit" or "LEO" as NASA calls it, which is about sixty miles above the ground here on earth.

He also knew that the rockets that carry the satellites automatically release them when they reach that hundred mile position at pre-arranged trajectory coordinates.

Those trajectory coordinates are voted on, and unanimously approved for designation by the Congressional satellite sub-committee, NASA, and the NSA; they are also completely hack proof.

"The Admiral is going to have some serious explaining to do" Jake said to himself as he typed incredibly fast on his laptop then hitting the "enter" button to get a big flashing red "ACCESS DENIED" on his screen.

Jake Mason was now criminally hacking into the National

Security Administration's main server, raising all kind of alarms back in DC and knowing his dad was going to be pissed.

His "Plan B" was to alter the trajectory coordinates of the Covington rocket/satellite; to send it somewhere else where it could crash safely away from populated areas.

Jake knew he had a seventy-five mile maximum window, beyond that the satellite would be launched automatically without any interference and Nathaniel Covington would have his "blackmail" application operational.

Jake continued to type getting "ACCESS DENIED" several times, until finally he got the software code through the NSA firewall to get "ACCESS GRANTED" flash on his screen.

Jake feverishly typed the keyboard, realizing that the NSA program he was hacking into only allowed the rocket trajectory to be altered to one of two places, either the place it took off from or the place that had it under automated control.

"I'm seriously out of a job for sure now" Jake said to himself a bit miffed but giggled at what he said; knowing he couldn't send it back to the Goddard Space Center because it would kill a lot of innocent people there.

He knew the ONLY place he could really send it was right where he was sitting; the Covington Industries building.

He continued typing on his computer for a few moments getting the coordinates from the rocket's current location which was just passing the fifty mile marker.

Jake quickly programmed the coordinates from the control room server and pressed "enter" seeing the rocket's trajectory start to turn on his computer screen.

A timer popped up immediately on his screen with 11:00:00 on it and started counting down to the point of impact; destroying the Covington Industries building.

"TERRIFIC; I have my dad, my Army buddies, and my two new sisters in a building that I just sent a twenty ton rocket full of flammable fuel into; and have eleven minutes to get everyone out before we're all crispy critters" Jake said out loud with a worried laugh but knowing his wife Linda, his son Parker, and Karen Tyler weren't in the building anymore.

"Better go tell my dad" he thought unlocking the control room door, grabbing his laptop, and then heading towards the stairwell.

"I wonder how he's going to feel about another building dropping on him" he said to himself knowing that the GBN building nearly fell on top of him before.

CHAPTER EIGHTEEN

Yuki Amikura opened the conference room door very slowly, her sword over her head in a defensive posture as she stepped inside; immediately closing and locking the door behind her.

The room was well lit and she could see her cousin Noki Amikura wearing a long-sleeved white collared shirt and sitting at the far end of a long table in the back of the room with a samurai sword laying on the table's surface in front of him.

Noki smiled at his young cousin as she looked at the lone mercenary wearing a mask sitting next to him; his handgun also sitting on the table top in front of him.

"He's not here to kill you; I am" Noki said to her grinning.

"He's just here in case there are any unexpected guests trying to interrupt our little family squabble" he continued, looking at the mercenary and smiling at him.

"I see you brought a sword; I guess since your men are all dead you'll have to fight on your own now" Yuki said staring at her cousin with contempt in her eyes knowing one of his men wounded Ochi.

"It doesn't have to be this way cousin" Yuki pleaded seeing the condescending grin on Noki's face.

"You can retire from the company and still live the rest of your life in luxury" she said hoping he would listen to reason before someone got killed.

"The company should be MINE; you never wanted it" he said getting up from his chair angry, pushing it back against the wall.

"Uncle thought you would ruin his company if you took over; and he was right" Yuki replied moving into the open space of the room.

"You have brought disrespect & dishonor to the Amikura name by lying down with known criminals like the Covington's" she continued, waiting for her cousin's first move towards her; knowing she was making him angrier.

"Then you're really going to be pissed off when I tell you I just sold $400 million dollars worth of missile guidance systems to the North Koreans" Noki replied smiling at her with an arrogant grin.

"They'll get refunded when I leave here" she said staring him in the eye.

Noki Amikura slowly picked up the sword from the table and pulled it from its scabbard. Slowly walking around the table he started swinging the sword left & right as if he was getting use to the weight of the sword in his hand for the first time.

"I see you came alone cousin; did my ninja kill your little pet outside?" he asked trying to provoke a response from Yuki who stood her ground in the open area of the room.

"Are you going to talk me to death cousin; I have a breakfast date in a couple of hours" she said sarcastically thinking about Crusher Davis outside the door waiting for her, then looking over at the mercenary now standing in the far corner of the room with his gun in his hand.

"Wanting to die quickly is a noble thing" Noki said as he playfully swung his blade at her several times hearing the "clang" each time she blocked his sword with her own.

Finally taking it seriously, Noki swung over & over again; being blocked each time by Yuki's agility and skill with a sword.

He pushed his blade against hers forcing their blades towards her blue uniform when Yuki kicked him hard in the chest with a forceful front-thrust kick that knocked him backwards separating their swords.

Noki stepped back and looked at his white shirt seeing a dirty boot print on the front of it and a smiling Yuki Amikura standing in front of him her sword over her head again.

"Looks like you're going to have to do laundry this week" she said with a smirk seeing the anger in his eyes and the boot print on his chest.

""Will you have something smart-ass to say as you take your last breath?" Noki asked as he prepared to attack again.

"Probably" she replied laughing as Noki ran up on her swinging his sword again going high, and then going low but still being counter blocked each time by a skilled Yuki. She ducked under a swing to her head coming back up and back-handing Noki in the jaw again knocking him backwards and finally hard enough to knock him off-balance and onto the floor.

Noki gets up quickly and comes after Yuki swinging his sword at her crazily; only to have her block each stroke easily; making him look more foolish in her eyes.

Yuki spin kicks Noki to the side of the head with lightning speed knocking him to the floor again causing him to roll over on his hands & knees; spitting blood out of his mouth this time onto the carpeted floor.

The mercenary, seeing Noki Amikura getting his ass kicked decides to kill her himself raising his gun and firing several shots at the blue dressed ninja girl.

Yuki dives under the conference table avoiding the bullets watching as the mercenary comes around the other side firing several shots into the top of the wooden table she is hiding under. The bullets barely miss her coming through the table as she rolls over to the other side away from the mercenary losing her sword.

"NOOOOO" Noki yells seeing the mercenary flip the big table over pushing it out of his way so he could have a clear shot at the young Asian woman.

Noki gets back on his feet; grabs his sword off the floor and runs to the mercenary aiming his gun at his defenseless cousin. He runs his sword through the soldier's back, and out his chest twisting the hilt as it stops; seeing him convulse, then slump on his sword killing him. Noki quickly pulls his blade out of the now dead mercenary to confront Yuki lying on the floor as the lifeless body falls to the ground beside her.

Yuki managed to roll into the open area, lying on the floor next to the wall; looking up at her cousin as she glances over at her sword just within arms reach now completely vulnerable.

Now standing over his fallen kin, Noki raises his sword above his head with blood still dripping from his mouth and now from his sword smiling; saying to his stunned cousin "Only I get to kill you".

Ochi Osaka was standing against the wall continuing to press down on her wound to keep it from bleeding again keeping her katana swords next to her as they leaned against the wall. She looked over at Crusher standing guard in the lobby seeing him keep an eye on her from a distance.

She and Crusher Davis understood why Yuki had to take on her cousin alone, but hated the idea of having to wait down the hallway from the conference room where Yuki & Noki Amikura were fighting, able to hear the continuous clash of steel blade against steel blade from down inside the room.

"SISTER" Ochi screamed when she heard the multiple gunshots from the conference room knowing that Yuki would NEVER use a gun against anyone.

She grabbed one of her Katana swords and ran gingerly to the door before Crusher could stop her kicking the door open with all she had left in her seeing a surprised Yuki lying on the floor as her cousin Noki stood over her his sword raised above his head ready for her deathstroke.

She threw her katana sword from the doorway towards Noki Amikura just as he turned and winked at her knowing she was watching him kill her best friend.

"YUKI" she screamed seeing the blade of her katana sword stick into the wall just above Yuki's head just as Noki's blade came down to strike her; instead he struck Ochi's blade embedded into the drywall giving Yuki a split second to grab her sword from the floor and plunge it deep into her cousin's chest as he went to raise his blade again.

Yuki slowly stood back up still holding her sword in Noki's chest staring into his dying eyes as he dropped his sword; the blood now pouring out of his mouth.

"That's what REAL family is about" she said knowing her best friend just saved her life even though she was seriously wounded herself.

She pulled the blade swiftly from his chest watching him fall to the floor; his dead eyes staring over at Ochi who had fallen down from the exertion of throwing her sword.

"OCHI" she yelled dropping her sword and running to her wounded friend.

Ochi smiled at her friend & companion and asked "Is that the end of all the family drama?" realizing Crusher Davis had caught her before she fell to the floor looking up at him smiling then back to Yuki saying "He's a keeper".

"Yeah, he is" Yuki replied grinning at the huge black soldier who gave her an agreeing grin.

"Ladies, we need to get out of here before it gets crazy again with more mercenaries & ninja's" Crusher stated slowly helping Ochi to her feet watching her put her arm around Yuki's neck to hold her up.

"What about Max Mason?" Yuki asked thinking her dad and brother Jake might need help with the Covington's.

"Admiral Mason, and the Captain can take care of themselves; he would want us to get out of here safely" Crusher replied as they started heading towards the stairwell door.

Max Mason walked out of the 5th floor stairwell with his XD handgun pointed everywhere he looked; finally coming to a hidden unmarked door to Nathaniel Covington's office.

He remembered earlier that morning; he, Tyler, and Linda used a direct elevator to his office thinking that Covington & Simon would be expecting him to use it to get to them; probably waiting at the elevator door with their guns drawn.

As he came up the stairwell knowing Covington was headed to his office Max asked Stacy to look at the floor plans to find him another way in that they wouldn't expect; finding the unmarked door.

Max slowly opened the door seeing Simon standing in front of the elevator door holding a MP-5 machine-gun, and Nathaniel Covington tearing through his desk looking for something. Neither saw him step inside the door as he quietly stood a few feet behind Simon his gun pointed at his head.

"Slowly, lower your gun; because I won't hesitate to kill you where you stand" Max said calmly to Simon glancing over at Nathaniel who looked up from looking into his desk drawers hearing Max's voice.

Simon slowly lowered the machine-gun, laying it on the floor at his feet then pushed it towards Max with his left foot now looking at Max Mason with a scowl on his face.

"You're to late Mr. Mason" Nathaniel Covington said smiling, looking up at the clock on his wall now saying 12:03am and knowing the rocket took off from the Goddard launch site already.

"Maybe, but I trust the ingenuity of my son to be able to stop your satellite; he's much smarter than you & I put together" Max replied grinning back at Nathaniel.

"You're so naïve Mason; my mother has already gotten away with taking your grandson; and in just a matter of minutes regardless if I'm in prison or not; OUR satellite will be operational" Covington said as Simon stood there looking for an opportunity to attack Max.

"Don't be so sure about a mother's love for her son" Max replied knowing Linda would give her last breath to save Parker from Evelyn Covington.

"And speaking of mother's, lets talk about yours for a moment" Max continued looking Simon in the eye with a grin.

"You don't get to talk about my mother asshole" Covington replied protecting her honor.

"Well, stop me if you've heard this one" Max said with a laugh still pointing his gun at Simon's head.

"Seems that my daughter found the buried hospital records Phillip Covington tried so hard to keep buried almost thirty years ago" Max started, continuing to smile at Simon who stood there and sneered at him.

"Looks like Evelyn Covington had a serious mental breakdown a couple of days after her baby boy was born; then finding out he suddenly died" he continued knowing that the child died of "sudden infant death" syndrome or "SID".

"When a nurse told her that her son had died; Evelyn tried to kill her with a pair of scissors, and was placed in the hospital's mental ward for almost a week" he said seeing Simon take a step towards him.

"Really asshole; you would rather die than tell him the truth?" Max asked Simon pointing his gun aggressively at his chest now seeing him step back again.

"What the Hell are you talking about Mason?" Nathaniel asked curious about where this was going still standing behind his desk.

"Seems that on the same day, another couple gave birth to a baby boy; but because of complications during the birth the mother died" Max replied watching Simon lower his head as he continued to talk.

"The father was so distraught over losing his wife that he basically struck a deal with the devil" Max continued looking over at Nathaniel Covington who was now engrossed in his story.

"I'll kill you for this Mason" Simon said angrily knowing Max wasn't finished with his story looking over at Nathaniel who looked at him confused.

"Phillip Covington paid the depressed, and now widowed father $10 million dollars to take the baby boy off his hands; giving the new born to his wife Evelyn to raise as her own" Max said watching Nathaniel sit down in his chair finally figuring out what he was saying.

Max could see Simon getting more agitated as he continued the story he was telling Covington, knowing Simon was about to do something stupid. Max took a couple of steps back.

"What are you saying Mason?" Nathaniel Covington asked confused at his story.

And sure enough, his face bright red with anger Simon slung his arms down and out to his sides to reveal two 18" razor sharp steel blades that slid out from metal rails attached to both of his forearms hidden by his large Na'rew jacket sleeves.

Simon spun around quickly swinging one of his blades at Max hitting the barrel of his gun and knocking it out of his hand and across the floor. Simon stood there smiling at Max seeing he was now unarmed then looked over at Nathaniel still sitting at his desk with a look of bewilderment on his face at what Max Mason had told him.

Max took a step backwards, and then reached behind his back pulling his two batons from their holsters slinging them both down towards the floor to extend them grinning back at Simon.

Max looked over at Nathaniel Covington seeing the confusion on his face about what he said about his family & his birth just staring into space.

Simon attacked swinging his blades back and forth at Max who blocked his every move with his steel batons finally sending Simon backwards with a hard front kick to his chest.

"The grieving husband & father agreed to accept the $10 million dollars for his son but wanted something else as well" Max said out loud knowing Covington was still listening as Max continued to stare Simon in the eye with his condescending smile.

Simon attacked again swinging his blades harder this time, finally getting through cutting Max through his tuxedo shirt on his left arm.

They both stepped back staring at one another; as Max looked down at his torn shirt starting to turn red with blood as it started dripping down his hand falling to the carpeted floor in small drops.

Max grabbed his arm to allow his white shirt to soak up some of the blood then looked at Simon smiling asking him "Do you want to tell him, or should I?".

Simon came at Max furiously swinging his blades erratically hoping to finally kill Max. However Max's expertise with swords and batons were no match for Simon when Max ducked under one of his strikes and came up swinging his baton hitting Simon across the jaw knocking him to the ground.

Max kept his eye on Simon laying there on the floor rubbing his jaw seeing the blood flow from the corner of his mouth; then looked over at Nathaniel Covington curious about whether Max Mason would continue his story.

"It seems that Phillip Covington bought the medical file from the doctor who delivered you" looking back at Simon slowly getting back on his feet.

"What Covington didn't know was a nurse had already sent a copy of the birth/death certificate to the state's Hall of Records the day the child was born" Max continued; seeing Nathaniel start to put the pieces together in his head.

"So according to our investigation, and the original birth certificate your REAL name is Jeffrey Ramsey; NOT Nathaniel Covington" Max said smiling at Nathaniel, then looking over at Simon knowing he was about to piss him off even more.

"And by the way, this is Simon Ramsey; your REAL father" Max said looking at Simon now with anger & contempt knowing they all played a part in kidnapping his grandson, and trying to kill his family.

Simon rushed him swinging his blades back and forth as Max blocked each of his swings as the loud sound resonated from the "clangs" of the blades hitting his steel batons. Max blocked his backhand swing with his baton then delivered a hard head butt to his head stumbling Simon backwards then falling to the ground toppling over.

Max stood over the downed bodyguard who was barely moving on the floor, finally seeing him slowly roll over on his back to show both him & Nathaniel that when he fell he impaled himself on his own blade. The blade had gone through the side of his abdomen and into his lungs.

"NOOOOOO" Nathaniel yelled running over to Simon from behind his desk going to his knees next to him; looking down at his mentor who was smiling up at him; blood starting to ooze from his mouth.

"MY SON; I have waited a very long time to call you that to your face" Simon said slowly dying. "Evelyn threatened to have you killed if I said anything to you about being my son" he continued, coughing up more blood. "I have always been so proud of you; only able to love you in silence" Simon said starting to gasp for air.

Simon looked up at Max standing over them both and said "I guess I have you to thank for bringing me & my son back together" seeing Max nod to the smile he gave him just as he took his last breath looking at Nathaniel.

Max stood there watching Nathaniel Covington, knowing he was Simon's son Jeffrey crying & holding the ONLY man he knew to be his friend & mentor slowly close his dead eyes laying his head softly down on the carpeted floor of his office.

Jake Mason ran in from the open doorway and stopped; seeing his dad standing there over a dead Simon and a emotionally tearful Nathaniel Covington.

He quietly approached his dad from the side saying in a low voice "We need to get the Hell out of here Pop".

Max looked at Jake and asked "Did you destroy the satellite?" watching Nathaniel Covington stand up in front of them both with anger on his face as tears continued to run down his cheeks.

"Bad news, good news, really bad news" Jake replied with a playful grin, but serious at what he was telling his dad.

"The rocket took off" Jake said seeing his dad wasn't to happy to hear that, but Nathaniel was with a big smile wiping the tears from his eyes and face.

"I managed to redirect it to crash somewhere else" he continued knowing the question his father was about to ask him as Covington stepped back from Simon still staring at him on the floor.

"I know I'm going to hate myself for asking this" Max said with a grin keeping one eye on Nathaniel who was a bit nervous standing there. Looking at Jake, Max asked "Where is it crashing Captain?" rolling his eyes already knowing the answer.

"HERE, in about ten minutes" Jake replied to his dad with a sheepish grin. "That's why we need to get the Hell out of here; NOW" he said seeing his dad smile at him knowing he did what was best to save lives.

Max turned to face Nathaniel saying "We can do this the easy way, or the hard way; I don't care which" tossing a plastic restraining cuff on the floor at his feet.

Nathaniel went into a fighting stance hearing Max say "Good, I wanted to beat the shit out of you" just as Nathaniel with precision, spun around and kicked Max upside his head. Max didn't move, in fact he didn't even flinch looking at Covington with anger in his eyes as he rubbed his cheek.

"You fucked up now dude" Jake said with a grin as he watched his dad use the same spin kick to knock Nathaniel about ten feet backwards landing hard against the wall.

Nathaniel slowly got up and walked towards Max swinging his fists with martial arts expertise but getting frustrated because Max blocked every punch he threw.

Max finally decided that he had enough; connecting to Nathaniel's jaw with a complete turning spin punch to his jaw knocking him to the floor again.

"Never piss off a grandfather by taking his grandson" Jake said watching Nathaniel Covington slowly getting back to his feet again.

"You're damn lucky it's a code today, and NOT a guideline" Max said looking over at his son smiling knowing he would understand what he meant by that.

Nathaniel was a bit wobbly from the punch he took taking a wild swing at Max who hit him square in the jaw with his right fist knocking him completely out watching him hit the floor unconscious.

Max looked at his son and asked "Howler?".

Jake looked at his dad saying solemnly "He won't be joining us" feeling bad that he had to kill him.

Max touched his ear bud as he bent over and flipped Nathaniel Covington over quickly putting the plastic cuffs on him saying out loud "Stacy do you copy?"

"I'm here daddy; are you & Jake okay, copy?" Stacy asked into his ear piece seeing on her screen they were both still inside Covington Industries.

"We're both fine; copy?" he said grinning at Jake as he picked Nathaniel Covington up off the floor and threw him over his shoulder.

"I need you to unlock the front door, patch into all the buildings loudspeakers, and tell everyone to get out & away from the building; copy?" Max said as both he & Jake hurried out the doorway with Covington over Max's shoulder.

"I also need you to find out who's in charge outside and have them meet us at the front door; copy?" he said, as he and Jake hurried down the emergency stairwell.

"Do you have locations on everyone else; copy?" Max asked hoping his team was out of the building already.

"Jose Martin & Crusher Davis have secured the other floors; copy?" she said to her father seeing the employees running out the front lobby door on her video screen, now that she unlocked the computerized magnetic locks.

"Crusher says Ochi was wounded by one of the ninja's she killed who was working for Noki Amikura; but its not life threatening, copy?" she continued saying to her dad.

"Roger that; and Yuki, copy?" Max asked hoping his other daughter was okay after her confrontation with her psycho cousin.

"She's good; her cousin not so much, copy?" Stacy replied in his ear with a slight giggle knowing her big sister killed him.

"Roger that, what about…?" Max didn't even get to say her name when he heard his daughter say.

"Both Tyler & Linda are out of the building, and near the stables going after Evelyn Covington and Parker; copy?" she replied knowing what he was about to ask.

Max let out a long sigh of relief knowing Tyler, Linda, and his grandson Parker weren't in the building anymore.

He could see Jose Martin, his daughter Yuki, and his new adopted daughter Ochi, who was being held up by Crusher Davis waiting in the lobby as he & Jake came through the stairwell door with Nathaniel Covington still unconscious over Max's shoulder.

"Lets go, everyone out of here" Max ordered looking around at everyone seeing the flashing lights of the police cars and emergency vehicles outside the large windows as they all headed to the building's front door.

CHAPTER NINETEEN

Karen Tyler continued lying on the grass between two bushes at the top of the hill still hidden from everyone as she looked through her rifle scope making sure there weren't any more of Howler's mercenaries moving around to interrupt Linda & Evelyn Covington's inevitable showdown.

The flames & smoke from the now burned out shell of the helicopter and fuel tank station continued to rise into the dark sky. She could see several large burning pieces of metal lying on the ground surrounding the fenced in corral area in front of the Covington's red & white barn as the fires lit up the area.

She slowly got up from her position and started walking down the hill towards Linda Mason who was standing in front of Evelyn Covington holding her son Parker with her arm now around his small neck.

The two angry women were staring at one another as Tyler gently & quietly moved up beside Linda keeping the red dot of her laser sight from her AR-15 sniper rifle motionless on Evelyn Covington's forehead.

Linda glanced over and smiled at Tyler not saying anything, just taking her hand and slowly lowering her friend's rifle from her target not wanting to kill the woman while she was holding her boy.

Linda pulled out her handcuffs from her gun belt and threw them on the ground in front of Evelyn saying "Please DON'T put these on" seeing the confusion on the rich matriarch's face at what she just said.

"See, if you put them on I don't get to kick your ass really bad" Linda said with an evil grin.

"I'm Evelyn Covington; I surrender to no one you smug bitch" the rich elder woman said holding Parker a bit tighter.

"MOMMY" Parker yelled starting to feel a little scared at what was happening around him as he struggled against her tight grip around his neck.

"Hey sweetheart, I've missed you; so has daddy & Grandpa Max" Linda replied smiling then getting down on one knee to talk to her son on his level.

"Say the word sweetie and I will drop her where she stands" Tyler said raising her rifle back up and putting the red dot on Evelyn's forehead again making sure she said it loud enough for Covington to hear her.

"I can break this precious boy's neck before either one of you get to me" Evelyn said squeezing her arm a little tighter around the five year old's neck.

"Sweetie, do you remember what Grandpa Max said about bullies at school?" she asked her son not caring what Covington said.

Parker nodded to his mom understanding what she said then looked up at Evelyn Covington who looked down at him with a scowl on her face. He looked back at his mom who gave him a smile and a simple nod.

Parker looked to the ground then stomped on Evelyn's left foot really hard with his little right foot causing her extreme pain and immediately releasing her grip on the little boy who promptly ran to his mother still kneeling on the ground in front of him.

Linda remembered that Parker was having some "bullying" issues on the playground recently with a couple of boys at day care and he told his grandpa Max during one of their video chats.

She didn't like it at the time; but Max's advice was to stomp hard on the little boy's foot; and then go get the teacher; which he did twice, and the boys haven't bothered him since.

Linda hugged her son tightly kissing him affectionately as Tyler continued pointing her rifle at Evelyn Covington who was extremely angry at herself for allowing a little boy to get the best of her, causing her to lose the only leverage she had against the two armed women.

Tyler quickly motioned with her rifle to Evelyn Covington to raise her hands above her head which she did with disgust.

Linda looked up at Tyler and smiled looking at Parker with a big smile on his face happy to be with his mom again.

Linda stood up holding the little boys hand and said "This is your Grandma Karen; I want you and her to go find your Grandpa Max & daddy; okay sweetheart"

"Where are you going mommy?" Parker asked not wanting her to leave again.

Linda looked back at Evelyn Covington with anger in her eyes as the middle-aged woman arrogantly smiled at her replying "Mommy has to have a little talk with the lady, I'll be right back; I PROMISE".

Evelyn Covington grinned at what the young mother said replying to her statement with arrogance "A bit presumptuous of you, don't you think sweetheart".

"Okay mommy; come on Grandma, mommy isn't happy with that lady" Parker said grabbing her hand turning and walking towards the hill. Tyler looked down at the smart little boy and smiled as a tear came down her cheek thinking how smart & brave he was, just like his father; and Grandpa Max.

Linda stood in front of Evelyn Covington unbuckling her gun belt, dropping it to the ground with a confident grin. She slowly walked up to Evelyn who was smiling arrogantly at her staring her in the eyes.

"You kidnapped my son and tried to sell him bitch" Linda said angrily quickly punching her upside her jaw surprising the older woman knocking her backwards against the barn door.

Covington dusted her dress off then reached down and ripped the material up to her hip and tossing her heels to the side giving her easier mobility to fight.

She ran at Linda manically throwing precision punch combinations watching the well trained police officer block each one easily angering her even more.

Finally Evelyn kicked Linda in the abdomen forcing her to step back looking at the woman with contempt. "My son isn't the only one who learned how to fight over the years" she said laughing at Linda; then going back into a fighting stance.

"You hit like an old woman; WAIT, you are an old woman" Linda replied giving Covington her own laugh.

What Linda said infuriated Covington; her anger getting the better of her causing her to lose control and attack again with several spin kicks & punches that Linda blocked easily each time.

Linda finally had enough of deflecting Evelyn's aggressive attacks; spinning around quickly hitting Evelyn Covington hard in the jaw with her right fist knocking her to the ground.

"I know that had to hurt, didn't it?" Linda asked looking down at her lying in the dirt, blood pouring from her mouth.

Evelyn Covington looked up at Linda Mason from the ground; her beautiful dress now covered in dirt and screamed "YOU BITCH" as she slowly got up, wiping the blood from the corner of her mouth.

Linda walked up to the disoriented elderly woman and grabbed the front of her dress and jabbed with her right fist several times connecting to Evelyn's jaw & right eye socket knocking her to the ground again.

"That's for all the kids you kidnapped in the past you despicable low life" Linda said sternly standing over the bloody & bruised woman, her eye starting to swell from her punches.

Tyler stopped and turned back to see Linda standing over Evelyn Covington lying on the ground bleeding, then looked down at a smiling Parker saying "I think your mommy had a good talk with the lady" watching him look back at his mom who smiled at him.

Linda reached down and grabbed Evelyn Covington rolling her over on her stomach without any resistance pulling her hands behind her back.

She picked up the handcuffs she threw on the ground and quickly cuffed the woman's hands, securing them painfully tight around her wrists.

Linda grabbed the back collar of her dress and awkwardly helped the battered woman to her feet watching her spit blood out of her mouth and onto the ground at her feet.

She slowly walked her over to where Captain Hargrove was still sitting, awake now secured to the fence and looking up at the young officer with Evelyn Covington; shoving her down on the ground next to him.

"You two get to know each other; you'll both have prison in common real soon" she said looking down and smiling at the two captured criminals.

Tyler saw that Linda had arrested Covington after a good beat down and waited for her with Parker just a few feet away from where she pushed her down next to Hargrove.

"That looked like fun, did you get a couple of shots in for me and the other kids?" Tyler asked looking down at a bleeding Evelyn Covington. Linda again went to her knees hugging Parker, smiling up at her to acknowledge that she did.

Max Mason and his son Jacob hurried down the emergency stairwell with Nathaniel Covington still unconscious over Max's shoulder. They both knew they only had a few minutes to get out before the building came down on top of them from the Covington rocket heading towards it.

The three of them ran through the 1st floor door to find Jose Martin, Crusher Davis, Yuki Amikura, and a wounded Ochi Osaka standing just outside the stairwell waiting for them.

Max looked around the large room still cluttered with dead bodies from the fire fight Howler's men had with them earlier that evening figuring everyone else had gotten out by now.

"We need to get the fuck out of here; NOW" Jake said looking at his watch as everyone stared at Nathaniel Covington over Max's shoulder completely surprised they brought him with them.

Crusher picked up the still bleeding Ochi under her arm and headed towards the front lobby door with everyone else following; finally walking out the door and feeling the cold November air on their faces.

They all ran down the long sidewalk towards the parking lot trying to get as far away from the building as they could, seeing all the police & emergency vehicles with their bright colored lights flashing in the darkness.

Just as they got to the edge of the sidewalk where it met the driveway they were surrounded by both Federal & North Carolina State S.W.A.T. officers armed with AR-15 machine-guns yelling "SHOW US YOU'RE HANDS".

Everyone stopped where they were and raised at least one of their hands considering Crusher was holding up a still bleeding Ochi, and Max was carrying a still unconscious Nathaniel Covington over his shoulder.

"DON'T SHOOT, DON'T SHOOT" a familiar voice yelled loudly from behind the armed officers pointing their weapons at Max and his team.

Stacy Mason, along with Officer James Murphy moved in front of the officers as a young man wearing an F.B.I. insignia jacket followed them.

"Stand down everyone" he said waving his arms to lower their weapons as they slowly obeyed his orders.

The young F.B.I. agent turned looking at everyone, then at Max saying "Director Mason, I'm Agent Kyle Connors from the Raleigh office" extending his hand out to shake Max's.

"Admiral Cartwright & Lieutenant Mason explained the circumstances of the siege here tonight" Connors explained watching his men give their boss some space.

"Pop, we need to back these people up; NOW" Jake said to Max adamantly glancing at his watch again.

Max looked at Jakes anxious face and asked him "How much time before impact son?"

"About three minutes; we need to get all these people back more" he replied looking at all the SWAT, emergency people, and all their vehicles with flashing lights standing there in front of them.

Agent Connors heard what Jake Mason said and immediately yelled to his officers "GET THOSE VEHICLES AND EVERYONE BACK TO THE TREE LINE; NOW" seeing the tree line was near the compound's fence at least 200 yards from the building.

Crusher watched as two EMT's took Ochi from him and placed her gently on a gurney then quickly turned it towards one of the ambulances that was positioned near the front gate away from the Covington Industries building.

Yuki Amikura looked at the strong soldier with her sad eyes as he said "Go, she needs you". She smiled and ran after Ochi's gurney catching up to it, grabbing her frail hand as she glanced back at Crusher Davis giving him another smile.

"We need to move these people away from the building faster gentlemen" Max said seeing that the dressed up party guests weren't taking their direction very seriously.

Jake looked at his watch then looked up into the clear North Carolina sky seeing a small fireball hurdling through the clouds realizing it was the Covington rocket carrying the satellite almost upon them.

Jake grabbed Crusher & Jose by the arm looking at his dad yelling "TIME TO GO FELLA'S" as the four of them ran towards the trees.

Just as they got midway to the tree line the rocket hit the Covington building right in the middle of the roof causing the ground to tremble under everyone's feet. Max, Jake, Crusher, and Jose hit the ground hard as it rumbled underneath them.

Max looked up behind him to see the large fireball explode on top of the roof sending flames and building debris up into the sky with a tremendous roar.

The impact lit up the entire area around the building shooting flames out the windows; as the large satellite dishes attached to the roof top started falling off the sides and crashing to the ground below.

Jake got to his feet quickly lending a hand to help Jose up as they both stood there in shock looking at the burning and broken building. They looked at each other and grinned knowing they both survived.

"Another fine mess we got out of" Jose said to him with a grin.

"Yes sirrrr; looks like we get to climb another day" Jake replied laughing with his friend.

Crusher stood up beside Max as the four of them stood there fixated on the building; stunned at what had just happened because they were just in there a moment ago.

The fire started blowing out the rest of the windows on the lower floors; shooting through them into the night air, then suddenly the ground started shaking again; but not as intense as when the rocket first hit the building.

Everyone watched as the burning building started collapsing. One floor after another; fell on top of each other as smoke, concrete dust, and flames consumed the entire building rising into the night air until it was nothing more than a large pile of concrete rubble.

Emergency vehicles that had backed up to the tree line came rolling back up again to the front using hoses and water cannons to contain the building's many fires.

Stacy ran up to her dad and hugged him hard, glad to see him safe. Max smiled and kissed her on top of her head saying "I'm okay Princess".

She moved from her dad to her brother giving him a big hug as well then looking at them both grinning said to Jake "Really; you couldn't just blow the damn thing up in space, WE have to blow up ANOTHER building".

Max looked at his baby girl and pointed to Jake replying "He did it this time" laughing remembering the destruction they caused at the GBN building awhile back.

"My bad" Jake replied with a grin to his little sister.

"Like father, like son" Stacy said smacking Jake on the arm laughing.

"I take it Tyler & Linda are okay?" Max asked giving his daughter a serious look now.

"They haven't checked in since Linda blew up the helicopter; Tyler was giving her back up from the hill overlooking the stables" Stacy replied knowing that was the last time they spoke.

Max pulled out his handgun and checked the magazine then looked at his son Jake asking "Coming?"

"Yes sir" he replied replacing the magazine in his AR-15 machine-gun with a fresh loaded one nodding at his dad.

"Gentlemen, I'm sure the authorities could use a hand with some of the prisoners they've taken; I'd appreciate it if you'd help them out" Max said looking at both Crusher & Jose standing at attention saluting him in agreement.

"Really guys" Stacy said to the two soldiers, laughing at them as her father and brother headed over the hill towards the stables.

Agent Connors walks over to Max & Jake seeing them with guns in hand heading towards the other side of the demolished building and asks "Can I be of some help Director?" looking like they were headed for a fire fight.

"Actually, yes" Max replied smiling at the young F.B.I. agent. "We could use a couple of men to take charge of a couple of prisoners" he continued seeing the grin on his son's face.

"What makes you think there are prisoners Director?" Connors asked not understanding what he was asking.

"You haven't met OUR girls, have you Connors?" Max replied with a big grin looking over at Jake flashing the same grin.

Connors grabbed two of his men in full tactical gear and started walking towards the hill following Max & Jake keeping an eye on the burning, demolished building as they carefully walked passed it.

As the five of them got to the top of the hill they could see the burning helicopter & fuel station at the bottom, near the corral & stable barn. They could also see two women and a child standing over a man & woman sitting against the corral fence near the barn.

Max took the lead going down first. As he got to the bottom of the hill he could see Tyler, Linda, and little Parker standing there looking down at Evelyn Covington & Captain Hargrove; both still sitting on the ground leaning against the corral fence.

Parker was the first to see Max coming down the hill and ran towards his grandfather, as Linda & Tyler watched him; yelling "Grandpa, Grandpa".

Max got down on one knee and the little boy flew into his arms wrapping his arms around Max's sweaty neck holding on for dear life. Max smiled at Linda & Tyler as the two women approached, watching him squeezing his young grandson, and happy everyone was okay.

Tears of joy started running down both Linda & Tyler's face at what they both were watching.

Linda squeezed Tyler's hand and looked into her eyes saying "That's what being a Mason is really about; welcome to the family sweetie".

Max looked at his grandson's smiling face replying "Hey buddy, how you doin'?" as Jake walked up to the two of them. "Look who I found" he said with a smile to the little boy.

"DADDY" Parker yelled seeing his father walk up next to Max then looking back at his mom with a big smile.

"Hey little dude, I missed you" Jake replied hugging his son tightly and kissing him on the forehead.

"I missed you too, mommy got real mad at the lady" Parker said innocently.

Jake looked at his dad and laughed "I bet she did" seeing his wife roll her eyes looking back at a battered & bruised Evelyn Covington sitting in the dirt.

"Hey there stranger" Linda said to her husband as she jumped in his arms and kissed him hard.

"Hey yourself" Jake said hugging her tight continuing to kiss her.

Max looked at Tyler and realized how much he missed and worried about her, but knew she could take care of herself as he smiled. He grabbed her as she giggled and kissed her hard squeezing her tight.

He broke off his kiss and smiled at Tyler who looked up the hill to see the building in ruin asking "Really Mason; ANOTHER building, what do you plan on doing next; dropping a plane on someone?" she asked laughing.

"Nah, I've got something else in mind" Max replied with a mischievous grin.

A serious look came over Tyler's face as she asked him "What about Nathaniel Covington?"

"I left his sorry, unconscious ass with the Fed's" Max replied smiling at her. "Turns out it was a code today, lucky him" he said smirking at her.

One of Agent Connors men approached him and quietly spoke as the Mason family reunion continued. He motioned to the two armed men to pick up Captain Hargrove, and a still arrogant Evelyn Covington and escort them up the hill where they could be placed in custody and read their Miranda rights.

Everyone watched as the two Federal officers stood the two captured felons back on their feet pointing them towards the hill when Tyler spoke up "Hold up a minute" she asked stopping the two Fed's in their tracks holding on to Hargrove & Covington.

Tyler looked Evelyn Covington in the eye as she stood there nose to nose smiling at the smug look on her face saying "I'm going to make it my mission to bury you in the deepest, darkest hole I can find for what you did to all those innocent kids".

"Good luck with that" Covington said arrogantly. Just as she finished, Tyler hit her in the jaw with a hard right fist knocking the frail woman to the ground once again surprising her.

Everyone watched in shock at what Tyler did as the officer picked Evelyn off the ground again causing the older woman to give Tyler an evil look as she got up.

Max, Tyler, Linda, and Jake holding Parker in his arms watched as the two officers dragged the two people responsible for kidnapping their son/grandson up the hill towards the demolished Covington Industries building.

Max put his arm around Tyler's neck and they started walking towards Agent Connors who waited for them. Max smiled at her and asked "Do you feel better?" seeing the grin on her face.

"Actually I do, thank you" she replied smiling over at Linda who nodded to her new friend in agreement.

"Director, I have orders from the President & Admiral Cartwright to put you ALL on a plane to DC this morning; for debriefing" Connors said remembering what his officer told him.

"Yeah, I kinda figured that" Max replied with a grin to everyone knowing that Admiral Cartwright would want his team questioned & documented on everything that happened here, on his desk as soon as possible; especially since his son crashed a multi-million dollar government-issued rocket into a corporate building; destroying them both.

Everyone returned to the top of the hill where they met Stacy, Crusher, Jose, and Officer Murphy waiting together for their return; as police, fire, and emergency personnel quickly worked on containing the injuries & fires surrounding the destroyed Covington building

Stacy ran to her brother holding Parker who yelled her name "Aunt Stacy" when he saw her.

"Where have you been you little bug" Stacy asked him smiling, glad to see he was safe as Jake slowly put him down on the ground so she could hug her nephew.

"Mommy & Grandma got mad at the lady" he replied looking

over and smiling at his mom & Tyler standing there with grins on their faces hearing what he said to his aunt.

Stacy looked over at a bleeding, bruised, and tattered Evelyn Covington seeing her handcuffed and being dragged towards one of the SUV's belonging to the F.B.I.

She turned her head and looked at the two women with a sheepish grin both smiling at one another then they playfully shrugged their shoulders at Stacy as if to say "She deserved it".

Max looked around the area thinking what a big mess he and his team caused then snickered as he watched Nathaniel Covington being escorted by two F.B.I. agents towards another SUV parked next to the one Evelyn was being taken too.

Evelyn Covington saw Nathaniel, happy that he was alive and screamed "Nathaniel, Nathaniel; help your mother please" as she aggressively fought the two agents trying to put her in the backseat of the large black government car wanting to talk to her son.

Evelyn could see the anger & contempt in her son's eyes as he stood next to the opened car door staring at her not understanding why he was acting this way towards her.

She screamed again "Nathaniel, HELP your mother" this time being stern and angry at him for ignoring her.

"My name is Jeffery, Jeffery Ramsey and you're NOT my mother" he said to the disgraced elderly woman with shock on her face now understanding what he meant.

He looked at Evelyn one last time and slowly got into the backseat as the agent put his hand on the back of his head to help him in; hearing her sobbing as she yelled "Nathaniel, Nathaniel" then hearing her stop and call out "Jeffery, Jeffery, help mommy" closing his eyes as the door shut.

After watching the sad & pathetic show with the Covington's Tyler looked at Max with a smirk and asked "A code huh?" knowing that torturing the two of them this way would be better than letting them die, something they both deserved.

Max smiled at her, then turned and looked at Stacy asking "Where are your sisters?" not seeing either Yuki or Ochi with them.

"Yuki went with Ochi to the hospital to get some stitches" she replied to her father knowing he had some concerns about Ochi being wounded.

"The EMT said it was a flesh wound, not life threatening; that Crusher had saved her life" Stacy continued seeing relief come over her father's face.

"Well that's great news" Max said happy that his new adopted daughter would be okay.

"However; we ALL need to be in DC this morning for debriefing; orders from the Admiral" he said repeating what Agent Connors said to him earlier looking around at everyone relieved they were all safe; including his girlfriend, daughters, son, daughter-in-law, and his precious grandson; all smiling at him right now.

CHAPTER TWENTY

Max stood looking out his office window, now back in DC; he was holding his half-full cup of coffee having spent almost two full days giving account depositions, going over crime scene photos, questioning the rescued guests, interrogating arrested mercenaries, looking at the Covington Industries financial records, and finally identifying Howler, Simon, and the rest of the dead bodies left in the building's rubble; finally pulled out by fire & rescue teams.

It was now Wednesday afternoon and everyone on Max's team was cleared of any wrong doing allowing them all to relax for a couple of days until they're responsibilities caught up to them that following Monday morning, or before.

He knew his daughter Stacy had to head back to the Persian Gulf Saturday morning, to catch up with her ship; sad that he wouldn't see his baby girl again for the next seven months while she fulfilled her naval at-sea obligation.

Master-Sergeant Crusher Davis had to return to his state government job back in Tennessee, while Detective Jose Martin was to return to his job with the Fairfax County Police Department that coming Monday.

Admiral Cartwright gave them both a letter to their employers that stated they were involved in reserve military training exercises so not to be disciplined for not being at work the past few days without an excuse.

Max was told by Stacy that her sister's Yuki Amikura & Ochi Osaka needed to return to Japan and Amikura Electronics. Yuki called for a Monday morning board meeting to explain the death of her cousin Noki and his nefarious actions within the global conglomerate.

Max's son Jake was now between jobs, but relished the idea of taking care of his son Parker while his wife Linda temporarily took over the Captain's job at her precinct in Raleigh. The Admiral recommended her to the North Carolina State police, and Raleigh's city town council; both approving of her taking temporary control there. Her first official act as Captain was promoting Officer James Murphy to Lieutenant for his bravery & loyalty to her family and his badge.

Max remembered that Murphy saved his daughter's life which made him a bit more open to allowing him to date his daughter; just a "little" bit more open he thought with a smirk.

She was an adult now and didn't need his permission anyway, but smiled thinking she would always be his "princess".

The Covington's and Captain Hargrove were awaiting trial in a Federal detention facility close by without bail; on fifty counts of human trafficking, kidnapping, child endangerment, wire fraud, the murder of Jonah Singh, conspiracy to commit murder, attempted murder of a law enforcement officer, and a whole lot of other charges. If convicted the three of them could serve life in prison without possibility of parole only because none of them actually killed Singh; a now dead Howler did.

Max knew it was a couple of weeks away from the Thanksgiving Day holiday but thought this was the perfect occasion to have Thanksgiving dinner right now; since everyone he loved, his "family"; was right here in town, at least until Saturday.

Max & Tyler had a long discussion about what Max wanted to do agreeing that it was the perfect idea before everyone left. Max knew he had to get Tyler's approval because he wanted to have this dinner party at "they're" house to make it more special for everyone; he knew she wouldn't say no.

They discussed they're idea with EVERYONE, getting them all to agree to come Thursday afternoon; as if it was the normal Thanksgiving Day.

Max & Tyler got everyone's input on what should be served other than the traditional turkey & stuffing. Max wanted to call a caterer to provide the food but Tyler, Linda, and Stacy refused to let him; saying they were going to cook the feast themselves with everyone's help.

That evening Max, Tyler, Linda, Stacy, Jake, and Parker all went to the Mega Superstore near the house and bought everything they needed for the next day's dinner including a "very big" thirty-five pound turkey that was thawed and ready to go in the oven.

That Wednesday night Max watched as Tyler laid her head on his shoulder gently falling asleep as they watched the late night news on television together.

Jake & Linda were staying in one of the upstairs guestrooms, and had already put Parker to bed. Linda said "Goodnight" to them both heading up the stairs.

Jake leaned over and gave his dad a "fist bump" saying "Goodnight Pop" then followed his wife upstairs. Max smiled watching his son go up the stairs one more time, like he had done so many times before he got married.

He thought to himself this was probably going to be the last time his entire family would be together for a VERY long time; wanting to make the most of it. He smiled at a sound asleep Karen Tyler still lying on his shoulder seeing how peaceful & beautiful she looked knowing what he had to do to make this dinner a lot more special for everyone.

Stacy & Yuki were double-dating that night with James Murphy & Crusher Davis; while Ochi Osaka recovered from her wounds overnight in the hospital.

While Stacy stayed in Max's other guestroom, Yuki had a suite with Ochi at the Washington Majestic hotel in downtown DC. Murphy & Crusher were staying with Jose Martin at his house in Arlington; everyone knew to be at Max's house at 12 noon, and that dinner would be served at 2pm.

Max could see how incredibly beautiful & safe Tyler looked sleeping in his arms and knew right then he wanted to spend the rest of his life with her. He gently nudged her saying "Let's get you to bed sweetheart" seeing her eyes half open with a smile on her face helping her off the couch and up the stairs.

Thursday morning came quickly, as Max woke up and rolled over in bed to find Tyler missing. He looked over at his alarm clock seeing it was a still dark 6am, figuring she was in the bathroom when he started smelling something good from the downstairs kitchen.

He remembered when he was a kid waking up to his mom's wonderful cooking on Thanksgiving Day. She would get up so early to start cooking, and baking bread filling their house with delicious aromas before anyone even got out of bed.

Max got up and put his robe on over his pajama pants and t-shirt knowing there were others in the house that may not want to see that, and slowly made his way downstairs.

He stood quietly in the kitchen archway to find Tyler & Linda completely showered, dressed, and wearing full length aprons around their necks; fussing over the large turkey they had bought the night before.

He watched amusingly as they were both putting pads of butter into the turkey's stretched out skin just liked his mom use to do bringing a big smile to his face.

"Good morning ladies" he said smiling at Tyler who had her hands full of butter while Linda stuffed her side of the bird with her handful.

Tyler smiled at him seeing him wearing the robe she bought him saying "Hey handsome, there's coffee, and chocolate-chip muffins Linda baked for breakfast" looking over at the stove where the muffins were her hands still full of butter.

"Mornin' Max" Linda said smiling at her father-in-law who poured himself a cup of coffee then walked over to Tyler and kissed her with another smile.

"Morning sweetheart" he replied to Linda leaning down to kiss her on the cheek. "Why are you two up so early?" he asked figuring they both agreed to get up together at this time.

"This damn bird needs to be in the oven for about seven hours; fifteen minute's a pound" Linda said remembering how her mother taught her to cook a turkey for Jake & Parker the last couple of Thanksgiving's; then looked over at Tyler rolling her eyes wondering why Max bought such a big turkey. Tyler just smiled at the two of them as Max sheepishly grinned at her.

"Yes ma'am" Max replied knowing he never actually cooked a turkey for his family. He picked up his coffee cup, one of the muffins, and a paper towel and smiled at the two hardworking ladies going into the family room next to the kitchen to get out of their way.

He sat down on the couch and turned on the large screen TV they had up on the wall and watched as the early morning news came on announcing several big name politicians resigning last night including Texas Congressman Harold Jenkins; the man who tried to take Max's agency away from him.

Max recognized most of the names from Nathaniel Covington's blackmail list as Tyler and Linda stood behind the couch standing over him listening to the reporter's story.

Someone had sent an anonymous flash drive to the television station last night with a list of political names, and their documented crimes from all over the country.

Tyler put her hand on Max's shoulder saying "I'm glad you took his name off the list" looking down at him with a smile. Max smiled back reaching up to hold her hand understanding what she said.

"He's been our friend and our leader" he said smiling at the two women.

"I owe it to him to at least give him the benefit of the doubt" he continued, taking a sip of his coffee.

Finally, everyone got up and started helping with the festivities; including Parker, who helped lick the spatula with leftover chocolate pudding on it after his mom made a pudding pie for dessert, along with the traditional pumpkin.

Jake & Stacy were both in the family room playing a racing video game with Parker when Max smiled at them both remembering they use to play like this when they were teenagers. He quietly gestured for them to come upstairs with him; both of them giving him a curious look. They both thought this was strange but decided to follow their dad to his bedroom anyway.

"Hey buddy, daddy & Aunt Stacy will be right back" Jake said to Parker who wasn't paying any attention to any of them continuing to play the video game as they both put their controllers on the table seeing their dad head up the stairs towards the bedrooms.

"I need to talk to you both" he said nervously standing there in front of them as Jake closed the bedroom door behind him.

"What did you do daddy?" Stacy asked with her hands on her hips figuring he said or did something to upset Tyler.

"Nothing, I swear" he said with a grin seeing Jake laugh at the exchange between him and his sister. "I want to make this special for everyone today" Max said to them both then proceeded to tell them what he had planned for everyone at dinner.

They both smiled at their dad, each saying they approve of his plans as Stacy gave him a big hug and Jake gave him a pat on the arm grinning.

"Tell your two sisters when they get here; okay" he said looking at Stacy as they both headed out the bedroom door.

The three of them went back downstairs to help Linda & Tyler with the rest of the side dishes before everyone arrived; which was in about thirty minutes.

The doorbell rang and Max walked to the foyer and opened the door seeing Jose, Crusher, and Murphy standing on the front step with big grins on their faces each carrying a customary bottle of wine as a gift to the host.

"Wine drinker's huh?" Max asked with a smirk on his face seeing all the wine bottles.

"No sir; we figured we'd get all the ladies drunk" Jose said with a mischievous grin hoping his little joke didn't offend Max.

"I'm okay with that Detective" Max replied with a laugh moving to the side so the three men could come into the house.

Just as Max was about to close the door he noticed a black stretch limousine pull up to the curb and stop in front of the house. He curiously stepped out onto the porch watching as the well dressed driver got out and walked around to the passengers' door opening it and helping Yuki Amikura out of the car.

Yuki stood there smiling seeing Max standing there waiting on the front porch as the driver assisted Ochi Osaka out of the car. She was still a bit sore from her injury as she moved slowly up the driveway; with Yuki walking beside her, hovering like a big sister would.

When the two beautiful Asian women finally stood in front of Max they bowed to him in the traditional Japanese custom before entering a host's home.

Max could see it bothered Ochi to bow because of the injury to her abdomen but was impressed & honored that she made an effort too.

Not being much on ceremony's Max smiled at them both then proceeded to hug them one at a time seeing the surprise on both of their faces as he did.

"I'm so proud of you girls" Max said seeing them both smile at him. Just as he was about to say something else Stacy came to the door and quickly took them both inside, the three of them giddy as teenage school girls; who haven't talked to each other in days totally ignoring him now.

Now alone on the porch Max looked up into the bright sunny sky and said with a grin "Looks like it's going to be a beautiful day sweetheart" thinking about his lost wife Sylvia who he knew was looking down on all of them smiling today.

Everyone helped set the table with china, silverware, napkins, and finally all the food. Max earlier extended the dining room table to accommodate more chairs having Jake help him bring the others from the garage.

Everyone sat down at the table, drinks were poured, beers were brought in, and Max finally brought out the huge turkey cooked to perfection by Linda & Tyler; sitting it down in front of his chair at the head of the table to applause from everyone.

Just as Max was about to cut into the large roasted bird the doorbell rang. He smiled and said to everyone with a laugh "Leave it to the Admiral to show up AFTER all the work has been done" looking at the one empty chair waiting for him as he placed the large knife & fork down beside the turkey and walked to the door.

Max opened the door knowing it was Admiral Cartwright saying "Right on time Admiral; we just sat down" seeing Cartwright standing there without a smile on his face with two Secret Service agents standing behind him.

"Sorry Max; but he insisted on coming with me when he found out what we were all doing today" Cartwright replied standing aside to show a heavily protected President Keith Bradshaw standing there with sadness in his eyes.

Max immediately stood at attention and saluted his Commander-In-Chief who saluted him back and asked "May I come in and talk with you Max?".

"Absolutely sir" Max replied opening the door wide so the Admiral and the President could come inside.

Max escorted the two men into his living room and watched as Bradshaw turned to Cartwright and said "James, why don't you join the others and let Max & I talk for a moment" seeing the Admiral nod in agreement with him. Cartwright took off his coat and laid it on Max's living room chair and promptly walked towards the dining room where they could hear laughing and chatter.

Max stood in his usual at ease stance waiting to hear what the President wanted to discuss with him looking back as the Admiral found his way to everyone, hearing Stacy announce loudly "ADMIRAL

ON DECK" then him return "At ease everyone" hearing the chatter from the dining room continue.

"I'm sorry to come to your home unannounced and interrupt your family dinner Max" Bradshaw said his eyes sad with guilt and remorse.

"You are ALWAYS welcome in our home Mr. President" Max replied with a smile.

"I feel I need to explain what happened the night that got me on Nathaniel Covington's list" Bradshaw said turning red with embarrassment.

"You NEVER have to explain anything to me Mr. President" Max replied seeing how much this secret was hurting him inside.

"We have known each other for almost three years sir, I trust your dedication to the oath you took" he said looking the beleaguered President in the eye.

"But I'm not the one you have to explain to sir; there is a room full of people in there who would never question anything you asked them to do" he said pointing towards his dining room as they both could hear everyone continuing to laugh and talk to each other.

"May I then?" Bradshaw solemnly asked.

Max smiled at him approving of his request and extended his arm to direct him to everyone leading him down the hallway taking his coat as they walked.

Stacy glanced up seeing the President coming through the dining room doorway and stood up immediately standing at attention yelling above everyone talking "PRESIDENT ON DECK" saluting him as everyone looked towards the doorway just as they did for Admiral Cartwright.

Crusher Davis, Jose Martin, and Jake & Linda quickly stood at attention saluting President Bradshaw as he stood in the dining room.

Bradshaw waved his arms up & down slowly for everyone to sit down saying "Please have a seat everyone; I'll only take a minute of your time".

Everyone sat back down including Admiral Cartwright as Max stood behind the President eyeing Tyler with a smile on his face.

"First, your country & I appreciate what you all did this week and the emotional toll it took on some of you losing loved ones" Bradshaw started, looking at Yuki & Ochi on the other side of the table nodding to the young "ninja" girls in appreciation of their sacrifice.

"I want to explain why I was on Covington's list that most of you in this room already know about" Bradshaw started.

"I had just lost my wife to cancer; now a single father raising a young daughter alone, and just elected to the highest office in America; I know it's not a good excuse, but at the time it was a vulnerable time for me" he said looking over at Max who gave him a understanding & reassuring smile.

"After a fund-raiser, I met a woman in a restaurant eating alone; very elegant, and we hit it off" Bradshaw said looking around the table at everyone with guilt on his face.

"We ended up in her room after a couple bottles of wine, and the next morning we said goodbye and I haven't heard from her again; not until I got blackmail pictures from Nathaniel Covington a couple of weeks later" he said nervously. "The note inside said they would be in touch" he calmly said.

Everyone listened to him intently, occasionally looking over at Max who continued to stand proudly behind the ashamed President.

"I want you all to know that NEVER once did my allegiance stray from protecting this great country of ours; nor would I EVER put your dedicated lives in danger for any personal gain" Bradshaw said as he turned to Max and gestured for his coat.

"Thank you for allowing me to explain, please enjoy your dinner" he said taking his coat from Max and turning to leave the room.

"White meat; or dark meat?" Karen Tyler asked loudly as she stood up from her seat seeing Max smile at her.

KILLS OF THE FATHER

"Excuse me" Bradshaw asked as he turned facing Tyler who was smiling at him.

"Do you prefer white meat or dark meat of the turkey Mr. President?" she asked seeing the confusion on his face.

"I prefer white meat actually" Bradshaw said with a grin looking at her.

"Good, because Max bought a thirty-five pound turkey and I'm sure as hell not eating turkey sandwiches for the next couple of weeks; we would all be honored if you joined us for dinner sir" Tyler replied smiling seeing a big smile returned on the President's face. Tyler looked around the table seeing everyone give her an agreeing smile.

"I would like that; a lot actually, thank you" Bradshaw said looking around the table at all the smiling faces of approval.

Max already had a chair from the garage sitting in the kitchen in case he miss counted how many chairs they needed, coming back with it. He held on to it while watching everyone adjust their chairs a little closer to each other.

He placed it next to Admiral Cartwright's chair, and once again Bradshaw handed Max his coat looking down at James Cartwright who smiled and said "Sit down Keith, dinner's getting cold" looking up at the President as he sat down beside him. Just as he got situated Jose handed him the large bowl of mashed potatoes and a spoon.

Everyone was enjoying their Thanksgiving dinner of roasted turkey, mashed potatoes & gravy, stuffing, candied sweet potatoes with toasted marshmallows on top, fresh green beans, cranberry sauce, and fresh baked dinner rolls; an incredible Thanksgiving feast for all.

"What would you like to drink sir?" Max asked looking at Bradshaw from the kitchen doorway.

"Iced tea if you have it" Bradshaw replied.

"Live a little Keith; have a beer" Cartwright said with a laugh holding the bottle of beer he was drinking.

"Even the President of the United States is allowed a beer once in awhile sir" Max said seeing him grin when he handed him the ice cold bottle.

Max thought Linda, Tyler, and Stacy had out done themselves this evening; it was just perfect. Everyone was enjoying their meal, laughing, and talking like family does on a Thanksgiving Day.

Max stood up at the head of the table and tapped his beer bottle with his butter knife, the clanging getting everyone's attention. Everyone stopped talking and focused on what Max wanted to say.

"It's traditional on Thanksgiving Day to tell everyone what you're thankful for" he started, smiling at everyone as he looked around the full table.

"I know it's NOT Thanksgiving" he said laughing. "But I want to say what I am thankful for because everyone will be going their separate ways soon" he continued.

"I'm thankful for new friends" he said smiling as he tilted his beer bottle at Jose, Crusher, and James Murphy toasting them, then seeing them return his gesture.

"I'm SOOOO thankful for my extremely talented children; they have made me so proud at what they have become" Max said smiling at both Stacy & Jake.

"I am thankful to have the chance to renew a relationship I thought was lost forever; she and her friend have become incredible business women and I couldn't be more proud to call them both MY daughters" he said smiling at both Yuki & Ochi seeing tears come down both their faces.

"I know I'm dragging this on, but I'm getting to a point" he said laughing as everyone giggled with him.

"I'm thankful for a daughter-in-law who I have adored since my son brought her home to meet me; who gave me the most incredible gift of a grandson that loves us all unconditionally" he continued, looking over at Parker who was continuing to enjoy his sweet potatoes & marshmallows.

"It doesn't hurt, that the Mason bloodline continues with him either" Max said laughing with everyone.

"I'm thankful to work for two incredible men that I believe in; and they believe in us; you both make our country stronger with your guidance gentlemen" Max said tipping his bottle to President Bradshaw & Admiral Cartwright both returning the bottle tip.

"And though their not here, I'm thankful for my two teammates keeping me alive all these years" he laughed thinking of both Jordy & Mikey.

"But most of all; I'm thankful for someone who has never left my side, someone who has saved my life more than once, someone that loves me unconditionally, and she makes a pretty good turkey dinner" he said looking down at Tyler grinning who was starting to turn red with embarrassment at what he was saying about her in front of everyone.

Max reached into his pants pocket and pulled out his mother's large carat diamond engagement ring she gave him right before she died. He got down on one knee and smiled looking up at Tyler saying "I have loved you since the day I met you; I love waking up next to you & can't wait to come home to you" he said with love in his eyes.

"Karen Tyler will you marry me?" seeing a shocked & smiling Tyler with her hands over her mouth and tears starting to come down her cheeks.

"Oh Hell yes" she said grinning leaning down to kiss Max hard on the lips. "What took you so long Mason?" she asked smiling at him.

Everyone laughed, applauded, and whistled as Max slowly slid the ring on her left hand. Tyler stood up just as Max did and practically jumped in his arms kissing him again as she hugged her new fiance with all her might never wanting to let him go.

"I bought champagne, it's been getting cold in the fridge out in the garage" Max said to her leaning down to kiss her again with a sheepish grin.

Tyler looked over at Stacy with an evil grin and asked "Did you know about this?".

"Daddy asked Jake, Yuki, Ochi, and me for permission to ask you earlier today before dinner" she said with a big smile happy Tyler was going to be part of the family; FINALLY.

"I'm impressed you were able to keep this a secret" Tyler said to her new step-daughter with a big grin.

"Lady, you have NO idea" Stacy said laughing looking over at Yuki & Ochi smiling at them both.

Tyler sat back down and started showing off her new ring to all the ladies sitting around the table as the single guys started getting a bit nervous grinning at one another.

Max had come back from the garage and was now standing in the kitchen doorway holding two bottles of chilled champagne smiling at everyone sitting around the table happy, loving, and safe.

He continued to smile as he looked at his son Jake & his grandson Parker sitting at the table; thinking to himself "Sometimes the "Kills of the Father" can bring a family closer together" as he slowly walked back in smiling at Tyler, seeing everyone continue to laugh and talk with one another.

ABOUT THE AUTHOR

Charles Sisk's unique take on the crime thriller genre has resulted in two nominations for Best Thriller with the Author Academy Awards. His love for action movies and television fuel his enthusiasm to make Max Mason more than an action hero; he wants him to be an icon like Jack Reacher, Jack Ryan, and John McClane.

MAX MASON

RETURNS IN

"TIL' DEATH DO WE" KILL

The Misadventures of Max Mason

Printed in the United States
by Baker & Taylor Publisher Services